TRAFALGAR &
THE BATTLE OF
SALAMANCA

Two novels of the Spanish wars

First published 2019

Published under licence by Brown Dog Books and
The Self-Publishing Partnership, 7 Green Park Station, Bath BA1 1JB

www.selfpublishingpartnership.co.uk

ISBN printed book: 978-1-83952-075-4
ISBN e-book: 978-1-83952-076-1

Cover design by Kevin Rylands
Internal design by Andrew Easton

Printed and bound by CPI Group (UK) Ltd, Croydon, CR0 4YY

This book is printed on FSC certified paper

MIX
Paper from
responsible sources
FSC® C013604

TRAFALGAR & THE BATTLE OF SALAMANCA

Two novels of the Spanish wars

BENITO PÉREZ GALDÓS

Translated and with an introduction
and notes by Rick Morgan

BROWN
DOG
BOOKS

To Lizzie

Contents

Introduction   8

List of Maps   12

Timeline of historical events referred to in *Trafalgar*
and *The Battle of Salamanca*   16

Foreword to the 1881 Illustrated Edition   18

Trafalgar   20

Summary of events in the National Episodes between *Trafalgar*
and *The Battle of Salamanca*   163

The Battle of Salamanca   172

Endnotes to *Trafalgar*   435

Endnotes to *The Battle of Salamanca*   446

INTRODUCTION

Benito Pérez Galdós was born on 10th May 1843 in Las Palmas, Gran Canaria, and died on 4th January 1920 aged seventy-six in Madrid. He was a prolific writer and is widely considered to be Spain's greatest novelist after Cervantes. He published over thirty novels, twenty-three plays, and forty-six *Episodios Nacionales* (*National Episodes*), as well as a large body of journalism and other works.

He was the tenth child of an Army colonel. His mother was originally from Gipuzkoa, in the Basque Country. During his childhood, his father told him stories of his time as a soldier in Spain's War of Independence, the period covered by the first series of the *National Episodes*. He was educated in the Canary Islands and showed an early talent for drawing and was renowned for an excellent visual and literary memory. He also wrote articles and satirical verses for the local press.

In 1862 he moved to Madrid to read law at university but spent much of this time at the theatre and associating with writers. In 1865 and 1866 he witnessed the unrest in Madrid during the rebellion of Juan Prim which led to the abdication of Queen Isabel II in 1868. In 1867 he made his first trip abroad to Paris where he became familiar with the works of Balzac and Dickens, both of whom would be important influences on his own novel writing. In 1868 his translation of *The Pickwick Papers* (from a French edition) appeared in instalments in the *Nación* newspaper.

In the same year he gave up university and devoted himself to journalism and writing. His first novel *La Fontana de Oro* (*The Golden Fountain*) was published in 1870. Two further novels appeared before the publication of *Trafalgar*, the first of the *National Episodes*, in 1873. The *National Episodes* would become the lifetime achievement of Galdós (almost literally, since the last of them was published in 1912) and among his most popular works. They chronicle the history of Spain from 1805 until about 1880 through fictional characters appearing in historical events and interacting with historical persons.

His greatest works include *Doña Perfecta* (1876), a novel attacking religious bigotry in Spain, *Fortunata y Jacinta* (1886-87), the story of a bourgeois marriage and class relationships in contemporary Madrid, and *Miau* (1888), the tale of an honest civil servant who is a victim of others less scrupulous than him. These and others of his novels can stand with the best of European nineteenth-century fiction. From 1891 with the publication of *Ángel Guerra* he moved away from the influence of realism to that of spiritualism, having read and admired Tolstoy. During this period he published a series of novels including *Tristana* (1892), the inspiration for Luis Buñuel's film of the same name, and *Misericordia* (*Pity*), a novel about true charity and poverty.

In 1886 Galdós entered the Cortes as a deputy for Guayama in Puerto Rico (then ruled by Spain) for the Liberal Party, but his natural shyness meant that he did not speak often. In 1897, despite opposition from conservative elements, he was elected to the Spanish Royal Academy.

His final years were marked by financial problems (he had a costly legal case against his first publisher) and by progressive blindness. He became completely blind in 1912. In 1919 a statue of him by Victorio Macho was erected in the Retiro Park in Madrid by public subscription. He asked to be lifted up so he could feel the statue and wept with joy at feeling how well the sculptor had captured him. A year later over 30,000 people attended his funeral.

Galdós never married and he lived for a number of years with two sisters and then a nephew. He had a daughter in 1891 with Lorenza Cobián and probably had close relationships with a number of women. Certainly, there are many women protagonists in his work who are skilfully and sensitively drawn.

Galdós wrote throughout his working life, and he spent much time in researching his novels, travelling extensively, consulting historical records and visiting locales. His care in describing the settings of his novels is matched by an acute insight into human emotion and character, and the ability to tell a story and handle large casts of characters. He wrote in an easy, vigorous, often humorous style which continues to attract many readers almost a century after his death.

THE NATIONAL EPISODES

Galdós wrote forty-six historical novels which form the *National Episodes*. They are in five series, the first four consisting of ten novels each and the fifth series, which remained incomplete at his death, comprising six published novels and a sketch of one more. It is generally accepted that the first two series are of better quality than the last three series, where the impetus for their creation was probably more financial than purely artistic.

The two novels translated in this book are *Trafalgar*, the first novel in the first series, and the last novel in the first series, *La Batalla de los Arapiles* (I have given it the title *The Battle of Salamanca,* as this is the name the battle is known by in the English-speaking world).

The first series was published between 1873 and 1875 and follows the adventures of Gabriel Araceli, an orphan from Cádiz, during the War of Independence from 1805 until 1812.

The titles of the ten novels in the first series with their year of first publication are: *Trafalgar*, 1873; *La Corte de Carlos IV* (*The Court of Charles IV*), 1873; *El 19 de marzo y el 2 de mayo* (*The nineteenth of March and the second of May*), 1873; *Bailén*, 1873; *Napoleón en Chamartín* (*Napoleon at Chamartín*), 1874; *Zaragoza*, 1874; *Gerona*, 1874; *Cádiz*, 1874; *Juan Martín el Empecinado* (*Juan Martin the Undaunted*), 1874; and *La Batalla de los Arapiles* (*The Battle of Salamanca*), 1875.

The second series, published between 1875 and 1879, covers the period from 1814 until 1833.

The third series, published from 1898 until 1900, covers the period of the First Carlist War and the Regency of María-Cristina (1833-1843).

The fourth series, published between 1902 and 1907, covers the reign of Isabel II from her accession to power in 1843 until her deposition in 1868.

The six novels of the fifth series were published from 1907 until 1912. They deal with the "Glorious Revolution" that overthrew Isabel II, the reign of Amadeo I (1870-1873) and the short-lived First Republic (1873-1874), and finish in 1880 with the birth of the Infanta María de las Mercedes.

The care Galdós took in ensuring the National Episodes were historically accurate is shown by an incident he describes in his memoirs. In the summer of 1872 after he had acquired a history book on the Battle of Trafalgar in Madrid, he moved to Santander on the Cantabrian coast to prepare *Trafalgar*. A friend there mentioned to him that the last survivor of the Battle of Trafalgar, now aged eighty-three, lived there, and much to Galdós's joy he was introduced the following day to a former ship's boy on the *Santísima Trinidad*, the Spanish flagship. He was able to give Galdós a wealth of detail about life on board, which is used extensively in *Trafalgar*. Indeed, the hero Gabriel Araceli is on board the same ship in the battle.

Although each novel in the first series can be read on its own, it is better to read them in sequence. Because *The Battle of Salamanca* is the last of the series I have set out a summary of events in the novels between *Trafalgar* and *The Battle of Salamanca*. This will, I hope, make it easier to understand the references to past events in *The Battle of Salamanca*.

These translations are based on the texts of the first illustrated editions. The illustrated edition of *Trafalgar* was published in 1881 with illustrations by the brothers Enrique and Arturo Mélida. The illustrated edition of *The Battle of Salamanca* appeared in 1883 with illustrations by four artists, Arturo Mélida, Lizcano, Ferriz and Pellicer.

In *The Battle of Salamanca*, the words spoken by some of the French characters are occasionally written in French. I have kept the original wording but put a translation in footnotes.

I have been helped and encouraged by many friends and family members. I am very grateful to them all. I want to record my particular thanks to my brother Martin, my brother-in-law David Barrie and my wife Elizabeth Gibson for the patience and care they took in reading through drafts and the valuable comments they gave me. All errors and infelicities are entirely my own. I also want to thank Meirion Harries for his professionalism and benevolence in creating the images for the illustrations. Finally, I want to express my gratitude to the Casa-Museo Pérez Galdós in Las Palmas de Gran Canaria for their kind permission to reproduce the portrait of Galdós by Joaquín Sorolla on the cover of this book.

List of Maps

1. The Iberian Peninsula with principal places mentioned in the text   13

2. The surroundings of Cádiz   14

3. The battlefield of Salamanca   15

FRANCE

BURGOS

R. Ebro

GERONA

VALLADOLID

ZARAGOZA

BARCELONA

R. Duero

SALAMANCA

GUADALAJARA

ALMEIDA

CIUDAD
RODRIGO

MADRID

PORTUGAL

ARANJUEZ

R. Tagus

VALENCIA

LISBON

BADAJOZ

CÓRDOBA

BAILÉN

R. Guadalquivir

SEVILLE

GRANADA

100 MILES

CÁDIZ

CAPE
TRAFALGAR

GIBRALTAR

AFRICA

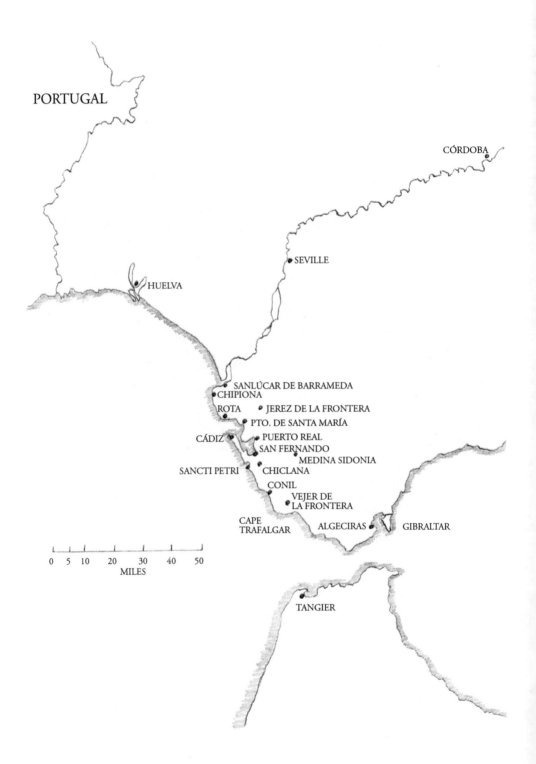

PORTUGAL

CÓRDOBA

SEVILLE

HUELVA

SANLÚCAR DE BARRAMEDA
CHIPIONA
ROTA   JEREZ DE LA FRONTERA
PTO. DE SANTA MARÍA
CÁDIZ   PUERTO REAL
SAN FERNANDO
MEDINA SIDONIA
SANCTI PETRI   CHICLANA
CONIL
VEJER DE
LA FRONTERA
CAPE
TRAFALGAR   ALGECIRAS   GIBRALTAR

0   5 10   20   30   40   50
MILES

TANGIER

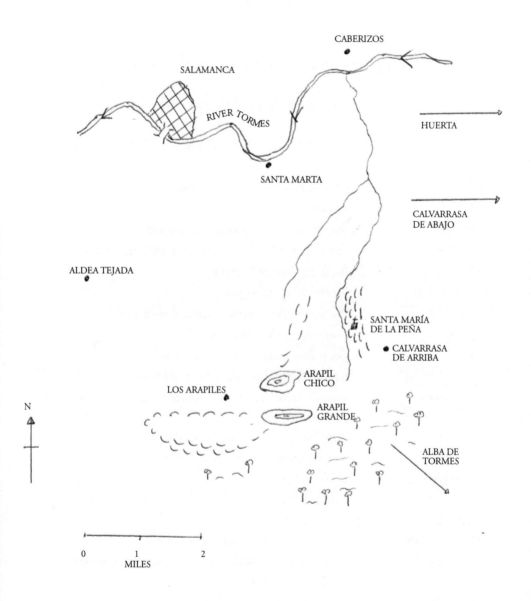

Timeline of historical events referred to in

TRAFALGAR and THE BATTLE OF SALAMANCA

1788	Charles IV becomes king of Spain
1789	French Revolution
1793-95	War of Roussillon between France and Spain
18.8.1796	Treaty of San Ildefonso between France and Spain
14.2.1797	Battle of Cape St Vincent
13/14.7.1801	Second Battle of Algeciras
25.3.1802	Peace of Amiens between Great Britain and France
2.8.1802	Napoleon made Consul for life
18.5.1803	Great Britain declares war on France
22.10.1803	Subsidy Treaty between France and Spain
5.10.1804	Moore's interception of Spanish treasure fleet off Cape Santa María
2.12.1804	Napoleon crowned emperor of the French
14.12.1804	Spain declares war on Great Britain
19.10.1805	Battle of Ulm
21.10.1805	Battle of Trafalgar
2.12.1805	Battle of Austerlitz
November 1807	French occupy Portugal under Junot
19.3.1808	Riot of Aranjuez. Abdication of Charles IV in favour of his son Ferdinand VII
23.3.1808	French troops occupy Madrid

2.5.1808	Uprising in Madrid against French occupiers
7.5.1808	Joseph Bonaparte declared King of Spain as José I
19.7.1808	Battle of Bailén
1.8.1808	Joseph Bonaparte leaves Madrid
December 1808	Napoleon restores Joseph in Madrid
December 1808 to February 1809	Second siege of Zaragoza
23.1.1809	Napoleon returns to Paris
22.4. 1809	Sir Arthur Wellesley arrives in Lisbon as commander of the British forces
28.7.1809	Battle of Talavera
May to December 1809	Third siege of Gerona
20.1.1812	Wellington captures Ciudad Rodrigo
19.3.1812	Constitution of Cádiz declared
6.4.1812	Wellington captures Badajoz
24.6.1812	Napoleon invades Russia
22.7.1812	Battle of Salamanca
12.6.1813	French evacuate Madrid

FOREWORD TO THE 1881 ILLUSTRATED EDITION OF
BOOKS ONE AND TWO OF THE NATIONAL EPISODES
TO THE READER

Friend and master,

*Before these twenty novels became reality, when the first of them was not yet written, nor even thought through, and all this work of seven thousand pages was just an artistic aspiration, I considered and decided that the **National Episodes** should, sooner or later, be an illustrated work. The multitude and variety of characters, the charm of the locations, the countless events in the action, divided between the historical and the domestic, the scenes, either real or imagined, which were to appear throughout the whole course of the work, were an important* reason for my lack of confidence in proceeding with the idea of this long-drawn-out narrative if I did not have the assistance of talented pencils that would give to the book all the strength, all the emphasis and all the spirit that was necessary to fulfil the supreme objective of pleasing you. There are works to which illustrations, however good they may be, add nothing. This, on the other hand, is one of those that, helped by drawing, can acquire an extraordinary splendour, and create enchantments that with the best will in the world you surely would not find in a simple text.

It not having been possible to bring about this precious alliance in the first editions, which for various reasons I always considered to be provisional, I was stimulated to work by the hope of offering you, in the fullness of time, an edition such as the present one, in a beautiful and elegant form, worthy of your eyes and in addition perfected by the graphic text which, in my opinion, is almost an intrinsic requirement of the **National Episodes**.

This hope, dear sir and friend, has become reality and as I happily hand over this graphic text, I can only attribute its principal merit, not to my perseverance, but to the good fortune of having found in the Mélida brothers such effective partners, who with their drawings have given an interpretation to my words that is superior to the words themselves, to such an extent that they have equalled here the great artists, whose main gift is to exalt and enrich subjects.

Dressed in magnificent finery, the **National Episodes** appear once more today. These are the twenty little books that have wandered here and there for eight years, ugly and naked, dressed in nothing more than the dalmatic of the nation, as old as it is many-coloured. Humble then, they enjoyed your kindness; courtiers now, they believe they are entitled to win your favour.

And, since there is nothing more tedious than long prologues, I decree and command, in your honour, that this one shall be the very shortest. I have prepared a long and prolix piece on the origin of this work, its aims, the historical and literary elements which I made use of, the facts and anecdotes I collected; in short, a little bit of history or rather literary memories, with the addition of some thoughts for free on the contemporary novel. But realising that these things are of only marginal interest and are better suited to a postscript than to a prologue, I am keeping them to the end of the work where you can see them, read them and enjoy them if you have absolutely nothing better to do.

The brevity of my Preface entitles me to your gratitude. For the continued kindness you show me, mine is very great.

Benito Pérez Galdós
Madrid, March 1881

TRAFALCAR

I

Before I tell about the great event I witnessed, let me say a few words about my childhood and explain the strange way that life's chances led me to be present at the terrible catastrophe suffered by our Navy.

In speaking about my birth, I will not imitate most

of those who write about the deeds they have done, those who begin by naming their relations, nearly always noble, and never less than gentlemen, even going so far as to claim they are descendants of the Emperor of Trebizond[1] himself. For my own part, I cannot adorn my book with sonorous family names; and apart from my mother, whom I knew only for a short time, I have no knowledge of any of my ancestors, except for Adam, whose kinship seems to me to be indisputable. So I will start my story like Pablos, the thief of Segovia[2] – fortunately God granted that this was our only similarity.

I was born in Cádiz, in the famous district of La Viña,[3] which is no academy for decent people, neither today nor then. Memory throws no light on me or on what I did as a child until the age of six and if I remember this date, it is because I associate it with a naval incident which I heard about at that time: the Battle of Cape St. Vincent,[4] which occurred in 1797.

Looking at a confused and sketchy image in the picture of things that have happened, with the curiosity and interest typical of someone observing himself, I see myself playing on La Caleta[5] with other boys of my age, more or less. That was for me life in its entirety; more than that, it was the normal life for our privileged sort, and those who did not live like me seemed to be exceptions to mankind, since in my childish innocence and ignorance of the world I believed that man had been raised for the sea, Providence having assigned to him swimming as the supreme exercise for his body and, for the constant employment of his mind, the pursuit and catching of crabs, then tearing off and selling their prized claws, known as "Bocas de la Isla",[6] both for its own satisfaction and as a tasty treat, so combining the enjoyable with the useful.

The society in which I grew up, then, was the roughest, most primitive and lowest that could be imagined, so much so that we lads from La Caleta were regarded as being more of a rabble than those who pursued the same industry and defied the elements with the same resolution in Puntales.[7] And because of this difference, both sides thought of themselves as rivals, and at times our forces would meet at the Puerta de Tierra[8] in great and noisy fights with stones, where the ground would be stained with heroic blood.

When I was old enough to start business on my own account, with the aim of earning an honest penny, I remember performing my tricks on the breakwater, acting as a Head of Protocol[9] to the many English who visited us then, as they do now. The breakwater was an Athenian academy for getting ahead within a few years, and I was not one of the less diligent pupils in that vast branch of human knowledge, nor did I

stop excelling in the pilfering of fruit, where the Plaza de San Juan de Dios offered ample opportunity for our initiative and great speculations. But I want to bring this part of my story to an end, since I am now greatly ashamed of my degradation and I thank God that He soon liberated me from this and raised me to a nobler path.

One of the impressions kept firmly in my memory is the keen pleasure I took at the sight of the warships when they anchored off Cádiz or in San Fernando.[10] Because I could never satisfy my curiosity by coming close to those huge structures, my ideas about them were fantastic and absurd, and I imagined they were full of mysteries.

Eager to imitate the great affairs of men, we boys also made our own squadrons, with small, crudely shaped boats on which we put sails of paper or rags, navigating them with great determination and solemnity on any sort of puddle in Puntales or La Caleta. So that everything should be perfect, whenever some coin came into our hands through one of our special industrial processes, we would buy some powder at Old Ma Coscoja's, in Calle Horno de Santa María, and with this ingredient we had a complete naval celebration. Our fleets were launched to catch the wind on oceans three yards across; they fired their guns of reeds; they struck against each other as if in bloody boardings where their imaginary crews fought gloriously; covered by smoke, with a glimpse of flags, made from the first scrap of coloured rag found on the rubbish dump, and, all the while, we would be dancing with delight on the shore, to the thunder of the artillery, imagining ourselves to be the nations to which those ships belonged and believing that, in the world of men and great things, the nations would dance the same way when watching the victory of their cherished squadrons. Boys see everything in

an odd way.

It was a time of great naval combats, since there was one every year and some skirmish every month. I thought that the squadrons fought each other purely and simply because they liked doing so, or to prove their bravery, like two toughs who arrange to meet outside to slash each other with knives. I laugh when I recall my outlandish ideas about things of that time. I heard a lot about Napoleon, and how do you think I imagined him? Well, nothing more than just one of those smugglers from the Campo de Gibraltar[11] who were always to be seen in the La Viña district. I imagined him on his Jerez colt, with his shawl, leggings, felt hat and the appropriate carbine. I had the notion that, in this rig and followed by adventurers of the same sort, this man, whom everyone described as extraordinary, had conquered Europe, that is to say a large island, in which there were other islands which were the nations, namely England, Genoa, London, France, Malta, the land of the Moor, America, Gibraltar, Mahón, Russia, Toulon, etc. I had formed this geographical notion in accordance with the most frequent ports of origin of the ships whose passengers I had dealings with, and I don't need to tell you that of all these nations or islands, Spain was the very best, because of which the English, somewhat in the manner of highwaymen, wanted to seize it for themselves. When speaking of this and other diplomatic affairs, I and my pals from La Caleta used to say thousands of phrases inspired by the most ardent patriotism.

But I don't want to tire the reader with trifles that refer only to my own impressions, and I will finish talking about myself. The only person who made up for the misery of my existence with a selfless affection was my mother. The only thing I remember of her is that she was beautiful, at least she seemed so to me. Since becoming a widow, she kept herself and me by washing and mending clothes for some sailors. Her love for me must have been very great. I fell gravely ill from yellow fever which was devastating Andalusia at that time, and when I became well again she took me in procession to mass in the old cathedral, where she made me go along the pavement on my knees for over an hour, and on the same altarpiece where we had heard mass, she placed, as a form of *ex-voto,* a wax child which I believed to be a perfect portrait of me.

My mother had a brother, and if she was good, he was bad and cruel to boot. I cannot remember my uncle without a feeling of terror, and because of various separate incidents I can recall, I concluded that the man must have committed a crime at the time I am referring to. He was a sailor and when he was in Cádiz and on shore, he would come home drunk as a lord and treat us savagely: his sister with words, using the foulest language towards her, and me, with deeds by punishing me for no reason. My mother must have suffered a lot because of her brother's atrocious behaviour, and that, together with her arduous and poorly paid work, hastened her end, which left an indelible impression on my spirit, although my memory today can only perceive it vaguely.

During that time of misery and vagrancy I spent my time simply in playing by the sea and running through the streets. My only troubles were those caused by a hard slap from my uncle, a scolding from my mother or some mishap in the organisation of my squadrons. My spirit had yet to experience any strong and truly deep emotion, until the loss of my mother introduced me to a very different dimension of human existence that I had not experienced until then. Because of that the shock I felt has never been wiped from my soul. Even after so many years have passed, I still remember, like the fearful images remembered from nightmares, that my mother was lying prostrate with some ailment I do not know; I remember having seen some women come into our home, I cannot state their names or status; I remember hearing wails of grief, and feeling myself in the arms of my mother; I also remember cold hands, really cold hands, touching me all over my body. I believe they then took me away from there and these vague memories are linked with the sight of some yellow candles that gave off a frightening light in the middle of the day, the sound of prayers, the whispering of some old gossips, the loud laughter of drunk sailors and, after that, the sad notion of being an orphan, the idea of finding myself alone and abandoned in the world, an idea that overpowered my poor spirit for some time.

I cannot recall what my uncle did at that time. I only know that his cruelty to me redoubled to such a point that, tired of his bad treatment, I escaped from home wanting to find my fortune. I went to San Fernando; from there to Puerto Real.[12] I joined up with

D. Alonso Gutierrez de Cisniega.

the lowest of the low on those shores, a breeding ground for masters of trickery, and how or why I do not know, but I went with them to set up in Medinasidonia,[13] where one day we were in a tavern when a press gang of marines came in and we fled, each one hiding where he could. My lucky star led me to a house whose owners took pity on me, showing a great interest in me, no doubt because of the tale I told, on my knees, bathed in tears and with pleading gestures, of my sad state, my life and, above all, my misfortune.

That couple took me under their protection and freed me from the press gang, and afterwards I remained in their service. I went with them to Vejer de la Frontera,[14] the place where they lived as they were only passing through Medinasidonia.

My guardian angels were Don Alonso Gutiérrez de Cisniega, a captain in the Navy, retired from the service and his wife, both of advanced years. They taught me many things I did not know, and as they took a liking to me, before long I assumed the role of page to Don Alonso and accompanied him on his daily walk, as the worthy invalid could not move his right arm, and his right leg only with great difficulty.

I do not know what they found in me to awaken their interest. No doubt, my tender years, the fact that I was an orphan and also the docility with which I obeyed them played a part in justifying the kindness for which I have been profoundly grateful throughout my life. As well as those reasons for that affection, it should be added (although I feel bad about mentioning it) that despite having lived until then in contact with the shabbiest dregs of society, I had some innate culture or sensitivity which in a short time made me change my manners to the point where, some years later, despite my complete lack of education, I was in the position of being able to pass for a well-born person.

I had been about four years with them when what I am about to describe happened. The reader will not demand the accuracy I believe to be impossible, dealing with events that occurred in my youth and narrated in the evening of my existence, when close to my end, after a long life, I feel the ice of old age slow my hand as it holds the pen, while my frozen understanding attempts to deceive itself by looking for a fleeting rejuvenation in sweet dainties or glowing memories. Like those old rakes who believe they can awaken their slumbering voluptuousness, deceiving their senses by looking at paintings of beauties, I want to give liveliness and interest to the withered thoughts of old age, warming them up with the representation of past greatness.

And the result is immediate. What a marvellous trick of imagination! Like someone leafing through pages long since folded up from a book that he once read, I look at the years that were with curiosity and wonder; and while the magic of this contemplation lasts, it seems that a friendly genie has come and taken the affliction of the years from me, lightening the load of my old age which was weighing down my body as well as my soul.

This blood, this tepid and lazy humour which today barely animates my worn-out body, fires up, gets excited, circulates, boils, runs and beats in my veins with a quickened pulse. It seemed as if a great light had come into my brain and illuminated and brought forth a thousand unknown marvels, like the traveller's torch which lights up the darkness of the cave and reveals the wonders of geology so quickly that it seems it is creating them. And at the same time, my heart, dead to all great feelings, rose up, Lazarus called by the divine voice, and my breast shook, making me sad and joyful at the same time.

I am a young man; time has not passed; I have before me the principal deeds of my youth; I shake the hands of old friends; in my mind the happy and terrible emotions of my young days return, the ardour of triumph, the heaviness of defeat, the great joys as well as the great sorrows brought together in memory as they are in life. One emotion dominated all the others, one that always guided my actions during that eventful period between 1805 and 1834. Close to the grave, and considering myself to be the most useless of men, you can still bring tears to my eyes, oh sacred love of my country! In return, I can still dedicate some words to you, cursing the shabby doubter who disowns you and the corrupted philosopher who confounds you with short-term interests.

I dedicated my manhood to this emotion and to it I dedicate this task of my final years, taking as the tutelary spirit or guardian angel for my written life, the one that had been mine for my real life. I will tell of many things. Trafalgar, Bailén,[15] Madrid,[16] Zaragoza,[17] Gerona,[18] Arapiles![19] I will say something about all of these if you are patient.[20] My tale will not be as fine as it should be, but I will do all I can to make it truthful.

Gabriel, ¿eres tú hombre de valor?

II

On a day in early October of that ill-fated year (1805), my noble master called me to his room and, looking at me with his usual severity (a quality that was in appearance only as his character was of the utmost mildness), said to me,

'Gabriel, are you a man of courage?'

At first I did not know how to answer, since, to tell the truth, at fourteen years old I had not yet had any opportunity to astonish the world with any heroic deed; but hearing myself called "a man" filled me with pride, and as it also seemed to me to be unbecoming to deny I was courageous in front of someone who so clearly was, I replied with boyish arrogance,

'Yes, my master, I am a man of courage.'

Then that worthy man who had shed his blood in a hundred glorious combats, not that this meant he disdained to treat his loyal servant with trust, smiled at me and motioned me to sit down. He was just going to let me know of some important decision when his wife and my mistress, Doña Francisca, suddenly came into the office so that she could take more of a part in this conference and she began speaking harshly as follows,

'No, you will not go; I can assure you, you will not be going to the fleet. Whatever next!? At your age and after you have retired from the service as an old man! Oh Alonsito, you're seventy now and this is really no time for joking.'

It seems as if I can still see before me that lady, respectable as much as she was irate, with her large bonnet, her organdie dress, her white ringlets and a hairy mole on one side of her chin. I mention these four diverse details because without them my memory cannot imagine her. She was a beautiful woman in her old age, like the Saint Anne of Murillo,[21] and her great beauty would have been perfect, and the comparison with the mother of the Virgin exact, if my mistress had been silent like a painting.

Don Alonso, somewhat cowed as usual whenever he heard her, replied,

'I have to go, Paquita. According to the letter which I have just received from that good man Churruca,[22] the Combined Fleet[23] must either leave Cádiz to provoke a fight with the English or wait for them in the bay if they dare to enter. One way or another, the thing is going to come about.'

'Well, I am glad', Doña Francisca responded. 'Gravina,[24] Valdés,[25] Cisneros,[26] Churruca, Alcalá Galiano[27] and Álava[28] are there. I hope they smash those English dogs to bits. But you have become an old crock and are no use for that sort of damned thing. You still can't move your left arm which they dislocated for you at Cape St. Vincent.'

My master moved his left arm in a stiff and warlike gesture to prove that he could use it freely. But Doña Francisca, unconvinced by such a feeble argument, continued shouting,

'No, you won't be going to the fleet, because they don't need any scarecrows like you there. It would be one thing if you were forty years old, as you were when you went to Tierra del Fuego[29] and brought me those green necklaces from the Indians… But now… I know that idiot Marcial has been getting you worked up by talking to you last night and this morning about battles. It seems that Mr. Marcial and I are going to have to quarrel. Let him go back to the ships if he wants to so that they can take off the leg he still has. Oh blessed Saint Joseph! If only I had known when I was fifteen what seafarers were. What a torment! Not one day of rest! A woman marries so she can live with her husband, and then when you least expect it a dispatch from Madrid arrives and in two shakes they've sent him away from me to I don't know where, to Patagonia, to Japan or to Hell itself. Then it's ten or twelve months without seeing him and finally, if the savages haven't eaten him, he returns a wreck, so ill and yellow that a woman has no idea what to do to get his natural colour back… but you cannot catch old birds with chaff, and suddenly another little dispatch from Madrid… You're off to Toulon, to Brest, to Naples, here and there, wherever that great rascal of a First Consul[30] feels like. Ah, if everyone did as I say, that little gentleman who has stirred up the world so much would soon be paid out!'

My master looked with a smile at a bad engraving fixed on the wall which, clumsily coloured by an unknown artist, showed the Emperor Napoleon as a rider on a young charger with the famous redingote daubed with vermillion. No doubt, the impression left with me by that work of art which I contemplated for four years, was the reason I changed my ideas about the bandit costume of the great man, and afterwards I pictured him dressed like a cardinal and mounted on a young charger.

'This is no way to live,' continued Doña Francisca, waving her arms, 'God forgive me, but I hate the sea, even though they say it is one of His greatest works. I don't know what the Holy Inquisition is for if it doesn't turn those diabolical warships into ashes! Just let them come and tell me what's the point of putting cannon ball after cannon ball, just like that, onto four planks of wood which, if they break, throw hundreds of poor devils into the sea! Isn't that tempting God? And these men go crazy when they hear a cannonade! Goodness gracious! I shudder when I hear them, and if everyone thought like me, there wouldn't be any more wars at sea and all the cannons would be turned into bells. Look, Alonso,' she added, stopping in front of her husband, 'it seems to me that they have already defeated you several times. Do you want another battle? You and the others as crazy as you, haven't you had enough after the Fourteenth?'[31]

Don Alonso clenched his fists on hearing of that sad memory and refrained from uttering a sailor's oath only out of respect for his wife.

'The one to blame for your stubbornness in wanting to join the fleet,' added the lady, getting angrier all the time, 'is that rogue Marcial, that devil of a sailor who should have drowned a hundred times, and has been saved a hundred times just to torment me. If he wants to go back to sea again with his wooden leg, his broken arm, his missing eye and his fifty wounds, let him go off and do so, and God grant that he never appears here again. But you will not be going, Alonso. You will not be going because you are sick and because you have already served the King enough, and he has certainly rewarded you very badly, and if I were in your place, I would throw those captain's stripes which you've had for ten years into the face of the Generalísimo of Land and Sea.[32] In truth, they should have made you an admiral at least: you very much deserved it when you went on the expedition to Africa[33] and brought me those blue beads which I used with the Indian necklaces to decorate the case of Our Lady of Mount Carmel.'

'Admiral or not, I have to join the fleet, Paquita,' my master said. 'I cannot miss that fight. I have an account to settle with the English.'

'Well, you're in a fine position to settle that account,' replied my mistress. 'A sick man and half-crippled.'

'Gabriel will be going with me,' my master said, giving me a look which filled me with courage.

I made a gesture which indicated my agreement with such a heroic project, but took care that Doña Francisca did not see me as she would have made me feel the irresistible weight of her hand if she had seen my bellicose disposition.

Seeing that her husband seemed determined, she became more enraged; she swore that if she were reborn, she would never marry a sailor; she said awful things about the Emperor,[34] our beloved King,[35] the Prince of Peace,[36] all the

signatories to the Subsidy Treaty,[37] and finished by assuring the valiant sailor that God would punish him for his foolish temerity.

During this dialogue that I have related, but without answering for its accuracy as I based it only on vague memories, a loud cough like that of a dog in the next room announced that Marcial, the old man that caused the upset, had been listening for some time to my mistress's fiery declamation, during which she had made quite a few unflattering remarks about him. Wanting to take part in the conversation, something that the trust he enjoyed in the house allowed him to do, he opened the door and came into my master's room.

Before continuing, I want to say something about my master and his noble consort, so that you will have a better understanding of what is going to happen.

III

Don Alonso Gutiérrez de Cisniega belonged to an ancient family from Vejer itself. He was intended for a naval career, and in his youth, as a midshipman, he distinguished himself honourably in the English attack on Havana in 1748.[38] He took part in the expedition from Cartagena against Algiers in 1775 and was also present at the attack on Gibraltar by the Duke of Crillon in 1782.[39] Later he sailed on the expedition to the Straits of Magellan[40] in the sloop *Santa María de la Cabeza*, commanded by Don Antonio de Córdova.[41] He also took part in the glorious combats of the Anglo-Spanish squadron against the French off Toulon in 1793 and, finally, he ended his glorious career at the disastrous encounter of Cape St. Vincent in command of the *Mejicano*, one of the ships that had been forced to surrender.

Afterwards, my master, who had not risen as high in the ranks as his hard and wide-ranging career deserved, retired from the service. As a result of the wounds he received on that sad day, he became sick in his body and more seriously in his soul as a consequence of grief over the defeat. His wife cured him with love, although not without some shouting as curses on the Navy and seafarers came from her mouth as often as the sweet names of Jesus and Mary came from the mouths of the devout.

Doña Francisca was an excellent lady, exemplary, of noble origin, devout and God-fearing like all women of that time, charitable and discreet, but with the sharpest and wickedest temper I ever came across. I really do not think she was born with that irascible temperament, but on the contrary it was created by the troubles she suffered from the disagreeable profession of her husband; and it should be admitted that she was justified in her complaints, since that marriage which over fifty years could have given twenty children to the world and to God, had to be satisfied with just one, the enchanting and peerless Rosita, of whom I will tell later. For these and other reasons, Doña Francisca asked Heaven in her daily prayers to annihilate all the fleets of Europe.

Meanwhile, the hero wasted sadly away in Vejer, looking at his laurels eaten by moths and gnawed by mice, while he constantly thought and spoke about an important topic,

namely that if Córdova, the commander of our squadron, had ordered them to luff to port instead of ordering them to go to starboard, the *Mejicano, San José, San Nicolás* and the *San Isidro* would not have fallen into the possession of the English, and the English admiral Jervis would have been beaten.[42]

His wife, Marcial and even I, exceeding the limits of my knowledge, told him that the matter was beyond doubt with the hope that, considering us as convinced, the intense ardour of his obsession would lessen, but even so, his obsession accompanied him to the grave. Eight years had passed since that disaster and the news that the Combined Fleet was going to have a decisive encounter with the English seemed to rejuvenate him in his excitement. This then blossomed into the idea of him having to join the fleet so that he could be present at the undoubted defeat of his mortal enemies and, although his wife tried to dissuade him, as I have related, it was impossible to deflect him from his eccentric plan.

So that the strength of his desire can be understood, it is sufficient to say that he dared to oppose, although avoiding any quarrel, the firm wish of Doña Francisca, and I have to point out, so that you have an idea of my master's obstinacy, that he had no fear of the English, nor of the French, nor of the Algerians, nor of the savages on the Straits of Magellan, nor of the angry sea, nor of sea monsters, nor of the crashing storm, nor of the heavens, nor of the earth; he was afraid of nothing created by God except for his saintly wife.

Doña Francisca.

It remains for me to speak about Marcial the sailor, the object of the deepest hatred on the part of Doña Francisca, but tenderly loved like a brother by my master Don Alonso, with whom he had served.

Marcial (I never knew his surname), known as *Half-a-man* among the sailors, had been a bosun on warships for forty years. At the time of my tale this hero of the seas was the strangest sight imaginable. Picture, ladies and gentlemen, an old man, of middling height, with a wooden leg, his left arm completely cut off well below the elbow, one eye missing, his face scrawled with a multitude of disorderly gashes in all directions, the marks of all sorts of enemy weapons, a tanned and weather-beaten complexion like that of all old sailors, with a husky, booming and slow voice quite unlike that of any sensible inhabitant of dry land, and you will get an idea of this character, whose memory makes me regret the plainness of my palette, since in truth he deserved to be painted by a skilled portrait painter. I cannot say if his appearance made you laugh or commanded respect; I believe both at the same time and depending on how you looked at each other.

What can be said is that his life was the history of the Spanish Navy in the final part of the last century and the beginning of this one; a history in whose pages glorious actions alternate with pitiful calamities. Marcial had sailed in the *Conde de Regla*, the *San Joaquín*, the *Real Carlos* and the *Trinidad*,[43] and in other heroic and unfortunate ships with whose old timbers, on meeting their ends in honourable defeat or treacherous destruction, sank the naval might of Spain. As well as taking part in campaigns with my master, *Half-a-man* was present at many others, such as the expedition to Martinique,[44] the action off Finisterre[45] and before them, the awful episode in the Strait of Gibraltar

37

Marcial.

during the night of 12th July 1801[46] and the fight at Cape Santa María on 5th October 1804.[47]

At the age of sixty-six he retired from the service, not for want of spirit, but because he was now completely dismasted and out of action. He and my master became two good friends ashore, and as the bosun's only daughter had got married to a former servant of my master, with a grandson resulting from this union, *Half-a-man* decided to cast anchor for good, like an old hulk of no use for war, and even went so far as to deceiving himself that he liked peace. You just had to look at him to see that the most difficult job that could be given to that glorious wreck of a hero was looking after children, and in fact, Marcial did nothing else but carry, amuse and put his grandson to sleep, for which task his shanties seasoned with some oath characteristic of his profession sufficed.

But learning that the Combined Fleet was preparing for a great battle, he felt his deadened enthusiasm revive in his breast and dreamt that he was giving orders to the crew in the forecastle of the *Santísima Trinidad*. As he noticed the same signs of recrudescence in Don Alonso, he unbosomed himself to him, and after then they would spend most of the day and night telling each other the news they had heard as well as their own feelings, referring to past deeds, speculating about future ones and daydreaming, like two ship's boys calculating in intimate confidence how they are going to become admirals.

In these private retreats, which very much alarmed Doña Francisca, was born the plan to join the Fleet so that they could be there at the coming battle. You already know the view of my mistress and the thousand rude things she said about that trickster sailor, and you also know that Don Alonso intended to carry out that bold plan, accompanied by his page, and now it remains for me to tell of what everyone said when Marcial turned up to defend the war against the shameful *status quo* of Doña Francisca.

IV

'Mister Marcial,' she said with redoubled fury, 'if you want to go to the fleet and give it your finishing touches, you can join up whenever you want, but this one will not be going.'

'Good,' the sailor replied, having sat down on the edge of a chair, occupying only the space necessary to support himself, 'I will go on my own. The Devil take me if I don't fix my spyglass onto this party.'

Then he added joyfully, 'We have fifteen ships, and the Frenchies have twenty-five vessels. If they were all ours, you wouldn't need so many…. forty ships and great heart aboard!' Like the flame that passes from a wick to another one nearby, the enthusiasm that radiated from Marcial's eye lit up my good master's two eyes, deadened by age.

'But "*el Señorito*",[48] continued *Half-a-Man*, 'will have a lot as well. That's how I like things: plenty of wood to shoot cannon balls at and lots of powder *zmoke* to warm up the air when it's cold.'

I had forgotten to say that Marcial, like nearly all sailors, used a vocabulary made up of the strangest linguistic monstrosities, since it is customary for seafarers of all nations so to disfigure their native tongue as to change it into a caricature. Noting most of the words used by sailors, it is apparent that they are simply corruptions of the most common words, adapted to their excitable and energetic temperament, always prone to cut short all life's functions, and especially language. Hearing them speak, it seemed to me sometimes that their tongue was an organ that got in their way.

Marcial, as I say, would change nouns into verbs, and the latter into nouns, without consulting the Academy.[49] In the same way he applied the vocabulary of sailing to everything in life, assimilating a ship with a man by virtue of a forced analogy between the parts of the former and the members of the latter. For example, talking about the loss of his eye, he would say that he had closed the "starboard gangway", and to express the breaking off of his arm he would say that he had been left without his "port cathead". For him, the heart, seat of valour and heroism, was the "powder magazine" and in the same way the stomach was the "hardtack store". At least sailors understood these phrases, but there were others, daughters of his own philological inventiveness, known and fully appreciated only by him. Who could understand the meanings of "pedigumify", "hoochiness"[50] and other frightful names of the same ilk? I believe, but I'm not certain, that the first meant to doubt and that the second meant sadness. He used thousands of different terms for getting drunk, the most common of which was "to put on the coat", an idiom my readers will not be able to understand unless I explain to them that, having bestowed the honorific title of "greatcoats" onto the English sailors, no doubt because of their uniforms, by saying "put on the coat" for getting drunk Marcial intended to express a common and regular activity among his enemies. He gave foreign admirals eccentric names, made up by him and translated in his own way, based on similarities in their sounds. He called Nelson "*el Señorito*", a word which indicated some consideration or respect; Collingwood[51] "*el tío Calambre*",[52] a phrase which seemed to him an exact translation from English; Jervis he named "Old Fox" like the English themselves; Calder,[53] "*el tío Perol*",[54] because he found a lot of similarity between the two names; and following completely the opposite linguistic system, he gave Villeneuve, head of the Combined Fleet, the nickname of *Monsieur Corneta*, a name taken from a comic show Marcial had gone to in Cádiz. The language that came out of Marcial's mouth was so absurd that, to avoid tedious explanations, I have felt obliged to substitute his phrases with the proper ones when I refer to conversations of his that I remember.

So let us now continue. Doña Francisca, crossing herself, said,

'Forty ships! That is tempting Divine Providence! Dear Jesus! It means there will be at least forty thousand cannons for these enemies to kill each other with.'

'The thing is that, as Monsieur Corneta has the powder magazines well stocked,' Marcial replied, pointing to his heart, 'then we'll make those greatcoats laugh: this time won't be like Cape St. Vincent.'

'One must take into account,' said my master with pleasure, seeing that his favourite topic had been mentioned, 'that if Admiral Córdova had ordered the *San José* and the *Mejicano* to turn to port, Jervis would not have been called Earl of St Vincent. I'm sure of that and I have the facts to prove that with the manoeuvre to port we would have been victorious.'

'Victorious!' exclaimed Doña Francisca scornfully. 'As if they could have done any more…. these braggarts seem to want to swallow up the whole world, but however much they go out to sea they never seem to have enough ribs to take poundings from the English.'

'No!' said *Half-a-man* with energy and clenching his fist in a threatening manner.

'It's only because of all their clever ways and dirty tricks! We always go against them with our souls on a reach, well, with nobility, our flag hoisted and with clean hands. The English don't *come out in the open*,[55] they always attack by surprise, looking for bad seas and stormy weather. That's how it was in the Strait,[56] which cost us dearly. We were sailing without suspecting anything, as there was no fear of treachery even from

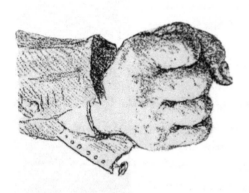

heretical Moorish dogs, *never mind* from the English who are *civil* and a sort of Christian. But no, someone who attacks treacherously is not a Christian, but a highwayman. Picture it, Señora,' he added, turning to Doña Francisca to win her goodwill. 'We left Cádiz to help the French squadron which had sought shelter in Algeciras, pursued by the English. This was four

years ago now, but I'm still so angry that my blood *boilers* when I remember it. I was in the *Real Carlos*, 112 guns, commanded by Ezguerra, and we had as well the *San Hermenegildo*, also 112 guns, the *San Fernando*, the *Argonauta*, the *San Augustín* and the frigate *Sabina*. Together with the French squadron, which had four ships, three frigates and a brigantine, we left Algeciras for Cádiz at midday, and as there was a gentle breeze we were this side of Punta Carnero at nightfall. The night was darker than a barrel of pitch, but as the weather was good, we did not mind sailing in the dark. Nearly all the crew was asleep; I remember that I was in the forecastle, talking with my cousin Pepe Débora who was telling me about his mother-in-law's dirty tricks, and from there I saw the lights of the *San Hermenegildo*, which was sailing on the starboard beam about a cannon shot away. The rest of the ships were ahead. *Well*, the last thing we were expecting was that the greatcoats had left Gibraltar behind us and were in pursuit. And how could we have seen them anyway as they were blacked out and closing up on us without us being aware? Suddenly, although the night was very dark, I thought I saw – I have always had *peepers* like a lynx's – I thought a ship was passing between us and the *San Hermenegildo*.

"José Débora," I said to my companion, "either I'm seeing *ghosties* or we've got an English ship to starboard."

José Débora looked and said to me, "May the mainmast fall through the scuttle and split me in two if there's any ship to starboard apart from the *San Hermenegildo*."

"Well, whether there is or there isn't," I said, "I'm going to tell the officer on watch."

No sooner had I said this, when *Bang!* we heard the *musiquade* of a full broadside which they discharged into the side of our ship. Within a minute the crew was awake... everyone at his post... What a din, Señora Doña Francisca! I just wish you could have seen it so that you could know what these things are like. We were all swearing like devils and asking God to put a cannon on each of our fingers to reply to the attack. Ezguerra went up to the quarterdeck and gave the order for a broadside to starboard... *Cerrash!* The starboard broadside fired off immediately, and they answered shortly after... But in this shindig we didn't see that with the first discharge they had fired some damned *comestible* (he meant combustible) material on board which fell onto the ship as if it was raining fire. Seeing that our ship was burning, our fury was redoubled and we loaded another broadside, and another, and another. Things had got to a pretty state! Our captain ordered us to close up to starboard so we could board the enemy ship. I wish you could have seen me there... I was in my element... in the wink of an eye we had the axes and pikes ready for boarding.... the enemy ship was coming up to us, which *goatified* (gladdened) my spirits because we would be grappling with each other sooner... close up, close up to starboard... terrifying! It was beginning to get light, the yardarms were now touching each other; we were already arranged in groups when we heard swearing in Spanish on board the enemy ship. Then we all went rigid with horror when we saw that the ship we had been fighting with was the very same *San Hermenegildo*.'

'Well, that really was a fine thing,' said Doña Francisca, showing some interest in the story. 'How could they have

La mar es grande.

been such asses that each of them…'

'I can tell you that we had no time for any chit-chat. The fire on the *Real Carlos* carried over to the *San Hermenegildo*, and then… Virgin of Carmel… all hell broke out! There were many shouts of "To the boats!" The fire was now at the level of the magazine, and that little lady doesn't mess about…[57] we were swearing, shouting, insulting God, the Virgin and all the saints. Because that seems to be the way you speak your mind when you're full to the hatches with courage.'

'Jesus, Mary and Joseph! How horrible!' exclaimed my mistress. 'Did they escape?'

'Forty of us escaped in the gig and six or seven in the jolly boat and they picked up the number two from the *San Hermenegildo*. José Débora made himself fast to a piece of mast and made it to the shores of Morocco more dead than alive.'

'And the others?'

'The others… the sea is big and has room enough for many people. Two thousand men *put out their fires* that day, including our Commander Ezguerra and Emparán, the commander of the other vessel.'

'God preserve them!' said Doña Francisca. 'Even though it served them right for going off to play these stupid games. If only they had stayed at home nice and quiet as God ordains…'

'Now the cause of this disaster,' said Don Alonso, who liked to interest his wife in dramatic events like these, 'was as follows: the English, taking advantage of the darkness of the night, ordered the *Superb*,[58] the swiftest of the vessels they had, to put out her lights and place herself between our two fine ships. And that's what she did – fired her two broadsides, put her rig smartly aback, at the same time luffing up to get away from the response. The *Real Carlos* and the *San Hermenegildo*, finding themselves under attack unexpectedly, opened fire; and they carried on fighting each other until shortly before dawn and, when they were about to board, they recognised each other and then the events happened which Marcial has told you about in detail.'

'Oh, and how well they played you!' said the lady, 'It was well done, even though it's not a thing honourable people would do.'

'What else would you expect?' added *Half-a-Man*. 'At that time, I didn't much like them, but since that night… if any of them are in Heaven, I don't want to go to Heaven, even if that condemns me for all *entirety...*'

'And what about the capture of the four frigates that were coming from the River Plate?' said Don Alonso, encouraging Marcial to carry on with his tales.

'That was one I was involved in as well,' the mariner replied, 'and where I was left without a leg. They took us by surprise then as well, and as we were at peace, we were sailing very much at our ease, already counting the hours to our arrival when suddenly… I'll tell you what happened, Señora Doña Francisca, so you can understand the evil ways of those people. After the affair in the Strait, I joined the *Fama* bound for Montevideo, and we had been there for a long time when the commodore received an order to transport some valuables from Lima and Buenos Aires to Spain. The voyage was good and we didn't have any mishaps other than some slight fevers which weren't enough to kill any man… We were carrying a lot of money belonging to the King and to private individuals, and also what we call "the pay chest", which are the small savings of the troops serving in the Americas. In all, if I'm not mistaken, it was something like five million pesos, and if that wasn't enough, we were also carrying some wolf skins, vicuña wool,[59] dried cacao husks, bars of tin and copper, and fine woods. So, sir, after fifty days' sail, we saw land on 5th October[60] and were planning to come into Cádiz the following day, when hey presto, four lady frigates appear from the north-east. Though it was peacetime and our captain, Don Miguel de Zapiaín, didn't seem to have any damned suspicions, I, old sea dog that I am, called over to Débora and told him that the weather smelt to me of powder… Well, when the English frigates were close by, the admiral gave the order to clear for action; the *Fama* was ahead and in a short time we were a pistol shot from one of the English frigates to windward.

Then the English captain called us with his speaking trumpet and told us – and I must say I admired his plain speaking – he told us to heave to because he was going to attack us. He asked us a thousand questions but we told him that we did not care to answer. All this time, the three other enemy frigates had come closer to ours in such a way that each of the English ones had a Spanish one on the leeward side.'

'Their position could not have been better,' my master pointed out.

'I agree entirely,' Marcial continued, 'the commander of our squadron, Don José Bustamente,[61] was not very prepared, and if it had been me… Well, sir, the English *comodón*[62] (he meant 'commodore') sent on board the *Medea*, one of those little codfish-tailed officials, who, without beating about the bush, said that, '*though* war had not been declared, the *comodón* had orders to seize us. That's what you really call being English! The fight began shortly after. Our frigate received the first broadside on the port side; the salute was answered and cannon shot went to and fro… The fact of the matter is that we didn't overpower those heretics *given that* those devils went and set fire to the magazine of the *Mercedes*, which exploded in an instant, and when this happened all of us were greatly distressed, feeling so humiliated… not for want of courage, but for what they call… *morale*, so… then at that very moment we felt we were lost. The sails on our frigate had more holes than an old cape, our ropes broken, five feet of water in the hold, the mizzen-mast down, three shot holes on the waterline and many dead and wounded. Despite this we carried on our *beano* with the English, but when we saw the *Medea* and the *Clara*, unable to withstand the roasting, strike their colours, we stretched sail and retired, defending ourselves as best we could. The damned English frigate pursued us and as she was faster than our ship, we couldn't escape and we, too, had to strike the rag at three in the afternoon, after they had already killed many of us and I was half-dead on the lower deck as a cannon ball had decided to remove my leg. That ruddy lot took us to England, not as prisoners, but as detainees; but letters went to and fro between London and Madrid; the fact is they kept the money, and it seems to me that another leg would have sprouted on me, before the King of Spain saw any one of those five million pesos.'

'Poor man! So then you lost your leg?' Doña Francisca said to him sympathetically.

'Yes, ma'am. The English, knowing that I was no ballet dancer, believed that one was enough for me. They looked after me well during the crossing; in a town called *Plinmuf* (Plymouth) I was six months on a hulk, pegging out and my warrant for the next world in my pocket, but God did not intend I should sink so soon; an English doctor fitted me with this wooden leg, which is better than the other one because that one aches with damned rheumatism, whereas this one doesn't hurt even if it was hit with a charge of shrapnel. As for its hardness, I think it is hard enough, although I still haven't tested it by standing before the stern of any English ship.'

'You are very brave,' said my mistress, 'may God grant that you don't lose the other one as well. Whoever looks for danger…'[63]

Marcial's tale having ended, the dispute about whether my master would go to the fleet started up again. Doña Francisca continued to be negative, and Don Alonso, who was like a lamb in the presence of his worthy spouse, looked for excuses and invoked all sorts of reasons to persuade her.

'We will only go to see, nothing more, just to see,' the hero said with a pleading look.

'Let's do without the soothing words,' his wife replied. 'You two are a proper pair of nonsense peddlers.'

'The Combined Fleet,' said Marcial, 'will stay in Cádiz and they will try and force an entry.'

'So in that case,' my mistress added, 'you can see the thing from the walls of Cádiz;

but as for what is in those little ships… no, no and no is what I say, Alonso. You have never seen me cross in forty years of marriage (he saw her cross every day), but I swear to you now that if you go on board… understand that Paquita will not be here for you.'

'My dear!' exclaimed my master with pain. 'Then I have to die without that pleasure.'

'A fine pleasure, great God! Look how those madmen kill each other! If the King of Spain[64] paid attention to me, he would send the English packing and tell them: "My beloved vassals are not here for you to amuse yourselves with. Go and do your work with one another if you want to play". What do you think of that? Although I am a foolish woman, I know very well what's going on here, it's the First Consul, Emperor, Sultan or whatever he is that wants to attack the English and as he doesn't have enough brave men to do the job, he has tricked our good king into lending him ours, and the truth is that he's harming us with his naval wars. You two tell me, what has Spain got to do with this? Why does there have to be gunfire after gunfire every day for a trifle? Before those dirty tricks that Marcial told us about, what harm had the English done to us? Ah, if they paid attention to what I say, that Mister Bonaparte would be making war on his own, or if not, he wouldn't be making war!'

'It is true,' said my master, 'that the alliance with France is causing us a lot of harm since any advantage benefits our ally while all the disasters happen to us.'

'Well, then, you complete fools, why are you so keen on this war?'

'The honour of our nation is at stake,' Don Alonso replied, 'and once caught up in this affair, it would be unworthy to withdraw. When I was in Cádiz last month for the baptism of the daughter of my cousin, Churruca said to me: "This alliance with France and the wretched Treaty of San Ildefonso,[65] which, through Bonaparte's cunning and Godoy's weakness, has been turned into a treaty of subsidies, will be our ruin, the ruin of our fleet, unless God saves us, and therefore the ruin of our colonies and Spanish trade in America. But in spite of everything, we have to carry on."'

'I always say,' added Doña Francisca 'that this Prince of Peace gets himself into things he does not understand. It's obvious that he is a man without any education! My brother, the archdeacon, who is a supporter of Prince Ferdinand,[66] says that this man Godoy is a complete idiot and that he never studied Latin or theology, so all he knows about is playing the guitar and the twenty-two ways to dance the gavotte. It seems that he was made prime minister because of his pretty face. That's how things are done in Spain, next, hunger and more hunger… everything so expensive… yellow fever destroying Andalusia… Oh yes, this is all very fine… and it's all of you who are

to blame for this,' she continued, raising her voice and getting redder in the face. 'Oh yes, you who offend God by killing so many people; you, who if instead of getting involved with those damned ships, went to church and said the rosary, Old Nick would not be going so freely about Spain making mischief.'

'You can go to Cádiz as well,' said Don Alonso, anxious to arouse some enthusiasm in his wife's breast. 'You can go to Flora's and from the balcony you will be able to see the battle in comfort: the smoke, the explosions, the flags… it is a great sight.'

'No thank you! I would drop dead with fright. We will be peaceful here, since he who looks for danger will perish from it.'

And so ended that dialogue, whose details have stayed in my memory, despite the time that has passed. But it is often the case that things which happened long ago, in the time of our childhood, stay more sharply engraved in our imagination than things we witnessed when grown up and when reason predominates over all our faculties.

That night Don Alonso's and Marcial's discussions continued during the short periods that the suspicious Doña Francisca left them alone. When the latter went to the parish church to attend the novena,[67] as was her pious custom, the two sailors breathed freely like rowdy schoolboys when teacher is out of sight. They shut themselves up in the study, took out some charts and began examining them with great attention; then they read some papers on which were noted the names of many of the English ships with the number of cannon and crew, and during their enthusiastic conference, in which reading alternated with the most energetic commentaries, I noticed that they were devising the plan for a naval battle.

Marcial imitated, with gestures of his arm and a half, the advance of the fleets, the explosions of broadsides; with his head, the rolling of combatant ships; with his body, the falling side of a ship which was going to sink; with his hand, the raising and lowering of signal flags; with a soft whistle, the command of the bosun; with thwacks of his wooden leg on the floor, the thunder of cannon; with his leathery tongue, the oaths and strange sounds of battle and as my master was helping him in this task with the utmost gravity, I wanted to add my twopenn'orth as well, encouraged by example and giving free rein to that overpowering need to make a noise which dominates a boy's temperament with absolute power. Unable to contain myself and seeing the enthusiasm of the two seafarers, I began whirling round the room, given that the way I was treated without any formality by my master gave me leave to do so; I mimicked with my head and arms the disposition of a ship working to windward, at the same time uttering, with lowered voice, booming monosyllables that seemed most like the sound of cannon shot, such as *Boom! Boom! Boom!* My respected master and the mutilated sailor, children just like me on that occasion, paid no attention to what I was doing, so taken over were they by their own ideas. How I laughed when recalling that scene and how true it is, as far as my playmates in that game were concerned, that the enthusiasm of old age turns old men into children, repeating the mischievous tricks of the cradle at the very edge of the tomb!

They were utterly absorbed in their discussion when they heard the steps of Doña Francisca who was returning from the novena.

'She's coming!' Marcial exclaimed in terror.

And immediately they put away the plans, hiding their excitement, and began talking about unimportant matters. But I, either because young blood could not calm down easily, or because I did not notice my mistress's arrival in time, carried on displaying my rapture in the middle of the room with phrases such as these, expressed with the greatest self-confidence: 'Starboard tack! Down helm! Broadside to leeward! Fire! *Boom. Boom!*' She came up to me, furious, and without any warning discharged into my stern a broadside with her right hand, and with such a good aim that it made me see stars.

'You as well!' she cried, beating me without mercy. 'You see,' she added, looking at her husband with flashing eyes, 'you have taught him to lose all respect. Do you think you are still in La Caleta, you wretched ne'er-do-well?'

The hiding continued so: me, going to the kitchen, weeping and ashamed, having lowered the flag of my dignity and without any thought of defending myself against such a superior enemy; Doña Francisca, behind me in pursuit and testing the scruff of my neck with repeated blows of her hand. In the kitchen, I cast anchor, in tears and reflecting on how badly my naval battle had ended.

V

In opposing the foolish determination of her husband, Doña Francisca did not just base herself on the reasons stated above; as well as those, she had another, much more powerful one, that I did not mention in the previous dialogue, perhaps because it was understood too well.

But the reader does not know it and I will tell you what it is. I believe I have written that my master and mistress had a daughter. Well, then, this daughter was called Rosita, slightly older than me, as she had just passed her fifteenth birthday, and it had been agreed that she would marry a young officer of the Artillery called Malespina, from a family of Medinasidonia, distantly related to my mistress's family. The wedding had been fixed for the end of October and it could be readily understood that the absence of the bride's father would have been inappropriate for such a solemn occasion.

I will now tell you about my young lady and her fiancé, about their love, their planned union and … Ah, here my memories take on a melancholy tone, evoking in my fantasy troubling and exotic images that seem to have come from another world, wakening in my tired breast sensations which, truth to tell, I do not know whether they bring joy or sadness to my spirit. These burning memories, which today seem to fade away in my mind, like tropical flowers transplanted to the frozen north, sometimes make me laugh, and sometimes make me reflect… but enough of this, the reader will tire of these irritating reflections which are of interest to one mortal alone.

Rosita was extremely pretty. I remember her beauty perfectly, although I would find it very difficult to describe her features. It seems as if I see her smiling before me. The singular expression on her face, unlike that of anyone else, is for me, because of the clarity with which it opens up to my understanding, like one of those primitive notions that we seem to have brought from another world, or which have been instilled into us from the cradle by a mysterious power. And yet, I do not intend to describe her, because what was real has become an indeterminate idea in my brain and nothing fascinates us more, nor does anything elude so subtly all descriptive appreciation, than an ideal loved one.

When I joined the household I believed that Rosita belonged to a higher order of beings. I will tell you why I thought this so that you can marvel at my simplicity. When we are children and a new being comes into the world in our house, the adults tell us that they had brought him or her from France, Paris or England. Mistaken, like all children, about such a strange way to perpetuate the species, I believed that children came by order, packed up in a little box, like a collection of trinkets. Well, then, gazing at the daughter of my master and mistress for the first time, I thought that such a beautiful person could not have come from the factory we all came from, that is, from Paris or England, and I persuaded myself of the existence of some enchanting region where divine craftsmen knew how to fashion such lovely examples of humankind.

As we were both children, although of different status, we soon treated each other with the informality of our age, and my greatest happiness consisted in playing with her, suffering all her peevishness, which was great, since in our games the classes were never confused: she was always the young lady and I always the servant; so it was that I always came off worst, and if there were blows I do not need to say here who was on the receiving end.

My heart's desire was to go and meet her when she left school and accompany her home; and when some unexpected occupation meant that someone else was charged with carrying out such a sweet commission, my grief was so deep that I treated it as equal to the worst hardships that a man could experience in life and I would say, "It's impossible that I will suffer greater misfortune when I'm grown up." To climb up the orange tree in the patio at her order to pluck the orange blossom from the highest branches was my greatest delight, a position or pre-eminence superior to that of the greatest king on earth seated on his golden throne, and I cannot recall any joy comparable to that I felt having to run after her in that divine and immortal game called hide-and-seek. If she ran like a gazelle, I flew like a bird to catch her more quickly, catching hold of her by whichever part of her body was closest to hand. When our roles changed, when she was the pursuer and I was the one to be caught, the pure and innocent delights of that sublime game were repeated, and the darkest and vilest hiding place, where hidden and palpitating I awaited the touch of her arms, anxious to grasp me, was for me truly paradise. I should add that during these episodes I never had a thought or sensation that did not emanate from the most refined idealism.

And what can I say about her singing? Since a very young girl she was in the habit of singing the *olé*[68] and the *cañas*[69] with the skill of nightingales, which know everything

about music without having been taught. Everyone praised her for that ability and they would form a ring around her to hear her, but the applause of her admirers displeased me and I would have wished she had remained silent for everyone else. That style of singing was a melancholy trilling, even though modulated by her child's voice. The note, which repeated itself, twisting and then unwinding itself like a thread of sound, lost itself as it rose and grew fainter as it faded away, only to return descending in a low timbre.

It seemed to be emitted by a little bird that first ascended into the sky and then sang for our ears alone. My soul, if I may be permitted to use a commonplace simile, seemed to extend itself as it followed the sound and then contract as it drew back before it, but always hanging on the melody and associating the music with the beautiful singer. So striking was the effect that hearing her sing, above all in the presence of others, was all but mortification for me.

We were both more or less the same age, as I have said, since she was older than me by only some eight or nine months. But I was a stunted little thing, while she developed strongly, so that after I had been three years in the house, she seemed much older than me. Those three years passed without us suspecting that we were growing up and our games continued without interruption, but then she was naughtier than me and her mother would scold her, trying to control her and get her to work.

At the end of those three years I noticed that the shapes of my adored young lady were expanding and becoming more rounded, perfecting the beauty of her body; her face became more glowing, fuller, more distant; her large eyes, brighter, even though her expression was less variable and unpredictable; her walk more unhurried; her movements, whether more or less nimble I do not know, but certainly different, although I could not then, nor can I now, say where the difference lay. But none of these features confused me as much as the transformation in her voice, which acquired

a sort of sonorous gravity, very different from that mischievous and happy squeal she used to call me with before, upsetting my good sense and obliging me to forget my chores to take part in games. The rosebud had changed into a rose.

One day, one a thousand times ill-fated, a thousand times mournful, my young mistress appeared before me in a long dress. That transfiguration produced such an effect on me that I did not utter a word the whole day. My composure was solemn like that of a man who has been vilely cheated and my anger towards her was so great that, talking to myself, I proved with strong arguments that the rapid growth of my young mistress was a crime. The fever of reasoning was woken in me and I argued passionately with myself on this matter in the silence of my sleeplessness. The thing that stunned me most was seeing how a few yards of cloth had completely changed her character. On that day, one a thousand times miserable, she spoke to me stiffly, ordering me in a severe and even bad-tempered manner to do the chores I least liked, and she, who so often had been an accomplice in my idleness and had covered up for me, then reprimanded me for being lazy. Meanwhile, not even a smile, no skips, no silliness, no quick races, not even a little *olé*, no hiding away from me so that I could find her, no pretending to be cross and then laughing, no little spats, not even a tap on my neck from her little white hand! A terrible crisis of existence! She had changed into a woman and I continued to be a child!

It goes without saying that there were no more frolics or games; I no longer climbed the orange tree whose blossoms grew in peace, free from my amorous rapacity, spreading its leaves luxuriantly and its inviting fragrance profusely. No longer did we run along the patio, nor did I make any more trips to school to bring her home, so proud of my commission that I would have defended her against an army if they had tried to take her away from me. Since then, Rosita would go about with great circumspection and dignity; on many occasions I noticed that when she went upstairs ahead of me, she took care to show neither a line nor an inch above her beautiful ankle, and this system of deceitful concealment was an insult to the dignity of one whose eyes had seen things higher up. I laugh now when I think how those things broke my heart.

But more terrible misfortunes had yet to come. One day in the year of her change, Martina, Rosario the cook, Marcial and other servants became concerned about some grave matter. Applying my assiduous sense of hearing, I then learnt that an alarming rumour was going about: the young lady was going to marry. The thing was ridiculous since I did not know that she had any fiancé. But in those days the parents arranged everything, and the strange thing is that sometimes everything did not turn out badly.[70]

So a young man from a great family asked for her hand in marriage and my master and mistress granted it to him. This young man came to the house accompanied by his parents who were some sort of counts or marquises with a resounding title. The suitor wore his uniform of the Navy, in which honourable body he served, but despite such elegant trappings, his look was very disagreeable. That is how he must have seemed to my young mistress, since from the start she displayed an aversion to that marriage. Her mother tried to persuade her, but without success, and painted for her a most accomplished picture of the fiancé's good qualities, his elevated lineage and great riches. Her daughter was not persuaded and countered these reasons with other very sensible ones.

But the naughty girl did not mention the main reason, and the main reason was that she had another sweetheart, whom she truly loved. This other was an officer in the Artillery called Don Rafael Malespina, who had an impressive bearing and elegant figure. My young mistress had got to know him in church, and perfidious love had taken hold of her while she prayed, since the church, as a poetic and mysterious place, was a very suitable location for opening wide the soul's doors to love. Malespina would hang about the house, which I observed on a number of occasions, and he spoke so much about this love affair in Vejer that the other one found out about it and they challenged each other. My master and mistress found out everything when news came to the house that Malespina had mortally wounded his rival.

The scandal was great. The religiosity of my master and mistress was so scandalised by that event that they could not hide their anger and Rosita was the principal victim. But months and then more months passed, the wounded man recovered, and as Malespina was also a well-born and rich person, indications appeared in the political atmosphere of the house that young Don Rafael would join it. The parents of the wounded man gave up the engagement, and instead the victor's father came to the house to ask on behalf of his son for the hand of my dear young mistress. After some delays, it was granted.

I remember when Malespina senior went there. He was a very dry and pompous man, with a multi-coloured waistcoat, lots of flaps on his watch, a large doublet and a very long and sharp nose with which he seemed to sniff people who were engaged in conversation with him. He talked nineteen to the dozen and did not let anyone else get a word in edgeways; he seemed to have all the answers and one could not praise anything without him instantly saying that he had a better one. Since then, I branded him as a vain and very deceitful man, something I had occasion to see clearly later. My master and mistress gave him a royal welcome, as well as to his son who came with him. After then the fiancé kept coming to the house every day on his own or accompanied by his father.

D. Rafael Malespina.

A new change in my young mistress. Her indifference towards me was so marked that it bordered on disdain. Then I began to see clearly for the first time, cursing it, the lowliness of my condition; I tried to understand the right to superiority which those who really were superior had, and I asked myself, full of anguish, if it was fair that others were noble and rich, whereas I had La Caleta as my inheritance, my person as my only fortune, and I hardly knew how to read. Seeing the reward for my burning love, I realised that I could not aspire to anything in the world and only later did I acquire the firm conviction that great and constant effort from me might perhaps give me everything I lacked.

In view of the coolness she showed to me, I lost confidence and I did not dare to open my mouth in her presence, and she instilled in me much more respect than her parents. Meanwhile, I carefully observed the signs of the love that ruled over her. When he was late, I saw her impatient and sad, when the slightest sound indicated that someone was approaching, her beautiful face lit up and her black eyes sparkled with anxiety and hope. If it eventually was him who came, it was impossible for her to hide her joy and then they would be chatting for hours and hours, always in the presence of Doña Francisca, as my young lady was not allowed to have conversations on her own or through screens.

They also wrote to each other at length and the worst thing about it was that I was the postman for the two lovers. This made my blood boil! In accordance with instructions, I would go out to the square and there I would meet, more punctual than a clock, master Malespina who would give me a note to deliver to my young lady. I carried out my commission and she would give me another one to take to him. How many times was I tempted to burn those letters and not take them to their addressee! However, luckily for me, I had the serenity to overcome such a nasty notion.

D. José Malespina.

Needless to say, I hated Malespina. When I saw him come in, I felt my blood rise up, and whenever he ordered me to do something, I did it as badly as possible, wanting to make known to him my deep anger. This indifference, which to them seemed a lack of breeding and to me an outburst of moral integrity peculiar to elevated souls, earned me some reprimands and above all, was the origin of a phrase said by my young lady which struck into my heart like a painful thorn. On one occasion I heard her say, "This boy has become so bad that he must be sent away from the house."

Finally the wedding day was fixed, and a few days before that day what I have already related happened, as well as my master's scheme. One can therefore understand that Doña Francisca had strong reasons, in addition to her husband's poor health, for preventing him from joining the Fleet.

VI

I remember very well that on the day after the cuffing I had received from Doña Francisca, provoked by the spectacle of my irreverence and her deep hatred of naval warfare, I went out to accompany my master on his midday walk. He gave me his arm and Marcial was at his side; the three of us were walking slowly, in keeping with the unsteady gait of Don Alonso and the clumsiness of the sailor's artificial leg. We looked like one of those processions where a group of old and moth-eaten saints, on a wobbly palanquin, threatened to fall to the ground as soon as those carrying them walked a bit faster. The two old men had nothing quick or sharp about them other than their hearts, which functioned like machines that had just left the workshop. They were magnetic needles which, despite their great power and exact movement, could not get the old and damaged hulls in which they were embarked to sail well.

During the walk, my master, after having affirmed with his habitual gravity that if Admiral Córdova, instead of ordering to go to starboard, had ordered to go to port, the Battle of the Fourteenth would not have been lost, began to talk about the famous project, and, although they did not clearly state their plan, no doubt because I was in front, I understood from the odd word that they were going to try and carry it out on the sly and just leave the house one morning without my mistress being aware.

We returned home and there was much talk then about very different things. My master, who was always complaisant towards his wife, was never more so than on that day. Whatever Doña Francisca said, however insignificant, he celebrated with inappropriate hilarity. I think that he even gave her some trinkets, showing in everything he did his desire to keep her happy. No doubt because of this same officious indulgence, my mistress was more intractable and irritable than I had ever seen her be. No honourable compromise was possible. For some trivial reason or other, she quarrelled with Marcial and ordered him to leave the house immediately; she said terrible things to her husband and during dinner, although he praised every dish with unusual warmth, the implacable lady did not stop grumbling.

The hour for saying the rosary came, a solemn ceremony which took place in the dining room with everyone in the house present, and my master, who on other occasions would go to sleep, lazily murmuring the *Paternosters*, something that would earn him a few reprimands, was very wide awake that evening and prayed with real eagerness, making his voice heard among all the others.

Another thing happened that has remained very much in my mind. The walls in the house were decorated with two sorts of objects: engravings of saints and maps; the heavenly kingdom on one side and all the sailing directions for Europe and America on the other. After eating, my master was in the gallery looking at a chart and tracing the lines on it with an unsteady finger, when Doña Francisca, who suspected something about the escape plan and anyway always made a great fuss when she surprised her husband in his nautical enthusiasm *in flagrante delicto*, came up behind him and, raising her arms, exclaimed:

'In God's name! You really are looking for it… I swear to you that if you are looking for trouble, you'll get it!'

'But my dear,' my master replied, trembling, 'I was here looking at the course of Alcalá Galiano and Valdés in the schooners *Sutil* and *Mejicana* when they went to explore the Juan de Fuca Strait.[71] It was a very fine voyage, I think I have told you about it.'

'I tell you I'll burn all those useless bits of paper,' Doña Francisca added. 'A curse on voyages and the Jewish dog that invented them![72] You would do better by thinking about the things of God since, when all's said and done, you're not a child anymore. What a man, dear God, what a man!'

She did not stop there. I happened to be passing nearby, but I don't remember exactly if my mistress vented her anger on my humble person by demonstrating to me again the elasticity of my ears and the agility of her hands. The thing is that these caresses happened so frequently that I cannot recall if I received some on that occasion. What I do remember is that my master, despite having redoubled his efforts to be nice, did not succeed in mollifying his wife.

I haven't said anything about my young mistress. Well, you should know that she was very sad because Mister Malespina had not put in an appearance that day, nor had he written any letter, all my attempts to find him in the square having failed. Night came and with it a sadness in the soul of Rosita as there was no hope of seeing him until the following day. But all of a sudden and after the order had been given for supper, there was a loud knocking on the door. I ran to open it and there he was. Before doing so, my hatred had known it was him.

It is as if I can still see him when he appeared before me, shaking his cloak, wet from the rain. Whenever I recall him, he seems to me as I saw him on that occasion. Speaking impartially, I can say he was a truly handsome young man, with a noble presence, graceful manners, a pleasant expression, somewhat cold and reserved in appearance, rarely smiling and exceedingly polite, with that grave and slightly conceited politeness of the nobility of long ago. That night he was wearing a jacket with tails, short breeches with boots, a Portuguese hat and the richest scarlet cloak with silk lining, which was the most elegant article of clothing among the young gentlemen of the period.

As soon as he entered, I knew something serious was afoot. He went to the dining room and everyone was astonished to see him at that hour as he had never come before in the evening. The joy of my young mistress lasted only so long as it took to realise that the reason for such an unexpected visit could not be a pleasant one.

'I have come to take my leave,' said Malespina.

Everyone was stunned with Rosita whiter than the paper I am writing on; then bright scarlet and later, deathly pale again.

'But, what's happening? Where are you going to, Don Rafael?' my mistress asked him.

I must have said that Malespina was an officer in the Artillery, but I did not mention that he was stationed at Cádiz and on leave in Vejer.

'As the fleet is short of personnel,' he added, 'they have ordered our embarkation for service aboard. A battle is believed to be inevitable and most of the ships are lacking gunners.'

'Jesus, Mary and Joseph!' exclaimed Doña Francisca in mortal terror. 'They're taking you as well? Well, I like that! But you are based on land, my young friend. Tell them to sort it out themselves; if they don't have enough people, they'll have to find them. This really is a fine joke to play!'

'But, my dear,' Don Alonso said nervously, 'don't you see that it's necessary....'

He was unable to continue because Doña Francisca, who was getting carried away with her anger, apostrophised all the powers of the earth.

'You think everything is fine as long as it's for your blessed ships of the line. But who, who is this Devil from Hell that has ordered Army officers to go on board? Don't let them tell me: it's the doing of Mister Bonaparte. No one from here could have devised such devilry. Just go and say that he's going to get married. Now,' she continued, turning to her husband, 'write to Gravina and tell him that this young man cannot join the fleet.'

And when she saw her husband shrugging his shoulders to indicate that the matter was extremely serious, she exclaimed,

'You are useless. Jesus! If I wore breeches, I would plant myself in Cádiz and get you out of this fix.'

Rosita did not say a word. I was watching her closely, and knew how greatly alarmed she felt. Her eyes did not leave her fiancé and if etiquette and good form had not prevented it, she would have wept loudly, relieving the pain of her oppressed heart.

'Military men,' said Don Alonso, 'are slaves to their duty and our country requires this young man to go to sea to defend it. In the coming battle you will attain great glory and make your name illustrious with some deed which will remain in History as an example to future generations.'

'Yes, yes, that's right,' said Doña Francisca, imitating the grandiloquent tone in which my master had just pronounced these words. 'Yes. We know all that, but why? Just because of a whim of those idiots in Madrid. Let them come and fire the cannons themselves and make war… and, when are you leaving?'

'First thing tomorrow. My leave has been cancelled and I have been ordered to report immediately to Cádiz.'

It is impossible to portray in words or write about what I saw in the look of my young mistress when she heard those phrases. The engaged couple looked at each other and a long and sad silence followed the announcement of the impending departure.

'This is intolerable,' said Doña Francisca. 'They will end up by taking civilians and even women if they take a fancy to… Lord,' she continued, looking to Heaven in the posture of a priestess, 'I do not believe I will offend you if I curse the man who invented ships, curse the sea on which they sail, and doubly curse the man who made the first cannon whose blasts drive a woman mad and kill so many poor fellows who did no harm.'

Don Alonso looked at Malespina, trying to find in his face an expression of protest against these insults directed at the noble Artillery. Afterwards he said,

'What is bad is that the ships are also in want of good equipment; it would be regrettable…'

Marcial who was listening to the conversation from the door could not contain himself and came in, saying,

'How could anything be lacking? The *Trinidad* has a hundred and thirty guns: thirty-two of thirty-six, thirty-four of twenty-four, thirty-six of twelve, eighteen of eight, and howitzers of twenty-four. The *Príncipe de Asturias,* a hundred and eighteen; the *Santa Ana*, a hundred and twenty; the *Rayo*, a hundred, and the *Nepomuceno, the San….*'[73]

'Who asked for your opinion, Mr. Marcial?!' yelled Doña Francisca. 'Not that we care whether they have fifty or eighty!'

Despite this Marcial continued with his military statistics, but with a lower voice and directing himself only to my master who did not dare show his approval.

She carried on speaking,

'But, Don Rafael, you must not go, for God's sake. Say that you are for the land and that you are going to get married. If Napoleon wants a war, let him have it on his own; let him go and say, 'Here I am, either kill me, you English, or be killed by me.' Why does Spain have to answer to the whims of that gentleman?'

'I must admit,' said Malespina, 'that our union with France has been disastrous up to now.'

'Well, then, why did they do it? They are right when they say that Godoy is someone without any education. How can he think of governing a nation by playing the guitar!'

'Following the Peace of Basel,'[74] the young man continued, 'we found ourselves obliged to become enemies of the English, who beat our fleet at Cape St. Vincent.'

'Stop there,' my master declared, striking the table heavily with his fist. 'If Admiral Córdova had ordered the ships in the vanguard to luff to port, in accordance with the most basic laws of strategy, victory would have been ours. I have proved that over and over and I gave my opinion at the time of the battle. Still, it's the case that everyone should keep to their own station.'

'The fact is that the battle was lost,' Malespina continued. 'This disaster would not have had such grave consequences if the Spanish Court had not entered into the Treaty of San Ildefonso with the French Republic, which put us at the mercy of the First Consul, obliging us to help him in wars which were only of interest to him and to his great ambition. The Peace of Amiens[75] was only a truce. England and France declared war on each other again and then Napoleon demanded our help. We wanted to be neutral since that treaty put no obligations on us in the second war, but he asked for our co-operation so vigorously that, to placate him, the King had to agree to give France a subsidy of one hundred million reales, which was a high price for buying neutrality. But we still did not buy it with this. Despite such a great sacrifice we were dragged into the war. England forced us into it, inopportunely seizing four frigates that were coming from America laden with riches. After that act of piracy, the Court in Madrid had no other choice than to throw themselves into the arms of Napoleon, which was just what he wanted. Our Navy remained at the discretion of the First Consul, now the Emperor, who, hoping to defeat the English by deception, ordered the Combined Fleet to set out for Martinique with the aim of removing the sailors of Great Britain from Europe. With this stratagem he hoped to realise his longed-for landing on that island, but all this clever plan served to do was to demonstrate the inexperience and cowardice of the French admiral,[76] who, having returned to Europe, did not want our ships to share in the glory of the Battle of Finisterre. Now, according to the orders of the Emperor, the Combined Fleet is to proceed to Brest. They say that Napoleon is furious with his admiral and that he intends to relieve him immediately.'

'But, according to what they say,' Marcial suggested, '*Monsieur Corneta* wants to show off and find some military action which will make his mistakes be forgotten. I'm pleased because this way we'll soon see who can take it and who can't.'

'What is without doubt,' Malespina continued, 'is that the English fleet is approaching and intends to blockade Cádiz. The Spanish naval officers are of the opinion that our fleet should not leave the bay, where there is a chance of victory. But it seems the Frenchman is determined to go out.'

'Let's see,' my master said. 'Whatever happens,

the battle will be glorious.'

'Glorious, yes,' Malespina replied. 'But who can be sure that it will be fortunate? The naval officers are building up false hopes and perhaps because they are too closely involved they are not aware of the inferiority of our armament compared to that of the English. As well as superiority in artillery, they have everything necessary for quickly repairing any damage. Best not to say anything about personnel; that of our enemies cannot be bettered, all of whom are old and very experienced sailors, whereas many of the Spanish ships are crewed in the most part by levies who are always slackers and hardly know what their job is; the Marine Corps is not much of an example either, since the vacancies have been filled by soldiers from the Army: very brave no doubt, but they get seasick.'

'Well, then,' my master said, 'within a few days we will know how this will all turn out.'

'I already know how it will turn out,' Doña Francisca observed. 'Those gentlemen, while they will have achieved great glory, will come home with their heads broken.'

'My dear, what do you understand about this?' said Don Alonso, unable to contain a fit of anger, which only lasted a moment.

'More than you!' she replied sharply. 'But may it please God to preserve you, Don Rafael, so that you return safe and sound.'

This conversation took place during supper, which was a very sad occasion. After this, the four of them did not say a word. Once supper was over, it was time to say farewell, which was a most tender one and, as a special favour fitting for such a solemn occasion, the kind-hearted parents left the engaged couple on their own, allowing them to say farewell to each other at their ease and without witnesses so that dissimulation would not force them to omit any swooning as an outlet for their deep anguish. No matter what I did, I was not able to be present at the ceremony and so I am ignorant about what happened then, but it is easy to guess all the tender words imaginable that they would have said to each other.

When Malespina came out of the room he was paler than a corpse. He quickly took his leave from my master and mistress who embraced him with great affection and he left. When we turned to where my young mistress had gone, we found her in a sea of tears; her sorrow was so great that her loving parents could not calm her spirit with ingenious reasoning or temper her body with the cordials that I hurriedly brought from the pharmacy. I confess that I, too, was deeply pained at the sight of the misfortune of the poor lovers, and the tinges of resentment that Malespina inspired in my breast diminished. A child's heart forgives easily and mine was no less inclined to gentle and expansive sentiments.

VII

The following morning a great surprise was waiting for me and, for my mistress, the greatest tantrum that I think she ever had in her life. When I got up Don Alonso seemed to be excessively amiable and his wife more irritated than usual. When the latter went to mass with Rosita, I noticed that he was in a great hurry to pack into a case some shirts and other articles of clothing, among which went his uniform. I helped him and this smelt to me of a secret getaway, although I was surprised not to see Marcial anywhere. However, it did not take me long to understand his absence since Don Alonso, once he had sorted out his meagre baggage, became very impatient until at last the sailor appeared, saying,

'Here is the coach. Let's go before she comes.'

I picked up the case and in a jiffy Don Alonso, Marcial and I left through the gate of the yard so that we would not be seen;[77] we got into the chaise and this set off at the highest speed permitted by the scragginess of the nag that was dragging it and the tempestuous configuration of the road. This, if it was bad for horses, was wicked for coaches, but in spite of the heavy jolts and our retching, we hurried along and while the town was still in sight, the torture suffered by our bodies did not diminish in the slightest.

This journey made me extraordinarily happy, because any novelty delights all boys. Marcial was beside himself with joy and my master, who in the beginning was almost more joyful than me, began to get sad when the town could no longer be seen. From time to time he would say,

'And she was so opposed to this! What will she say when she comes home and doesn't find us there!'

As for me, my breast swelled at the sight of the countryside, with the joy and freshness of morning and, above all, with the thought of soon seeing Cádiz and its incomparable bay filled with ships, its busy and merry streets, its Caleta which at one time symbolised for me the most beautiful thing in the world: liberty, its square, its

quay and other places much loved by me. We had not gone three leagues when we caught sight of two horsemen mounted on magnificent sorrel horses who, coming up behind us, soon joined us. We instantly recognised Malespina and his father, that tall, pompous and very talkative gentleman I have spoken about before. Both were surprised to see Don Alonso and even more so when he told them that he was going to Cádiz to join the fleet. The son received the news with sorrow, but the father, who as I later learnt was an out and out braggart, congratulated him with overblown pomposity, calling him the flower of navigators, the model of a sailor and an honour to his country.

We stopped to eat in the inn at Conil.[78] The gentlemen were given what they had, and Marcial and I were given what was left over, which was not much. Since I was serving at the table I could hear the conversation and so I got to know better the character of Malespina senior, who if at first was in my eyes an impostor full of vanity, then seemed to me to be the most amusing teller of tall stories that I had ever heard.

The future father-in-law of my young mistress, Don José María Malespina, who was no relation to the famous sailor of the same surname,[79] was a retired colonel in the Artillery and took the greatest pride in knowing like no one else all about that terrible weapon and how to handle it. Speaking about this topic seemed to spark his imagination and his facility for lying the most.

'Artillerymen,' he said without ceasing for a moment from gobbling down his food, 'are indispensable on board ship. What use is a ship without artillery? But where you can see the effect of this admirable invention of human intelligence is on land, Don Alonso. During the War of Roussillon[80]… you know of course that I took part in that campaign and that all the victories were due to my skill in handling artillery… the Battle of Masdeu,[81] how do you think we won it? General Ricardos[82] placed me on a hill with four guns, ordering me not to open fire until he gave me orders to do so. But I, who saw things differently, waited stealthily until a French column began to position itself before me in a disposition that meant my fire could enfilade them from one end to the other. The French formed the line perfectly. I took careful aim with one of the guns, fixing the sight on the first soldier's head… Do you understand? As the line was so perfect, I fired and bang! The shot removed a hundred and forty-two heads and it was only because the end of the line moved a bit that more of them didn't fall. This caused great consternation among the enemy, but as they had no idea of my strategy, nor could they see me where I was located, they sent another column to attack the troops which were to my right and that column suffered the same fate, then another and another until the battle was won.'[83]

'Amazing!' said my master, who was aware of the enormity of the fib but nevertheless did not want to contradict his friend.

'Then in the second campaign, with Count de la Unión[84] in command, I taught the republicans another good lesson. The defence of Boulou[85] did not turn out well for us because we ran out of ammunition; I, in spite of everything, wreaked great destruction by loading a gun with the keys of the church, but there weren't many of these and in the end, as a desperate measure, I put into the barrel of the cannon my keys, my watch, my money, some trinkets I found in my pockets and finally, even my medals. The remarkable thing is that one of these went and planted itself onto the chest of a French general where it stayed on as if stuck without harming him. He kept it and when he went to Paris, the Convention[86] sentenced him, I'm not sure, either to death or to exile for having accepted a decoration from the government of an enemy.'

'What devilry!' my master murmured, amused by such droll tales.

'When I was in England,' Malespina senior continued, '… you know of course that the English government summoned me to improve that country's Artillery… I used to dine every day with Pitt,[87] Burke,[88] Lord North,[89] General Cornwallis[90] and other important persons who used to call me "the Spanish Wit". I remember one occasion, we were in the Palace, when I was asked to demonstrate a bullfight and I had to wave the cape at, stick and kill a chair, which greatly amused all the Court, especially King George III[91] who was a real old chum of mine and who was always telling me to order some good olives from my country. Oh, he was on very close terms with me! He was absolutely determined that I should teach him some Spanish words, above all, some from this our graceful Andalusia. But he could never learn  more than "another bull" and "bring on those five", which was the phrase he greeted me with every day when I went to have whiting and some small glasses of sherry with him for lunch.'

'He had that for lunch?'

'It's what he liked best. I had to bring the whiting from Cádiz, bottled; it keeps very well with a specific I invented, I have the recipe at home.'

'Amazing. And did you improve the English Artillery?' my master asked, encouraging him to continue because he was entertaining him so much.

'Completely. When there I invented a cannon which never got to be fired because the whole of London, including the Court and the ministers, begged me not to do the trial for fear that lots of houses would fall to the ground from the shaking.'

'So in the end was that great cannon just consigned to oblivion?'

'The Emperor of Russia[92] wanted to buy it, but it was impossible to move it from where it was.'

'Well, you could get us out of our difficulty by inventing a cannon that would destroy the English fleet in one shot.'

'Ah,' Malespina replied, 'that's just what I'm thinking of and I believe I will be able to carry out my plan. I can show you the calculations I have already made, not just to increase the calibre of the guns by a fantastic amount, but also to build tough plates to defend ships and forts. It has been my lifelong plan.'

By now they had finished eating. Marcial and I wolfed down the leftovers in a trice and we continued our journey, they on horseback with stirrups, and we as before in our worn-out chaise. The meal and the frequent drinks with which he had sprinkled it stirred up the inventive vein in Malespina senior even more and for the whole journey he continued to transfix us with his copious nonsense. The conversation returned to the theme on which it had started: the War of Roussillon and as Don José was hastening to recount some new exploits, my master, now tired of so much lying, wanted to divert him from that subject and said,

'A disastrous and imprudent war. It would have been much better if we had never embarked upon it!'

'Ah,' Malespina exclaimed, 'the Count of Aranda,[93] as you know, condemned this ill-fated war with the Republic from the start. How we spoke about this question! We have been friends since childhood, you see. When I was in Aragón we spent seven months together hunting in the Moncayo.[94] It so happens that I had a special shotgun made for him....'

'Yes, Aranda was always opposed to it,' said my master, cutting him short on the dangerous path of ballistics.

'Yes indeed,' the liar continued, 'and if that eminent man defended the peace with the republicans with so much passion, it was because I advised him to do so, persuading him of the inopportuneness of the war. But Godoy, who was already the royal favourite, persisted in carrying it on, just to annoy me, as I heard later. The most amusing thing is that Godoy himself was forced to end the war in the summer of ninety-five when he realised how ineffective it was and then he awarded himself the resounding title of *Prince of Peace*.'

'How much we need, my old friend,' said my master, 'a great statesman who is equal to the circumstances, a man who does not get us involved in useless wars and who maintains the dignity of the Crown unharmed!'

'Well, when I was in Madrid last year,' the storyteller went on, 'it was suggested to me that I should assume the post of Prime Minister. The Queen[95] was very keen on it and the King[96] said nothing... every day I went with him to the Pardo[97] for a bit of shooting... even Godoy himself would have agreed, knowing my superiority; and if he had not, I would not have been short of a little castle where I could have shut him up in so that he couldn't tell me what to do. But I refused, preferring to live quietly in my village, and I left public affairs in the hands of Godoy. There you have a man whose father looked after mules on the estate of my father-in-law in Extremadura.'

'I did not know that,' Don Alonso said. 'Although he came from obscure origins, I thought the Prince of Peace belonged to a noble family, one with a meagre fortune, but with good principles.'

And so the dialogue continued: Señor Malespina telling tales as tall as houses and my master listening to them with the patience of a saint, sometimes seeming to be irritated, other times pleased at hearing such absurd nonsense. If I remember correctly, Don José María also said that he had advised Napoleon to carry out the bold coup of 18th Brumaire.[98]

Talking of these and other things we arrived in Chiclana[99] at nightfall and my master, totally exhausted and shattered by the movement of that apology for a gig, stayed in that town while the others carried on, wanting to arrive in Cádiz that night. While they had supper, Malespina subjected them to new lies and I could see that his son was listening to them painfully as if he was embarrassed to have the greatest storyteller in creation as his father. They said farewell and we rested until dawn the following day when we continued on our road, and since it was much quicker and more comfortable from Chiclana to Cádiz than the previous stretch, we arrived at our journey's end at about eleven o'clock in the morning, our health intact and with joy in our hearts.

VIII

I cannot describe the excitement that the return to Cádiz awoke in my heart. As soon as I had some free time, after my master had been installed at the house of his cousin, I went out onto the streets and ran down them in no fixed direction, intoxicated by the atmosphere of my beloved city.

After such a long absence, things that I had seen so many times enchanted me as though new and extremely beautiful. In all the people I met as I passed I would see a friendly face and everything for me was charming and cheerful; the men, the women, the old people, the children, the dogs, even the houses, which my youthful imagination saw as somehow alive and gay, and I imagined them to be living beings, and it seemed to me that they shared the general happiness in my arrival, their balconies and windows mimicking the features of a jubilant face. My soul saw its own joy reflected in everything external.

I ran through the streets with great anxiety as if I wanted to see them all in one minute. On the Plaza de San Juan de Dios I bought some sweets, not so much for the pleasure of eating them, but more for the satisfaction of showing myself, now regenerated, to the saleswomen, to whom I spoke as an old friend, recognising some as ones who had treated me well in my former misery, and others as victims, as yet unappeased, of my innocent fondness for prowling around. Most of them did not remember me, but some received me with abuse, recalling the exploits of my youth and made witty remarks about my new appearance and how serious I looked, so that I had to clear off in a hurry, although not without my dignity being wounded by some expertly thrown fruit peel landing on my new suit. As I was aware of how formal I looked, these jokes filled me much more with pride than with pain.

I then went along the city walls and counted all the ships at anchor that I could see. I spoke with some sailors that I came across on my way and I told them that I was going to the fleet as well and asked them in a pompous tone whether Nelson's fleet had been sighted. Then I told them that *Monsieur Corneta* was a coward and that the coming show would be a good one.

At last I arrived at La Caleta and there my joy was boundless. I went down to the beach and, taking off my shoes, I jumped from rock to rock. I looked for my former friends of both sexes, but only found very few: some were already grown up and had embraced better careers; others had been press-ganged onto ships and those that remained hardly recognised me. The changeable surface of the water awakened voluptuous feelings in my breast. Powerless to resist the temptation and compelled by

the mysterious attraction of the sea, whose eloquent sound has always seemed to me, I do not know why, a voice that gently courts in calm conditions and imperiously calls in the storm, I quickly got undressed and threw myself into it like someone throwing themselves into the arms of a loved one.

I swam for more than an hour with a feeling of indescribable pleasure, then, having got dressed, I continued my walk towards the district of La Viña in whose edifying taverns I came across some of the most noted degenerates from my golden days. When speaking to them, I put on the airs of a man of worth and as such I spent the few coins I had in treating them. I asked them about my uncle, but they gave me no news about his lordship, and then after we had chatted a bit, they made me drink a glass of brandy that instantly knocked my poor body to the floor.

While my drunkenness was at its worst I believe those rogues laughed at me to their heart's content, but once I had sobered up a bit, I left the tavern deeply ashamed. Although I found walking very difficult, I wanted to go by my old home, and in the doorway I saw an old woman in rags who was frying some blood and tripe. Moved by being at the abode of my birth, I could not stop crying, something which made that woman, who had no such feelings, think was mockery or a stratagem to steal her fried food. So I had to escape from her hands through my lightness of foot, leaving the relief of my feelings for a better occasion.

I then wanted to see the old cathedral, which was linked to one of the tenderest memories of my childhood, and I went in; the place seemed enchanting to me and I have never gone through the nave of any church with such religious veneration. I believe it gave me a great desire to pray and that is indeed what I did, going on my knees before the altar on which my mother had placed an *ex-voto* for my salvation. The wax figure that I believed to be a perfect portrait of me was hanging there, taking its place with the gravity of holy things, but they seemed to me like chalk and cheese. That little doll, which symbolised piety and maternal love, filled me, however, with the deepest respect. I prayed for a while on my knees, recalling the sufferings and death of my dear mother who was now at ease with God in Heaven, but because my head was hurting from the fumes of the accursed brandy, I fell over when I got up and a heartless sacristan threw me smartly out onto the street. In a few ticks I got to the house in Calle del Fideo[100] where we were staying and my master, when he saw me come in, reprimanded me for having been away so long. If this transgression had been committed with Doña Francisca, I would not have escaped a severe beating, but my master was tolerant and never punished me, perhaps because he was conscious that he was just as much a child as I was.

We had gone to stay in the house of my master's cousin, a lady whom the reader will permit me to describe at some length, as she is someone who deserves such treatment. Doña Flora de Cisniega was an old lady who was determined to stay young; she was over fifty but she put into practice every imaginable artifice to deceive the world, pretending to be half that appalling age.

To describe how much she concocted science and art into harmonic consort to achieve that objective is a task for which my feeble forces are unequal. To enumerate the curls, ribbons, bows, clothes, preparations, rouges, waters and other strange bodies that contributed to the great opus of her monumental restoration would tire the most fertile imagination; so let this be left to the novelists' pens, it is not for History, inquiring into great affairs, to appropriate such a splendid matter. In relation to her appearance, what I remember most is the composition of her face on which it seemed that dawn's rosy hues had been placed by all the brushes of academicians past and present. I also remember that when she spoke she would pout, and purse her lips with the aim either of gracefully making her wide mouth smaller or covering up the ruin of her teeth, from whose ranks a couple of teeth would desert every year, but that supine stratagem of conceit was so ill-fated that it made her uglier rather than more beautiful.

Her clothes were luxurious and her hair was filled with bushels of powders and as she was quite plump, judging by the display of broad cleavage and what could be seen

Doña Flora.

through the gauze, all her ambition was directed to showing off those parts which were less susceptible to the harmful action of time, something for which she had a marvellous skill.

Doña Flora was a person much taken with the old ways; she was very devout, although not with the holy piety of my Doña Francisca and she was very different from my mistress in that as much as the latter loathed all types of naval glory, the former was keen on all military men in general and sailors in particular.

Inflamed by love of her country, now that her advanced years meant that she could not aspire to the warmth of any other love, and proud in the extreme as a woman and as a Spanish lady, patriotic emotion was associated in her mind with the roar of the guns and she believed that the greatness of peoples was measured in pounds of gunpowder. Not having any children, her life was filled by the neighbours' gossip, picked up and passed around by a small circle of two or three chatterboxes like her, and she entertained herself with her passion for discussing public affairs. At that time there were no newspapers and political ideas, like the news, circulated by word of mouth and were more distorted then than now, because it was always the greatest lie that left its mark.

In all the big cities, and especially in Cádiz which in those days was the most cultured, there were many idlers who were depositories of news from Madrid and Paris and who were diligent vehicles for taking and distributing it, swelling with pride at having a mission which gave them great importance. Some of these, like living newspapers, would meet at that lady's home in the afternoons and this, as well as the good chocolate and the better pastries, attracted others anxious to know what was happening.

Doña Flora, now that she could no longer inspire any serious passion nor shake off the heavy weight of her fifty years, would not have exchanged this role for anything else, since being the main hub for news was almost equivalent in those days to the majesty of a throne.

Doña Flora and Doña Francisca loathed each other cordially, as anyone will understand from the intense militarism of the one and the pacific timidity of the other. This was why, when talking to her cousin on the day of our arrival, the good lady said to him,

'If you had always listened to your wife you would still be a midshipman. What a woman! If I was a man and was married to a woman like that I would explode like a bomb. You have done well not following her advice and coming to the fleet. You're still young, Alonso, you can still reach the rank of commodore, which you would certainly have done by now if Paca hadn't wedged the gate shut on you like we do to stop chickens leaving the yard.'

Then, after my master, driven by his great curiosity, had asked her about any news, she said to him,

'The main thing is that all the sailors here are very dissatisfied with the French admiral who has proved his ineptitude in the voyage to Martinique and the Battle of Finisterre. He is so timid and is so afraid of the English that when the Combined Fleet arrived here last August he did not dare to seize the English cruisers commanded by Collingwood, who only had three ships.[101] All our officers are very unhappy about having to serve under the orders of such a man. Gravina went to Madrid to say this to Godoy, warning of great disasters if someone more suitable was not appointed to lead the Fleet, but the minister just told him any old thing because he does not dare to decide anything, and because Bonaparte is deeply involved with the Austrians,[102] he doesn't make any decisions either... They say that he, too, is very dissatisfied with Villeneuve and has decided to dismiss him, but in the meantime... Ah, Napoleon should entrust the command of the Fleet to some Spaniard, to you, for example, my dear Alonso, and throw in three or four promotions, which you truly deserve.'

'Oh, I am not suited for that,' my master said with his habitual modesty.

'Either Gravina or Churruca, who they say is such a good sailor. If not, I fear that this will end badly. There are no Frenchmen to be seen here. Just imagine, when Villeneuve's ships arrived they were without supplies and munitions and in the arsenal they didn't want to give them any. They turned up in Madrid to complain, and since Godoy only does what the French ambassador, Monsieur de Bernouville, wants him to do, he gave the order to provide our allies with whatever they needed. But even that didn't work. The Intendant of the Navy and the Commander of Artillery said they would give nothing unless Villeneuve paid for it in cash upfront. And it seems to me they were right to say that. The last thing we need is those gentlemen, without so much as a by your leave, taking away what little we have! Fine times we live in! Everything today costs an arm and a leg; there's yellow fever in one place and bad weather in another; they've made such a mess of Andalusia that the whole of it is not worth a floorcloth, and then on top of all that the disasters of war. National honour does in truth come first and we need to carry on to avenge the wrongs we have suffered. I have no wish to recall the affair at Cape Finisterre where through the cowardice of our allies we lost the *Firme* and the *Rafael*, fine ships both, nor the blowing up of the *Real Carlos*, an act of treachery that wouldn't happen even among the Moors of Barbary, nor the theft of the four frigates, nor the fight at Cape...'

'The thing is this...' said my master, interrupting her excitedly. 'It is essential that everyone stays in his place. If Admiral Córdova had given the order to turn to....'

'Yes, yes. I know,' said Doña Flora, who had heard my master say the same thing many times, 'they need a good beating and I know you will give it to them. I believe you will cover yourself in glory. And we'll infuriate Paca.'

'I'm no use for the battle,' my master said sadly. 'I have come just to be present at it, out of pure devotion and the enthusiasm inspired in me by our beloved ensigns.'

The day after this talk my master received a visit from a commodore in the Navy, an old friend, whose features I will never forget, even though I saw him only on this occasion. He was a man about forty-five years old, with a handsome and pleasant face and with such an expression of sadness that it was impossible to look at him without feeling an irresistible urge to love him. He did not wear a wig and his abundant blond hair, which had not been tortured by the barber's tongs into the shape of a pigeon's wing, was drawn together with some abandon into a large pigtail and was inundated with powders with less art than the typical expectations of the age demanded. His eyes were large and blue; his nose, very fine, a perfect shape and slightly long without making him ugly, seemed rather to ennoble his expressive features. His beard, shaved with care, was somewhat pointed and augmented the melancholy set of his oval face, which suggested sensitivity rather more than energy. This noble bearing was enhanced by a courtesy in his manners, by a grave politeness which you will find hard to form an idea of, given the pompous fatuity of fashionable gentlemen and the fickle elegance of our gilded youth. He was short, thin and seemed sickly. Rather than a warrior, he appeared to be a man of learning, and his brow, which no doubt contained high and refined thoughts, did not seem at all suitable for facing the horrors of battle. His frail constitution, which no doubt contained an exceptional spirit, seemed destined to succumb, shaken at the first blow. And yet, as I learnt later, this man had as much courage as intelligence. It was Churruca.[103]

The uniform of the hero showed, without being old or threadbare, some years of honourable service. Then, when I heard him say, without any tone of complaint certainly, that the Government owed him nine months' back pay, I understood that wear and tear. My master asked him about his wife and from his reply I deduced that he had got married not long before, and I felt sorry for him on account of this, as it seemed cruel to me to send him into battle at such a happy time. He then spoke about his ship, the *San Juan Nepomuceno*, to which he displayed the same affection as to his young wife, because, he said, he had arranged and fixed the ship to his own taste as a special privilege, making her one of the foremost ships in the Spanish Navy.

They then discussed the usual topic of those days: whether the fleet would go out or not, and the sailor spoke at length in the following terms, whose substance I have kept in my memory and later, with dates and historical information, I was able to reconstitute as exactly as possible:

'The French admiral,' Churruca said, 'not knowing what decision to take, and wanting to do something that would make his mistakes be forgotten, has shown himself, since we have been here, to be in favour of going out in pursuit of the English. On 8th October he wrote to Gravina, telling him that he wanted to hold a council of war on board the *Bucentauro*[104] to agree on what would be most advantageous. Gravina did indeed attend the council, bringing with him Vice Admiral Álava, Rear Admirals Escaño[105] and Cisneros, Commodore Galiano and me. From the French fleet there were Admirals Dumanoir[106] and Magon,[107] Captains Cosmao,[108] Maistral,[109] Villiegris[110]

and Prigny.[111] After Villeneuve had indicated he wished to go out, all of us Spaniards were opposed. The discussion was very lively and heated and Alcalá Galiano exchanged some pretty heated words with Admiral Magon that would have led to a duel if we had not calmed them down. Our opposition greatly annoyed Villeneuve and in the heat of the discussion he also said some angry words to which Gravina responded in a very forceful manner... it's curious how eager those gentlemen are to go to sea in search of a powerful enemy when at the Battle of Cape Finisterre they abandoned us, depriving us of the chance of victory, if they

Churruca.

had come to our assistance in good time. Besides, there are other reasons, which I gave at the Council: that the season is advanced; that it is more advantageous for us to stay in the bay, forcing them into a blockade which they won't be able to sustain, especially if they also blockade Toulon and Cartagena. We have to acknowledge with regret the superiority of the English Navy, the perfection of the armaments, the excellent crews on their ships, and above all, the way their fleets operate as a unit. We, with on the whole less skilful men, with imperfect armaments and under the command of a leader who displeases everyone, could nevertheless conduct a defensive war within the bay. But we will have to obey, in accordance with the blind submission of the Court of Madrid, and to put ships and sailors at the mercy of the plans of Bonaparte, who has not given us, in exchange for this slavery, a leader worthy of such sacrifices. We will go out, if Villeneuve is determined to do so, but if the outcome is disastrous, it will be laid at our door for having opposed the foolish plan of the leader of the Combined Fleet. Villeneuve has given himself over to desperation; his master has said some harsh words to him and the news that he is going to be relieved leads him to commit greater follies, hoping to reclaim in one day his lost reputation either by victory or death.'[112]

This is how my master's friend expressed himself. His words made a great impression on me since, being a child, I was very interested in these events and later, reading in History about what I had witnessed, I supplemented my memory with real facts and I can tell my tale with sufficient accuracy.

When Churruca left, Doña Flora and my master praised him greatly, extolling above all his expedition to South America to chart those seas.[113] According to what I heard them say, Churruca's worth as a scholar and sailor was such that Napoleon himself gave him a precious gift and heaped attention on him. But let's leave the sailor and return to Doña Flora.

Two days after we had been there I became aware of a phenomenon that disgusted me greatly, which was that my master's cousin began to take a fancy to me; that is to say, she found me to be just right to be her page. She did not stop making all sorts of endearments to me, and once she found out I, too, was going to the fleet, she wailed about it, swearing that it would be dreadful if I lost an arm, a leg or some other no less important part of my body, let alone if I lost my life. I was indignant at such unpatriotic

compassion and I even believe that I said some words to show how inflamed I was with warlike ardour. My bravado amused the old lady and she gave me thousands of sweets to rid me of my bad mood.

The next day she forced me to clean the cage of her parrot, a shrewd animal that spoke like a theologian and woke us all up in the morning, shouting, "English dog, English dog." Then she took me with her to mass, making me carry her stool, and in the church she kept turning around to see if I was there. Later she made me wait on her at her toilet, an operation which appalled me, when I saw the catafalque of curls and coils that the hairdresser put onto her head. Noticing the obvious astonishment with which I watched the skill of the master, a true architect of hair, Doña Flora laughed out loud and told me that instead of thinking about joining the fleet, I should stay with her and be her page, adding that I should learn to arrange her hair and that with the office of master hairdresser I could earn my living and be a really important person. These propositions did not tempt me and I told her pretty plainly that I preferred to be a soldier rather than a hairdresser. This pleased her, and as I surrendered the comb to her for the sake of matters patriotic and military, her affection towards me was redoubled. Despite my being made a fuss of there, I confess that I had more than my fill of Doña Flora and that compared to her sugary compliments, I preferred the hard cuffs of my irascible Doña Francisca.

It was inevitable: her ill-timed affection, her affectations, the persistence with which she sought my company, telling me that my conversation and my person enchanted her, prevented me from following my master on his visits on board ship. A servant of his cousin accompanied him on such sweet occupation, whereas I, with no freedom to run about Cádiz as I would have wished, got bored at home in the company of Doña Flora's parrot and the men who went there in the afternoons to talk about whether the fleet would go out or not and other tedious and much more frivolous things.

My vexation reached the point of desperation when I saw Marcial coming to the house and my master going aboard with him, even though not definitively joining a ship; and when this happened and my afflicted spirit still cherished the faint hope of forming part of that expedition, Doña Flora insisted on taking me on her *paseo* up and down the avenue and also to the Carmelite church to hear vespers.

This was unbearable for me, even more so as I dreamt of putting into effect a certain little plan which consisted of me visiting, on my own account, one of the ships, taken there by some sailor that I knew, whom I hoped to run into on the quayside. I went out with the old lady and when we went along the ramparts I lingered to look at the ships, but I was not able to devote myself to the delights of that spectacle because of having to respond to the thousands of questions from Doña Flora, and I became quite dizzy. During the *paseo* some young men and older gentlemen joined her. They seemed very grand and were the fashionable people of Cádiz, all of them very discriminating and elegant. One of them was a poet, or rather, all of them wrote verses, even if bad, and it seemed to me I heard them talk about some sort of Academy[114] where they would meet to fire away at each other with their stanzas, an entertainment that did no harm to anyone.

As I observed everything, I paid attention to the extraordinary image of those men, their effeminate gestures and above all their clothes, which seemed extremely strange to me.

Not many people in Cádiz dressed like that and when I thought later about the difference between their attire and the ordinary clothes of the people I had always seen, I realised that the latter dressed in the Spanish way, whereas Doña Flora's friends followed the fashions of Madrid and Paris. The first thing that caught my eye was the oddity of their sticks, which were twisted clubs with a very thick knob. You could not see their beards because they were hidden by a cravat, a sort of scarf,

which, having made a few turns round the neck and extending up to the lips, formed a sort of basket, a tray or rather a basin, in which the face rested. Their hairstyle was one of artificial disorder and rather than a comb, it seemed as if they had used a broom to prepare it; the tips of their hats touched their shoulders; their frock coats, with a very high waist, almost smeared the ground with their tails; their boots were pointed; a multitude of medallions and seals hung from the pockets of their waistcoats; their striped breeches were tied at the knee with an enormous bow, and so as to make these figures completely grotesque, they all carried a monocle and at various times during a conversation they would bring it up to the right eye and close the left eye, even though they could see perfectly well with both.

The conversation of those characters was about the departure of the fleet, alternating this topic with an account of some sort of dance or party which they spoke highly of, one of them being the object of much praise for how well he did entrechats with his nimble legs when dancing the gavotte.

We left, having heard an irritating sermon, which they praised as a masterpiece; we recommended our *paseo* and the chatter continued in more lively fashion because we were joined by some ladies dressed in the same style, and between them all there rose up such a cacophony of gallantries, expressions and niceties mixed up with some insipid verse, that I can no longer remember them.

And meanwhile, Marcial and my dear master were trying to fix the day and the hour when they would definitely go aboard ship! And I was at risk of staying ashore, subject to the whims of that old lady who was sickening me with her insipid affection! Can you believe that on that very night she insisted that I should stay with her in her service for ever? Can you believe that she assured me that she loved me, and by way of proof embraced me and kissed me many times, telling me not to talk about it to anyone? How horrible are life's contradictions, I thought when I considered how happy I would have been if my young mistress had treated me in that way! I was totally embarrassed and I told her that I wanted to join the fleet, and that when I returned she could love me to her heart's desire, but that if she did not let me fulfil my wish I would hate her as much as this, and extended my arms to express a huge amount of hatred.

Then, when my master came in unexpectedly, I judged that the moment had come to achieve my ambition by means of an outburst of oratory that I had taken care to prepare and I went down on my knees before him and told him in the most pathetic tones that if he did not take me aboard, I would throw myself into the sea in despair.

My master laughed at the display; his cousin, mouthing affectionate remarks, pretended it was quite hilarious, making her desiccated face look ugly, but in the end she consented. She gave me thousands of sweets to be eaten on board; she charged me to flee from any place of danger and said nothing more against my embarkation, which took place very early next morning.

IX

October was the month and the eighteenth was the day. I am in no doubt about this date, because on the following day the fleet departed. We got up very early and went to the quayside, where we waited for a boat to take us aboard. Imagine my astonishment, what am I saying – my astonishment! – my enthusiasm, my rapture, when I found myself close to the *Santísima Trinidad*, the largest ship in the world, that wooden fortress, which seen from afar, I imagined to be some extraordinary and supernatural structure, a unique marvel worthy of the majesty of the seas. When our boat passed close to a ship, I would examine it with a sort of religious wonder, surprised to see how big were the hulls that looked so tiny from the ramparts; on other occasions they seemed smaller than my fantasy had made them. The restless enthusiasm which possessed me put me at risk of falling into the water when I contemplated with rapture a figurehead, the object that fascinated me more than any other.

At last we arrived at the *Trinidad*. As we were getting closer, the shape of that colossus was increasing and, when the launch came alongside, lost in the space of sea on which, in black and horrible crystal, the shadow of the ship was cast; when I saw how the immobile hull was immersed in the dark water that gently beat against the sides; when I looked up and saw the three lines of cannons showing their threatening muzzles through the gun ports, my enthusiasm turned into fear. I turned pale and remained motionless, gripping my master's arm.

But as soon as we went aboard and I found myself on deck my heart lifted. The airy and extremely high masts, the animation on the quarterdeck, the sight of the sky and the bay, the admirable order of so many things which filled the deck, from the hammocks arranged in a line on the bulwark to the capstans, pumps, hosepipes, hatches; the variety of uniforms; everything in fact filled me with so much wonder that for a good while I was absorbed in contemplating so beautiful a machine that I forgot everything else.

People today cannot understand those magnificent ships, even less the *Santísima*

Trinidad, from the bad prints with which they are represented. Nor are they at all similar to today's warships, covered with their heavy armour of iron, long, uninspired, black and with few features visible in their vast extent, all of which has sometimes made me think they are like immense floating coffins. Created in a positivist age and suited to the naval science of these times, which with the use of steam has overridden manoeuvres and trusted the outcome of battles to the power and thrust of the ships, the vessels of today are simply machines for war, whereas those of then were the warrior himself, fully armed with all weapons for attack and defence, but mainly relying on his skill and courage.

I observe when I see and I have always had the habit of associating, even to an exaggerated degree, ideas with images, things with people, even though they belong to the most disparate categories. Later, when I saw the so-called Gothic cathedrals of our Castile and those in Flanders, observing how with such imposing majesty their complex and subtle structure stood out from the buildings in the modern style, which were erected for utilitarian purposes, such as banks, hospitals and barracks, I could not but recall the different types of ships that I have seen in my long life, and I compared the old types to Gothic cathedrals. Their shapes which extended upwards; the predominance of vertical lines over horizontal ones; a certain inexplicable idealism, something both historical and religious, mixed with the complexity of the lines and the play of colours blended at the whim of the sun, caused this extravagant association, which I explain by the traces of romanticism left in the mind by the impressions of childhood.

The *Santísima Trinidad* was a ship with four decks. The biggest ones in the world had three. This colossus, built in Havana with the finest timber of Cuba in 1769, had thirty-six years of honourable service. She was 220 feet[115] (61 metres) in length, that is from stern to bow; 58 feet in the beam (wide) and 28 deep (height from the keel to the deck), extraordinary dimensions which no other ship in the world had at that time. Her mighty timbers, which were a veritable forest, supported four decks. In her sides, which were very strong wooden walls, 116 gun ports had been inserted when she was constructed; when she was altered, by enlarging her in 1796, there were 130 openings; and in 1805 after new guns had been mounted, she had in her sides, when I saw her, 140 muzzles of both cannons and carronades. The interior was marvellous in its distribution of the various compartments, whether decks for the guns, mess decks for the crew, storerooms for keeping supplies, cabins for the officers, galleys, a sickbay and other services. I was absorbed in running through the galleries and other hiding places in that Escorial[116] of the seas. The cabins located in the stern were a little palace inside and

from the outside a type of fantastic citadel; the rows of balconies, the sections at the corners of the stern, similar to the lanterns of an ogival castle, were like huge jaws open to the sea, and from which the eye could range over three-quarters of the horizon.

Nothing was grander than the yards and masts, those gigantic poles, flung skywards like a net into the storm. It seemed as if the wind would not need any strength to drive her enormous main topsails. The sight made you dizzy and you got lost in contemplation of the immense skein that was created among the yards and masts by the shrouds, stays, braces, backstays, lifts and halyards which were used to support and move the sails.

I was absorbed in contemplating this marvel, when I felt a hard blow to the back of my neck. I thought the mainmast had fallen on top of me. I turned round stunned and let out a cry of horror when I saw the man who was pulling me by the ears as if he wanted to lift me up in the air. It was my uncle.

'What are you after here, worm?' he said to me in his usual soft tone. 'Do you want to learn the trade? Hey, Juan,' he added, addressing a ferocious-looking sailor, 'get me this tortoise up onto the main yard so he can go along it.'

I avoided as best I could the obligation to go along the main yard and I explained to him with the utmost politeness that, being in the service of Don Alonso Gutiérrez de Cisniega, I had come aboard in his company. Three or four sailors, friends of my charming uncle, wanted to beat me up, so I decided to get away from such distinguished society and went off to the cabin in search of my master. The officers were making their toilet, no less difficult on board than on land and when I saw the pages occupied in powdering the heads of the heroes they were serving, I asked myself whether that operation was not the least suitable one on board ship, where every moment is precious and where everything that is not immediately necessary for the service is always an obstruction.

But fashion was as much a tyrant then as now, and even at a time like the present it imposed by way of compulsion its annoying absurdities. Even a soldier had to use up precious time in doing his pigtail. Poor things! I saw them arranged in a line one behind the other, each one arranging the pigtail of the one in front, an ingenious way to finish the operation in a short time. Next they pulled on a fur hat, a big, heavy thing whose purpose I could never understand, and then went to their posts if they were on guard duty, or if they were off duty to walk about on the waist. The sailors did not have that ridiculous appendage on their hair and their simple dress seems to me to have changed little since that date.

In the cabin my master was talking heatedly with the ship's commander, Don Francisco Javier de Uriarte[117] and with the Commodore, Don Baltasar Hidalgo de Cisneros. From the little that I heard, I was in no doubt that the French admiral had given the order to leave the following morning.

This made Marcial very happy and together with other old sailors in the forecastle, he would expound bombastically on the coming battle. This company pleased me more than that of my charming uncle, because the colleagues of *Half-a-Man*'s did not indulge in tedious jokes at my expense. This difference alone made you understand the diverse origins of the crewmen because while some of them were pure-bred sailors, brought there through the Register[118] or as volunteers, the others were press-ganged, and nearly always lazy, unruly, with bad habits and knowing little about their duties.

I got on better with the first than with the second ones and I attended all Marcial's lectures. If I were not afraid of wearying the reader, I would recount the explanation given by him for the diplomatic and political causes of the war, paraphrasing in the most amusing way what he had heard a few nights earlier from the mouth of Malespina at the home of my master and mistress. It was through him that I learnt that the fiancé of my young mistress had joined the *Nepomuceno*.

All the lectures ended up at one point alone: the coming battle. The fleet was due to leave the next day. What joy! To sail in this gigantic ship, the biggest in the world; to be present at a battle out at sea; to see what the battle was like, how the guns were fired, how the enemy ships were taken – such splendid fun! And then to return to Cádiz, covered in glory... to say to all who cared to listen to me, 'I was with the fleet, I saw everything.' To say it to my young mistress as well, telling her about the magnificent scene and exciting her attention, her curiosity, her interest... To say to her also, 'I was in the most dangerous places and that didn't make me afraid.' To see how she changed, how she grew pale and became frightened when she heard me tell of the horrors of battle, and then look disdainfully at everyone who said, 'Tell us, young Gabriel, about that tremendous affair!' Oh, this was more than enough to make my mind go crazy... I can honestly say that on that day I would not have changed places with Nelson.

It was dawn on the nineteenth, which made me very happy, and it had not yet got light when I was on the quarterdeck with my master, who wanted to watch the manoeuvre. After scrubbing the decks, the operation to get the ship underway commenced.

The great topsails were hoisted and the heavy windlass, turning with a piercing screeching, pulled up the mighty anchor from the bottom of the bay. The sailors ran along the yards; others handled the braces, quick to respond to the voice of the bosun, and all the voices on board, previously silent, filled the air with a terrifying din. The whistles, the bell at the bow, the discordant concerto of a thousand human voices mixed with the squeaking of the blocks; the crack of the ropes, the flapping of the sails as they whipped the masts before they filled out, driven by the wind; all these sounds accompanied the first paces of the colossal ship.

Small waves caressed her sides, and the ship, gigantic, majestic, began to glide along the bay without any pitching, without any rolling, in a grave and solemn progress, which could only be appreciated by observing in comparison the imaginary movement of the merchant ships at anchor and the scenery.

At the same time I looked all around and, good heavens, what a spectacle! Thirty-two ships, five frigates and two brigantines, Spanish and French, stationed ahead, aft and at our sides, were in full sail and making way driven, too, by the light wind. I have not seen a finer morning. The sun flooded the magnificent roadsteads with light; a faint tint of purple tinged the surface of the water to the east and the chain of hills and distant mountains which formed the horizon in the direction of the port were still lit by the fire of the passing dawn; the sky, clear, with just a few clouds reddened and gilded to the east; the sea, blue, was calm and on this sea and under this sky, the forty sailing ships with their white canvas, set out on their course, constituting the most spectacular squadron that could appear before human eyes.

The vessels did not all go at the same pace. Some went ahead, others took a long time to get going; a few passed close to us, while some had to remain in the rear. The slowness of their progress; the height of their rigging, covered in canvas; a certain mysterious harmony that my child's sense of hearing detected as coming from their proud hulls, a sort of hymn that was doubtlessly resonating within me; the brightness of the day, the freshness of the surroundings, the beauty of the sea, which outside the bay seemed to get rougher with charming merriment at the approach of the fleet, created the most impressive picture imaginable.

Cádiz, meanwhile, like a revolving panorama, became foreshortened

Nelson.

Gravina.

before our eyes, displaying to us in succession the various facets of its vast circumference. The sun, lighting up the glass in its thousand balconies, sprinkled the city with grains of gold, and its white bulk stood out so clean and pure above the water that it seemed as if it had just been created that moment, or drawn out of the water like the fantastic city of San Jenaro.[119] I saw the walls running from the quay to the Castle of Santa Catalina; I recognised the bastion of El Bonete, the bastion of Orejón, La Caleta and I filled with pride when I considered where I had come from and where I was now.

At the same time, I heard, like some mysterious music, the sound of the bells of the half-awake city, ringing for mass with that chattering clamour of bells in a big town. Now they were full of joy, like a wish for a safe journey, and I listened to the confused noise as if it were human voices saying farewell; now they seemed to me to sound sad and anguished, forewarning us of some misfortune and as we drew further away, that music continued to fade until it died out, diffused into immense space.

The fleet was leaving slowly; some ships took many hours to get out. During the departure Marcial was making comments on each ship, observing their progress, calling them names if they were slow-moving, encouraging them with paternal advice if they were swift and got underway quickly.

'Don Federico is such a slowcoach!' he said, looking at the *Príncipe de Asturias*, commanded by Gravina. 'There goes *Monsieur Corneta!*' he exclaimed, looking at the *Bucentaure*, the flagship. 'The fellow that *namified* you *Rayo* did well,' he said ironically as he looked at the ship of that name, which was the slowest in all the fleet.[120] 'Good for *Papa Ignacio*,' he continued, turning to the *Santa Ana*, which was under the command of Álava. 'Unfurl all the topsail, you lump of tunny,' he said, looking at Dumanoir's ship. 'This Frog uses a hairdresser to perm the topsail, and weighs down the candles with snuffers.'[121]

The sky became cloudy in the afternoon and at nightfall when we were already a long way out, we saw Cádiz gradually disappear in the mist until its final outlines became lost in the inky night. The fleet took a course south.

In the night I did not leave Marcial, once I had left my master well settled in his cabin. Surrounded by two colleagues and admirers, he explained Villeneuve's plan to them as follows.

'*Monsieur Corneta* has divided the fleet into four units. The vanguard, which is commanded by Álava, has seven ships; the centre which comes to seven and which *Monsieur Corneta* commands in person; the rearguard, also with seven, which is commanded by Dumanoir, and the reserve, consisting of twelve ships, which is commanded by Don Federico. It seems to me that this is not at all badly thought out. Assuming that the Spanish ships are mixed up with the Frogs so that they can't leave us in a jam, as happened at Finisterre. According to what Don Alonso told me, the Frenchman has said that if the enemy appears from leeward, we will form line of battle and fall on him... That's all very nice, said in the cabin, but really... will *el Señorito* be such an ass and come to us from leeward? Yes, because his lordship has so little *lantern* (intelligence) that he will let himself be caught out like that... *We'll see to see if we see* what the Frenchman is hoping for... If the enemy comes from windward and attacks us we have to wait for him in line of battle and as he will have to split up to attack us, if he doesn't manage to break our line, it will be very easy for us to defeat him. Everything seems easy to that gentleman. (Murmurs.) He also says that he won't give any signals and that he expects everything of each captain. We're certainly going to see what I've been preaching about since those damn *Surmises* treaties,[122] and that's... I'd better shut up... please God! I've already told you that *Monsieur Corneta* hasn't a clue and that he can't get his head around fifty ships. Beware of an admiral who summons his captains the day before a battle and tells each of them to do whatever takes their fancy... *and then after that* (Great expressions of agreement). Well, let's see what happens... but you tell me, if we Spaniards want to knock the bottoms out of some English ships, can't we do it ourselves and aren't there more than enough of us to do so? Then *why on earth* do we have to ally ourselves with Frenchmen who don't let us do *what we have a mind to do* but instead we have to follow their lordships under tow? *Every time* we've gone with them, *every time* we end up *uncorked*... Well, then, may God and the Virgin of Carmel be with us and deliver us from our French friends for ever and ever amen. (Great applause.)

Everyone agreed with his view. His lecture went on to a late hour, ascending from the Naval Profession to the Science of Diplomacy. The night was clear and we were sailing with a fresh wind. I may be allowed to say *we* when talking about the fleet. I was so proud to be on board the *Santísima Trinidad* that I began to imagine that I would play some important role on such an exalted occasion, and because of this I was always strutting about with the sailors, letting them see that I was there for some useful purpose.

X

At dawn on the 20th the wind was blowing with a lot of strength and this had caused the ships to become very far apart from each other. But the wind having eased slightly after midday, the flagship signalled for the formation of five columns: the van, the centre, the rear and two squadrons which made up the reserve.

I delighted in seeing how those great bulks obediently came into formation, and even if, because of the diversity in their seaworthiness, the manoeuvres were not very fast and the lines formed were not perfect, there was always something to admire when watching this exercise. The wind was blowing from the south-west, according to Marcial, something he had predicted since the morning and the fleet, with the wind coming from starboard, moved in the direction of the Strait of Gibraltar. At night some lights were seen and at dawn on 21st we saw twenty-seven ships to windward, among which Marcial made out seven three-deckers. At about eight, the thirty-three ships of the enemy fleet were in sight, formed into two columns. Our fleet formed a very long line and it seemed that the two columns of Nelson, arranged in the form of a wedge, were advancing as if they intended to cut our line between the centre and the rear.

Such was the situation of both contestants, when the *Bucentaure* made the signal to wear ship. Perhaps you do not understand this, but I can tell you that it involves changing to the diametrically opposite direction, which means that if before the wind was driving our ships from starboard, after this manoeuvre it came from port so that we were going in almost the opposite direction to before. The bows were headed north and this action, whose purpose was to have Cádiz to leeward so as to put in there in case of ill fortune, was heavily criticised on board the *Trinidad* and specially by Marcial who said,

'Now the line of battle has gone and done the *splitters* so that if it was bad before, it's worse now.'

In fact, the van turned into the rear and the reserve squadron, which was the best as I had heard tell, remained at the end. As the wind was light, the ships of various speeds and crews with little skill, the new line could not be formed with any rapidity or precision: some ships went very quickly and rushed up to the one ahead; others hardly moved and lagged behind or went off course, leaving a large gap which broke the line before the enemy had to take the trouble to do so himself.

The order was given to reform the line; but however obedient a ship may be, it is not as easy to handle as a horse. Because of this, as he watched the manoeuvres of the nearest ships, *Half-a-man* said,

'The line is longer than the Camino de Santiago.[123] If *el Señorito* cuts it then that's goodbye to my flag; there's no way we could sail in any order even if they made our hair into canons. Gentlemen, they are going to hit us in the centre. How can the *San Juan* and the *Bahama* come and help us when they are at the tail-end, and the *Neptuno* or the *Rayo* can't either as they are at the head? (Murmurs of agreement.) Also, we're to leeward and the greatcoats can choose their spot where to attack us. We'll have enough to do to defend ourselves as best we can. What I say is may God get us out of this and deliver us from Frenchmen for ever and ever, amen Jesus.'

The sun was advancing towards the zenith and the enemy was already upon us.

'Call this a time to start a battle? At twelve noon!' the sailor angrily exclaimed, although he did not dare to publicise his display too widely, nor did his lectures extend beyond a small circle, into which I had introduced myself, driven as always by my insatiable curiosity.

I don't know why but I seemed to see expressions of displeasure on everyone's faces. The officers on the quarterdeck and the sailors and bosuns on the forecastle were watching the ships which were to leeward and out of line, among which were four belonging to the centre.

I have forgotten to mention an operation before the battle that I took part in. After the ship had been cleared for action in the morning, and everything necessary for servicing the guns and for their handling had been prepared, I heard them say,

'The sand, spread out the sand.'

Marcial pulled me by the ear and, lifting me onto a hatch, put me in a line with some press-ganged sailors, ship's boys and other more or less lowly types. From the hatch to the bottom of the hold they had placed some sailors at intervals on the lower decks and in this way they were taking out sacks of sand. One would give to another at his side, and this one to the next one and in this way as many sacks as were wanted were quickly and easily taken out. Passing from hand to hand a multitude of sacks came up from the hold and I was greatly surprised when I saw them empty them onto the deck, the quarterdeck and the forecastle, spreading out the sand so that it covered all the planks. They did the same on the lower decks. To satisfy my curiosity, I asked the ship's boy next to me.

'It's for the blood,' he answered me indifferently.

'For the blood!' I repeated, unable to repress a shudder of terror.

I looked at the sand; I looked at the sailors who were noisily busying themselves with that task and for an instant I felt a coward. However, the imagination which held sway over me at that time, drove all fear from my mind and all I thought of was triumphs and happy surprises.

The gun crews were ready and I noticed that the ammunition passed from the powder magazines on the lower deck by means of a human chain like the one that had brought the sand from the bottom of the ship.

The English were advancing to attack us in two groups. One was heading towards us and had at its head, or at the apex of the wedge, a large ship with an admiral's pennant. Later, I learnt that this was the *Victory*, and that she was commanded by Nelson. The other had at its front the *Royal Sovereign*, commanded by Collingwood.

All these men, as well as the strategic details of the battle, were studied by me later.

My memories, which are as clear as a picture about everything I experienced, can hardly serve me in respect of the operations that I did not understand at that time. What I frequently heard from the mouth of Marcial, coupled with what I learnt later, made me understand the formation of our fleet and so that you can get a good idea of it, I have set out here a list of our ships, showing those that went off course leaving a gap; the nationality and the way in which we were attacked. This is how it was, more or less:

	Neptuno S.	
	Scipion F....	
	Rayo S.........	
	Formidable F.	Van
	-------Duguay F.	
	Mont-Blanc F.....	
	Asís S...................	

First Squadron		Agustín S...............	
Commanded by Nelson		Héros F...................	
		Trinidad S................	
	Victory	Bucentaure F...........	Centre
		------Neptune F......	
		Redoutable F.............	
		Intrépide F.................	
		------Leandro S..........	

Second Squadron		-------Justo S.................	
Commanded by Collingwood		-------Indomptable F...	
		Santa Ana S............	
	Royal Sovereign	Fougueux F.............	Rear
		Monarca S.................	
		Pluton F....................	

	Bahama S...................	
	-----------Aigle F.............	
	Montañés S.................	
	Algeciras S....................	
	Argonauta S..................	
	Swift-Sure F...................	Reserve
	Argonaute F....................	
	Ildefonso S......................	
	--------Achille F.............	
	Príncipe de Asturias S.......	
	Berwick F...........................	
	Nepomuceno S....................	

It was a quarter to twelve. The terrible moment was approaching. The anxiety was general and I don't say this just because of what was passing through my own mind, since I was concentrating so much on the movements of the ship on which Nelson was said to be, that for a good while I was not aware of what was going on around me.

Suddenly our captain gave a terrible order which was repeated by the bosuns. The sailors ran to the lines, the blocks screeched, the topsails flapped.

'Flat aback, flat aback!' shouted Marcial, letting out a string of oaths. 'That damned idiot wants to put us astern.'

Instantly I understood that the command to slow the *Trinidad* had been given in order to narrow the gap with the *Bucentaure*, which was following, because the *Victory* appeared to be getting ready to cut the line between the two ships.

When I saw how our vessel manoeuvred, I noticed how most of the crew did not have that confidence peculiar to sailors familiar, like Marcial, with wars and storms. I saw some of the soldiers suffering from seasickness and gripping the shrouds to stop themselves falling. It's true that there were some very determined men, especially among the volunteers, but generally they were all press-ganged, obeyed orders unwillingly, and I'm sure they didn't have the least amount of patriotism in them. The only thing that made them fit for battle was the battle itself, as I later learnt. Despite the various levels of morale among those men, I believe that in those solemn moments before the first cannon shot the idea of God was in everyone's head.

As far as I was concerned, I had never experienced in my soul feelings like the ones of that moment. Despite my few years, I was in a position to understand the gravity of the event and for the first time since I was born, my mind was filled with lofty ideas, elevated images and noble thoughts. The certainty of victory was so rooted in my spirit that I was almost sorry for the English and I admired them when I saw them seeking certain death with such zeal.

I perceived then for the first time with complete clarity the idea of my homeland and my heart responded to it with spontaneous feelings, hitherto unknown, in my soul. Up till then I imagined my homeland through the persons that ruled the nation, such as the King and his famous minister, whom I did not treat with equal respect. As I knew no more history than what I had learnt in La Caleta, I took it as law that one should be delighted on hearing that the Spanish had first killed lots of Moors and then a great crowd of Englishmen and Frenchmen. So I imagined that my country was very brave, but bravery as I understood it was as similar to barbarity as one egg is to another. With thoughts like those, patriotism for me was no more than the pride of belonging to that breed of Moor slayers.

But in that moment preceding the battle I understood the full meaning of that divine word, and the idea of nationality made its way into my spirit, illuminating it and revealing infinite wonders, like the sun which drives away the night and produces a beautiful landscape from the darkness. I saw my country as an immense land inhabited by peoples who were all united in brotherhood; I saw society divided into families, in which there were wives to support, sons to educate, property to maintain, honour to defend; I realised there is a pact established between so many beings to help and sustain each other against attack from abroad and I understood that for the sake of all these, ships had been built to defend the homeland, that is: the soil in which they set their plants; the furrow watered with their sweat; the house where their old parents lived; the garden where their children played; the colony discovered and conquered by their ancestors; the port where they tied up their boat worn out by her long voyage; the store where they deposited their riches; the Church, sarcophagus of their elders, living space of their saints and coffer of their beliefs; the square, place of their happy amusements; the family home, whose old furniture handed down from generation to generation seems to symbolise the perpetuity of nations; the kitchen, within whose smoky walls it seems that the echo of tales told by grandmothers to calm the mischief and fear of their grandchildren will never die away; the street, where friendly faces are seen filing past; the countryside, the sea, the sky, everything which from birth is joined to our existence, from the manger of a loved animal up to the throne of patriarchal kings; all the objects in which our soul prolongs its life, as if our own body was not enough.

I also believed that the issues Spain had with France and England were always because one of those nations wanted to take something from us, in which I was not far wrong at all. It seemed to me therefore that defence was as legitimate as aggression was brutal and as I had heard it said that justice triumphed always, I was in no doubt about victory. Seeing our red and yellow flags, whose combination of colours best represented fire, I felt my breast swell; I could not contain some tears of emotion; I remembered Cádiz and Vejer; I remembered all the Spaniards, whom I thought of as leaning from a great terraced roof, anxiously watching us; and all these ideas and feelings finally drew my spirit to God to whom I offered a prayer, which was not Our Father or Ave Maria, but something new which came into my head then. A sudden crash took me out of my trance, making me shudder with the most violent shaking. The first cannon shot had sounded.

XI

A ship in the rear fired the first shot against the *Royal Sovereign*, commanded by Collingwood. While the *Santa Ana* engaged in combat with this ship, the *Victory* turned towards us. On the *Trinidad* everyone was very anxious to open fire, but our captain waited for the most favourable moment. As if some of the ships had communicated it to the others, like fireworks connected by a common fuse, the firing ran from the *Santa Ana* to the two extremities of the line.

The *Victory* first attacked the *Redoutable*, a French ship; repelled by the latter, she came and stationed herself opposite our side to windward. The terrible moment had arrived; a hundred voices said, 'Fire!' repeating like an infernal echo that of the captain, and the broadside hurled fifty projectiles onto the English ship. For a moment the smoke made me lose sight of the enemy. But the latter, blind with courage, came upon us before the wind. When she came in gunshot range, she luffed and discharged her broadside into us. In the intervals between one exchange and another, the crew, who could see the damage done to the enemy, redoubled their enthusiasm. The guns were served with alacrity, even if slowing up somewhat, a result of the lack of practice of some gun-captains. Marcial would happily have taken on responsibility for the task of serving one of the guns on deck, but his mutilated body was not capable of responding to the heroism of his spirit. He contented himself with watching over the supply of ammunition, and with voice and gestures encouraged those serving the guns.

The *Bucentaure*, which was at our stern, was firing equally at the *Victory* and the *Temeray*,[124] another powerful English ship. It seemed as if Nelson's ship was going to fall to us, because the *Trinidad*'s guns had destroyed the rigging and we saw with pride that she had lost her mizzen-mast.

In the heat of that first encounter I hardly noticed that some of our sailors were falling wounded or dead. Having put myself in a place where I thought I'd be less in the way, I continued to watch the captain, who commanded from the quarterdeck with heroic serenity and I was amazed to see my master, with less calm but with more enthusiasm, encouraging the officers and sailors with his husky little voice.

'Ah,' I said to myself, 'if only Doña Francisca could see you now!'

I will confess that I had moments of terrible fear when I would have hidden myself away in nothing less than the depths of the hold, and others of a sort of delirious fearlessness when I put my life at risk by watching that great spectacle from places of the greatest danger. But, leaving to one side my humble self, I will tell about the most terrible moment of our struggle with the *Victory*. The *Trinidad* was destroying her with much good fortune, when the *Temeraire*, executing a most skilful manoeuvre, came between the two combatants, saving her companion from our cannon balls. Immediately, she turned to cut the line by the stern of the *Trinidad* and as the *Bucentaure*, during the exchange of fire, had got closer to the latter to the point where their yardarms touched, there was a large opening, through which the *Temeraire* dashed and then promptly tacked and, placing herself on our port quarter, fired at us on that side, up till then untouched. At the same time, the *Neptune*,[125] another powerful English ship, stationed herself where the *Victory* had been earlier; the latter fell to leeward so that in a moment, the *Trinidad* found herself surrounded by enemies who were peppering her with shots from all sides.

From my master's face, the sublime rage of Uriarte and the swearing of Marcial's sailor friends, I realised that we were lost and the idea of defeat grieved my soul. The line of the Combined Fleet had been broken at various points and the most terrible disorder had succeeded to the imperfect order in which it had formed after the order to wear. We were encircled by the enemy, whose guns launched a terrifying rain of cannon balls and shrapnel onto our ship, as well as onto the *Bucentaure*. The *Augustín*, the *Héros* and the *Leandro* were fighting far from us, in a somewhat comfortable position, while the *Trinidad*, along with the flagship, unable to move and caught in a terrible skirmish by the genius of the great Nelson, fought heroically, no longer in search of an impossible victory, but stirred by the urge to perish with honour.

The grey hairs which cover my head today still stand on end when I recall those dreadful hours, particularly from two to four in the afternoon. I imagine the ships, not as blind war machines obedient to man, but as real giants, living and monstrous beings fighting on their own account, putting into action, like agile limbs, their sails and those terrible weapons, the mighty guns in their sides. Watching them, my imagination could do no less than personalise them and even today I seem to see them approaching and challenging each other, luffing smartly to discharge their broadsides, rushing to board the enemy with daring movements, falling back with ardent fighting spirit to gather more strength, scorning and upbraiding the enemy; I seem to see them expressing the pain of a wound, or nobly exhaling a dying groan, like the gladiator who does not forget his honour in his death throes; I seem to hear the murmur of their crews, like a voice coming from an inflamed breast, sometimes an enthusiastic yelling, sometimes a low howl of despair, the precursor of extermination; now a hymn of joy which signals a victory; next a furious roar which fades away in the air, giving way to a terrible silence announcing the shame of defeat.

The inside of the *Santísima Trinidad* presented a scene from Hell. Manoeuvres had been abandoned as the ship was not moving, nor could it move. All effort was given to serving the guns as rapidly as possible, thus responding to the destruction caused by the enemy projectiles.

The English shrapnel ripped the sails as if great and invisible nails were tearing them into shreds. Pieces of bulwark, chunks of wood, thick shrouds, cut off like sheaves of corn; blocks which were falling, bits of canvas, ironwork, ropes and other debris torn from their position by the enemy guns filled the deck where there was hardly any space to move. Minute by minute a multitude of men full of life fell to the ground or into the sea; the blaspheming of the combatants became so mixed up with the laments of the wounded that it was impossible to tell if those dying were insulting God or if those fighting were calling to Him in distress.

I had to help in one of the saddest tasks, carrying wounded men to the hold where the sickbay was. Some died before getting there and others had to undergo painful operations before they could rest their exhausted bodies for a moment. I also had the indescribable satisfaction of helping the carpenters, who very quickly had plugs applied to the holes in the hull; but because I was not very strong my help was not as effective as I would have wished.

The blood ran copiously over the main deck and the other decks and, despite the sand, the movement of the ship carried it here and there making ominous patterns. The cannon balls, fired at such close range, mutilated bodies horribly and one frequently saw people rolled along, their heads completely cut off, if the violence of the projectile had not hurled the victim into the sea, in whose waves the final idea of life would lose itself almost without pain. Other cannon balls ricocheted off a mast or the bulwarks, sending up a hail of splinters which wounded like arrows. The firing from the tops and the shrapnel from the carronades scattered a slower and more painful death, and it was rare that someone did not come out of it more or less seriously scarred by the lead and iron of our enemies.

Assailed by such a fate and without being in any way able to return the same destruction, the crew, that soul of the vessel, felt they were expiring, and endured their death agony with desperate courage, and the ship itself, that glorious frame, shuddered with the blows of the cannon balls. I felt her shake in the terrible struggle: her timbers creaked, her beams cracked, her pillars grated in the manner of limbs twisted by pain and the main deck vibrated under my feet with a loud throbbing as if the anger and suffering of her crew had communicated itself to the whole immense frame of the vessel. Meanwhile, water was penetrating through the

thousands of holes and cracks in the riddled hull and was starting to flood the hold.

The *Bucentaure*, the flagship, surrendered before our eyes. Once the admiral had given up, what hope remained for the ships? The French ensign disappeared from the stern of that brave ship and she ceased firing. The *San Agustín* and the *Héros* were still holding out and the *Rayo* and the *Neptuno*, members of the van, that had come to help us, were trying in vain to rescue us from the enemy ships that were blockading us. I could see the part of the battle that was closest to the *Santísima Trinidad*, as it was impossible to see anything else of the line. The wind seemed to have died and the smoke remained above our heads, enveloping us in its thick whiteness, which our eyes could not penetrate. We made out only the rigging of a few distant vessels, enlarged in some inexplicable way by an optical effect unknown to me or because the terror of that sublime moment made everything larger.

For a moment the dense shadow broke up, but in such a terrible way!

A frightening detonation, more powerful than the thousand guns of the fleet being fired at once, paralysed everyone, causing general terror. When our ears received such a powerful impression, the clearest visibility had illuminated the broad space occupied by the two fleets, stripping away the veil of smoke and presenting before our eyes a complete panorama of the battle. The terrible explosion had occurred towards the south, in the area previously occupied by the rear.

'A ship has blown up,' everyone said.

Opinions varied and there was uncertainty whether the ship that had blown up was the *Santa Ana*, the *Argonaute*, the *Idelfonso* or the *Bahama*. Later it became known that it was the French ship called *Achille*. The expansion of the gases scattered into a thousand pieces over sea and sky what moments before had been a fine ship with 74 guns and a crew of 600 men.[126] A few seconds after the explosion we were already thinking of no one else but ourselves.

With the surrender of the *Bucentaure*, all the enemy's fire was turned onto our ship, whose loss was now certain. My enthusiasm of the first moments had gone and my heart was filled with a paralysing terror that smothered all faculties of my mind, except curiosity. This was so irresistible that it forced me to go out to the most dangerous places. My meagre assistance was now of little use since they weren't even taking the wounded to the hold as there were so many of them and the guns required service from those who still had some strength. Among the latter I saw Marcial who was everywhere at once, shouting and moving about as much as his limited agility allowed and he was at the same time bosun, sailor, gunner, carpenter and whatever else he had to be in those terrible moments. I never believed that someone who could be thought of as being only half a human body could perform the functions of so many men. A blow from a splinter had wounded him in the head and the blood, which was marking his face like ringworm, made him look dreadful. I saw his lips move as he drank some liquid which he then spat out angrily beyond the gangway as if he wanted to injure our enemies with gobbets of spit.

The thing that surprised me most – and frightened me a bit – was how Marcial, even in that scene of desolation, would joke; I don't know whether it was to encourage his dispirited comrades or because this was the way he used to encourage himself.

The foremast fell with a sound of thunder, filling the forecastle with its mass of rigging, and Marcial said,

'Lads, bring out the axes. Let's put this furniture into the bedroom.'

Immediately they cut the ropes and the mast fell into the sea.

When he saw the fire getting worse, he shouted at a storekeeper who had been transformed into gun-captain,

'Pedro Abad, send the wine over to those greatcoats so that they leave us in peace.'[127]

And to a soldier who was lying as if dead from the pain of his wounds and the anguish of seasickness, he said as he applied the linstock to his nostrils,

'Sniff a little leaf of orange blossom, mate, to stop you fainting. Do you want an outing in the boat? Off you go, Nelson has invited us to have a few jars.'

This was going on in the waist. I looked up to the quarterdeck and saw that admiral Cisneros had fallen. Two sailors hastily carried him down to the cabin. My master remained immobile at his post but a lot of blood was running from his left arm. I ran towards him to help him, but before I got to him an officer had approached him trying to convince him to go down to the cabin. He had just said a couple of words when a shot took away half of his head and his blood spattered my face. Then Don Alonso withdrew, as pale as the corpse of his friend which was lying mutilated on the quarterdeck.

When my master went below, the captain remained alone on deck, showing such spirit that I could not stop watching him for a time, astonished at so much courage. With his head uncovered, his face pale, his look fiery and his gestures energetic, he remained at his post directing this hopeless action that could not now be won. Such a horrendous disaster had to take place with order and the captain was the authority that was regulating heroism. His voice led the crew in that fight of honour and death.

An officer who was commanding in the first battery came up to obtain orders and before he could speak, fell dead at the feet of his captain; another midshipman who was at his side also fell badly wounded, and in the end Uriarte remained entirely on his own on the quarterdeck which was covered with dead and wounded. Even then his eyes did not stop watching the English ships or the activity of our guns, and the impressive appearance of the quarterdeck and the poop, where his friends and junior officers were in their death throes, did not shake his manly breast or break his determined resolution to continue firing until he perished. Ah, recalling later the serenity and stoicism of Don

Francisco Javier Uriarte, I could understand everything they tell us about the heroic captains of antiquity. At that time I did not know the word *sublime*, but when I saw our captain, I understood that every language must have a beautiful term to express that grandeur of the soul which seemed to me a favour rarely granted by God to miserable man.

In the meantime, most of the guns had stopped firing as half the men were out of action.

Perhaps I might not have known this was the case, if, having come out of the cabin, driven by my curiosity, I had not heard a terrifying voice say to me:

'Young Gabriel, here!'

Marcial was calling me. I went quickly and found him busy serving one of the guns that had no men. A shot had carried off the end of *Half-a-man*'s wooden leg, which led him to say,

'As long as I can keep the one of flesh and bone...'

Two dead sailors were lying beside him; a third, gravely

Uriarte

wounded was trying to carry on serving the gun.

'Mate,' Marcial said to him, 'you can't even light the end of a cigar.'

He snatched the linstock from the wounded man's hands and gave it me, saying, 'Take it, young Gabriel; if you're afraid, jump into the water.'

While saying this, he loaded the cannon as fast as he was able, helped by a ship's boy who was practically unharmed; they primed it and aimed; both exclaimed, 'Fire!' I put the match to it and the cannon fired.

The operation was repeated for a second and a third time and the sound of the cannon, fired by me, reverberated in an extraordinary way in my soul. My considering myself no longer a spectator but a determined actor in such a magnificent tragedy banished fear for a moment, and I felt I was someone of great mettle, at least I had the firm resolution to appear as if I was. From that time I realised that heroism is nearly always a sort of self-respect. Marcial and the others were watching me; it was essential I made myself worthy of their attention.

'Ah!' I said to myself proudly. 'If my young mistress could only see me now... How brave I am firing off cannon shots like a man! I'm sure I've sent at least two dozen Englishmen to the next world.'

But these noble thoughts did not occupy me for long because Marcial, whose tired nature began to exhaust itself after its exertion, breathed heavily, dried the blood which was flowing copiously from his head, closed his eyes, his arms reached out limply, and he said,

'I can't go on: the powder has come up to my poop (head). Gabriel, bring me some water.'

I ran off to look for some water and when I brought him some he drank thirstily. He seemed to gain new strength with this; we were about to carry on when a huge noise left us motionless. The mainmast, cut off at the deck hole, fell on top of the waist and across the mizzen-mast. The ship was full of debris and the mess was dreadful.

Luckily, I was in a recess and received nothing more than a light wound to my head, which, although it stunned me at first, did not prevent me from clearing away the bits of sail and ropes that had fallen on top of me. The sailors and soldiers on deck struggled to remove such an enormous mass of useless stuff, and from then on only the guns on the lower decks carried on firing. I emerged as best I could, looked for Marcial, could not find him, and having turned to look at the quarterdeck, I noticed that the captain was no longer there. Gravely wounded by a splinter in the head, he had fallen lifeless and immediately two sailors came up to take him down to the cabin. I ran there, too, and then a fragment of shrapnel hit me in the shoulder, scaring me terribly and I believed the wound was mortal and that I was going to breathe my last. My alarm did not stop me from going into the cabin, where, because of the amount of blood flowing from my wound, I grew weaker and for a moment I fainted.

During that fleeting lethargy, I still heard the din of the cannons of the second and third gun decks and then a voice shouting angrily,

'Boarders! Pikes! Axes!'

Then the confusion was so great that I could not distinguish what were human voices in that enormous concert. But, how I do not know – and without coming out of that somnolent state – I realised that they believed everything was lost and that the officers were in the cabin to agree the surrender; and I can assure you, unless it was an invention of my imagination, confused at the time, that a voice from the waist resounded with the words,

'The *Trinidad* will never surrender!'

It would certainly have been Marcial's voice, if someone actually did say such a thing.

I became fully awake and saw my master laid out on one of the sofas in the cabin, his head hidden in his hands in a gesture of despair and without a care for his wound.

I approached him and the unhappy old man could find no better way to show his distress than by embracing me paternally, as if we were both close to death. He, at least, I believe thought himself about to die from pure grief, as his wound was not at all serious. I consoled him as best I could, telling him that, even though the action had not been won, it wasn't because I had failed to kill enough Englishmen with my little cannon, and I added that next time we would have more luck; childish reasoning that did not calm his agitation.

Going out in search of water for my master, I witnessed the act of striking the colours which were still flying at the spanker, one of the few parts of rigging that remained standing along with the trunk of the mizzen-mast. That glorious piece of cloth, already holed in a thousand places, sign of our honour, that gathered beneath its folds all combatants, descended the mast to be hoisted no more. The idea of humbled pride, of an exhausted spirit that succumbs to superior forces, can have no more perfect image to represent itself to human eyes than the one of that oriflamme which goes down and disappears like a setting sun. And on that saddest of evenings, the sun reached the end of its course at the moment of our surrender and illuminated our flag with its last ray.

The firing stopped and the English came aboard the conquered vessel.

XII

When the spirit, resting from the excitement of battle, had time to give way to pity, to the cold terror produced by the sight of such great ruin, those of us who were still alive saw the scene on the ship in all its awful majesty. Up till then, everyone had been fully occupied in defence, but when the firing stopped, it was possible to see the great destruction done to the hull which, letting in water through the thousands of places it had been damaged, was sinking and threatening to entomb all of us, living and dead, at the bottom of the sea. Hardly had the English come aboard, when a single cry went up from our sailors,

'To the pumps!'

All of us that could went to them and worked eagerly, but those imperfect machines removed much less water than was coming in. Suddenly, a cry even more terrible than the previous one filled us with horror. I have already said that the wounded had been taken to the lowest deck, the orlop, a place safe from the effect of shot as it was below the waterline. The water was rapidly invading that area and some sailors appeared at the hatch shouting,

'The wounded are going to drown!'

Most of the crew hesitated between carrying on pumping out the water and going to help those unfortunate ones, and I don't know what would have become of them if men from an English ship had not come to our aid. Not only did they carry the wounded to the third and second gun decks, they also put hands to the pumps, while their carpenters tried to repair some of the damage to the hull.

Overcome by tiredness and thinking that Don Alonso might need me, I went to the cabin. I then saw some Englishmen engaged in raising the British ensign at the stern of the *Santísima Trinidad*. As I count on the gentle reader having to forgive me for recording my impressions here, I can say that this made me think a bit. I had always thought of the English as veritable pirates or highwaymen of the seas, a mercenary tribe that was no nation and lived off marauding. When I saw the pride with which they hoisted their ensign, saluting it with hearty cheers, when I saw the joy and the satisfaction that capturing the largest and grandest vessel that had hitherto ploughed the waves gave them, I thought that they, too, had their beloved homeland, which had entrusted the defence of its honour to them; it seemed to me that in that land, mysterious for me, called England there must also exist, as in Spain, many worthy people, a paternal king and the mothers, daughters, wives and sisters of such brave sailors, who, hoping anxiously for their return, were praying to God to give them victory.

In the cabin I found my master much quieter. The English officers who had come in there treated our ones with delicate courtesy and, as I heard, they wanted to transfer the wounded to some enemy ship. One of those officers approached my master as if he recognised him and greeted him in tolerably correct Spanish, reminding him of their former friendship. Don Alonso answered his polite words gravely and then wanted to know from him the details of the battle.

'But what became of the reserve? What did Gravina do?' my master asked.

'Gravina withdrew with some ships,' the Englishman replied.

'Only the *Rayo* and the *Neptuno* came to help us from the van.'

'The four French ships, *Duguay Trouin*, *Mont-Blanc*, *Scipion* and *Formidable* are the only ones that were not in action.'

'But Gravina, Gravina, what about Gravina?' my master persisted.

'He withdrew in the *Príncipe de Asturias*, but as we gave chase to him, I do not know if he has reached Cádiz.'

'And the *San Ildefonso*?'

'She was captured.'

'And the *Santa Ana*?'

'She was captured, too.'

'Good God!' Don Alonso exclaimed, unable to disguise his anger. 'I'll wager that the *Nepomuceno* hasn't been captured…'

'She has been as well.'

'Oh! Are you sure of that? And Churruca?'

'He was killed,' the Englishman replied sadly.

'Oh! Killed! Churruca killed!' my master exclaimed in distressed bewilderment. 'But the *Bahama* must have got back untouched to Cádiz.'

'She was captured as well.'

'As well! Galiano is a hero and a learned man.'

'Yes,' the Englishman replied sombrely, 'but he was killed as well.'

'And what about the *Montañés*? What happened to Alcedo?'[128]?'

'Alcedo… he was killed as well.'

My master could not hold back his feelings of profound grief; and as his advanced age diminished his presence of mind in such terrible moments, he had to undergo the slight bitterness of shedding some tears, a sad honour to his comrades. Weeping is not inappropriate in great souls; on the contrary, it shows the fruitful association of delicacy in sentiment with energy in character. My master wept like a man, after he had done his duty as a sailor; but recovering himself from this depression, and looking for some way to repay the Englishman for the sorrow the latter had caused him, he said,

'But you will have suffered no less than us. Our enemies will have had considerable losses.'

'One, above all, irreparable,' the Englishman replied with as much distress as that of Don Alonso. 'We have lost the first of our sailors, the bravest of the brave, the heroic, the divine, the sublime Admiral Nelson.'

And with as little fortitude as my master, the English officer had no care to hide his immense grief; he covered his face with his hands and wept, with all the frank expression of true sorrow, for his chief, protector and friend.

Nelson, mortally wounded in the middle of the battle, as I later learnt, by a musket ball that went through his chest and lodged in his spine, said to Captain Hardy,

'It is over; they have succeeded at last.'

His agony continued until late afternoon; he did not miss any details of the battle, nor was his military and naval genius extinguished until the final fugitive throb of life vanished from his wounded body. Wracked by terrible pain, he continued to give orders, informing himself about the movements of both fleets and when he was told about the triumph of his one, he exclaimed,

'God be praised. I have done my duty.'

A quarter of an hour later the premier sailor of our century expired.[129]

Please forgive me for this digression. The reader will be surprised that we did not know the fate of many of the vessels in the Combined Fleet. There is nothing more natural than our ignorance, on account of the excessive length of the line of battle and, in addition, the system of separate fights adopted by the English. Their ships had mixed with ours and as the contest was at musket range, the enemy vessel that beat us hid the rest of the fleet from view; in addition, the extremely thick smoke prevented us from seeing anything that was not close by.

At nightfall, when the cannon fire had still not stopped, we made out some ships which were passing at a distance like ghosts, some with half their masts and rigging, others completely dismasted. The mist, the smoke and the very confusion in our heads prevented us from telling whether they were Spanish or the enemy and when the light of a huge explosion far away lit up here and there that frightful panorama, we saw that the struggle was continuing ferociously between groups of isolated ships, that others were running in disarray and aimlessly, driven by the storm, and that one of our ships was being towed by another English ship towards the south.

Night came and with it the seriousness and horror of our situation increased. One would think that Nature should be kind to us after such misfortunes, but, on the contrary, the elements unchained themselves with fury, as if Heaven believed that the depth of our wretchedness was not great enough. A severe storm broke and the wind and the sea, now thoroughly rough, lashed the vessel which, unable to manoeuvre, vacillated at the mercy of the waves. The motion was so strong that it made work difficult, which, together with the weariness of the crew, made our condition get worse hour by hour. An English ship, which I later learnt was called *Prince*,[130] tried to take the *Trinidad* in tow, but her attempts were fruitless and she had to move away for fear of a collision which would have been disastrous for both vessels.

In the meantime it was impossible to have any food or drink and I was dying of hunger, because the others, indifferent to anything other than danger, hardly bothered about such an important matter. I did not dare to ask for a piece of bread for fear of appearing annoying and at the same time, I am not ashamed to admit it, my keen powers of observation were directed to all the places where I concluded there could be food supplies. Driven by necessity, I took the risk of paying a visit to the hard tack store and imagine my surprise when I saw Marcial there, decanting into his stomach the first thing that came to hand. The old man was not seriously wounded, and although a shot had carried off his right foot, as this was none other than the tip of his wooden leg, Marcial's body was only slightly more crippled through this mishap.

'Have some, young Gabriel,' he said, filling me in the trough with biscuits.[131] 'A boat without ballast doesn't sail.'

He immediately lifted up a bottle and drank with delight.

We came out of the storeroom and I saw that we were not the only ones visiting that place, since everything indicated that some disorderly pillaging had taken place there a few moments earlier.

My strength restored, I was able to think of being of service, putting my hands to the pumps or helping the carpenters. Some damage was laboriously being made good with the help of the English who were watching over everything, and as I later understood, they did not let any of our sailors out of sight because they feared that they might rise up and recapture the ship, which was something that showed our enemies had more suspicion than good sense, since one would have had to have lost one's reason to try and retake a vessel in such a state. The fact is the *greatcoats* were everywhere and did not miss any movement.

Night came and finding myself frozen to the marrow I left the deck where I could hardly stand up, and where I also ran the risk of being knocked down by the heavy sea, and retired to the cabin. My initial intention was to sleep a bit, but who slept that night?

Everything was confusion in the cabin, the same as in the waist. Those who were fit helped the wounded and the latter, troubled by their pains and at the same time by the movement of the vessel, which denied them any rest, presented such a sad sight that on seeing them it was impossible to abandon oneself to rest. On one side of the cabin, covered by the national flag, lay the dead officers. Amid such desolation, faced with the sight of so much pain, there was something enviable in those bodies; they were the only ones at rest on board the *Trinidad*, and they were beyond everything, weariness and sorrow, the shame of defeat and the sufferings of the body. The flag that served as their illustrious shroud seemed to place them beyond that sphere of responsibility, loss and desperation in which we found ourselves. They were not affected by the danger threatening the ship, because she was now nothing more than their coffin.

The dead officers were: Don Juan Cisniega, first lieutenant, who was not related to my master, despite having the same surname; Don Joaquín de Salas and Don Juan Matute, also first lieutenants; lieutenant colonel in the Army Don José Graullé; second lieutenant Urías; and midshipman Don Antonio de Bobadilla. The dead sailors and soldiers, whose bodies lay in disorder on the gun decks and the main deck, reached the dreadful total of four hundred.

I will never forget the moment when those bodies were cast into the sea by the order of the English officer who was in charge of the ship. The sad ceremony took place at dawn on the 22nd, an hour when the storm seemed to have grown worse on purpose in order to increase the horror of such a scene. The bodies of the officers were taken out onto the main deck, the priest hurriedly said a prayer for the dead, because this was no occasion for fancy words, and the solemn ceremony followed immediately. Wrapped in their flag, and with a cannon ball tied to their feet, they were cast into the sea, without this, which ordinarily would have made everyone sad and dismayed, upsetting at the time any of those present. Their spirits had been so hit by misfortune that the spectacle of death was merely a matter of indifference to them! Funeral rites at sea are sadder than those on land. A body is placed in the grave and there it stays; those who are interested

know that there is a corner of the earth where those remains lie and they can mark them with a gravestone, with a cross or a rock. But in the sea… the bodies are cast into the moving immensity and it seems they cease to exist at the moment of falling; the imagination cannot follow them on their journey to the depths of the abyss and it is difficult to think of them being somewhere when they are at the bottom of the Ocean. I had these thoughts as the bodies of those illustrious warriors disappeared, the day before full of life, the glory of their homeland and the delight of their families.

The dead sailors were cast overboard with less ceremony; the Ordinance required them to be wrapped up in a hammock,[132] but on this occasion there was no time to waste in complying with the Ordinance. Some were shrouded as required, but most were thrown into the sea without any covering or shot at their feet, for the simple reason that there was not enough for everyone. There were four hundred, approximately, and in order to finish the operation of burying them as soon as possible, it was necessary for every able man aboard to take part to complete it sooner. Much to my disgust I had to offer to help in such a sad task and some bodies fell into the water, released overboard by my hand, helping other stronger ones.

Then something happened, a coincidence that terrified me greatly. A horribly disfigured body had been grasped by two sailors, and at the moment they lifted it up, some of those present made crude jokes, which would have been unsuitable on any occasion, but were vile at this moment. I don't know why the body of that unfortunate man was the only one that caused them to lose respect for death with such lack of shame, but they said: "That's certainly settled his hash… he won't be coming back to play any of his tricks," and other vulgarities of the same kind. This angered me, but my anger changed into astonishment and an indefinable feeling, a mixture of respect, sorrow and fear when I looked carefully at the mutilated features of that corpse and recognised my uncle… I shut my eyes in terror, and I did not open them until the violent splash of water on me told me that he had disappeared for ever from human sight.

That man had behaved very badly to me, very badly to his sister; but he was my close relative, the brother of my mother; the blood that ran through my veins was his blood and that internal voice which prompts us to be kind to the faults of our family could not remain silent after what happened before my eyes. At the same time, I had been able to see in the bloodied face of my uncle some physical features of my mother's face and this increased my affliction. At that moment I did not remember that he had been a great criminal, still less the cruelties he inflicted on me during my unfortunate childhood. I can assure you, and I have no hesitation in saying so, even though it is to my credit, that I forgave him with all my soul and that I raised a prayer to God, asking Him to forgive him for all his faults.

I learnt later that he had behaved heroically in the battle, without this making him liked by his comrades who, considering him to be the wickedest of men, had no word of affection or pity for him, not even at the supreme moment when all faults are forgiven, because they imagined the criminal giving an account of his actions before God.

Later on that day, the *Prince* tried again to take the *Santísima Trinidad* in tow, but with as little success as the night before. The situation did not get worse, despite the storm continuing with equal strength, as much of the damage had been repaired and it was believed that once the weather had calmed, the hull could be saved. The English were very keen to do this, because they wanted to take the largest ship yet built as a prize to Gibraltar. For this reason they worked assiduously day and night at the pumps, allowing us to rest for a while.

Throughout the 22nd the sea stirred itself into a frenzy, lifting and carrying the hull of the ship as if it were a frail fishing boat; and that mountain of wood proved the strength of the joints in her solid timbers, when she failed to break into a thousand pieces on receiving the tremendous pounding of the waves. There were moments when, with the sea collapsing onto her, it seemed the ship was going to sink for ever, but the wave, aroused as if by the thrust of an intense whirlwind, lifted her proud bow, adorned with the lion of Castile, and we breathed again with the hope of saving ourselves.

On every side we could make out scattered ships, most of them English, not without heavy damage, all of them trying to reach the coast for shelter. We also saw Spanish and French ships, some dismasted, others being towed by an enemy vessel. Marcial recognised one of these as the *San Ildefonso*. We saw floating in the water lots of wreckage and debris, such as topmasts, tops, broken longboats, hatches, pieces of railing, ports and finally we made out two wretched sailors, who, badly stowed on a large mast, were carried off by the waves and would have perished if the English had not immediately gone to their aid. Brought on board the *Trinidad*, they came back to life, which, won back from feeling themselves in the arms of death, is equivalent to being born again.

The day passed between torment and hope; first we thought transfer to an English vessel was essential if we were to be saved, then we thought it was possible to keep ours. In any event, the idea of being taken as prisoners to Gibraltar was awful, if not for me, for honourable and stubborn men like my master, whose moral suffering on that day must have been unprecedented. But these sad alternatives ceased to exist in the evening at the time when everyone came to believe that if we did not tranship we would all perish in the vessel, which now already had fifteen feet of water in the hold. Uriarte and Cisneros received this news calmly and serenely, demonstrating that they did not find much difference between dying in their own home and being prisoners in a foreign one. Immediately afterwards the transfer began in the poor light of dusk, something that was not an easy task, it being necessary to get about three hundred wounded men on board. The crew who were fit amounted to some five hundred men, the number to which the one thousand five hundred and fifteen individuals that made up the crew before the battle had been reduced.

The transfer started hastily with boats from the *Trinidad*, the *Prince* and from three other vessels of the English fleet. Preference was given to the wounded, but although they tried to avoid hurting them in any way it was impossible to carry them from where they were without seriously affecting them, and some shouted loudly to leave them in peace, preferring death to a voyage that increased their pain. Urgency did not yield to compassion and they were taken to the boats with as little pity as the cold corpses of their comrades had been thrown into the sea.

Captain Uriarte and Rear Admiral Cisneros went aboard the boats of the English officers and, having urged my master to board them as well, the latter steadfastly refused, saying that he wanted to be the last to abandon the *Trinidad*. I could not help being annoyed by this because, the patriotic glow inside me, which at the beginning made me somewhat fearless, having vanished, I was thinking of nothing else than saving my life, and staying on board a vessel that was about to sink in moments was not the best way to achieve that noble aim.

My fears were not groundless, as when not even half the crew were off, a dull rumble of alarm and fear resounded in our ship.

'We're sinking! To the boats, to the boats!' some shouted while everyone, overcome by the instinct of self-preservation, ran to the gunwales, looking with eager eyes for the returning boats. All work was abandoned; no more thought was given to the wounded and many of the latter, already taken out on deck, were dragging themselves about it in raving wanderings, looking for a gangway to throw themselves into the sea from. Through the hatches came a pitiful cry, which still seems to resonate in my brain, freezing the blood in my veins and making my hair stand on end. It was the wounded left on the first gun deck, who, finding themselves drowning in the water which was coming into that section, were crying out for help whether to God or to men, I do not know.

Asking the latter was in vain, since they thought of nothing but their own salvation. They threw themselves headlong towards the boats and this confusion in the darkness of the night slowed down the transfer. One man alone, impassive in such great danger, remained on the quarterdeck paying no attention to what was happening around him and walking up and down preoccupied and meditative, as if those planks on which he placed his foot were not being summoned by the vast deep below. It was my master.

I ran up to him utterly terrified and said to him,

'Sir, we're going to drown!'

Don Alonso paid no attention to me and I actually believe, if my memory is not playing tricks on me, that without stopping what he was doing he said some words that were so inappropriate to the situation like,

'Oh, how Paca will laugh when I come home after this great defeat!'

'Sir, the ship is sinking!' I exclaimed again, no longer describing the danger, but pleading with gestures and shouts.

My master looked at the sea, at the boats, at the men who, desperately and blindly, were throwing themselves at them, and I looked with anxious eyes for Marcial and I called him with all the force of my lungs. Then it seemed I lost all sensation of what was going on, I got confused, my eyes clouded and I do not know what happened. In recounting how I escaped, I can only base myself on very vague memories, like images in a dream, since, no doubt, terror had made me unconscious. It seems that a sailor came up to Don Alonso while I was speaking to him and seized him in his strong arms. I, too, felt myself being taken, and when my clouded mind had cleared a bit, I found myself in a boat, reclining on the knees of my master, who held my head in his hands with paternal affection. Marcial was clutching the tiller; the boat was full of people.

I looked up and saw, about four or five yards away, to the right, the black side of the ship, on the point of sinking; from the ports which the water had not yet reached came a faint light, that of the lamp lit at nightfall, which still kept watch, a tireless guardian, over the remains of the abandoned vessel. Also moans coming from the gun ports reached my ears; it was the poor wounded whom it had not been possible to save and who found themselves suspended over the abyss, while that sad light let them see each other, communicating to each other with their eyes the terror in their hearts.

My imagination transported itself again to the interior of the vessel; it just needed an inch of water to break the delicate equilibrium that still kept her afloat. How would those unfortunate people be watching the water rising! What would they say at that terrible moment!? And if they saw those fleeing in the boats, if they heard the creaking of the oars, how bitterly would their suffering souls lament! But it is certain, too, that that cruel martyrdom purified them of all sin and that the mercy of God filled the whole ship at the moment she sank beneath the waves for ever.

The boat drew away and I carried on looking at that huge, shapeless mass, although I suspect it was my imagination and not my eyes which gazed at the *Trinidad* in the darkness of the night and I even believe I saw in the black sky a great arm which came down to the surface of the waters. It was doubtlessly the image of my thoughts, reproduced by deep feelings.

XIII

The boat proceeded – but where to? Even Marcial himself did not know where we were heading for. The darkness was so deep that we lost sight of the other boats and the lights of the *Prince* vanished behind the fog as if a puff had blown them out. The waves were so big and the storm so severe that the frail craft made very little progress and thanks to some skilful handling capsized only once. All were silent and most stared sadly at the place where it was supposed that our abandoned comrades were fighting at that moment against death in dreadful agony.

This voyage did not pass without me, as was my custom, making some reflections, which I might venture to describe as philosophical. Many will laugh at a fourteen-year-old philosopher, but I will not be embarrassed by ridicule and will have the temerity to write down here my reflections at that time. Children, too, are in the habit of thinking great things; and on that occasion, faced with such a spectacle, what brain, unless it was that of an idiot, could remain calm?

Well, then, in our boats were Spaniards and Englishmen, although the former were greater in number and it was curious to see how they fraternised, supporting each other against the common danger, not remembering that on the previous day they were killing each other in a horrendous struggle, more like wild beasts than men. I looked at the English, rowing with as much determination as our men; I saw in their faces the same signs of terror and hope and above everything the true expression of the heavenly sentiment of humanity and charity, which was the motive of one and all. With these thoughts I said to myself,

'My God, what is the point of wars? Why can't these men be friends at all times in life as they are in times of danger? Doesn't what I am seeing prove that all men are brothers?'

But all of a sudden the idea of nationality, that system of islands which I had concocted, cut across these considerations and then I said,

'But now I get it; this thing about the islands wanting to take some bit of land from each other, ruins everything and no doubt in each of them there must be some very evil men who are the ones that wage wars for their own advantage, either because they are ambitious and want to be in charge, or because they are greedy and long to be rich. These evil men are the ones who deceive the rest, all those unfortunate ones that go off to fight; and so that the deception is complete, they urge them to hate other nations; they sow discord, stir up envy and here you have the result. I am certain,' I added, 'that this cannot go on; I bet two to one that in a short while the men in all the islands must realise that they are making a great blunder in waging such terrible wars and there will come a day when all will embrace, everyone agreeing that we are nothing more than just one family.'

That is what I thought. Since then, I have lived seventy years and I have not seen that day arrive.

The boat advanced laboriously through the violent sea. I believe that Marcial, if my master had allowed him to do so, would have done the following deed: throw the English into the water and head for Cádiz or the coast, even with the almost inescapable prospect of drowning on the voyage. It seemed to me he suggested something like this to my master, speaking quietly in his ear, and Don Alonso had to give him a lesson in gentlemanly conduct, because I heard him say to him,

'We are prisoners, Marcial; we are prisoners.'

The worst of the matter was that we could not make out any vessel.

The *Prince* had moved away from where she had been; no light indicated to us the presence of an enemy ship. Eventually, we caught sight of a light, and shortly afterwards, the vague bulk of a ship running before the storm to windward in the opposite direction to us heaved in sight. Some thought she was French, others English, and Marcial maintained she was Spanish. They strained the oars and not without some labour we came within hailing distance.

'Ahoy!' our men shouted.

Immediately there was an answer in Spanish.

'It's the *San Augustín*,' said Marcial.

'The *San Augustín* was sunk,' replied Don Alonso. 'It seems to me she will be the *Santa Ana*, which was captured as well.'

Sure enough, once we got closer, everyone recognised the *Santa Ana*, commanded in the battle by Vice Admiral Álava. Immediately the English who were guarding her got ready to give us help and before long we were all safe and sound on deck.

The *Santa Ana*, a ship of 112 guns, had also suffered a lot of damage, although not as serious as the *Santísima Trinidad*, and, even though she was completely dismasted and without a rudder, the hull had survived not too badly. The *Santa Ana* lasted for another eleven years after Trafalgar and would have lasted still longer if, for want of careening, she had not sunk in Havana Bay in 1816. Her action during the days I am talking about was glorious in the extreme. As I have said, she was under the command of Vice Admiral Álava, head of the van, which, after the order of battle had been changed, became the rear. You already know that the column commanded by Collingwood headed for battle against the rear, while Nelson went against the centre. The *Santa Ana*, assisted only by the *Fougueux*, a French ship, had to fight the *Royal Sovereign* and four other English ships and, despite the unequal forces, each side suffered as much as the other, Collingwood's ship being the first to be put out of action, so that he had to transfer to the frigate *Euryalus*.[133] According to what they reported there, the fight had been horrendous, and the two powerful ships, their yardarms touching, were destroying each other over the space of six hours until, with Admiral Álava wounded, Captain Gardoqui[134] wounded, five officers and ninety-seven hands dead, with more than one hundred and fifty wounded, the *Santa Ana* had to surrender. Captured by the English, it was almost impossible to steer her on account of her poor state and the violent storm that burst in the night of the 21st; so that when we came aboard her the situation was pretty critical, although not hopeless, and she floated at the mercy of the waves, unable to sail in any direction.

Naturally, I was comforted by seeing how everyone's faces there showed their fear of an early death. They were sad and quiet, enduring with dignity the sorrow of defeat and the shame of finding themselves prisoners. I noticed one detail which drew my attention, which was that the English officers who were watching over the vessel were not, by a long chalk, as kind and good-natured as those carrying out the same duties aboard the *Santísima Trinidad*. On the contrary, those on the *Santa Ana* were some very grim and disagreeable gentlemen, who humiliated our men to excess, making too much of their own authority and finding fault with everything with great fussiness. This seemed to offend our captive crew greatly, especially the sailors, and I even thought I heard some alarming muttering, which would not have been very reassuring to the English if they had heard it.

As to the rest, I do not want to talk about incidents of navigation that night, if wandering about haphazardly, at the mercy of the waves, without sails or rudder can be called navigation. I do not want to tire my readers either by repeating things that we have already witnessed on board the *Trinidad*, and I will move on to telling you about entirely new things which will surprise you as much as they surprised me.

I had lost my fondness for going to the waist and the forecastle and so, once I found myself on board the *Santa Ana*, I took refuge with my master in the cabin, where I could rest a little and have some food, as I was very much in need of both things. However, many wounded were there, who needed looking after and this occupation, very welcome to me, did not allow me all the rest my exhausted body demanded. I was engaged in putting a bandage on the arm of Don Alonso, when I felt a hand resting on my shoulder; I turned round and came face to face with a tall, young man, wrapped up in a long, blue cloak and at first, as often happens, I did not recognise him, but looking at him closely for the space of a few seconds, I gave an exclamation of amazement: it was the young Don Rafael Malespina, the fiancé of my young mistress.

Don Alonso embraced him with great affection and he sat down at our side. He was wounded in the hand and was so pale from fatigue and loss of blood, that the emaciation completely disfigured his face. His presence produced very strange sensations in my mind and I must confess to all of them, even though one of them does me little credit. At first I felt a sort of joy to see someone I knew who had survived the horrendous battle unscathed; a moment later the old hatred which that fellow inspired in me awoke in my breast like a dormant pain that returns to torment us after a period of respite. I admit it with shame: I felt a certain anguish at seeing him safe and sound; but I will say in my defence that this anguish was a momentary and fleeting emotion like a flash of lightning, truly a flash of black lightning that darkened my soul, or rather, a slight eclipse of the light of my conscience, which soon shone again with radiant brilliance.

The wicked side of my character dominated me for a moment; but in another moment I was able to silence it and pen it up in the depths of my being. Can everyone say the same?

After this moral combat I looked at Malespina with joy because he was alive and with sadness because he was wounded, and I can still recall with pride how much I tried to display to him these two emotions. My poor young mistress! How great her anguish must have been in those moments! My heart ended up by being eternally full of kindness; I would have run all the way to Vejer to tell her,

'Mistress, Doña Rosa, your Don Rafael is fine and healthy.'

Poor Malespina had been transferred to the *Santa Ana* from the *Nepomuceno*, also a captured ship, where there were so many wounded that it was necessary, as he said, to share them out to prevent all of them perishing from lack of care. Immediately father-in-law and son-in-law exchanged initial greetings, devoting a few words to their absent families; the conversation then turned to the battle; my master related what had happened on the *Santísima Trinidad* and then said,

'But nobody has told me for sure where Gravina is. Was he taken prisoner or did he withdraw to Cádiz?'

'The admiral,' Malespina replied, 'sustained horrendous fire from the *Defiance* and the *Revenge*. He was supported by the *Neptune*, French, and the *San Ildefonso* and the *San Justo*, ours; but the enemy's forces doubled with the help of the *Dreadnought*, the *Thunderer* and the *Polyphemus*, after which any resistance was impossible. The *Príncipe de Asturias* having all her rigging cut, with no masts, riddled with shot and Admiral Gravina and his rear admiral, Escaño, having been wounded, it was decided to break off the fight, because any resistance was senseless and the battle was lost. From the remains of a mast Gravina gave the signal to withdraw and accompanied by the *San Justo*, the *San Leandro*, the *Montañés*, the *Indomptable*, the *Neptune* and the *Argonauta*, he steered for Cádiz, but with the sadness of not having been able to save the *San Ildefonso*, which remained in the possession of the enemy.'

'Tell me what happened on the *Nepomuceno*,' my master said with the greatest interest. 'I still find it hard to believe that Churruca has died and, although everyone takes it as a fact, it is my belief that wonderful man must be alive somewhere.'

Malespina said that, unfortunately, he had witnessed the death of Churruca and promised to give an exact account. A number of officers formed a ring around him and I, more curious than they, became all ears so as not to miss a word.

'After we had left Cádiz,' said Malespina, 'Churruca had a foreboding of this great disaster. He had given his opinion against going out because he knew our forces were inferior and in addition he had little confidence in the ability of the leader Villeneuve. All his predictions became true, all of them, even his death, since there's no doubt he had a premonition of it, certain as he was that he could not achieve victory. On the nineteenth he said to his brother-in-law Apodaca:[135] 'Rather than surrender my ship, I have to blow her up or sink her. This is the duty of those who serve King and Country.' The same day he wrote to a friend of his, telling him, 'If you get to hear that my ship has been captured, say that I have died.' One could see from the great sadness on his face that he foresaw a disastrous outcome. I believe that this certainty and the physical impossibility of avoiding it, yet having the strength for it, deeply disturbed his soul, capable of great deeds as well as great thoughts. Churruca was a religious man, because he was a superior man. On the twenty-first, at eleven o'clock in the morning, he ordered all hands and troops on deck: he made them get on their knees and solemnly told the chaplain, 'Perform your ministry, Father, and give absolution to these brave people who do not know what awaits them in the battle.' The religious ceremony having concluded, he ordered them to stand up, and speaking firmly and with conviction, exclaimed: 'My sons, in the name of God, I promise eternal bliss to anyone who dies doing his duty! If anyone fails in his duties, I will have him shot immediately and if he escapes my eyes or those of the brave officers I have the honour to command, his remorse will follow him, as the rest of his days drag out, a miserable and ruined wretch.' This speech, as eloquent as it was simple, which brought together the doing of military duty with religion, enthused all the crew of the *Nepomuceno*. Such pitiful valour!

Everything was lost like treasure sinking to the bottom of the sea. Once the English had been sighted, Churruca regarded the initial manoeuvres ordered by Villeneuve with great displeasure, and when the latter signalled that the fleet should reverse course, something that everyone knew would disrupt the order of battle, he revealed to his second in command that he considered the action was already lost with such a clumsy strategy. Naturally, he understood the bold plan of Nelson, which was to cut our line in the centre and the rear, surrounding the Combined Fleet and attacking some of their vessels in such a way that they would be unable to offer any assistance. The *Nepomuceno* came to be at the extremity of the line. Firing broke out between the *Santa Ana* and the *Royal Sovereign*, and one after the other all the ships were joining the battle. Five English ships from Collingwood's division steered towards the *San Juan*, but two of them carried on and Churruca had to face forces of no more than three to one. We held out vigorously against such superior foes until two in the afternoon, with much suffering, but inflicting double the damage in return on our opponents. The great spirit of our noble captain seemed to have communicated itself to our soldiers and sailors, and the handling as well as the firing was done with astonishing speed. The ones from the levy had taught themselves heroism after no more than two hours' apprenticeship, and our ship, because of its glorious defence, was not only the terror but also the wonder of the English. The latter needed new reinforcements; they needed six against one. The two ships that had attacked us first returned and the *Dreadnought* put herself alongside the *San Juan* to pound us at less than half a pistol shot. Imagine the fire from these six colossuses, vomiting cannon balls and shot onto a 74-gun vessel. It seemed as if our ship was getting bigger, growing in size as the fearlessness of its defenders grew. It seemed as if their bodies also took on the dimensions of giants, as did their spirits, and seeing how much terror we instilled into forces six times superior, we thought we were something more than men. Meanwhile, Churruca who was our mind, directed the action with astonishing serenity. Realising that skill had to take the place of strength, he economised on firing and entrusted everything to good marksmanship, thus ensuring that every ball caused real damage to the enemy. He attended to everything, he decided everything, and the shrapnel and cannon balls shot over his head without him losing his self-possession even once. That man, weak and sickly, whose handsome and sad features did not seem born to brave such terrifying scenes, filled all of us with a mysterious courage just with the flash of his glance. But God did not want him to come out alive from the terrible struggle. Seeing that it was not possible to harass a ship that was doing mischief to the *San Juan* at the bow with impunity, it was he himself that aimed the cannon and managed to dismast his opponent. He was coming back to the quarterdeck when a cannon ball hit him on the right leg with such good aim that it almost removed it in the most painful way at the upper part of the thigh. We ran to support him and the hero fell into my arms. What a terrible moment! I still seemed to feel under my hand the violent throbbing of a heart that even at that terrible instant was beating only for the sake of our country. His physical decline was very rapid; I saw him make an effort to raise his head which was bowed down on his chest; I saw him try to lighten his face with a smile, already clouded with a mortal pallor, while in a voice hardly altered, he cried out, 'This is nothing. Carry on firing.' His spirit was rebelling against death, disguising the great pain of a mutilated body, whose dying palpitations were being extinguished second by second. We tried to take him down to the cabin, but it was not possible to get him off the quarterdeck. Finally, yielding to our entreaties, he realised it was necessary to give up command. He called for Moyna, his second in command, and they told him he was dead; he called for the captain of the first battery, and the latter, although seriously wounded, came up to the quarterdeck and took over command. From that moment the crew shrank: from giants they changed into dwarves; courage disappeared and we realised that it was essential that we surrendered. The consternation that possessed me once I received the hero of the *San Juan* in my arms did not prevent me from noticing the terrible effect this misfortune had on everyone's sprit. As if a sudden moral and physical paralysis had overcome the crew, they all became frozen and silent, without the grief occasioned by the loss of such a beloved man giving rise to the shame of surrender. Half of the men were dead or wounded; most of the cannons knocked out; the masts, apart from the foremast, had fallen and the rudder did not work. In such a pitiful condition an attempt was even made to follow the *Príncipe de Asturias*, which had hoisted the signal to retire, but the *Nepomuceno*, mortally wounded, could not steer in any direction. And despite the ruin and destruction of the vessel; despite the dejection of the crew; despite such unfavourable circumstances to our detriment, not one of the six English ships dared to attempt to board. They feared our ship, even after having defeated her. Churruca, in the paroxysms of death, ordered the flag to be nailed to the mast and that the ship should not be surrendered while he lived. This time could not be anything alas but very short, because Churruca was dying as quickly as possible and all those of us who were present were astonished that a body in such a state could still take breaths and this was how it conserved the strength of his spirit, devoted with irresistible drive to life, since for him at that moment to live was a duty. He did not lose consciousness until the last moments; he did not complain of his pains nor show regret

for his approaching end; on the contrary, he was determined
above all that the officers should not know the gravity of his condition and that
no one should fail in their duty. He thanked the crew for their heroic conduct; he said

some words to his brother-in-law Ruiz de Apodaca, and after dedicating remembrances to his young wife and raising his thoughts to God, whose name we heard pronounced many times through his dry lips, he expired with the peace of the just and the fortitude of heroes, without the satisfaction of victory, but also without the bitterness of the defeated, combining duty with dignity and making a religion of discipline; resolute as a soldier, serene as a man, without complaining about or accusing anyone, with the same dignity in death as in life. We gazed at his body, still warm, and it seemed untrue; we believed he must wake up to lead us again and in weeping for him we showed less fortitude than he did in dying, because on expiry, all the courage, all the enthusiasm he had instilled into us, was taken away. The *San Juan* surrendered and when the officers of the six ships that had destroyed us came aboard, each one claimed for himself the honour of receiving the sword of the dead admiral. All said, 'She was surrendered to my ship,' and for a moment they quarrelled, claiming the honour of victory for one or other of the vessels to which they belonged. They wanted the temporary commander of the *San Juan* to decide the question and say to which of the English ships she had been surrendered and the former replied, 'To all, as the *San Juan* would never have surrendered to one alone.' In the presence of the corpse of the late lamented Churruca, the English, who knew him from his reputation for courage and learning, displayed deep sorrow and one of them said this or something like it, 'Illustrious and worthy men like him should not be exposed to the hazards of a battle, but indeed should be taken good care of for advances in the science of navigation.' Then they ordered the funeral to take place, forming up the English troops and sailors by the side of the Spanish ones and in all their actions they showed themselves to be gentlemen, magnanimous and generous. The number of wounded on board the *San Juan* was so considerable that they transferred us to other vessels of theirs or prizes. It fell to my lot to come to this one, which was one of the most damaged ones, but they reckon on being able to tow her to Gibraltar before any other, now that they cannot take the *Trinidad*, the largest and most coveted of our ships.'

Malespina stopped here, having been listened to with close attention while he spoke about what he had witnessed. From what I heard, I realised that on board every vessel there had occurred a tragedy as dreadful as the one I had witnessed, and I said to myself,

'What a disaster, dear God, caused by the mistakes of a single man!'

And, although I was then just a youngster, I remember that I thought the following,

'One stupid man is not capable at any time in his life of making the blunders that nations led by hundreds of talented men sometimes do.'

XIV

A good part of the night passed with the accounts of Malespina and of other officers. My interest in those narrations kept me awake and so excited that it was only much later that I managed to get to sleep. I could not get out of my mind the image of Churruca, just as I had seen him, fine and well in the home of Doña Flora. And in fact on that occasion I had been surprised by the intense sadness on the face of the illustrious sailor, as if it presaged his painful and approaching end. That noble life had been extinguished at the age of forty-four after twenty-nine years of honourable service in the Navy as scholar, military man and navigator, since Churruca was all of these, as well as a perfect gentleman.

I was thinking of these and other matters when my body finally surrendered to fatigue and I remained asleep until the dawn of the 23rd, my youthful nature having overcome my curiosity. During my sleep, which must have been long and not tranquil, rather, agitated by images and nightmares characteristic of the excitement in my brain, I heard the thunder of gunfire, the shouts of battle, the sounds of rough waves. At the same time I dreamt that I was firing the cannons, that I went up aloft, that I ran along the batteries encouraging the gunners and even that I was giving orders on the quarterdeck like an admiral. I don't have to tell you that in that bitter struggle, made inside my own brain, I defeated all the English present and future with as much ease as if their vessels were cardboard and their shot were breadcrumbs. I had under my flag a thousand or so ships, all larger than the *Trinidad*, and which moved as I pleased with the same precision as the toys which my friends and I played with in the puddles of La Caleta.

But in the end, all these glories vanished, which, as they were purely dreams, is nothing strange, since we find that the real ones also vanish. It all came to an end when I opened my eyes and realised how small I was compared to the magnitude of the disasters I had witnessed. Yet, there was something odd! I was awake and still heard gunfire; I heard the terrifying noise of a brawl and shouts which announced great activity in the crew. I thought I was still dreaming; I sat up on the couch where I had been sleeping, paid great attention and a deafening shout of "*Long live the King!*" definitely reached my ears, leaving me with no doubt that the *Santa Ana* was fighting once more.

I went outside and took stock of the situation. The weather had become much calmer; to windward some unrigged ships could be seen and two of them, English ones, were firing at the *Santa Ana*, who was defending herself with the support of two others, a Spanish one and a French one. I could not understand this sudden change in our situation as prisoners; I looked at the stern and saw our flag flying in place of the English one. What had happened, or rather, what was happening?

On the quarterdeck was someone I realised was Admiral Álava, and, although wounded in various parts of his body, he had sufficient strength to lead this second battle, intended perhaps, as far as the *Santa Ana* was concerned, to make the misfortunes of the first one be forgotten. The officers were encouraging the ship's crew who were loading and firing those guns that remained serviceable, while some of them were engaged in watching over, and keeping in line, the English, who had been disarmed and penned up on the first 'tween deck. That nation's officers, who had been our guards, had changed into prisoners.

I understood it all. The heroic commander of the *Santa Ana*, Don Ignacio M. de Álava, seeing the approach of some Spanish ships, which had come out of Cádiz with the intention of retaking the captured vessels and saving the crews of those close to sinking, addressed his downcast crew with patriotic language. They responded to the voice of their leader with a supreme effort; they forced the English who were guarding the vessel to surrender; hoisted the Spanish flag once more and the *Santa Ana* became free, although engaged in a new battle, more perilous perhaps than the first.

This outstanding daring, one of the most honourable episodes in the action of Trafalgar, took place on a dismasted vessel, without a rudder, with half of her men dead or wounded and the rest in a completely pitiful state of morale and physically. Once that deed had been done, it was necessary to face up to the consequences: two English ships, also in a bad state, were firing at the *Santa Ana*; but the latter was getting timely help from the *Asís*, the *Montañés* and the *Rayo*, three of those that had withdrawn with Gravina on the 21st and which had come out again to rescue the prizes. Those noble invalids were engaged in a new and desperate struggle, perhaps with more courage than in the first, because the unstaunched wounds inflamed the fury in the souls of the combatants and these seemed to fight with greater ardour because they had less life to lose.

The vicissitudes of the terrible day of the 21st repeated themselves before my eyes: enthusiasm was great but the men few, which meant that effort had to be redoubled. It is regrettable that such a heroic deed has filled no more than a brief page in our history, even if it is true that, compared to the great event known today as the *Battle of Trafalgar*, these episodes shrink and almost disappear as faint glows in a horrible night.

Then I witnessed a deed which brought tears to my eyes. Not being able to find my master anywhere and fearing that he might be in some sort of danger, I went down to the first battery and found him occupied in aiming a cannon. His quivering hand had taken the linstock from those of a wounded sailor, and with the weak sight of his right eye, the unfortunate man was searching for the spot he wanted to send the cannon ball to. When the gun fired, he turned towards me, trembling with pride and in a voice I could hardly hear, said to me:

'Oh! Now Paca won't be laughing at me. We will enter triumphant into Cádiz.'

In short, the contest ended happily, because the English realised the impossibility of retaking the *Santa Ana*, who was helped, as well as by the three ships mentioned, by two other French ones and a frigate, which arrived in the thick of the fight.

We were free in the most glorious manner; but at the point that feat was accomplished, the danger we faced became clear as the *Santa Ana* would have to be towed to Cádiz because of the poor condition of her hull. The French frigate *Thémis*[136] threw us a cable and put her bow to the north, but what strength could that vessel have to tow another one as heavy as the *Santa Ana*, and which could only help herself with the tattered sails that remained on her foremast? The ships that had rescued us, that is, the *Rayo*, the *Montañés* and the *San Francisco de Asís*, wanted to carry on with their heroic deeds and made sail to rescue as well the *San Juan* and the *Bahama*, which were manned by the English. So we remained on our own, with no more help than that of the frigate which was hauling us along, a child leading a giant. What would become of us if the English, as it was to be supposed, recovered from their setback and returned with reinforcements to pursue us? However, it seemed as if Providence was smiling on us since the wind, favourable to the course we were taking, drove our frigate onwards, and behind her, lovingly led, the ship drew closer to Cádiz.

Five leagues separated us from the port.

What indescribable satisfaction! Soon our troubles would be at an end; soon we would be able to put our feet on dry land, and if we were bearing news of great disasters, we were also bringing joy to many hearts that were suffering mortal anxiety, believing that those who returned alive and well had been lost for ever.

The fearlessness of the Spanish ships had no results other than the rescue of the *Santa Ana*, since the weather turned against them and they had to withdraw without being able to chase the English ships that were escorting the *San Juan*, the *Bahama* and the *San Ildefonso*. We were still four leagues distant from the end of our voyage when we saw them withdraw. The strong winds had increased and the general opinion on board the *Santa Ana* was that if we delayed in arriving, we would have a very bad time. New and more terrible hardships. Once more hope lost in sight of port and when only a few more paces over the terrible element would have put us into complete safety within the bay.

What's more, night was bearing down with a very bad look: the sky, overloaded with black clouds, seemed to have rolled flat over the sea and the electrical discharges which lit it up at brief intervals gave a dreadful colouring to the twilight. The sea, increasingly turbulent, a fury still not appeased by so many a victim, roared with rage and its insatiable voracity demanded a greater number of prizes. The remains of the most numerous fleet which at that time had defied its fury together with that of the enemy, did not escape the anger of the element, stirred up like an ancient god, pitiless to the very end, as cruel in the face of fortune as in the face of misery.

I noticed signs of deep sorrow on the face of my master as well as on that of Admiral Álava, who, despite his wounds, was fully alert and ordered a signal to be made to the frigate *Thémis* to increase her speed if it was possible. Far from responding to his justified impatience, our tug prepared to reef and take in sail to weather the furious east wind better. I shared the general sorrow and in my innermost thoughts considered how easily destiny mocks our best-laid plans and how quickly the greatest luck turns to ultimate misfortune. But there we were on the sea, a majestic emblem of human life. A little wind transforms it; the gentle wave which rocks the vessel with a soft stroke changes into a liquid mountain which shatters her and tosses her about; the pleasant sound of the small undulations in the water made in fair weather is then a voice which grows hoarse and shouts, cursing the fragile craft and the latter, hurled headlong, submerges with the feeling she has lost the support of her keel, only to mount up again, thrown upwards by the rising wave. A calm day brings on a frightening night, or, on the contrary, a moon which embellishes space and calms the spirit will often precede a terrible sun before whose brightness Nature breaks up in formidable confusion.

We were experiencing the misery of these alternatives as well as that produced by the works of man. After a battle we had suffered a shipwreck; saved from the latter, we found ourselves once more engaged in a fight, which finished well and then, when we thought we had come to the end of so many troubles, when we greeted Cádiz full of joy, we found ourselves again in the power of the storm, which was drawing us away, wanting to finish us off. This series of misfortunes seems absurd, doesn't it? It was like the cruel aberration of a divinity determined to cause the most harm possible to beings who had lost their way... but no, it was the logic of the sea, together with the logic

of war. Once these two terrible elements are joined together, who but a fool would be amazed to see them produce the greatest misfortunes?

A new circumstance increased the sorrows of that evening for me and for my master. After the *Santa Ana* had been recovered, we had not seen the young Malespina. At last, after having looked for him for a long time, I found him curled up on one of the couches in the cabin.

I approached him and saw that he was very pale; I asked him some questions but he was unable to answer me. He tried to get up and fell down again out of breath.

'But you are wounded!' I said. 'I'll get someone to treat you.'

'It's nothing,' he replied. 'Could you bring me a little water?'

I immediately called my master.

'What is it? The wound in your hand?' the latter asked while examining the young man.

'No, it's something else,' Don Rafael replied sadly and pointed to his right side, close to the waist.

Then, as if the effort used in showing his wound and saying those few words was too much for his weakened nature, he shut his eyes and remained for some time without speaking or moving.

'Oh, this looks serious,' Don Alonso said with dismay.

'It's more than serious,' added a surgeon who had come to examine him.

Malespina, deeply saddened at finding himself in such a state and believing there was no cure for him, did not even report his wound and withdrew to that spot where his thoughts and memories occupied him. Believing himself to be close to death, he refused to let them give him any treatment. The surgeon said that, although serious, the wound did not seem to be mortal; but he added that if we did not get to Cádiz that night, so that he could be properly attended to on land, his life, as well as those of the other wounded, would be in great danger. In the Battle of the 21st the *Santa Ana* had had ninety-seven killed and a hundred and forty wounded; the resources of the sickbay had been exhausted and some essential medicines were completely lacking. Malespina's misfortune was not the only one following our rescue and it was God's will that another very dear to me should suffer a similar fate. Marcial had been wounded, even though in the first few moments he felt hardly any pain or distress, because his strong spirit kept him going. However, it was not long before he went down to the lower deck, saying that he felt very bad. My master sent for the surgeon to attend him and the latter confined himself to saying that the wound would have been nothing to a young man of twenty-four: *Half-a-man* was over sixty.

Meanwhile, the *Rayo* was passing to port and within hailing distance. Álava gave the order to ask the frigate *Thémis* if she believed she could enter Cádiz and, having replied flatly no, he asked the same question to the *Rayo*, which being hardly damaged, reckoned she could make it safely to port. So, various officers having met together, they agreed to transfer to that ship Captain Gardoqui, who was seriously wounded, and many other naval and military officers, including the fiancé of my young mistress. Don Alonso ensured that Marcial was also transferred, having regard to his great age which made him considerably worse, and he gave me the job of accompanying them as a page or medical orderly, ordering me not to leave their side for a moment until I left them in Cádiz or Vejer, in the hands of his family. I was preparing to obey and tried to persuade my master that he, too, should transfer to the *Rayo* to be safer, but he did not even want to listen to such a proposal.

'Fate,' he said, 'has brought me to this vessel and I will stay with her until God decides whether or not we escape. Álava is very ill; most of the officers are wounded and here I can be of some service. I am not one of those that run away from danger; on the contrary, I have been searching for it since the twenty-first and I want to find an opportunity where my presence with the fleet can be of use. If you arrive before me, which I hope you do, tell Paca that a good sailor is a slave to his country, and that I have done very much the right thing by coming here, and that I am very happy that I came, and that I am not sorry, absolutely not, I am not sorry... quite the opposite... tell her that she'll be happy when she sees me, and that my comrades would have missed me if I had not come... how could I have been absent? Don't you think that I did the right thing by coming?'

'Well, it's obvious, what doubt could there be?' I replied, trying to calm his agitation, which was so great that he could not see the inappropriateness of discussing such a serious question with a wretched page.

'I see that you are a reasonable person,' he continued, feeling comforted by my approval. 'I see you have an elevated and patriotic outlook... but Paca can only see things from her own selfish viewpoint; and as she has such a remarkable temper and as she has got it into her head that fleets and cannons are good for nothing, she cannot understand that I... well, then... I know that she'll get furious when I return, then... as we didn't win, she'll say all sorts of things... she'll drive me crazy... but, pshaw... I won't pay any attention to her. What do you think? Isn't it right that I shouldn't pay her any attention?'

'Rather!' I replied. 'Your lordship has certainly done the right thing by coming here; it proves that your lordship is a brave sailor.'

'Well, go and give that message to Paca and you'll see how she answers you,' he replied, becoming increasingly agitated. 'Well, then, tell her that I'm well and unharmed and that my presence here was very necessary. The truth is that I played a very major role in the rescue of the *Santa Ana*. If I hadn't aimed those guns so well, who knows, who knows!? And what do you think? I might still be able to do something more; it might still be that if the wind is favourable to us, we rescue a couple of ships tomorrow... Yes, indeed... I'm working out a definite plan now... Let's see, let's see... So then, young Gabriel, goodbye. Careful what you say to Paca.'

'No, I won't forget. She will know that if it wasn't for your lordship the *Santa Ana* wouldn't have been retaken and she'll also know that with any luck your lordship may bring us two dozen ships into Cádiz.'

'Two dozen, no, my boy,' he said, 'that's a lot. Two ships, or perhaps three. Well, I think I truly did do the right thing by coming to the fleet. She will be furious and she will drive me crazy when I return; but I believe, I'll say it again, that I truly did do the right thing by going on board.'

Having said this, he left me. A moment later, I saw him seated in a corner of the cabin. He was praying, counting the rosary very furtively, as he did not want to be seen occupied in such an exercise of devotion. I assumed from his final words that my master had gone off his head and seeing him praying made me realise the weakness of his spirit, which had struggled in vain to overcome his tired old age and, not being able to continue the struggle, he turned to God in search of forgiveness. Doña Francisca was right. My master, for many years, had been good for nothing but praying.

In accordance with what had been agreed, we trans-shipped. Don Rafael and Marcial, along with the other wounded officers, were lowered with a lot of effort onto one of the launches by the arms of strong sailors. The large waves interfered with this operation a lot, but eventually it was done and the two boats steered towards the *Rayo*. The crossing from one ship to the other was the very worst, but in the end, although there were moments when I thought the boat was going to disappear for ever, we arrived at the side of the *Rayo* and with the greatest effort we went up the ladder.

XV

'We've jumped out of the frying pan into the fire,' said Marcial when they put him down onto the deck. 'But where the captain rules, a sailor has no sway. They gave the *Rayo* to this damned man because he's useless. He says that he'll enter Cádiz before midnight, and I say that he won't. We'll see.'

'What are you saying, Marcial, that we won't arrive?' I asked with great anxiety.

'You, young master Gabriel, don't understand anything about this.'

'It's that when my master Don Alonso and the officers of the *Santa Ana* believe the *Rayo* will enter port tonight, she is bound to enter port. If they say it's going to happen, then that is what will happen; everyone knows that.'

'And you don't know, *sardine-io*, that those gentlemen on the poop deck *lampify* (make mistakes) more easily than us sailors in the waist. If not, what was the head of all the fleet, *Monsieur Corneta*, may the Devil take him, all about? You've seen how he had no idea at all about leading an action. Do you think that if *Monsieur Corneta* had done what I said he would have lost the battle?'

'So do you think we won't get to Cádiz?'

'What I say is that this ship is heavier than lead itself, and treacherous to boot. Her trim is bad, she steers badly and it seems she's as crippled, one-eyed and one-armed as me, since if you put the helm one way, she goes the other.'

In fact, the *Rayo*, in general opinion, was one of the least seaworthy vessels. But, despite this and her advanced age, which was getting on for fifty-six years, because she was in a good state, she did not seem to be in any danger, since even if the gale was getting stronger all the time, the port was also close. In any event, wasn't it logical to assume that a greater risk was being run by the *Santa Ana*, dismasted, rudderless and compelled to proceed under tow to a frigate?

Marcial was put on the lower deck and Malespina in the cabin. When we left him there with the other wounded officers, I heard a voice I recognised, although I could not at first think whose it was. I approached the group from which that booming talk was coming and I was astonished to recognise Don José María Malespina himself in person. I ran up to him to tell him his son was here, and the good father stopped the pack of lies he was telling to go to the side of the wounded young man. Great was his joy to find him alive, since he had left Cádiz because impatience was devouring him and he wanted to know his whereabouts at all costs.

'What you've got is nothing,' he said, embracing his son, 'a simple scratch. You're not used to suffering wounds; you're a lady, Rafael. Ah, if you had been old enough to come with me to the War of Roussillon, you'd have seen some good ones. Those were proper wounds. You know about the ball that came in through my forearm, went up to my shoulder, went all round my shoulder and ended up coming out at my waist. Ah, what an outstanding wound! But in three days I was fit again, commanding the Artillery in the attack on Bellegarde.'[137]

Then he explained how he came to be on board the *Rayo* as follows,

'On the night of the twenty-first we knew in Cádiz the outcome of the battle. I might say, gentlemen, that no one paid any attention to me when I spoke about reform of the Artillery, and here you have the consequences. Anyway, once I knew and I had found out that Gravina had withdrawn with some ships, I went to see if the *San Juan*, which you were on, was among them, but they told me she had been captured. I cannot describe to you my anxiety: I had almost no doubt that you were dead, especially after I knew of the large number of losses on your ship. But I am a man that doesn't give up easily and knowing that they had arranged for some ships to go out with the intention of recovering the disabled ships and rescuing prisoners, I decided to remove any doubts immediately and join one of them. I explained my intention to Solano,[138] and then to the Rear Admiral of the Fleet, my old friend Escaño, and not without some hesitation they let me come. On board the *Rayo*, which I joined this morning, I asked for you, the *San Juan*, but I was told nothing comforting, in fact, quite the opposite, that Churruca had been killed and that his ship, having fought gloriously, had fallen into the hands of the enemy. Imagine how worried I was! I had no idea at all today that when we rescued the *Santa Ana*, you would be on board! If I'd known it for certain, I would have redoubled my efforts in the orders I gave, with the leave of these gentlemen, and Álava's ship would have been free in two minutes.'

The officers who surrounded him looked at him sarcastically when they heard the latest boastful opinion of Don José María. From their laughter and whispering I understood that throughout the day they had been enjoying the stories of that fine gentleman, who could not halt his voluble tongue even in the most critical and distressing circumstances.

The surgeon said it was important to let the wounded man rest and not to carry on any conversation in his presence, above all one that was about the past disaster. Don José María, who heard this, maintained that, on the contrary, it was important to revive the wounded man's spirit by conversation.

'In the War of Roussillon, when we were seriously wounded (and I was many times), we would order the soldiers to dance and play the guitar in the sickbay and I am sure that this treatment cured us more quickly than all the poultices and medicine chests.'

'So, in the French Republican Wars,' said an Andalusian officer who wanted to put Don José

María to shame, 'it was the case that in the field hospitals for the wounded there would be a complete corps de ballet and an opera company, and with this one could do without any doctors or apothecaries, since with a couple of arias and two dozen entrechats en sixte, everyone would be as good as new.'

'Now, halt!' Malespina exclaimed. 'A likely story that is, my young sir. How can wounds be cured by music and dance?'

'That's what you said.'

'Yes, but that only happened once, and it's unlikely to happen again. Is it at all likely that there will be another war like that of Roussillon, the bloodiest, the best planned, the most strategic one that the world has seen since Epaminondas?[139] Of course not, since everything was extraordinary there and I can testify to that as I was present from the *introito* until the *ite, missa est.*[140] It's to that war that I owe my knowledge of artillery. Haven't you heard of me? I am sure you must know me by reputation. Well, you should know that I have here in my head a grand project and such a one that if one day it is realised, there will be no more disasters like that of the twenty-first. Yes, gentlemen,' he added, looking gravely and smugly at the three or four officers who were listening to him, 'it is essential to do something for one's country; something surprising urgently needs to be invented, something that will give us back in a tick everything that we have lost and assure our navy of victory for ever and ever amen.'

'I say, Señor Don José María,' one officer said, 'explain to us what your invention is.'

'Well, at the moment I'm busy with the method of constructing three hundred-pounder cannons.'

'Three hundred-pounders!' the officers exclaimed, bursting into mocking laughter. 'The largest ones we have on board are thirty-six.'

'Those are children's toys. Imagine the destruction that those three hundred-pounder guns would do firing on the enemy fleet,' Malespina said. 'But what the devil is this?' he added, holding on tight so as not to fall to the ground, since the rolling of the *Rayo* was such that it was very difficult for someone to keep upright.

'The gale is getting stronger and it seems to me we won't get into Cádiz tonight,' an officer said and left.

Only two were left and the storyteller continued with his long-winded speech as follows,

'The first thing that would have to be done would be to build vessels of two hundred and sixty to two hundred and seventy-five feet long.'[141]

'Good heavens! That little launch would be quite something, don't you think?!' one of the officers said. 'Two hundred and seventy-five feet! The *Trinidad*, may she rest in peace, was one hundred and ninety feet, and everyone thought she was too long. She beat badly, and handling her was always very difficult.'

'I can see, young sir, that you are easily frightened,' Malespina continued. 'What are two hundred and seventy-five feet? Much bigger vessels still could be built. And I have to warn you that I would build them from iron.'

'From iron!' exclaimed the two listeners, unable to stop laughing.

'Yes, from iron. Perhaps you are not aware of the science of hydrostatics? In accordance with it I would build an iron vessel of seven thousand tons.'

'And the *Trinidad* was only four thousand!' an officer said. 'And that seemed too many. But don't you understand that to move that bulk you would have to have such a colossal rig that it would be beyond human strength to handle her?'

'Easily done! Ah, my good sailor, why do you think I would be so stupid as to move this vessel by means of the wind? You don't know me. If you knew what sort of idea I have… but I have no wish to explain it to you as you would not understand me.'

At this point in his discourse, Don José María had such a tumble that he ended up on all fours. But even this did not shut him up. Another one of the officers left and only one remained, who had to carry on the conversation.

'What ups and downs!' the old man continued. 'It seems indeed that we are going to be smashed to pieces on the coast… Anyway, as I said, I would move this bulk I invented by means of… haven't you guessed? By means of steam. For this one would build a special machine where the steam, compressed and expanded, alternatively, inside two cylinders, would move some wheels… then…'

The officer had no wish to hear any more; and, although he had no position on the vessel, nor was he on duty, as he was one of the rescued ones, he went to help his colleagues who were very busy with the increasing storm. Malespina remained alone with me and I thought that he would then stop talking, judging me to be someone unsuitable for carrying on the conversation with. But it was my misfortune that he valued me more than I did myself and carried it on with me as follows,

'Now you understand what I mean, don't you? Seven thousand tons, the steam, two wheels… then….'

'Yes, sir, I understand perfectly,' I replied, hoping he would become silent since I was neither in the mood to listen to him, nor did the violent rolling of the boat, foreboding great danger, dispose my mind to a discourse extolling the Navy.

'I can see that you know me and understand my inventions,' he continued. 'You will have already realised that the vessel I invent will be invincible, whether in attack or in defence. With four or five shots it would have defeated the thirty English ships on its own.'

'But wouldn't the guns on those ships have caused damage to it as well?' I said timidly, pointing this out to him more out of politeness than because the thing interested me.

'Ah, your observation, young sir, is most pertinent, and proves that you understand and appreciate great inventions. To prevent the enemy artillery having any effect, I would cover my vessel with thick plates of steel, in other words, I would put a cuirass onto it, like the ones used by the warriors of old. In this way it could attack and the enemy projectiles would have no more effect on its sides than a broadside of bread pellets thrown by a child would have. The idea I have come up with is a marvellous one. Imagine if our country had two or three vessels like that. Where would the English fleet be then with all their Nelsons and Collingwoods?'

'But even if those vessels could be built here,' I said with spirit, knowing the force of my argument, 'the English would have them also and then the chances in the fight would be the same.'

Don José María seemed stunned by this reasoning, and for a moment he was perplexed and did not know what to say, but his inexhaustible talent soon suggested some new ideas to him and he replied testily,

'And who has told you, impudent rascal, that I would be capable of disclosing my secret? The vessels would be built in the greatest secrecy without a word said to anyone. Let us suppose that there was a new war. The English provoked us and we told them, 'Yes indeed, we are ready, we shall fight.' The ordinary ships went out to sea, the fight started, and, just imagine it, suddenly there appeared on the waters of the battle two or three of these iron monsters, belching smoke and going here and there paying no heed to the wind; they get everywhere they want, the thrust of their tapering bows makes matchwood of the opposing vessels, and with a couple of cannon shots... Just think, everything would be over in quarter of an hour.'

I did not want to raise any more objections, because the idea that we were in great danger prevented my mind being occupied by thoughts other than those directed to such a critical situation. I thought no more of the formidable imaginary vessel, until thirty years later I knew about the use of steam in navigation and even more so when after half a century I saw in our glorious frigate *Numancia*[142] the perfect realisation of the eccentric schemes of the storyteller of Trafalgar.

Half a century later I remembered Don José María Malespina and said,

'It seems impossible that the nonsense thought up by a liar or storyteller ends up becoming wonderful reality with the passage of time.'

Since I witnessed this coincidence I have never dismissed in the slightest any utopia and all liars seem to me to be men of genius.

I left Don José María to see what was happening and as soon as I stepped outside the cabin I realised the awkward situation the *Rayo* was in. The gale was not only stopping her from getting into Cádiz, but driving her towards the coast, where she would certainly run aground, dashing her onto the rocks. However bad the fate of the *Santa Ana*, which we had left, it could not be worse than ours. I observed the faces of the officers and sailors attentively to see if I could find something to indicate hope, but, to my dismay, in all of them I saw signs of great dejection. I consulted the sky and saw it was absolutely awful; I consulted the sea and found it was very angry. There was only God to turn to, and He had hardly been well disposed to us since the 21st!

The *Rayo* ran northwards. According to the information given by the sailors, whom I was with, we passed before the Marrajotes Bank, Hazte Afuera, Juan Bola,[143] before Torregorda,[144] and, finally, before the castle of Cádiz. All the manoeuvres necessary for making for the inside of the bay were executed in vain. The old ship, like a frightened steed, refused to obey; the wind and the sea, which were running with violent fury from south to north, carried her along and nautical science could do nothing to prevent it.

We quickly went past the bay. To our right Rota, Punta Candor, Punta de Meca, Regla and Chipiona[145] soon appeared. There was now no doubt that the *Rayo* was heading straight for an inevitable collision with the coast close to the mouth of the Guadalquivir. It goes without saying that the sails had been taken in, and that this measure not being enough for such a violent storm, the upper masts had also been lowered. Finally, it was thought necessary to cut the masts to avoid the ship being thrown under the waves. With big storms, a vessel needs to make itself smaller, the tall holm oak must change itself into lowly grass, and as the masts could not bend like the branches of a tree, there came the sad requirement to amputate them, leaving no limbs to save life.

The loss of the vessel was now inevitable. With the mainmast and the mizzen-mast cut, everyone lost heart and the only hope was to be able to anchor her near the shore, for which purpose the anchors were got ready and the cables strengthened. Two cannon shots were fired to ask for help from the beach, now close by, and as we clearly saw some bonfires on the shore, we rejoiced, thinking that there would be someone who could help us. Many were of the opinion that some Spanish or English ship had run aground and that the bonfires we saw had been lit by the shipwrecked crew. Our fear grew moment by moment and, as for me, I have to say I thought I was close to a calamitous end. I paid no attention to what was happening on board, nor in the confusion of my mind could I think of anything other than death, which I judged to be inevitable. If the vessel were to be wrecked, who would be able to cross the space of water that would separate her from the land? The most dreadful place in a storm is where the waves are attacking the land, and it seems they are digging into it to carry off chunks of the shore into the depths of the abyss. The forward thrust of the wave and the violence with which it drags itself back are things that no human force can overcome.

Finally, after a few hours of mortal fear, the keel of the *Rayo* struck a sandbank and she came to a stop. The entire hull and the remains of her masts and spars shuddered for an instant as if they intended to overcome the obstacle placed in her way; but the latter was bigger and the vessel, heeling over to one side after the other, sank by the stern and, after an almighty crack, remained motionless.

It had all come to an end, and now the only thought was to save our lives, crossing the space of sea that separated us from the coast. This seemed almost impossible to do in the boats that we had on board; but there was hope that they could give us help from land, since it was clear that the crew of a recently wrecked vessel was bivouacked on shore and one of the sloops of war, that the naval authorities in Cádiz had got ready for such cases, could not be far away… The *Rayo* fired cannons again and we awaited rescue with great impatience, because, unless they came quickly, we would all perish with the ship. This unfortunate invalid, whose bottom had opened up when she grounded, threatened to break into pieces through her own convulsions, and it could not be long until the moment came when, the fastening on some of her frames having become unfixed, we would be at the mercy of the waves, with no support other than what the dismembered remains of the vessel might give us.

Those on land could not help us; but God willed that the alarm signal of cannon fire had been heard by a sloop that had put out to sea from Chipiona, and she approached us at the bow, keeping a good distance. Once we had caught sight of her large mainsail we saw that our salvation was certain and the captain of the *Rayo* gave orders so that the trans-shipment would be carried out without any upset in such dangerous moments.

My first intention, when I saw that it was a case of trans-shipment, was to run to the side of the two people there I was interested in: young Malespina and Marcial, both wounded, although the second one not seriously. I found the Artillery officer in a pretty bad way, and he said to those around him,

'Don't move me; let me die here.'

Marcial had been carried onto the deck and was lying on the ground so cast down and dejected that his appearance caused me real fear. He looked up when I approached him and taking me by the hand, he said in a shaky voice,

'Don't leave me, young Gabriel.'

'Ashore! We're all going ashore!' I exclaimed, trying to encourage him. He, however, sadly shaking his head, seemed to presage some misfortune.

I tried to help him get up, but after one attempt his body then collapsed exhausted and finally he said,

'I can't.'

The bandages on his wound had fallen off and in the chaos of that difficult situation he couldn't find anyone who could put them on again. I tended to him as best I could, comforting him with encouraging words and I even tried laughing and ridiculing him for what a sight he looked, to see if this would revive him. But the poor old man did not move his lips; rather, he lowered his head with a sad grimace, insensible of my jokes as well as of my consoling words.

While I was occupied in this, I did not notice that they had started the embarkation into the boats. Almost the first to be lowered into them were Don José María Malespina and his son. My first impulse was to go after them, following my master's orders; but the image of the wounded and abandoned sailor held me back. Malespina did not need me, whereas Marcial, who could almost be considered dead, grasped my hand with his frozen one, saying to me,

'Don't leave me, Gabriel.'

The boats came alongside with difficulty, but despite this, once the wounded had been trans-shipped, the embarkation was easy, because the sailors launched themselves into them by slipping down a line or throwing themselves in with one leap. Many flung themselves into the water and swam to them. The thought of which of those two procedures I would use to save myself crossed my mind as a terrible problem. There was no time to lose, because the *Rayo* was falling apart: nearly all the stern was submerged and the bursting of the beams and the half-rotted ribs signalled that very soon that bulk was going to be a vessel no longer. Everyone ran with alacrity to the boats and the sloop, manoeuvring skilfully to withstand the sea, picked them up. The craft returned empty in a short while, but it was not long before they were full again.

I saw how *Half-a-man* had been abandoned and, choking and crying, I went up to some sailors asking them to take up Marcial and save him. But they were quite absorbed with saving themselves. In a moment of desperation, I even tried to put him on my back, but with my limited strength I hardly managed to lift his limp arms from the ground. I ran all over the deck looking for a charitable soul and some were on the point of yielding to my entreaties, but the danger led them away from such a fine intention. To understand this inhuman cruelty you have to have been in such terrible straits as these: sentiment and charity disappear in the face of the instinct of self-preservation, which completely dominates a man and at times makes him resemble a wild beast.

'Ah, those villains don't want to save you, Marcial!' I cried in great anguish.

'Forget them,' he said. 'It's the same on board as it is on land. You must go: run, lad, or they'll leave you here.'

I do not know which idea mortified me more: either that of staying on board, where I would inevitably perish, or that of going and leaving that unfortunate man on his own. Finally, the voice of Nature was stronger than any other and I went a few paces towards the gunwale. I turned back to embrace the poor old man, and then ran quickly to the place where the last sailors were embarking. There were four of them; when I arrived I saw that all four had launched themselves into the sea and were swimming up to the boat, which was some ten or twelve yards away.

'What about me?' I cried out in distress, seeing that they were leaving me. 'I'm coming, too, me, too!'

I shouted with all my strength, but they did not hear me, or did not want to pay me any attention. Despite the darkness, I saw the boat; I saw them get into it, although you could hardly make out this operation. I got ready to throw myself into the water to follow the same destiny, but in the very instant that I made up my mind to take this course, my eyes no longer saw the boat and the sailors, and before me there was only the horrible darkness of the water.

All means of rescue had disappeared. I looked all about me and saw nothing but the waves which were shaking the remains of the vessel; not even a star in the sky; not even a light on the shore. The sloop had disappeared as well. Beneath my feet, which were stamping with rage, the hull of the *Rayo* was breaking into pieces, and only a part of the bow remained complete and in one piece, with the deck full of debris. I was standing on a shapeless raft which threatened to break apart in moments.

Finding myself in this situation, I ran towards Marcial, saying,

'They've left me behind, they've left us behind!'

The old man pulled himself up with much effort, leaning on his hand; raised his head and ran his worried eye over our gloomy surroundings.

'Nothing!' he exclaimed. 'Nothing to be seen. No boats, no land, no lights, no shore. They won't be coming back.'

When he said this, a terrible crack was heard under our feet in the depths of the fore lower deck, now completely flooded. The forecastle leant wildly to one side and we had to grip tightly to the base of a windlass to stop ourselves falling into the water. We couldn't stand up: the final remains of the *Rayo* were about to be swallowed by the waves. But as hope never leaves us, I still thought this situation would last until dawn without getting worse and I was comforted by seeing that the foremast was still upright. With the firm intention of getting onto it when the hull was about to sink, I looked at that proud tree on which were flying bits of rope and tatters of sail, and which endured, a colossus dishevelled in desperation, asking Heaven for mercy.

Marcial let himself fall to the deck and then he said,

'There's no hope now, young Gabriel. They don't want to come back, nor would the sea let them if they tried. As it is what God intends, we two have to die here. It's of no importance for me: I am an old man and no use for any damned thing… but you… you are a child, and…'

When he said this, his voice became unintelligible with emotion and hoarseness.

Soon after I clearly heard him say these words,

'You don't have any sins because you are a child. But me… Still, when one dies like this… what shall I say… like a dog or a cat, you don't need a priest to come and give you *solution*, all that's needed is that you make your peace with God yourself. Haven't you heard that?'

I do not know what I replied; I believe I said nothing and I began to cry inconsolably.

'Cheer up, young Gabriel,' he continued. 'A man must be a man and now is the time when you find out what you're made of. You don't have any sins, but I certainly do. They say that when a person dies and there's no priest he can confess to, he has to tell the first person he meets what he has on his conscience. So I'm telling you, young Gabriel, that I'll make my confession to you and that I'll tell you my sins and trust that God is listening to me behind you and that He will forgive me.'

Silenced by terror and the solemn words I had just heard, I hugged the old man, who continued as follows,

'Well, then, I state that I have always been a Catholic, *Postolic*, Roman Christian and that I have always had and have a devotion to the Virgin of Carmel, to whom I call for help at this moment; and I also state that if I haven't been to confession or received communion for twenty years, it wasn't because of me, but for the *sake* of the damned service and because of always putting it off to the next Sunday. But now I am sorry that I didn't do it, and I state, declare and perjure myself that I love God, the Virgin and all the saints and may they punish me for all that I have done to offend them, since if I haven't been to confession or received communion this year it was because of that *matter* of the damned *greatcoats*, who made me go to sea when I had the *projection* of fulfilling my religious obligations. I have never stolen, not even a pinhead, nor have I said any lies other than one or two as a joke. I repent of the beatings I gave my wife thirty years ago, although I believe they were well deserved, since she was as disobedient as a *churra*[146] ewe and had a temper sharper than a scorpion. I didn't deviate by one jot from what the Regulations require; I detest no one more than the *greatcoats*, whom I'd have liked to see made into mincemeat; but, as they say, we are all children of God, I forgive them and *similarwise* I forgive the French, who brought this war on us. I won't say any more, because I think I'm going away under full sail. I love God and I am at peace. Embrace me, young Gabriel, and hug me closely. You have no sins and you will be *culminatering* with the angels in Heaven. It's better to die at your age than to live in this *wretchified* world… So then, courage, lad, it's coming to an end. The water's rising and it's the end of the *Rayo* for ever. The death of someone who drowns is very easy: don't be scared… hug me. In a short while we will be free of sorrow, me accounting to God for my peccadillos and you happy as a sandboy, dancing in Heaven, which is carpeted with stars, and there it seems that happiness never ends, because it's eternal, or as somebody else said: tomorrow and tomorrow and tomorrow, and the next one and for ever…'

He could speak no more. I clung tightly to *Half-a-man's* body. A furious sea shook the bow of the ship and I felt the water whip across my shoulder. I shut my eyes and thought of God. At the same moment I lost all feeling and did not know what happened.

XVI

I do not know when, but the notion of life dimly illuminated my mind once more; I felt intensely cold and it was only because I had that feeling that I knew I was still alive, since I had no memory of what had happened, nor could I understand my new situation. When my thoughts were gradually clearing and the lethargy in my senses vanished, I found myself lying flat on the beach. Some men were round about me, observing me with interest. The first thing I heard was,

'Poor little thing! He's coming round now.'

Little by little I was coming back to life, and with that, the memory of what had happened. I remembered Marcial and I believe that the first words that passed my lips were to ask after him. Nobody could give me an answer. Among those surrounding me I recognised some sailors from the *Rayo*; I asked them about *Half-a-man* and they all agreed that he had perished. Then I wanted to find out how they had rescued me; but they could not give me any information either.

They gave me something or other to drink; they carried me to a nearby house and there, next to the fire and cared for by an old woman, I recovered my health, although not my strength. Then they told me that, another sloop having gone out to reconnoitre the wreckage of the *Rayo* and of a French ship that had suffered the same fate, they found me by the side of Marcial and were able to save my life. My companion in death was dead. I also learnt that a number of unfortunate men had perished while swimming from the shipwrecked vessel to the shore.

I wanted to know what had happened to Malespina, but there was no one who could give me any information about the father or the son. I asked about the *Santa Ana* and they told me she had arrived safely in Cádiz, upon which news I decided to leave immediately to rejoin my master. I was some distance away from Cádiz, on the coast which joins up with the right bank of the Guadalquivir River.[147] I needed then to start off immediately to cover such a long distance as soon as possible. I waited for two more days to recover and eventually, accompanied by a sailor who was going the same way,

I set off towards Sanlúcar. I remember we crossed the river on the morning of the 27th and then we carried on our journey on foot without leaving the coast. As the sailor who accompanied me was outspoken and cheerful, the journey was as pleasant as I could have hoped for, given my state of mind, still depressed by the death of Marcial and the final scenes which I witnessed on board. On the way we would talk about the battle and the shipwrecks which followed it.

'He was a good sailor, was *Half-a-man*,' said my travelling companion. 'But who made him to go to sea with a cargo of more than sixty years? The end he came to served him right.'

'He was a brave sailor,' I said, 'and so fond of war that not even his ailments held him back once he had decided to join the fleet.'

'Well, no more fleet for me,' the sailor continued. 'I don't want any more sea battles. The King pays badly and then, if you end up crippled or disabled, it's goodnight to you – and have I met you? I don't remember it. I'm surprised how badly the King treats those who serve him. Would you believe it? Most of the captains who fought on the twenty-first have not been paid for months. Last year there was a post-captain in Cádiz who, not knowing how to maintain himself and his children, took a job as a waiter in an inn. His friends discovered him, and, even though he tried to disguise his poverty, they finally succeeded in getting him out of such a degrading position. This happens with no other nation in the world. And then they are amazed when the English beat us! Well, as for the armament. The arsenals are empty and however much money you ask Madrid for, not even a farthing. It's a fact that all the treasure of the King is used to pay the salaries of the gentlemen at Court and the one among them that eats up the most is the Prince of Peace, who collects a whacking forty thousand *duros*[148] as Councillor of State, as Secretary of State, as admiral and as major general of the marines… I stand by what I said: I do not want to serve the King. I'm off home to my wife and children, since I've done my service and in a few days they'll have to pay me off.'

'Well, you can't complain, my good friend, if you ended up on the *Rayo*, a ship that hardly saw any action.'

'I was not on the *Rayo*, but on the *Bahama*, which without doubt was one of the vessels that fought best and longest.'

'She was captured and her commander died, if I remember rightly.'

'Aye, that's what happened,' he replied. 'And it still makes me weep when I think of Don Dionisio Alcalá Galiano, the bravest admiral in the Navy. Yes; he was a strong character and he would not tolerate the slightest fault; but his great severity made us love him more, because a captain that makes himself feared for being strict, if strictness is accompanied by justice, instils respect and eventually wins the affection of people. It can also be said that there has been no greater and more generous gentleman in the world than Don Dionisio Alcalá Galiano. That's why when he wanted to honour

his friends he didn't do things by halves, and once in Havana he spent ten thousand *duros* on some banquet that he gave on board his vessel.'

'I've also heard say that he was very knowledgeable about navigation.'

'About navigation? He knew more about it than Merlin and all the doctors of the Church. Why, he had made no end of charts and had discovered I don't know how many lands all the way down to Hell itself! And they send men like that to battle so that they can die like a ship's boy! I'll tell you what happened on the *Bahama*. Once the battle had begun, Don Dionisio Alcalá Galiano knew we were bound to lose it, because of that damned order to wear round... We were in the reserve and remained at the rear. Nelson, who was no fool, saw our line and said, 'So if I cut through it in two distinct places and get them between two broadsides, not even one of their ships will escape me.' And that's what that devil did, and as our line was so long, *the van could not succour the rear.*[1][149] He defeated

Alcalá Galiano.

us bit by bit, attacking us in two solid columns arranged in the form of a wedge, which is, so they say, the way of fighting used by the Moorish captain Alexander the Great and they say that Napoleon also uses it today. The fact is that he surrounded us and divided us and gradually finished us off vessel by vessel in such a way that we could not help each other and each ship was obliged to fight against three or four. So you see, the *Bahama* was one of the first to open fire.

Alcalá Galiano reviewed the crew at midday, inspected the batteries and delivered an address to us in which he said, pointing at the flag, 'Gentlemen, you will all be aware that this flag is nailed.' We already knew what type of man commanded us and so this

---

1   * Nelson's words *[author's note]*.

language did not shock us. Then he said to midshipman Don Alonso Butrón, who was responsible for it: 'Take care to defend it. No Galiano surrenders and a Butrón should not do so either.'[150]

'It is a shame,' I said, 'that these men did not have a leader worthy of their valour, seeing that they weren't given command of the fleet.'

'It is indeed a shame, and you'll see what happened. The set-to began, and you'll know it was a fine affair if you were on board the *Trinidad*. Three ships peppered us with shot from port and starboard. From the first moments the wounded fell like flies and the captain himself was badly hurt in the leg and then he received a blow in the head from a splinter, which severely injured him. But do you think this frightened him or that he indulged in any ointments or sticking plasters? Of course not! He remained on the quarterdeck regardless, although people very dear to him fell at his side to rise no more. Alcalá Galiano was directing operations and the guns as if we were giving a salute in front of a square. A small ball of no significance took away his telescope, which made him smile. It's as if I can still see him now. The blood from his wounds was staining his uniform and hands; but he paid no more attention to this than if it were salt water spray sprinkled by the sea. As his nature was somewhat violent and his temper lively, he shouted out his orders and with such fighting spirit, that if we had not obeyed them because it was our duty, we would have obeyed them from fear... But finally, everything suddenly came to an end, when a medium-calibre ball hit him in the head, killing him instantly. With this, enthusiasm was finished, but not the fight. When our beloved commander fell, they hid him so that we would not see him, but nobody failed to realise what had happened and after a desperate fight, sustained by the honour of the flag, the *Bahama* surrendered to the English who took her to Gibraltar unless she sank beforehand, as I suspect.'[151]

On concluding his account and after telling how he had passed from the *Bahama* to the *Santa Ana*, my companion gave a big sigh and remained silent for a long time. But as the way was long and tedious, I tried to start up the conversation again and I began by telling him about what I had seen and, finally, my transfer on board the *Rayo* with the young Malespina.

'Oh,' he said, 'is he a young Artillery officer who was transported to the sloop and from the sloop to land on the night of the twenty-third?'

'The same one,' I replied, 'and what's more no one has given me any information on his whereabouts.'

'Well, he was one of those that perished in the second boat, which could not make land. They saved some of the fit ones, including the father of that Artillery officer, but all the wounded drowned, which is to be expected as those unfortunate men could not swim to the shore.'

I was lost in thought at hearing of the death of young Malespina and the idea of the grief that awaited my unhappy and adored young mistress filled my heart, smothering all feelings of resentment.

'What a terrible misfortune!' I exclaimed. 'And will it be me that takes such sad news to his grieving family? Are you sure about what you've said?'

'I saw with my own eyes the father of that young man groaning bitterly and recounting the details of the unfortunate incident with such anguish that it broke your heart. According to him, he had saved everyone in the boat, and confirmed that if he had wanted to save just his son, he could have done so at the cost of the lives of the rest. He preferred, nevertheless, to give life to the greater number, even if it meant sacrificing his son's life for the sake of many, which is what he did. He seems to be a man with a great soul and exceedingly clever and brave.'

This saddened me so much that I spoke no more of the matter. Marcial dead, Malespina dead! What terrible news I would be bearing to my master's home! For one moment almost I had decided not to return to Cádiz, leaving it to fate or rumour to take such a distressing message into the hearth of the home, where so many hearts were palpitating with worry. However, I needed to report to Don Alonso to give him an account of my conduct.

We finally arrived in Rota, where we took a boat for Cádiz. You cannot imagine how agitated the population was by the news of the fleet's disasters. Little by little news of what had happened would arrive, and by now the fate of most of the vessels was known, although the whereabouts of many sailors and crewmen were still unknown. In the streets at any moment there were scenes of grief when someone who had just arrived told of the dead he knew about and named those who were not going to return. The crowd invaded the quay to identify the wounded, hoping to find a father, a brother, a son or a husband. I saw scenes of wild joy, mixed with moments of grief and terrible distress. Hopes vanished and suspicions were confirmed in most cases, and the number of those who won in that agonising game of fate was very small, compared to those who lost. The bodies that appeared on the Costa de Santa María settled the doubts of many families, while others were still hoping to find their loved ones among the prisoners taken to Gibraltar.

In honour of the people of Cádiz, I have to say that no other community was so determined to give help to the wounded, making no distinction between Spaniards and the enemy, rather treating all equally under the broad standard of charity. Collingwood recorded this generosity of my countrymen in his memoirs.[152] Perhaps the magnitude of the disaster extinguished all bitterness. Is it not sad to reflect that it is only misfortune that makes men brothers?

In Cádiz I was able to find out about the action in its entirety, which, despite having participated in it, I knew nothing about except for particular incidents, since the length of the line, the complexity of the movements and the varied fates of the ships permitted nothing else. From what they told me there, as well as the *Trinidad*, the *Argonauta*, 92 guns, commanded by Don Antonio Pareja, and the *San Augustín*, 80 guns, commanded by Don Felipe Cajigal, also sank. Together with Gravina in the *Príncipe de Asturias*, the *Montañés*, 80 guns, commanded by Alcedo, who died in the battle together with his second in command Castaños; the *San Justo*, 76 guns, commanded by Miguel Gastón; the *San Leandro*, 74 guns, commanded by José Quevedo; the *San Francisco*, 74 guns, commanded by Don Luis Flores; the *Rayo*, 100 guns, under the command of Macdonell, had returned to Cádiz. Of these, the *Montañés*, the *San Justo*, the *San Francisco* and the *Rayo* went out on the 23rd to recapture the ships that were visible; but the latter two were lost on the shore, the same as the *Monarca*, 74 guns, commanded by Argumosa; and the *Neptuno*, 80 guns, whose heroic commander, Don Cayetano Valdés, already famous for the Expedition of the 14th,[153] was on the point of death. Those captured were the *Bahama,* which broke up before reaching Gibraltar;[154] the *San Ildefonso*, 74 guns, commanded by Vargas, which was taken to England; and the *Nepomuceno*, which

remained for many years at Gibraltar, kept as an object of veneration or sacred relic. The *Santa Ana* arrived successfully in Cádiz on the same night that we left her. The English also lost some of their great ships, and not a few of their senior officers shared the glorious end of Admiral Nelson.

As for the French, it goes without saying that they suffered as many losses as we did. With the exception of the four ships that retreated with Dumanoir without firing a shot, a stain that the Imperial Navy could not rid itself of for a long time, our allies conducted themselves heroically in the battle.

Villeneuve, wanting his mistakes to be forgotten in one day, fought bravely until the end, and was taken as a prisoner to Gibraltar. Many other captains fell into the hands of the English, and some died. Their ships suffered the same fate as ours: some withdrew with Gravina; others were taken as prizes and many were lost on the shore. The *Achille* blew up in the middle of the battle, as I described in my account.

But, despite these disasters, our ally, proud France, did not pay as dearly as Spain for the consequences of that war. If she lost the flower of her Navy, in those same days she achieved sensational triumphs on land. Napoleon had transferred the Grand Army in a short time from the shores of the English Channel to Central Europe and executed his colossal plan of campaign against Austria. On 20th October, one day before Trafalgar, on the battlefield of Ulm he watched the march past of the Austrian troops, whose generals surrendered their swords to him, and two months later on 2nd December of the same year, he won the most brilliant action of his reign on the fields of Austerlitz.

In France these triumphs attenuated the defeat of Trafalgar; Napoleon himself ordered the newspapers not to mention the matter and when he was informed of the victory of his implacable enemies the English, he shrugged his shoulders and said, 'I cannot be everywhere.'

XVII

I tried to put off the moment of reporting to my master; but in the end, hunger, the penniless state I found myself in and the lack of shelter forced me to go. As I approached the house of Doña Flora, my heart was beating so strongly that at every step I paused to catch my breath. The immense grief that I was going to cause by announcing the death of the young Malespina weighed on my soul with such awful heaviness, that if I had been responsible for that disaster, I would not have felt more wretched. Eventually I arrived and went into the house. My presence in the courtyard produced a great sensation; I heard loud steps on the upper galleries and I had no time to say even a word before I was embraced tightly. I recognised at once Doña Flora's face, more daubed that day than a painting and savagely disfigured by the joy that my presence caused in the spirit of that excellent old lady. The sweet names of *bonny child, naughty monkey* and *little angel* and more, which she showered on me with great generosity, did not make me smile. I went in and everyone was moving about. I heard my master say, 'There he is! Thank God.' I entered the drawing room and Doña Francisca rushed towards me and asked me with mortal anxiety,

'What about Don Rafael? What has happened to Don Rafael?'

I remained bewildered for a long time. My voice died in my throat and I did not have the courage to say the fatal news. They repeated the question and then I saw my young mistress coming out of an adjoining room, with a pale face, frightened eyes, displaying in her attitude the distress that possessed her. The sight of her made me break into bitter tears and I did not need to say a word. Rosita gave a terrible cry and fell down in a faint. Don Alonso and his wife ran to help her, hiding their sorrow in the depths of their hearts.

Doña Flora grew sad, called me to one side so that she could make sure that my person had returned intact, and said to me,

'So then, that young gentleman has died? I thought that would happen and I told Paca so, but she, by no end of praying, believed she could save him. But why would

God be concerned with such a thing…? Now you, safe and sound, what joy! You're not missing anything?'

The consternation that reigned in the house is impossible to describe. For the space of quarter of an hour nothing was heard except for weeping, cries and sobbing, because Malespina's family was there as well. But how strange are the ways God uses to achieve his ends! As I said, a quarter of an hour had passed since I gave the news, when a loud and shrill voice reached my ears. It was that of Don José María de Malespina who was shouting in the courtyard, calling his wife, Don Alonso and my young mistress. What most surprised me was that the braggart's voice sounded as merry as usual, something that seemed to me highly indelicate after the misfortune that had occurred. We ran to meet him and I was astonished to see him as happy as a sandboy.

'But Don Rafael…' my master said to him in surprise.

'Fine and healthy,' Don José María replied. 'That is to say, not healthy, but out of danger, yes, certainly, because his wound no longer gives concern. The fool of a surgeon thought he was going to die, but I knew very well that he wouldn't. What are these poor little surgeons to me! I cured him, gentlemen; me, me, with a new unused procedure which only I know about.'

These words, which suddenly transformed the situation in such a radical way, left my master and mistress astounded; then intense happiness succeeded the earlier sadness and finally when their great excitement allowed them to reflect on the mistake, they interrogated me severely, scolding me for having given them such a big shock. I apologised, saying that I had been told about it just as I have related and Don José María became furious, calling me an unreliable person, a liar and a mischief-maker.

Sure enough, Don Rafael was alive and out of danger; but he had remained in Sanlúcar at the house of some acquaintances, while his father came to Cádiz in search of his family to take them to the side of the wounded man. The reader will not understand the origin of the mistake that made me announce in good faith the death of the young man; but I bet that whoever reads this will suspect that some stupendous lie of the elder Malespina brought the news of the supposed misfortune to my ears. That was so, neither more nor less. According to what I learnt after accompanying the family to Sanlúcar, Don José María had concocted a novel about the heroism and skill he had displayed; in various small groups of people he had recounted the strange case of his son's death, adding particulars and circumstances so dramatic that for some days the fake protagonist was the object of everyone's praise for his unselfishness and bravery. He told how, the boat having foundered, he had to choose between the rescue of his son and of all the others, opting for the latter because it was more generous and humanitarian. He adorned his legend with details so extraordinary, so interesting and at the same time so credible, that many believed him. But the fraud was soon revealed and the deception did not last long, although long enough for it to come to my ears, so that I had to pass it on to the family. Although I already had a very poor view of the elder Malespina's veracity, I would never have believed that he could have lied about such serious things.

Once those strong emotions had passed, my master fell into deep melancholy; he hardly spoke; one would say that, his final dream having vanished, he had closed all his accounts with the world and was preparing for the final voyage. The definitive absence of Marcial took away from him the only friend of that childlike old age of his, and having no one to play toy ships with, he wasted away in deep sorrow. Even the sight of him so downcast did not stop Doña Francisca in her task of mortification and on the day of my arrival I heard her saying to him,

'A nice job you all did... What do you think? Still not happy, are you? Well, go off to the fleet, then. Was I right or not? Oh, if only they had listened to me... Now will you learn? Don't you see how God has punished you?'

'Leave me in peace, please,' my master replied in distress.

'And now we're left without a fleet, without any sailors, and we won't even be able to walk about if we carry on joined up with the French... Would to God that those gentlemen don't pay us back badly. The one who has made a real mess of things is Señor Villeneuve. Well, Gravina also, if he had opposed the departure, as Churruca and Alcalá Galiano advised, he would have avoided this disaster which broke our hearts.'

'What do you understand about this? Don't mortify me,' my master said, extremely annoyed.

'So, I don't understand anything, then? I understand more than you. Oh, yes, I'll say it again. Gravina may be a fine gentleman and very brave; but to get us where we are now... he certainly did a good job.'

'He did what he had to do. Would you have had us branded as cowards?'

'As cowards, no, but as prudent men, yes. That's just it. I've said it once and I'll say it again: the Spanish fleet should not have left Cádiz, giving in to the brilliant ideas and egoism of *Monsieur* Villeneuve. Here they have said that Gravina, like his colleagues, advised against going out. But Villeneuve, who was decided on it, for the sake of doing some valiant act that would reconcile his master to him, tried to injure the pride of our men. It seems that one of the reasons that Gravina gave was the bad weather, and looking at the barometer in the cabin, he said: "Don't you see that the barometer is forecasting bad weather? Don't you see how it's falling?" Villeneuve then replied drily: "What's falling here is courage." When he heard this insult, Gravina got up blind with rage and threw into the face of the Frenchman his cowardly display at the action of Cape Finisterre. Some strong words were exchanged and finally our admiral exclaimed: "We'll go to sea first thing tomorrow!" But I do not think Gravina should have paid any attention to the bravado of the Frenchman, no, none at all, since prudence comes before everything, even more when knowing, as he did, that the Combined Fleet was not in a state to fight with the English fleet.'

This opinion, which at the time seemed to me to be an insult to our national honour, I thought later was well founded. Doña Francisca was right. Gravina should not have acceded to Villeneuve's demand. And I say this, damaging perhaps the halo that the people placed round the head of the commander of the Spanish fleet on that memorable occasion.

Without denying Gravina's excellence, I believe the praise given to him after the battle and at the time of his death was exaggerated. Everything showed that Gravina was a perfect gentleman and a brave sailor; but perhaps because he was too much a courtier, he lacked that resolution given by the constant habit of war and also that superiority which in difficult careers like the Navy one only reaches by assiduously studying the sciences that constitute it. Foresight, calmness and unshakeable firmness, the qualities necessary for those given to command great armies – only Don Cosme Damián Churruca and Don Dionisio Alcalá Galiano possessed them.

My master Don Alonso replied to his wife's last words, and when she left, I noticed that the poor old man prayed with as much piety as in the cabin of the *Santa Ana* on the night of our separation. From that day, Señor de Cisniega did nothing but pray and spent the rest of his life praying until he embarked in the ship that never returns.

He died long after his daughter married Don Rafael Malespina, an event that was arranged to take place two months after the great naval action that the Spanish call *the 21ˢᵗ* and the English the *Battle of Trafalgar*, because it happened near the cape of that name. My young mistress was married in Vejer at daybreak on a beautiful day, despite being winter, and they left immediately for Medinasidonia, where the house had been prepared for them. I witnessed her happiness during the days that preceded the wedding; but she did not notice the profound sadness that filled me, nor would she

have known its cause if she had noticed. All the time she was growing before my eyes and all the time I felt more humiliated in the face of her double superiority in beauty and class. Having got used to the idea that such an admirable union of favours could not and should not be for me, I managed to stop worrying, because resignation, giving up all hope, is a consolation similar to death and for that reason it is a great consolation.

They got married and on the same day on which they left for Medinasidonia, Doña Francisca ordered me to go there as well in order to put myself at the service of the newly-weds. I went at night and during my lonely journey I was struggling with my ideas and thoughts, which oscillated between accepting a post in the house of the married couple or rejecting it for ever. I arrived the following morning, approached the house, went into the garden, put my foot onto the first step of the door, and there I paused, because my thoughts were absorbing me completely and I needed to be still to think things over better. I think I remained in that position for over half an hour.

Profound silence reigned in the house. Husband and wife, married the day before, were no doubt having the first sleep of their peaceful love, still undisturbed by any sorrow. I could not help remembering those far-off days when she and I would play together. Then Rosita was number one in the world for me. For her, even though I was not number one, at least I was someone she loved and would miss if I were absent for an hour. How things change in such a short time!

Everything I was seeing seemed to express the happiness of the married couple and act as an insult to my loneliness. Although it was winter, I imagined that all the trees in the garden were covered in foliage and that the vine which shaded the door was unexpectedly full of young leaves to shelter them when they went out for a walk. The sun was very strong and the air became cooler, airing that nest whose first straws I myself had helped to gather when I was the messenger of their love. I imagined the rose bushes, stiff with cold, covered in roses and the orange trees with blossom and fruit that thousands of birds had come to peck, participating in the wedding feast. My thoughts and my imaginings were interrupted only when the profound silence reigning in the house was interrupted by the sound of a fresh voice that echoed in my soul, making me tremble. That happy voice produced in me an indefinable feeling, a feeling I did not know whether it was fear or shame; what I can be sure of, though, is that a sudden decision snatched me from the door and I ran out of the garden, like a thief fearing discovery.

My intention was unshakeable. Without losing any time I left Medinasidonia, having decided not to serve either in that house or the one in Vejer. After reflecting a short time, I decided to go to Cádiz and from there move to Madrid. And that's what I did, overcoming the allurements of Doña Flora, who tried to bind me with a chain of the withered roses of her love, and since that day how many things have happened to me that are worthy of retelling! My destiny, which had already taken me to Trafalgar, then took me onto other stages, glorious or wretched, but all worthy of memory. Do you want to learn about the rest of my life? Well, wait a bit and I will tell you some more in another book.

Madrid, January – February 1873

Summary of events in the National Episodes between *Trafalgar* and *The Battle of Salamanca*

THE COURT OF CARLOS IV (1807)

At the end of *Trafalgar* Gabriel Araceli left Cádiz to go to Madrid. There he entered the service of an actress, Pepita González, in 1805. He meets Inés, a fourteen-year-old seamstress who lives with her widowed mother, Doña Juana. Gabriel takes a liking to Inés, another poor young person trying to make a living and their mutual attraction then turns to love. By the time of this novel, through his work for Pepita González, Gabriel had entered the service of Countess Amaranta. Her family name and title are never told, but Galdós lets it be known that Goya painted her as a nude: she is clearly meant to be the Duchess of Alba. Amaranta is beautiful and involves Gabriel in intrigues at Court. Amaranta is a supporter of Prince Ferdinand, the son of Carlos IV, whose conspiracy against his father fails. Gabriel escapes from the clutches of the sinister lawyer Lobo who suspects his involvement in passing letters between conspirators.

Gabriel discovers that Amaranta has had a child with a minor noble who is supposed to have fled to France and the child has been abandoned. Gabriel refuses to carry out a spying mission for Amaranta as it offends his honour. Amaranta mocks him for his sense of honour and angrily dismisses Gabriel. Gabriel goes to the house of Inés to find that Doña Juana has just died and that on her deathbed she had confessed to her brother-in-law, the priest Don Celestino, that she was not the real mother of Inés and that Inés was the daughter of a great lady whose name she did not give. Inés is now to move with Don Celestino to Aranjuez where he has been appointed to a benefice under the patronage of Manuel de Godoy.

THE NINETEENTH OF MARCH AND THE SECOND OF MAY (MARCH TO MAY 1808)

Gabriel gets work in Madrid as a typesetter with a newspaper. Don Celestino reveals to Inés and Gabriel that he has received a letter from prosperous cousins of Doña Juana, Mauro Requejo and his sister Restituta, requesting that Inés come to live with them in Madrid where she can work in their shop and they will look after her well, even though they showed no interest in her while Doña Juana was alive. The Requejos visit them in Aranjuez. Don Celestino thinks this is a sign of God having made them charitable, but Gabriel is suspicious of their motives, believing that the Requejos have discovered the true parentage of Inés and want to profit from it. Inés moves to Madrid with the Requejos.

In Aranjuez, Gabriel is involved in the 'Riot of Aranjuez' of 19th March, an uprising that leads to the overthrow of Godoy's ministry and the enforced abdication of Carlos IV in favour of his son, now Fernando VII. Gabriel goes to Madrid where Inés is working (and being exploited) in the Requejos' shop. Gabriel gets work there, too, neither of the Requejos having recognised him from Aranjuez. Also working there as a clerk is Juan de Dios who has been employed by the Requejos for many years and is older than Gabriel. Juan de Dios is Basque and speaks French fluently, having been brought up there. Mauro Requejo plans that he will marry Inés and that Juan de Dios will marry Restituta.

Lobo, a neighbour of the Requejos, visits them and secretly informs Mauro that Inés's mother, a rich aristocrat, wants to find her daughter again and advises Requejo to treat Inés more kindly and not overwork her if he wants her to love him. Gabriel overhears this. Inés is kept a virtual prisoner and cannot disguise her disgust for the Requejos. Gabriel vows to save her and they confirm their love for each other.

French troops now occupy Madrid in all but name. While in the crowd of citizens welcoming Fernando VII to Madrid, Inés and Gabriel try unsuccessfully to escape from the Requejos, although Gabriel is able to tell Inés what he knows about her true mother and vows to restore her to her rightful position. Inés is kept locked in her room by Restituta Requejo. In the meantime, Juan de Dios confides to Gabriel that he loves Inés but is too nervous to declare it. Gabriel offers to help Juan de Dios free Inés and gives her some violets on his behalf, having first confirmed with Inés that she loves only Gabriel. Restituta overhears Inés declaring in her sleep that she loves only one person and will marry him once she is free from her ferocious relatives. Restituta also finds the bunch of violets. Mauro is furious and vows to marry Inés that week whether she likes it or not, and Inés is kept locked up under the watchful eye of Restituta.

Gabriel's attempt to escape with Inés is thwarted by the obtuseness of Juan de Dios and the intervention of Lobo who stops Gabriel and Inés as they are trying to leave the house. Gabriel declares he is the one that Inés loves and Lobo recognises him as the messenger of the supporters of Godoy who had escaped him earlier. Mauro Requejo agrees to lock Gabriel in the shop cellar overnight before Lobo returns to take Gabriel for interrogation. Juan de Dios inadvertently frees Gabriel from the cellar and Gabriel manages to trick Restituta into going into the cellar in pursuit of Juan de Dios. Gabriel shuts them both in the cellar and he and Inés flee the house into the streets of Madrid.

They go to Gabriel's house and meet there Don Celestino who believes they will get help to flee from an unnamed marchioness who has expressed great interest in Inés.

Gabriel knows this marchioness from his time as Amaranta's servant and he leaves the house alone to make contact with her. She is Amaranta's aunt. It is the second of May. On the way he meets a friend, Chinitas, who tells him that the crowds are gathering to rise up against the French. Gabriel is roused to join the uprising. During the fighting, Gabriel ends up cornered in a house and escapes to the house next door, only to find a frightened Lobo and Juan de Dios; it turned out to be the Requejos' house. All of them flee from the French, Gabriel and Juan de Dios going to Gabriel's house to save Inés. They arrive to find Inés and Don Celestino holed up in the house with fierce fighting going on around it. Juan de Dios is ignored by Inés who embraces Gabriel. The fighting continues more fiercely and Juan de Dios faints from fear. Inspired by Don Celestino's oratory, Gabriel leaves the house to join the fight against the French, followed by Juan de Dios who is shamed by his earlier fear.

Gabriel survives the fight with light wounds, although many around him are killed, including Chinitas who gives Gabriel his knife before dying. He returns to his house to find only Juan de Dios who tells him that Inés and Don Celestino have been taken away as prisoners by the French. Gabriel and Juan de Dios look for them separately. After a fruitless search during which Gabriel sees scenes of terrible cruelty, Gabriel collapses from exhaustion. He revives and eventually comes to an enclosure where many prisoners are being held awaiting execution. He tries to enter the enclosure to look for Inés but after failing to get in by pleading, he produces Chinitas's knife saying that he has killed many Frenchmen with it and wants to kill Napoleon. He is seized and taken inside. Once there, he sees Don Celestino and Inés tied together about to be shot. Gabriel and Don Celestino plead with the French to release Inés as she is innocent. At that moment Juan de Dios arrives accompanied by Lobo and a French officer who was a regular visitor to Lobo in the Requejos' shop. Inés is taken away and Gabriel and Don Celestino fall before the firing squad.

BAILÉN (MAY TO JULY 1808)

Found by neighbours in Madrid, Gabriel miraculously escapes with his life from the firing squad, although Don Celestino is not so fortunate. Gabriel is recovering in the house of an old soldier, Don Santiago Fernandez, and his wife, Doña Gregoria. It turns out that Juan de Dios also lives there and had brought Gabriel to the house. Also present is Don Luis de Santorcaz, recently returned to Spain after many years in France. He extols Napoleon, the professionalism of the French Army and its generals, and predicts that Spain will fall completely under French power. He denies being a French agent, saying he has returned merely to deal with some family matters in Andalusia and will soon return to France. Juan de Dios then visits Gabriel and tells him that, having handed Inés over to the care of Lobo, he does not know where she is. Lobo had told Juan de Dios that he had handed Inés back to the custody of her parents who were noble.

Once restored to health, Gabriel finds out from a servant in the Madrid mansion of the marchioness, Amaranta's aunt, that Inés has been taken to Córdoba to be with the marchioness and her brother, a diplomat. Gabriel also meets Lobo who is surprisingly friendly to Gabriel, now that the French are in Madrid and the political climate has changed. Lobo encourages Gabriel to go to Córdoba in pursuit of Inés and tells him she was speaking tenderly of Gabriel as she was being taken there. Gabriel decides to go there as a travelling companion of Santorcaz who is also going to Córdoba.

On the way to Córdoba, they meet Andresillo Marijuán, a young man who is a servant of the Rumblar family, and he and Gabriel soon become good friends. Later they stop at Bailén in the house of the marchioness María de Rumblar, a widow of the old school who lives with her only son, Diego de Rumblar, and two daughters, Asunción and Presentación, and Diego's tutor, Don Paco. Gabriel decides to accompany Diego, Andresillo and other locals assembled by Doña María to join the army under General Castaños and they leave for Córdoba to enlist. Doña María asks them to deliver letters to her cousins and Gabriel is surprised to read on the envelopes that they are addressed to Amaranta and her aunt (who Gabriel now reveals is the Marchioness of Leiva). Santorcaz remains behind, saying he is waiting for some letters.

In Córdoba Gabriel is seen by Amaranta who pales when Gabriel mentions that he has been travelling with a man called Santorcaz. When Gabriel confesses to Amaranta that he and Inés love each other, she throws Gabriel out of the house in a fit of anger.

Some days later, Gabriel meets the diplomat who asks him to give a letter from the Marchioness of Leiva to Inés, who has shut herself away in a convent. Inés is pleased to see Gabriel and reads out the letter to him. In it the Marchioness tells Inés to leave the convent and come with them to Madrid because she and Amaranta are determined to preserve the family's inheritance by marrying her off to a young nobleman. Inés and Gabriel agree she should follow these instructions and Gabriel tells her he is joining the army to raise his status from that of a servant.

Gabriel, Andresillo and Diego de Rumblar leave Córdoba with the army and meet Santorcaz who joins them and acquires great influence over the impressionable Diego, instilling in him ideas of the Enlightenment and the French Revolution, which Diego does not fully understand. The party comes to the Rumblar house in Bailén, which has been pillaged by the French before they retreated. Doña María is horrified by Diego's talk of the Enlightenment and philosophy and his wish to be a professional soldier.

The party then leaves the Rumblar house to fight the French just outside Bailén. Santorcaz encourages Diego to snatch his intended fiancée from the convent in Córdoba once the battle is over. In the confusion of the battle, which is a Spanish victory, Gabriel mounts a stray horse. In the saddlebag he finds letters addressed to Santorcaz from Amaranta and the diplomat, and a miniature portrait of Inés. Gabriel deduces Santorcaz is the father of Inés. The letter from the diplomat tells Santorcaz that the Marchioness of Leiva, as head of the family, has forbidden Amaranta to marry Santorcaz as he had proposed in order to legitimise Inés, and that the Marchioness of Leiva and the Marchioness of Rumblar had agreed that Inés and Diego would marry to avoid a lawsuit over the family inheritance.

After the battle, Gabriel learns from Don Paco that the Marchioness of Leiva, her brother, Amaranta and Inés will be calling at the Rumblar house on their way to Madrid. They then arrive but Gabriel does not manage to see Inés.

Diego has not been seen since the battle and Gabriel joins his family in their search for him, with no success. They fear the worst. Two days after the battle, Don Paco and Gabriel then go to the French camp to see if Diego is being held prisoner.

They find Diego, who had been captured and made drunk by his captors. When he is brought back to the Rumblar house, he is introduced to an embarrassed Inés and then regales them with the merry time he had with the French, how they encouraged him when he said he wanted to go to France with Santorcaz and learn about new ideas, all to the horror of Doña María but to the amusement of Asunción and Presentación. He ends up by singing them a song he had been taught while a prisoner – the Marseillaise! Doña María leaves the room with her daughters and vents her anger by punishing them instead of Diego.

Gabriel follows Inés and her new family to Madrid, while Santorcaz departs with a band of guerrillas.

NAPOLEON AT CHAMARTÍN (JULY TO DECEMBER 1808)

Gabriel is once more in Madrid, living in the house of Don Santiago and Doña Gregoria, but Juan de Dios is no longer there. Don Diego is living a dissolute life in Madrid under the influence of Santorcaz. Gabriel is taken to Amaranta to report on Don Diego's activities, which are disturbing his prospective mother-in-law. Amaranta convinces Gabriel to abandon his pursuit of Inés because of his lowly status which he reluctantly agrees to, but refuses any financial reward from the countess for doing so, saying that he prefers to lead an honourable life as a soldier defending Madrid against the impending attack of Napoleon. He promises to leave Madrid and never see Inés again once the fight for Madrid is over.

Napoleon overcomes the resistance from Madrid and establishes himself at the palace in Charmartín just outside Madrid. Gabriel takes part in the fighting and Don Santiago is killed. Following the capitulation of the Spanish government, Santorcaz is appointed chief of police and Gabriel learns that Santorcaz wants to arrest him. He asks the countess's help to flee Madrid and she gives him a coach and a disguise. Just before he is to leave, Gabriel finds out from Don Diego that the latter wants to kidnap Inés and force her to marry him, an idea suggested by Santorcaz. Gabriel decides to warn the countess and uses the coach and disguise to go to the palace of El Pardo where Inés and the newly established court of José I, Napoleon's brother, are established.

Gabriel meets Inés there and warns her of Don Diego's plans. They renew their vows of eternal love. Gabriel falls into the hands of Santorcaz and he is sentenced to exile to France. Amaranta upbraids him for having broken his promise to her not to see Inés again.

ZARAGOZA (DECEMBER 1808-FEBRUARY 1809)

While being transported to France, Gabriel and some fellow captives escape from the French and go to Zaragoza which is about to suffer its second siege by the French.

The novel is taken up almost entirely by the siege and Gabriel's part in it. He leaves the city at the end of the siege, wounded and ill with the few remaining men of the garrison.

GERONA (MAY 1809 TO FEBRUARY 1810)

Gabriel makes his way to El Puerto de Santa María near Cádiz, where Spanish resistance to the French is concentrated. He is now a member of the Army of the Centre and meets Andresillo Marijuán again. Andresillo tells Gabriel about the Siege of Gerona which he had participated in.

Following Andresillo's account, Gabriel and a Portuguese officer, Figueroa, who has become a friend of Gabriel's, meet a strange woman who asks Gabriel to take her that night by boat to Cádiz. The woman later reveals herself to be Amaranta who is friendly towards Gabriel and very pleased to see him. Amaranta believes Doña María de

Rumblar is about to take Inés to Lisbon, and Amaranta wants to stop her. She says that much has changed in her life and she reproaches Gabriel for not contacting her since they last saw each other in Madrid. She mentions that she was pursued by Lord Byron while he was in Cádiz. The novel ends when they arrive at the house of Doña Flora de Cisniega (whom we met in *Trafalgar*) where Amaranta is lodging. Doña Flora is very happy to see Gabriel, now a handsome soldier of Spain.

CÁDIZ (1810-1812)

Amaranta tells Gabriel that Doña María de Rumblar and her family are in Cádiz and Inés is practically hidden away in their house. Inés is not allowed to see Amaranta (she does not know she is really her daughter) and Doña María is determined that Inés will marry her son Diego, who continues to lead a dissolute life, hiding this from his stern, deeply conservative mother. Amaranta tells Gabriel also that Inés has a suitor, an English nobleman, Lord Gray, a Byronic character, and Amaranta hopes this will improve her fortune.

Lord Gray calls regularly at the Rumblar house but not for the reason Amaranta thinks. Gabriel, jealous, also visits the Rumblar house. Against his will, Gabriel becomes friendly with Lord Gray and takes fencing lessons from him. In the meantime, Cádiz is under siege by the French and lively discussions are taking place in the Cortes that will lead to the declaration of the Constitution of Cádiz. Meetings of deputies to the Cortes and other politicians take place in the liberal house of Doña Flora and the strongly conservative house of Doña María.

Lord Gray is pursuing not Inés but Asunción, Doña María's daughter, who is intended for the convent. Asunción is taken in by Lord Gray's seductive talk and his promises to marry her and convert to Catholicism. She becomes infatuated with him and agrees to elope. They plan to leave the Rumblar house secretly at night. Gabriel learns of this and, thinking that Lord Gray is eloping with Inés, goes to the Rumblar house, too. He finds Inés, distracted and upset that Asunción has gone with Lord Gray. Inés asks Gabriel to accompany her to Lord Gray's house so that she can persuade Asunción to return before Doña María discovers she has gone.

They go to Lord Gray's house but he is not there. Inés fears the worst but Lord Gray returns angry, saying that Asunción is back at the Rumblar house as she had repented of her infatuation and wanted to return home. Inés asks Gabriel to take her back to Doña María. Instead of taking Inés back to the Rumblars, Gabriel borrows Lord Gray's coach and takes her to Doña Flora's house where Inés discovers that Amaranta is not her cousin as she had been told, but her mother.

When Doña María discovers Inés's absence she goes to Doña Flora's to accuse Amaranta and have her arrested by the authorities. Amaranta tells her that she wants Inés to live with her and that Inés came to her voluntarily, and that Inés had not been seduced by Lord Gray. Doña María says that the law does not recognise her as Inés's mother and then departs.

The next night Asunción is taken by force by Lord Gray and she is found the next day, beaten and with her clothes torn. Lord Gray has taken revenge on her for her refusal to go with him earlier. She is brought to Doña María who disowns her. The Marchioness of Leiva, who is also present at the Rumblar house, tells Gabriel in her capacity as head of the family that Inés will be returned to Doña María that night by the authorities.

Gabriel knows where Lord Gray is due to depart by boat that night from Cádiz and avenges Asunción by killing Lord Gray in a duel, his last fencing lesson. Figueroa, his second, advises Gabriel to flee as he will be wanted for the death of Lord Gray. Doña María, in disguise, witnesses the duel and thanks Gabriel but says she is disappointed in Inés whom she no longer considers worthy to be the wife of Diego, and says she knows that Gabriel loves her. Doña María tells him to take Inés away from her house and that she will start a legal action for the inheritance as the house of Leiva no longer has an heir.

Inés tells Gabriel that she and her mother will flee Cádiz, too, and help Gabriel escape from the authorities if he is pursued by them.

JUAN MARTÍN THE UNDAUNTED (1812)
Gabriel, as an officer in the regular army, is attached to a guerrilla band commanded by Vicente Sardina. He leaves Inés and Amaranta in Cifuentes, near Guadalajara, where Amaranta has a family property.

Sardina's guerrillas come under the direct command of Juan Martín. After a time some of the guerrillas, under a former priest Antón Trijueque, go over to the French. Although Trijueque hates the French he thinks he is the greatest strategist in history and that it is only by being with the French that he can achieve the recognition he thinks he deserves, and not by being a subordinate of Juan Martín.

In an ambush Juan Martín's forces are overcome by Trijueque's guerrilla band and Gabriel is taken prisoner and condemned to death. In prison he receives a surprise visit from Santorcaz, who invites Gabriel to defect to the French. Gabriel refuses. Santorcaz, thinking that Gabriel is now a dead man, tells him his plan to kidnap his daughter Inés to take revenge on Amaranta.

Gabriel manages to escape and goes on foot to Cifuentes, intending to get there before Santorcaz and the French. A series of unfortunate circumstances delays him and when he arrives at Amaranta's house he finds her prostrate on her bed, alone and ill. Inés has gone. Gabriel swears he will do everything to find her and kill Santorcaz. Amaranta thanks him and is reconciled with Gabriel, accepting that he has risen above his social class by merit and that he is her equal and now her only hope.

Gabriel rejoins the guerrillas of Juan Martín who survived the ambush. Trijueque surrenders to Juan Martín, asking that he be shot. Juan Martín tells him he must first ask for pardon and repent, but Trijueque's pride prevents him from doing so. Juan Martín then does what will most humiliate him: he spares his life and sets him free. Humiliated and mocked by his former subordinates, Trijueque hangs himself.

The Battle of Salamanca

I

The following letters, which can usefully replace my narrative, will allow me to take a brief rest.

Madrid, 14ᵗʰ March 1812

Dear Gabriel, if you have had no more luck than I, then we are both in a fine pickle. Until now the only thing that has come from my investigations is the sad certainty that the commissioner of police is no longer in this city, and that he is not in the service of the French, nor of anyone else unless it be the Devil. After his excursion to Guadalajara, he asked for leave, then gave up his post and at present nobody knows anything of him. Some think he is in Salamanca, his native place, some in Burgos or Vitoria, and others state he has gone to France, the former stage of his criminal adventures. Oh! Why did God make the world so large, so extremely large, that it is impossible to find in it the good that is lost! This immensity of creation favours only the scoundrels, who always find somewhere to hide the profits of their robberies.

My situation here has improved a little. I have surrendered, my friend; I wrote to my aunt telling her what had happened in Cifuentes, and the head of my illustrious family indicates to me in her last letter that she has pity on me. Her agent has received orders not to let me starve. Thanks to this and to my well-stocked old wardrobe, your poor countess will not have to beg for the present. I have tried to sell the gems, the laces, the tapestries and other jewelry that are not heirlooms, but nobody wants to buy them. No one has a peseta in Madrid and when bread costs from fourteen to sixteen reales[155], who do you think would fancy buying jewels? If this carries on, the day will come when I will have to exchange all my diamonds for a hen.

So that you can understand the glorious future that awaits my long-established family, one of the most brilliant stars in the heaven of this great monarchy, suffice it to say that the legal proceedings between our family and the Rumblar family have now started and in connection with this the Chancery of Granada has given birth to a mountain of sealed paper, which, if God does nothing about it, will grow so high that our grandchildren will see it with peaks higher than those of the Sierra Nevada itself. The Rumblar family is plunging into this sea of jurisprudence with delight. I can see what will happen. It will turn mankind into judges, scribes, bailiffs and code burrowers so that everything that breathes will be involved in their strife.

The lawyer Lobo, who visits me frequently with the double objective of enlightening me about my case and begging off me (today in Madrid the senior civil servants are asking for charity), has told me that in litigation such as this one there's enough material for it to last a nice little stretch, that is to say, at least a couple of centuries could go by before a judgment emerged or an order for further particulars, the pinnacle of delight. The aforesaid Lobo assures me as well that if we insist on transferring the rights of inheritance to Inés, we could easily lose the lawsuit in a few months, and then there would be no need to wait centuries before losing. The lack of formalities in the acknowledgment of the child and the indiscretion of my poor uncle, who has now gone to the grave, puts our heir in a very bad position to claim her rights of inheritance. Our part is now reduced, according to Lobo, to claiming the non-transfer of the inheritance to the Rumblar family, basing ourselves on various rights of *constructive possession, agnatic descent to and through males only, to males through males or females, to and through females only, inheritance outside lineal descent* and other fine phrases which I am learning for amusement in my sad loneliness and for entertainment in my final days.

My aunt says I am to blame for this disaster and cataclysm in which will sink this most glorious family that has defied the centuries and faced the erosion of time, without having ever produced a spendthrift until now, and she bases her anathema on my opposition to the proposed nuptials between our right and the right of the Rumblars. Really, my aunt is not wrong and no doubt some bitter torments are being prepared for me in Purgatory for having caused this conflict with my obstinacy.

I'm sending this letter to you in Sepúlveda. I think your searches anywhere along the road to France as far as Aranda will be fruitless. Try to get to Zamora. I continue my investigations here with indefatigable zeal and, displaying great enthusiasm for the French cause, I have become acquainted with senior and junior officials, mostly in the police and the secret police.

Let me know if you join the division of Carlos España. I think it would be better for your military career if you left those savage guerrillas, but for God's sake do not go to the Army of Extremadura. I believe that the light we are wishing for will not come from that quarter; continue in Castile while you can, my boy, and do not give up my holy undertaking. Write to me often. Your letters and the pleasure I have in answering them is my only consolation. I would die if I did not weep and if I did not write to you.

22nd March

You cannot imagine the dreadful poverty there is in Madrid. I've heard that a bushel of grain today is 340 reales. The rich can live, even though badly, but the poor are dying in the streets in their hundreds with nothing to be done to relieve their hunger. None of the charities are of any use and money goes in search of food without finding any. The destitute fight ferociously over a cabbage stalk and the leftovers from those few who still have a tablecloth on their table at home. It is impossible to go out onto the street, because the scenes before your eyes at every moment provoke feelings of horror and loss of faith in Divine Providence. At every step starving beggars come up to you, thrown out into the gutter and in such a state of emaciation that they seem like corpses in which the remains of a useless and miserable life have been left forgotten. The mire and filth of the streets and squares is their milk, and the only sound they make is to ask for bread that no one can give them.

If the police would allow it, they would curse the French, who hold a large stock of biscuit in their stores, while the nation starves. They say that since August they have buried twenty thousand corpses and I can believe it. Here you breathe death; the silence of the tomb reigns in Platerías, in San Felipe and the Puerta del Sol. Since they have demolished so many buildings, including Santiago, San Juan, San Miguel, San Martín, Los Mostenses, Santa Ana, Santa Catalina, Santa Clara and a number of the houses near the palace, the many ruins make Madrid look like a city that has been bombarded. What desolation, what sadness!

The French, plump and jolly, stroll around this cemetery and their police cruelly torment its peace-loving inhabitants. No groups are allowed on the streets, neither is stopping to chat, nor looking at the shops. Shopkeepers are fined 200 ducats if they let bystanders linger in doorways or in front of shop windows, so the poor shop assistants constantly have to come out and beat their customers away with their measuring sticks.

Yesterday the king ordered a bullfight to entertain the people – what a joke! I heard that the ring was deserted. I can just see the half a dozen skeletons in the arena, dressed in their costumes edged in silver and gold, more eager to eat the bull than to play it with the cape. Joseph was present, thinking that this was the way to win the favour of the people of Madrid.

They say they are trying to have a session of the Cortes in Madrid, I don't know whether this is also for the people's entertainment. Azanza,[156] the minister of His Bonapartian Majesty, told me that this would be *setting up an altar in front of the other altar*. I believe the altarpiece here will not have as many worshippers as the one we left in Cádiz.

Now they say that Napoleon is going to begin a war against the emperor of all the Russias. This will be favourable for Spain because they will take troops away from the peninsula, or at least they won't be able to replace the losses they are continually suffering. I see the French cause as being quite badly damaged and I have noticed that the more prudent ones among them no longer have any illusions about the final outcome of this war.

As for our matter, what can I tell you that is not sad and dispiriting? Nothing, my boy, absolutely nothing. My inquiries have led nowhere at all and I have been unable to find either the faintest light or the slightest clue. Nevertheless, I have faith in God and hope. I am sending this letter to Santa María de Nieva, as this is safest.

1st April

I have little or nothing to add to my letter of 22nd March. I am still in the dark but I have faith. How much of that one needs to stay in Madrid! This is a purgatory of poverty, loneliness and sadness and a hell of corruption, outrages and all types of immorality that the French have brought here. I do not believe, like the majority of people, that our customs were perfect before the invasion, but between that demure and contrite way of life and the shameless licence of today, the former is preferable by any reckoning. You can have no idea what a perverse institution the French police is without living here and seeing the execrable behaviour of this machine, placed in the hands of the vilest sort.

A multitude of superintendents and policemen, chosen from the dregs of society, is in charge of catching anyone they fancy and threatening them in the city jail, without any form of trial and no guidance other than arbitrariness and denunciation. The apparent reason for these abuses of authority is *complicity with the insurgents*, but the villains in one gang or another contrive to make use of this new Inquisition, whose good graces compel one to forget the charming ways of the old one. Anyone who wants to get rid of someone who is bothering them has an easy means to do so and there have even been some who, not content with seeing their enemy caught, have had him sent to the scaffold. Terrible things are spoken of, which I try not to believe, including the wickedness of a woman of this city, who, having quarrelled with her husband, denounced him as an insurgent and they dealt with the case in a matter of three days, all that was needed to go from Hangman's Alley to execution on the Plaza de la Cebada.[157] There is talk also of a certain Vázquez, who denounced his elder brother, and of a certain Escalera who ascended the stairs to the gallows because of his mistress's intrigues.[158]

There is a *Junta criminal* that inspires more terror than the judges of Hell. The low types that constitute it condemn to death those who read the papers of the insurgents, the *Empecinados*,[159] who are called here the *Madrid bumpkins*, and anyone suspected of links with the *spies, thieves, murderers, brigands, rustlers and… card-sharpers*, those that you would call guerrillas or soldiers of the fatherland.

One of the things the French are most criticised for, apart from their odious police, is the introduction of masked balls. This is somewhat overdone, since before such scandalous parties were instituted in our well-behaved country, there were intrigues and lots of ridicule about the vigilance of fathers and husbands. I do not believe that the masks have brought us all the sins, great and small, which are attributed to them. But decent and God-fearing people rage against this novelty and you hear of nothing else except how, with faces under wraps, there is now no marriage bed that is safe, no honourable household, no father that can be responsible for the honour of his daughters and no maiden that can preserve her soul clean and free from improper thoughts. I do not think this hostility to masks is fair; they are more comfortable and no more concealing than the old cloaks, and I think that many speak badly about masked balls because they do not find them as entertaining or as disreputable as the fairs of San Juan and San Pedro.[160]

But the novelty that angers and shakes up these good people the most is a game of chance called *roulette*, where it seems money dances for delight. The French are wicked to invent such bad and sinful things. They respect nothing, not even the venerable practices of antiquity, not even something that since remotest times has formed part of our model national existence. The right thing would have been to let our sons and fathers ruin themselves through cards, thereby following their patriarchal and perpetually unchanged customs, and not introduce *roulette* and other infernal devices. But the French say that *roulette* is an advance on playing cards, in the same way that the guillotine is better than the gallows, and the police much better than the Inquisition.

The worst of this is that, so they say, not only does the French government permit this devilish roulette, but they also own it and they get the lucrative winnings from it. In this way the French plan to pocket the little money they have left us in our coffers.

I cannot finish without telling you about a plan I have, which, if it comes off, I think will be more successful than all the inquiries and searches done up to now. The plan, my boy, is to get Joseph himself interested in supporting me. I intend to go to the palace where I will be received by Mister Bottles[161] who wants nothing more and would see the heavens open up for him when they announce to him that a grandee of Spain wants to see him. Up to now I have resisted all the suggestions from my various important friends who have insisted on presenting me to the King; but thinking it would be better, I have decided to go to court. In December 1808 I had dealings with both Bonapartes, and the kindnesses I received from Joseph makes me think the step I am taking will not be in vain, although at the risk of compromising myself with a cause I consider is lost. Goodbye: I will tell you everything.

22nd April

I have been to the palace, my boy, and prostrated myself before that Catholic Majesty of tinsel, who is served by a few Spaniards, moving about busily so as to seem many. If I were to tell any inhabitant of Madrid that Joseph I, known here as *one-eyed*, or as *Joe Bottles*, is a kind person, sensible, tolerant, with good manners and who desires nothing but good, they would think I was mad or perhaps sold to the French.

José 1.

Goblets received me with delight. The good man cannot hide it when some person of distinction, by visiting him, gives some sort of tacit assent to his usurpation. He no doubt thinks he can be master of Spain, conquering hearts one by one. You should see how diligent and extremely determined he is to be formal. It is true that his formality is less severe and mannered than that of our royal family, and rather than losing any dignity because of that, it actually increases it. He speaks almost to the point of familiarity, laughs, he also allows himself some gallant courtesies with the ladies, and occasionally cracks somewhat caustic jokes with great elegance, typical of Italians.

His foreign accent is the only thing that spoils his speech. He frequently confuses his native tongue with ours, and on occasions great efforts are needed to stop oneself from laughing.

His figure could not be better. Joseph is worth much more than that keg of a brother of his. His grave and expressive face is little short of perfection. He is generally dressed in black and his person is altogether very pleasant. I do not need to tell you that as much as they talk here about his binges, it's just a weapon invented by patriotism to help our national defence. Joseph is not a drunkard. Thousands of abominable tales which have to do with vices other than drunkenness are also told about him; but without flatly denying them, I find it hard to give them any credit. In summary, Bottles (we have got so used to calling him this name that it would be hard to call him something else) is a pretty good king, and having seen and had dealings with him, one cannot help deploring that instead of birth and right, it is usurpation and war that have brought him here.

His supporters here are few, so few that you can count them. This dynasty has no loyal subjects other than its ministers and two or three people appointed by them to senior positions. Those Spaniards who are in his service seem humiliated victims and do not have that triumphal and vainglorious air that those who have risen slightly above the rest through their own merit or through another's favour are wont to have. They live in shame or fear, no doubt because they can foresee that the *lord*[162] will ruin all of this. Some, however, build up their hopes and say that we will have Bottles, Magnums and Goblets world without end for ever and ever.

Moratín is not one of these and he is sadder and more faint-hearted than ever. He is no longer Secretary for the Interpretation of Languages,[163] but Chief Librarian,[164] a position he must fill splendidly. But he is not happy; he is afraid of everything and more than anything of the dangers of a second evacuation of the Court by the French. He has told me that the day the invader's power falls his hide will not be worth twopence, but I believe that his hypochondria and wretched disposition have darkened his soul and make him see enemies everywhere. He is ill and ruined, but he still works a little and just now he has given us *The School for Husbands*, translated from the French.[165] I haven't seen a performance nor have I been able to read it, because my mind cannot concentrate on anything like that.

Moratín frequently comes to see me with his friend Estala,[166] who is a rabid and passionate *afrancesado*,[167] while the former is a timid and melancholic one. Estala, who is not to be seen here, publishes furious articles in *El Imparcial*, and recently he wrote, alluding to Spain, that *those who are born in a country of slavery have no fatherland except in the sense that flocks of sheep destined for our consumption have one*. Because of this and other outrageous products of his talent which the *Gaceta* publishes, he is detested even more than the French.

Maiquez carries on at the Príncipe, and since Joseph has settled 20,000 reales a month on his theatre to help with its costs, they accuse him as well of being an *afrancesado*. At the moment, according to what I read in the newspapers, they are showing in turn *Orestes*, *The Great Piety of Leopold the Great* and a bad play adapted from the German whose title is *Conceal, by honour driven, the wound from the aggressor*.

Maiquez.

The theatre, so they tell me, is empty. Poor Pepilla González, whom you will not have forgotten, is dying of poverty because, not being able to perform on account of an illness she has contracted, she is without any salary, abandoned by her companions. She would end up like everyone else if I was not careful to send her every day just enough for her not to die. Pepilla, the venerable father Salmón and my confessor, Castillo, are the only people I can help, because the state of my property and the high prices of essentials stop me doing more. You will be astonished to learn that the opulent fathers of the Merced depend on charity to live, but public destitution in the capital of Spain has got to such a state that the fattest people have become as thin as rakes.

I have deliberately left our precious affair to the end of my letter because I want to surprise you. Have you not guessed that the tone of my language is less sad than usual? But I will not say anything until I am sure you will not be misled. Restrain your impatience, my son... Thanks to Joseph, they have supplied me with some valuable information and very shortly, as Azanza has just told me, this gleam of truth will become bright and clear light. Farewell.

21st May

Wonderful news, my dear friend, son and servant! At last the hiding place of our tormentor has been discovered. A thousand blessings on Joseph and that unknown Queen Julia,[168] whose name I invoked in order to win his favour! Santorcaz has not gone to France yet. Assuming, my dear one, that you are on the road westwards from here I can say to you, as they say to children playing blind man's buff, "you are getting warm". Yes, little one, stretch out your hand and you will catch the traitor. How often do we look for our hat and there it is on our head! Something we think is completely lost is often just nearby. The idea that this letter will not find you already in Piedrahíta frightens me. But God cannot be so unkind to us and when you receive this piece of paper, go immediately to Plasencia and, helped by your guile, your bravery, your ingenuity or all of them together, enter the residence of the scoundrel and snatch from him that stolen jewel that he always keeps with him.

How hard I have worked to find this out! Santorcaz left the service a long time ago. His character, his pride, his extravagance made him unbearable even to those who appointed him. He was tolerated for some time because of the good services he performed, but it was found out that he belonged to the society of the Philadelphians, which had its origin in the army of Soult and whose objective was to dethrone the Emperor and proclaim the republic.[169] He was removed from his position soon after he had robbed us of Inés, and since then he has wandered through the Peninsula founding lodges. He was in Valladolid, Burgos, Salamanca and Oviedo, but then his trail was lost and for some time it was thought he had gone to France. Finally, the French police (the worst thing in the world does something good) discovered that he is now in Plasencia, very sick and pretty much incapable of upsetting all the villages with his lodges and revolutionary conclaves. It is outrageous! The rakes, the rogues, the liars and the forgers want to change the world! It makes me so angry, my friend, it makes me so furious.

The one who completed my information about Santorcaz is an *afrancesado*, no less of a madman and intriguer than Santorcaz himself, José Marchena[170] – do you know him? He is one who passes here for a lax cleric, a sort of abbot who speaks more French than Spanish, and more Latin than French, a poet, an orator, a man of eloquence and wit, who is said to be a friend of Madame de Staël[171], and who appears really to have been one with Marat, Robespierre, Legendre, Tallien[172] and others of that rabble. He and Santorcaz lived together in Paris. They are still good friends and write to each other often. But this Marchena is a man of little discretion and answers every question he is asked. Through him I found out that our enemy is in poor health and that he only lives in towns occupied by the French and that when he goes from one place to another, he cleverly disguises himself so that he is not recognised. And we thought he was in France! And I told you not to go to the Army of Extremadura! Go, run, don't delay a single day. The *lord* must be somewhere there. I will write to you at the headquarters of Carlos España. Answer me immediately. Will you go where I tell you? Will you find what we are looking for? Will you be able to return it to me? I can hardly bear it.

Santorcaz.

II

When I received this letter I was on my way to join what was called the army of Extremadura, although it was not then in Extremadura, but in Fuenteguinaldo, in the province of Salamanca.

In April I had finally left the company of the guerrillas in order to return to the army. It fell to me to serve under the orders of a field marshal called Carlos Espagne, who later became the Conde de España, of mournful memory in Catalonia.[173] At that time, this young Frenchman who had been serving in our forces since 1792, was not famous, despite having distinguished himself in the actions of Barca del Puerto, Tamames, Fresno and Medina del Campo. He was an excellent soldier, very brave and tough, but with a changeable and uncontrollable temper. Commanding admiration in battle, his odd behaviour when he had no enemies in front of him, provoked laughter or rage. He had an unattractive figure and his face, consisting almost entirely of a parrot-beaked nose and big, dull eyes under eyebrows which were angular, unkempt and mobile, and in which every hair pointed in any direction it liked, betrayed a suspicious mind and burning passions, before which any friend or subordinate had to put himself on guard.

Many of his actions showed a lamentable emptiness in the chambers of his brain and if sometimes he did not set us fighting against windmills, it was because God held us in His hand. But it frequently happened that the alarm would be sounded in the middle of the night, we would rush hastily out of our lodgings, looking for the enemy who had disturbed our beauty sleep at such an unearthly hour, only to find that lunatic España yelling in the middle of the camp at his invisible fellow countrymen.

This man led a division belonging to the army under the command of General Carlos O'Donnell.[174] He had just been joined by the band of Julián Sánchez,[175] a very successful guerrilla in Old Castile, and was preparing to join the ranks of Wellington, who was based in Fuenteguinaldo, having captured Badajoz in late March. The French in Old Castile commanded by Marmont[176] were very disconcerted. Soult was operating in Andalusia but did not dare to attack the *lord* and the latter decided to advance boldly towards Castile. In summary, the war was not going too badly for us, whereas the imperial star seemed to be in evident decline following the blows suffered at Ciudad Rodrigo, Arroyomolinos and Badajoz.

I had received my commission as major in February of that year. Luckily, I commanded for some time a band of guerrillas (since I was also a guerrilla chief), which traversed the country around Aranda and later the *sierras* of Covarrubias and Demanda. By early March I was sure that Santorcaz was not in that region. I daringly extended my excursions to Burgos, occupied by the French, and entered the city in disguise, and I was able to find out that the former chief of police had lived there some months earlier. Coming down then to Segovia, I continued my inquiries, but orders obliged me to join the division of Carlos España.

I obeyed, and as it was just at the time I received the last of the letters I have faithfully copied, I considered this order sending me to Extremadura to be a special favour from Heaven. But, as I have said, Wellington, whom España was to join, had already left the banks of the Tiétar. We were to leave Piedrahíta to join him in Fuenteguinaldo or in Ciudad Rodrigo. From there I could easily go to Plasencia.

While various projects were revolving in my anxious and desperate mind, events took place which I cannot let pass in silence.

After a prolonged march during the afternoon and the greater part of a beautiful June night, España gave orders for us to rest at Santibáñez de Valvaneda, a village on the road from Béjar to Salamanca. We had relatively abundant supplies, considering the great scarcity of the time, and as the army was always ready to have some fun, there was much uproar and hilarity to be seen when we took possession of the houses at midnight, and along with the houses, the straw mattresses and cooking equipment.

It fell to me to have the best room in the house, which had the flavour of a palace and the trappings of an inn. My orderly prepared a comfortable bed for me and I don't mind telling you that I went to bed without anything extraordinary or poetical happening to me during that ordinary act of life. And it is also a fact, although equally prosaic, that when I went to sleep the only thing that made an impression on me in the twilight of my senses was the ancient ballad being sung in a low voice by my orderly in the adjoining room:

> "Bernardo is in the Carpio,
> the Moor is on the Arapil.
> As the Tormes goes between them,
> they cannot fight each other."[177]

III

I went to sleep, and you should not think that now ghosts will appear, or that the broken, coffered ceilings and ancient walls of the historic house, formerly a palace and now a country inn, will move apart to allow a deformed monster to enter, much less a tall maiden of perfect beauty coming to implore me to liberate her from her enchantment or to perform some other service for her, the hour when fables have dominion, the hour when realities are few. Do not expect either that any bearded matron, sickly dwarf or fierce giant will suddenly come and pay reverence to me and bid me follow them down long and dark corridors that lead to marvellous underground storehouses full of tombs or treasures. Those that listen to my tale will find none of this in it. They may only know that I went to sleep. For a long time, despite my deep sleep, the sensation of a noise coming from the lower part of the house did not leave me. The sound of the horses' hooves reverberated in my head with a distant echo, making a vibration like a deep earthquake. But these sounds gradually ceased and eventually everything fell silent. My mind submerged into that nameless sphere where everything, absolutely everything, external disappears and the mind alone remains, entertaining itself on its own or even playing games with itself.

But suddenly, I do not know the time or after how many hours' sleep, I was woken by a most peculiar sensation, which I could not figure out, because without any of my senses being affected, I quickly sat up in bed and said, 'Who is there?'

Now awake, I shouted at my orderly,

'Tribaldos, get up and make some light.'

Almost immediately I said this, I realised my mistake. I was completely alone. The only thing that had happened was that my mind, in one of its capricious tricks (since this is unquestionably what the phantasmagoria of dreams are), had done one of the commonest of all, which is to pretend to be two, by an illusory and false division, changing for an instant its eternal unity. This mysterious *me and you* often appears also when we are awake.

But if there was nothing odd going on in my bedroom apart from in my mind, as was demonstrated when Tribaldos came in with a light and looked about, something was going on in the lower part of the building, where the deep silence of the night was interrupted by the loud din of people, carriages and horses.

'Sir,' said Tribaldos, taking out his sabre and slashing from one side to the other in the air, 'these scoundrels don't want us to get any sleep tonight. Out, you villains! Did you think I was afraid of you?'

'Who are you talking to?'

'To the spirits, sir,' he replied. 'They've come to amuse themselves with your lordship, after they have played with me. One got me by the right leg, another one by the left leg and another one, uglier than Barabbas, tied a rope round my neck, and by pulling and tugging on it they flew off with me to my village so that I could see my Dorotea talking sweetly with Sergeant Moscardón.'

'You don't believe in spirits, do you?'

'Well, I don't have to believe in them, I've seen them! I've had more outings with them than the hairs on my head,' he replied with deep conviction. 'This house is full of their lordships.'

'Tribaldos, do me the favour of not killing any more mosquitoes with your sabre. Leave the spirits and go downstairs to see what is causing this infernal noise coming from the courtyard. It seems some travellers have arrived, but from the racket they are making, not even Sir Arthur Wellesley with all his train would have more people.'

The young fellow left, leaving me alone, but in a short while he appeared again, muttering menacing words through his teeth and with an unpleasant grimace on his face.

'You would think, sir, wouldn't you, that it must be Englishmen or travelling royalty that would thunder through the house in this way? Well, sir, they are actors, some cheap players on their way to Salamanca to perform at the festival of San Juan. I must have counted at least eight of them, leading men and ladies, and they have two wagons with painted canvases, costumes, gilded crowns, pasteboard armour and ridiculous masks. A fine lot! The innkeeper was going to throw them out onto the street, but they produced their money and no sooner had His Majesty Señor Chiporro seen the gold than he treats them like dukes.'

'Damn all actors! They are the worst breed of scoundrels crawling about in the world.'

'If I was Carlos España,' said my orderly, displaying the benevolent feelings lodging in his heart, 'I would seize the whole company, take them out to the yard, one after the other, and shoot every last one of them.'

'No, that's going too far.'

'That would put a stop to their antics. Pedrezuela and his fiendish wife María Pepa del Valle were actors. You had to see the talent with which he played his role of royal commissioner and she that of madam royal commissioner. They tricked everyone so well that they were believed in all the villages they went through and even in Tomelloso, which is mine and not a place of fools.'

'That Pedrezuela,' I said, feeling sleep overpowering me once more, 'was the man who condemned more than sixty people to death in various villages along the Tagus.'

'The very same one,' he replied, 'but he's settled all his accounts now because when General Castaños[178] and I went to help *the lord* at the siege of Ciudad Rodrigo, we got hold of Pedrezuela and his little woman and put them up against a wall and shot them. Since then, whenever I see an actor, my finger is itching to pull the trigger.'

Tribaldos left only to come back a moment later.

'I think they are leaving already,' I said, noticing an increase in noise, which indicated their departure.

'No, sir,' he replied, laughing. 'Sergeant Panduro and Corporal Rocacha have set fire to their cart which carries their theatrical gear. Just listen, sir, to the kings, princes and seneschals shrieking as they see their thrones, crowns and ermine cloaks burn. My goodness, how those princesses and grand duchesses can squawk! I'm going downstairs to see if that rabble can cry here as well as they can in the theatre… The headman of the troop can certainly shout… Can you hear him, sir? I'm going back downstairs to see them go.'

I heard that voice clearly among the other angry voices, and the strangest thing was that its timbre, although far off and disfigured by rage, made me shudder. I knew that voice.

I got up hurriedly and dressed with all speed, but the noises gradually died down, indicating that the poor victims of the soldiers' cruel joke were hastily leaving the inn. When I was going out, Tribaldos came in and said to me,

'That pick of the bunch of scoundrels has left, sir. The whole yard is full of burnt pieces of the palaces of Warsaw, pasteboard helmets and the scarlet soutane of the Doge of Venice.'

'Which way did those wretches go?'

'Towards Grijuelo.'

'So they're going to Salamanca. Get your gun and follow me immediately.'

'But, sir, General España wants to see your lordship right now. His Excellency's adjutant has brought the message.'

'The Devil take you, the message, the adjutant and the general… Why, I've put my cravat on the wrong way round… Give me that jacket, stupid… You didn't think I would go without it.'

'The general is waiting for your lordship. You can hear him down below stamping and shouting in his lodging.'

When I went down to the square, the annoying travellers had already disappeared. Carlos España met me as I came out and said to me,

'I have just received a

message from the *lord* ordering me to march to Sancti-Spíritus… Up, everybody, sound the call to arms.'

So ended an incident which I need not have related but for its connection to other more curious ones which will be told about later.

IV

Leaving the high road to the right, we went along a rough and winding track to cross the mountain range. Dawn came and a day on which nothing happened worthy of being marked by any white, black or yellow stone, but on the next day, I had an encounter which I regard as certainly being one of the most fortunate of my life.

We were marching lazily along at midday without any cares or taking any precautions, with the certainty that we would not meet any French in such wild places. The soldiers were singing and the officers were engaged in pleasant conversation about the campaign that had begun; we let the horses go at their natural and peaceful pace, without spurring them on or holding them back. The day was fine, in fact better than fine, quite warm, with the sun's rays on our shoulders, warming them more than was needed.

I was in the vanguard. When we came in sight of San Esteban de la Sierra, a small village, surrounded by the leafy greenness and welcome shade of trees, in whose shelter we had decided to take a siesta, I heard an uproar from the first groups of soldiers, who were marching ahead, in broken ranks and up to their old tricks with the villagers who appeared on the road.

'It's nothing, sir,' Tribaldos said in answer to my question about the reason for such outrageous shouting. 'It's Panduro and Rocacha who've come across an Augustinian friar, more importunate than Augustinian, and more villainous than importunate, who didn't get off the road when the troops were passing.'

'And what did they do to him?'

'Nothing more than play pelota[179],' he replied, smiling. 'His Paternity is crying and saying nothing.'

'I see that Rocacha is riding a donkey and racing towards the village on it.'

'It's his Paternity's donkey; his Paternity has a donkey with him loaded with rotten turnips.'

'Leave that poor man in peace, for the life of…!' I exclaimed angrily, 'and let him go on his way.'

I went on ahead and among the soldiers, who were tormenting him in thousands of ways, I could see a holy man with a hood, dressed in the Augustinian habit, upset and crying.

'Lord,' he said, looking piously towards Heaven with his arms crossed, 'may this be in atonement for my sins!'

His faded habit, which was full of holes, was a very good match for the miserable appearance of a thin and yellowish face, on which the dust mixed with tears or sweat formed a dark crust. Far from that miserable person displaying the comfort and satiety of the city monasteries, the best educators of people yet known, he seemed to be an anchorite of the desert or a beggar of the highway. When he found himself less harassed, he looked all around searching for his unfortunate companion in misfortune, and when he saw him returning at top speed puffing and blowing, his flanks crushed by the mighty Rocacha, he hurried forward to meet him.

Meanwhile, I was watching the good friar and when I saw him return, now pulling his recaptured ass with a thin rope, I could not help uttering an exclamation of surprise. That face which at first had wakened vague memories in my mind, finally revealed its secret, and despite the time that had passed and the damage done by the years and hardships, I recognised it as belonging to someone I was friendly with in other times.

'Señor Juan de Dios!' I exclaimed, holding up my horse until the friar came alongside me. 'Is it you I see in those habits and under that cloak of dust?'[180]

The Augustinian friar looked at me with a start, and after he had contemplated me for some time spoke to me in a mellifluous voice:

Juan de Dios.

'How does the Señor General know me? I am indeed Juan de Dios. I am grateful to Your Eminence for ordering them to return the donkey to me.'

'You address me as Eminence?' I replied. 'They haven't made me a cardinal yet.'

'In my confusion I did not know what I was saying. If Your Highness will permit me, I will depart.'

'First try to see if you recognise me. Has my face changed so much since that time we were together in the house of Don Mauro Requejo?'

This name made the good Augustinian shake and he stared at me with his feverish eyes and more astonished than surprised he said,

'Is it possible that I'm looking at Gabriel? My God! General, are you Gabriel, who in April 1808… I remember you well… Let me kiss your feet… So then you're actually Gabriel?'

'The very same. I'm so pleased we have met! You have become a poor friar…'

'To serve God and to save my soul. It has been some time since I embraced this life, as hard for the body as it is beneficial for the soul. And you, Gabriel? And your Excellency, Don Gabriel, you have gone in for the army? The life of arms is also an honourable one and God rewards good soldiers, some of whom have been saints.'

'That's my ambition, Father, but you seem as if you have already succeeded, because your poverty is no lie and your mortified face tells me that you fast every Friday during Easter.'

'I am a very humble servant of God,' he said, lowering his eyes, 'and I do the little my miserable strength allows. Now, General, I have had great pleasure in seeing you… and in recognising the generous young man who had been my friend, whereupon and with your leave, I will depart, since this army is going into the mountains and I am making for the high road.'

'I cannot allow us to separate so quickly, my friend, you are tired and you don't look as if you have obeyed that precept which requires charity to start with oneself. The regiment will rest in that village. Let's have whatever's available to eat and you can accompany me so that we can talk for a bit and revive old memories.'

'If the General commands me, I will obey because my destiny is to obey,' he said, walking beside me in the direction of the village.

'I see that the donkey has a better coat than its owner and doesn't mortify itself as much with fasts and vigils. It seems to be an animal that goes at a good pace and would carry you like a feather.'

'I will not ride him,' he replied without raising his eyes from the ground. 'I always go on foot.'

'That is too much.'

'I take this good animal with me so that it can help me carry alms and the sick people I collect in the villages to take them to hospital.'

'To hospital?'

'Yes, sir. I belong to the Order of Hospitallers that our holy father and patron the great San Juan de Dios founded in Granada, about two hundred and seventy or so years ago.[181] In our statutes we follow the rule of the great Saint Augustine and we have hospitals in various towns in Spain. We collect beggars from the roads, we visit the houses of the poor to tend to the sick who don't want to come to our house, and we live on charity.'

'An admirable life, brother!' I said, getting off my horse and, together with other officers and brother Juan, making my way towards a small wood at the edge of the village, where our orderlies were preparing a frugal meal for us under the welcome shade of some massive and cooling trees.

'Tie your donkey to the trunk of a tree,' I said to my old friend, 'and make yourself comfortable on the grass next to me so that we can give something to the body, as not everything has to be for the soul.'

'I will keep Don Gabriel company,' said Juan de Dios meekly after he had tied up his beast. 'I won't have anything to eat.'

'What do you mean you won't eat? Is it by any chance God's command not to eat? And how can an empty body be ready to help its neighbour? Come, Señor Juan de Dios, put aside this diffidence.'

'I don't eat any food that has been prepared in a kitchen, or anything hot or fancy that smacks of gastronomy.'

'Would you call this cold and dry mutton and this bread which is harder than rock gastronomy?'

'I cannot try that,' he replied, smiling. 'I live only on grasses of the field and wild roots.'

'Well, I admire you, but frankly… you'll have some wine to drink at the very least. It's from Rueda.'

'I drink nothing but water.'

'Good grief… water and weeds of the field! That's a nice hotchpotch. Still, if that's how someone is saved…'

'It's been some time since I made a very firm vow to live like this and until today, Don Gabriel, although not free of sins, I have the satisfaction of not having once broken my vow.'

'Well, then, I won't insist, my friend. You shouldn't be condemned on my account. The truth is I'm famished… Poor Juan de Dios.'

'Who would have said that we would meet again after so many years!? Isn't that right?'

'Yes, sir.'

'I thought you had passed to a better life. When you disappeared….'

'I entered the Order in January of '09. I completed my first exercises in March and received the first orders last year. I am still not a professed friar.'

'How many things have happened since we saw each other!'

'Yes, sir, how many!'

'You, retired from the world, live a beatific life with no sorrows or joys, happy with your estate...'

Juan de Dios sighed deeply and then lowered his eyes. I looked at him closely and saw the signs in his drawn face which showed it was no exaggeration to call this man of the wild grasses and the water of crystal streams devout. A very intense violet ring circled his eyes, which made his pupils shine more brightly and stand out from the bones in his face under the stretched and sallow skin. His expression was one of those souls exalted by a piety that also affects their spirit and their nervous system. Mysticism and sickness at the same time is a peculiar devotion which has elevated the finest figures to the heaven of human greatness. If at first I thought I saw something artificial and hypocritical in Juan de Dios, I soon became convinced of the opposite, and that holy man, cast into a contemplative and austere life by the world's tempests, was inflamed by burning and genuine fervour. It seemed as if he was on fire, one could watch the combustion of his body, gradually turning into ashes, burnt by the flame of spiritual fever; it seemed as if this man hardly touched the earth, at least the world of the living, and that the poor clay, which still weakly bound this noble soul, was falling apart and crumbling away bit by bit.

'It is admirable, my friend,' I said to him, 'that a man who was certainly not free of worldly passions has reached such a gratifying state of holiness.'

Friar Juan de Dios's features tightened with a slight shudder. But his face instantly composed itself and he said to me,

'Do you know what has become of that happy Requejo couple? I would be sorry if they had suffered any misfortune.'

'I haven't heard of them again. They are bound to be much richer, as villains are always successful.'

The friar gave no sign of assent.

'But God will have punished them in the end,' I continued, 'for the sufferings they inflicted on that unhappy girl...'

On saying this I noticed that in the veins of that wretched body of a man, which the grave was calling for its own, there still flowed some remnants of blood. Swelling blue veins shone for a moment through the skin of his face and a faint purplish tint coloured his austere forehead. I would not have been more surprised to see a wooden image blushing at the touch of kisses from the devout.

'God will know what has to be done with that Requejo pair, for their behaviour,' he replied.

'I believe you would not be indifferent to learn the fate which befell that unfortunate girl.'

'Indifferent, no,' he replied almost turning into a corpse.

'Oh, those people who are destined to suffer…' I said, closely observing the effect my words made on the holy man. 'That poor girl, so good, so pretty, so modest…'

'What?'

'She is dead.'

I thought that Juan de Dios would be shocked at hearing this, but to my great surprise I saw his face resplendent with serenity and beatitude. My astonishment was complete when with the utmost conviction, he said,

'I knew that. She died in the convent in Córdoba, where her family had shut her away in June 1808.'

'And how do you know that?' I asked, not correcting the poor Augustinian's mistake.

'We have extraordinary visions. God allows us, when our spirit is in a special state, to know about things that have happened in distant lands without anyone having told us about them. Inés died. I have seen her several times in my ecstasy, and there is no doubt that it is only the images of those persons who have had the fortune to leave this poor and miserable world for ever that appear to us.'

'That must be right.'

'Yes, it is, even though the dim eyes of the body create something else. Ah, those of the soul are the ones that never deceive because they always have in them a ray of eternal light. Bodily sight is an organ that the Devil uses as his spectacles to torment us. Often what we see with it is an illusion or a fantasy. I, Don Gabriel, suffer the most horrible torments from the continual trials that the Lord of Heaven and earth subjects my spirit to, and from the treacherous cunning of the angel of darkness, who, eager to ruin me, plays with my feeble senses and mocks this unfortunate creature.'

'Dear friend, tell me what happened to you. I, too, have sometimes been a plaything and object of ridicule of that Devil and I can give you some good advice on how to overcome him and to mock him instead of being mocked.'

V

'Since you have named a person who was a major reason for me abandoning these wicked times, and since you therefore know all my secrets, I must hide nothing from you. When God created me, he decided I should suffer, and I have suffered like no other mortal on this earth. Before I felt in my soul the divine ray of eternal grace, which illuminated for me the path of this new life, a worldly passion brought about my ruin. After I had embraced the holy cross for my salvation, the worries, weaknesses and agonies in my spirit have been such that I think this had been ordained by God so that I would know Hell and Purgatory while I lived before ascending to the resting place of the just… I loved a woman, but in such exaltation that my nature had become unhinged in that trance. When I realised that everything was over, I no longer had any sense, memory or will. I was a machine, sir, a stupid machine; my feelings were dead. I lived in darkness, seeing nothing, in a sort of lethargic fear. Various times afterwards I have wondered whether my stupor was the limbo where those who have just been born go to.'

'Exactly. That must be right.'

'When I came back to my senses, dear sir, I made a plan to become a friar. I had finished with the world. I made my confession with the utmost fervour. Father Busto enthusiastically approved my intention to devote the rest of my sad days to religion and as I displayed a wish to enter the poorest Order, one where the body would work hardest and where the spirit would be furthest removed from worldly attractions, he pointed me to this rule of hospitaller brothers. Ah, my soul received inexplicable consolation! I found out lonely places to meditate, and when meditating my head felt surrounded by a heavenly atmosphere. Such purity of light! Such sweetness and soft silence in the air!'

'And then?'

'Ah, then my misfortunes began again in a different form. God decreed that I should suffer, and suffering I am… hear me for a moment more. I began my studies and religious practices to enter the Order. One morning they received me at the monastery, where I put on layman's clothes. On that day I sat in my lessons happier than ever; I attended the sick as a servant in the infirmary and in the afternoon, taking the second volume of *The names of Christ*, by the master Brother Luis de León,[182] a book I enjoyed immensely, I went into the garden and in the quietest and most secret place there I surrendered my mind to the delights of reading. I had not yet finished that most beautiful chapter entitled *Description of human misery and the origin of its frailty*, when I felt a very intense chill run all over me, a feeling of great alarm and anxiety, then all my blood flooded into my breast and I felt a sensation which I cannot say was deepest joy or acute pain. A strange figure, vague shape or shadow came into my vision, I looked and saw her; it was her in person, seated on the stone bench at my side.'

'Who?'

'Do I need to say her name?'

'No, go on.'

'The book fell from my hands, I looked at the astonishing vision – since it was a vision – and worldly love was violently reborn in my breast like the explosion of a mine. I was entranced, sir, dumb and half-amazed, half-terrified. It was her in person, and she was looking at me with her sweet eyes, making me dizzy. She was about half a yard away from me, but I made no movement towards her, because the same astonishment, the wonder that such a prodigy of beauty produced in me, the same fire of love that consumed my being, held me enchanted and motionless. She was dressed in a very rich robe of a white and delicate fabric, which, as clouds mask the sun without hiding it, masked her beautiful body, blurring it rather than covering it. One of her delicate feet appeared naked from under the folds; her hair, arranged in curls with incomparable artistry, fell in beautiful locks on both sides of her face among strings of oriental pearls, and in her right hand she held a small bunch of fragrant flowers, whose scent reached the point of intoxicating my senses.'

'In truth, Señor Juan de Dios, I never saw Señorita Inés wear a dress like that, and it is certainly not suitable for strolling around in gardens.'

'What would you have seen her as being, if that image was not a physical and tangible form, but a deceptive fabrication of the Devil, who since that day has chosen me as a victim of his abominable experiments?'

'And that young lady with the naked foot and the bouquet of flowers said not a word?'

'Not even a tiny one, brother.'

'And you said nothing to her, nor crossed the half a yard space between the two of you?'

'I could not speak. I did indeed move closer to her, but in the same moment she disappeared.'

'What a dirty trick! But the Devil is like that, my friend: he offers, but does not give.'

'I took a long time to recover from the horrible feeling that thing had left in my soul. Finally, I picked up the book again and directed my thoughts to God. Ah, what a strange feeling! So strange that I cannot explain it to you. Just imagine, dear sir, that my thoughts, climbing up to Heaven, had taken material form, but were held back and driven off by a mighty hand. That is nothing more or less than what I felt. I wanted to think but my mind could only feel. Burning convulsions ran through my body like lightning flashes of movement... Ah, there is no way at all I can explain this... Something was smouldering in my body, like wicks which are dying down and whose ashes, half-flame and half-cinder, fall to the ground... I got up; I wanted to go into the church, but – can you believe that I couldn't? No, I could not. Someone pulled me out by the back of my habit. I ran to the cell they had assigned me and throwing myself to the ground, I put my forehead onto my hands and my hands onto the tiles. I remained like this for the whole night praying and asking God to free me from those horrible temptations, telling Him that I did not want to sin but to serve Him, that I wanted to be good and pure and holy.'

'Why didn't you tell other friars experienced in matters of visions and temptations about this event?'

'That's what I did immediately. That very evening I consulted Father Rafael de los Ángeles, a very pious and worthy man who showed great kindness to me, and he told me not to worry, since constant piety, unceasing mortification and unbounded humility were enough to strip the mind (that's exactly what he said) of that sort of imaginary and natural notions. He also told me that in his first years of monastic life he had experienced similar difficulties and predicaments, but that in the end through hard acts of penance and mystical readings he had convinced the Devil that his efforts to pervert him were useless, whereupon he left him in peace. He advised me that I should enter the active life of the Order, that I should seek out the miseries and woes of the world, gathering sick people from villages to take them to hospitals; that I should roam the fields, taking physical exercise and living on grass and roots, so that, deprived of all delicacies, the miserable and vile body will acquire that bareness and rigidity which banishes lustfulness. He also advised me to sleep little, and never on anything soft, but rather on hard rocks or sharp thorns, whenever I could; that in the same way I should withdraw completely from the company of friends, avoid talk of worldly matters, show no liking for anybody, but shun everybody so that I would think of nothing but the perfection of my soul.'

'And by doing this, have you succeeded...?'

'This is what I have done, brother, but I have hardly succeeded, if at all. Almost three years of mortification, penances, vigils, harshness, sleeping in the open fields and eating raw cabbage and hedge mustard have certainly strengthened my spirit, freeing me from that vague sensuality which initially drove my sanity to the edge of the precipice, but they did not free me from the continual attacks of the infernal angel who, from one day to the next, sir, in the open and indoors, in the sweet darkness of the sublime and sad night as well as in the dazzling light of the sun, placed before my eyes the image of the person I adored in the world. Ah, those days, when we were in the shop, I blasphemed, yes… I remember that one day I went into the church and kneeling before the Most Blessed Sacrament I said. 'Lord, I will hate you, I will reject you if you do not give her to me so that our souls and our bodies can be united for ever in life, in the grave and in eternity.' God is punishing me for having threatened Him.'

'So, all the time you…'

'Yes, all the time, all the time I see her, sometimes in this form, sometimes in another form, although the Devil does give me a rest for periods and I don't see anything. This ill-fated misfortune of mine has prevented me up to now from reaching the ultimate and most sublime stages in the sacraments of the Order, as I think I am unworthy for God to descend to my hands. It is a terrible feeling to have one's heart and mind completely prepared for holiness but be unable to reach that perfect state!

I despair and weep in silence when I see how happy the other friars of my Order are, the ones who enjoy in the purest peace the joys of blessed visions, which are the daintiest delights of spiritual sustenance. In their meditations some of them see before them  the image of the crucified Christ, looking at them with the most loving eyes; others delight in contemplating the holy figure of the Child Jesus; others are entranced by the presence of Saint Catherine of Siena or Santa Rosa of Viterbo, whose most chaste image and calm gestures inspire prayer and austerity, but I, unfortunate that I am, abominable sinner, who felt my bowels burnt up by a worldly love, and fed on that divine dew of passion, and steeped my soul in thousands of frivolities inspired by fantasy, I have become for ever sick with impurity, I have melted and been cast in an unknown crucible which has left me for ever in that despicable original form. I cannot be a holy man, I cannot throw off from me this second person that is my constant companion. Oh, my cursed tongue! I had said, 'I want to be united with her in life, in the grave and in eternity,' and this is what is happening.'

Friar Juan de Dios lowered his head and remained meditating for a long time.

'What are the new forms she has appeared in?' I asked him.

'One morning I was walking in the countryside when, having a raging thirst, I looked for a stream to quench it. Finally, under some leafy poplars whose old trunks stood straight up among blackish outcrops, I saw a clear stream which invited one to drink. After I drank, I sat on an outcrop and at the same instant I felt that peculiar anxiety which always announced to me the power of the angel of evil. A shepherdess was at a short distance from me; her in person, sir, as beautiful as the cherubim.'

'And was she tending some cows or a flock of sheep?'

'No, sir, she was on her own, sitting like me on an outcrop, with her snow-white feet in the water, which she noisily shook about, making cold drops splash up and wet my face. She had loosened her hair which she was combing. I cannot remember well all the details of her dress, but it was certainly a dress that did not cover much. She looked at me smiling. I wanted to speak but I could not. I took a step towards her and she disappeared.'

'And then?'

'I saw her again in various places. I was in Ciudad Rodrigo when the *lord* attacked it in January this year. I was serving in the hospital when the siege began and so some other good fathers and I went out to help the many wounded Frenchmen who had fallen on the walls. I was appalled as I had never seen such carnage and I did not cease asking for the intercession of the Blessed Mother of Our Lord so that the fury of the Anglo-Portuguese would abate.[183] On the 18th, the outwork, where I was, gave me a good idea of what Hell is like. The convent of San Francisco, where we were putting the wounded, blew up into a thousand pieces… The French mocked me, and because they showed much ill will towards us friars, believing us to be behind the resistance to them, they treated me badly in word and deed… Oh! When the allies entered the square, I was wounded, not by the bullets of the besiegers, but by blows from the besieged. The English, Spanish and Portuguese came in through the breach. I felt very frightened when I heard victorious curses roared out in three different languages. They were smashing each other like wild beasts… I was lying lifeless and moribund in a pool of blood and mud and surrounded by dead bodies. I was dying of a raging thirst, a thirst, my dear sir, so burning that it was as if my veins were full of fire, and as if my mouth, tongue and palate, instead of being live and moist flesh, were dry and inert burlap. What torture! I said to myself. 'Thank you, Lord, who has deigned to lift me up to Your bosom. The hour of my death has come.' I had just said that, or rather, I had just thought that, when I felt on my lips the heavenly touch of fresh water. I sighed and my spirit shook off its funereal torpor. I opened my eyes and saw touching my burning lips a white hand in whose hollowed palm the clear liquid sparkled as fresh and pure as if gushing from a country spring.'

'So, what form did Señorita Inés come in that time?'

'She came as a nun.'

'And nuns give drinks in the hollow of their hand?'

'That one did, certainly. It would be impossible for me to describe to you how beautiful her face was, surrounded by the white coif and how well the austerity of the poor serge of the habit suited her. I had hardly looked at her, when she suddenly flew off, leaving me thirstier than before.'

'One thing occurs to me, Señor Juan de Dios,' I said, feeling deeply moved by the strange illness of the unfortunate hospitaller, 'which is, seeing that that person is an artifice of the most evil, the most villainous and shameless spirit created by God, and having caused you so much sorrow, grief, mortal anguish and many heated outbursts, it would seem to be more natural for you to detest her and that you should see her as being dreadfully and horribly ugly, rather than being that marvel of beauty you extol with such delight.'

Friar Juan de Dios sighed sadly and said to me,

'The Evil One never displays repulsive or abhorrent things for us to see, but on the contrary things which are beautiful, fragrant, or pleasing to the palate, to the senses of smell, of hearing and of touch. He knows very well what works. If you have read the life of Madre Santa Teresa de Jesús,[184] you would have seen that the Devil once painted a picture of Our Lord Jesus Christ before her to trick her. She herself says that the Evil One is a great painter, and adds that when we see a very good picture, even though we know that a bad man had painted it, we would still admire it.'

'That is very well said... something else occurs to me. If I had been tormented in this heartless way by the Evil Spirit, who I'm beginning to see is an out and out villain, I would have tried to pursue the image, touch it, speak to it, to see whether it really was an empty illusion or a physical being.'

'I did that, dear sir and my friend,' replied the hospitaller in a voice already weak from having spoken so much, 'but I was never able to get my hands on her, having only succeeded once in touching the skirt of her costume. I can assure you that when I saw her she always appeared to me to be a human being with her natural solidity, sturdiness and the brilliance and gentleness of the eyes, the sweet breath of the mouth, and in addition the dress floating with the wind; in short, everything was put together in such a way that it was impossible not to believe she was a living person and like the rest of our species.'

'And did she always appear alone?'

'No, sir, there were some times when I saw her in the company of other girls, as for example in Seville last year. They were all empty creations of infernal industry, since they disappeared with her, like a multitude of lights that go out with just one puff.'

'And do they always disappear in that way like a light going out?'

'No, sir, there are times when she runs ahead of me and I follow her and either she loses herself among the crowd or goes so far ahead that I cannot catch her up. One day I saw her on a fine steed that ran faster than the wind, and yesterday I saw her in a cart.'

'Which also ran like the wind?'

'No, sir, well, it hardly ran since it was a poor cart. There is something special about yesterday's vision which frightens me and which demonstrates to me that the evil I suffer from is serious and getting worse.'

'Why?'

'Because she spoke to me yesterday.'

'What?' I exclaimed, smiling, but not surprised at how extreme my friend's mad fantasies had become.

'The young lady with the naked foot, the shepherdess, the nun of Ciudad Rodrigo has spoken at last?'

'Yes, sir. She was travelling in the company of some actors who were apparently coming from Extremadura.'

'In a cart! ... With some actors! ... From Extremadura!'

'Yes, sir; I see that you are astonished and I understand that, and with good reason in this case. Some men on horseback went in front, next came a cart with two women and then another cart with theatre scenery and equipment, all burnt and in pieces.'

'Brother, you are making fun of me,' I said, getting up suddenly and sitting down again, driven by a burning anxiety.

'When I saw her, my dear sir, I felt that feverish chill, that sensation of pleasure and pain that accompanies my terrible crises.'

'And how was she?'

'Sad, wrapped up in a black cloak.'

'And the other woman?'

'Another trick of the imagination, no doubt, accompanied her in silence.'

'And the men who were on horseback?'

'There were five, and one of them was dressed as a juggler with tri-coloured breeches and a peaked cap. They were quarrelling and another one of them, who seemed to be in charge of them all, was an elegant person with good presence, with a pointed beard like the Devil's.'

'Didn't you catch any smell of sulphur?'

'Nothing like that, sir. The men were talking animatedly and mentioned some soldiers who had burnt their infernal trash.'

'I fear, dear brother Juan,' I said in alarm, 'that you are no longer the only one that has been bedevilled, but I am as well, since those actors, and those women, those carts and those pieces of theatre junk are real and actual, and, although I did not see them, I know that they were in Santibáñez de Valvaneda. Could there be any explanation for you thinking that one of the actresses was the same well-known person, other than that it was a most nimble trick on the part of his infernal majesty?'

'I did say,' the friar continued simply, 'that this apparition today is the most extraordinary and frightening one I have experienced in my life, since diabolical handiwork has displayed such tokens, signals and glimpses of reality in it that it would deceive the most intelligent and impartial person. This is also the first time that this beloved image, as well as taking the solid body of a woman, has copied the human voice.'

'She spoke?'

'Yes, sir, she spoke,' said the hospitaller, terrified. 'Her voice is not the same as the one which still echoes in my ears, since I heard her at the Requejos', in the same way that her appearance today seemed to me to be more beautiful, more robust, more complete and better formed. When I saw her in the convent, in the wood, in the church and in Ciudad Rodrigo she was almost a child, but today...'

'But if she spoke, what did she say?'

'I went up to the cart, looked at her, she looked at me, too... Her eyes were rays which burnt my body and soul. Then she seemed surprised, very surprised... Ah, her lips moved and pronounced my own name. 'Señor Juan de Dios,' she said, 'have you become a friar?' I thought I was going to die at that very moment. I wanted to speak but could not do so. She made as if to give me a donation and immediately the man who seemed to be in charge of everyone, as if becoming aware of my presence by the actors' cart, stopped his horse and coming back said to me roughly, 'Clear off, you worthless loafer.' She then said, 'He's a poor mendicant asking for alms.' The man raised his stick as if to hit me and she said, 'Father, don't hurt him.''

'Are you sure she said that?'

'Yes, I am sure, but the wretch, like the infernal creature that he was, a natural enemy of persons dedicated to the service of God, called me a loafer again and at the same time I received such a blow on the head that I fell down senseless.'

'Señor Juan de Dios,' I said to him after reflecting a short while on the strangeness of that adventure, 'swear to me that what you said is true and that it is not your intention to make fun of me.'

'Me, make fun of you, my dear officer!' the hospitaller exclaimed, on the verge of tears seeing that his truthfulness was in doubt. 'What I have told is the truth, and as clearly as the Devil is in Hell and as God is in Heaven, so the number of cases of obsession in the world is infinite, and every day we hear tell of new outrages and stupendous tricks by the mortifier of mankind.'

'And are you able to say precisely where that affair with the actors' cart took place?'

'After Santibáñez de Valvaneda, about three leagues. They were going at a good pace on the road to Salamanca.'

The unhappy hospitaller could not be lying, and as for the Devil's involvement in the abovementioned matters and people, I had my reasons for believing there was some difference between the friar's first encounters and the most recent one.

Once more I urged him to have something, but for the second time he refused to give his body any treat. We were getting ready to leave when I saw him turn pale, inasmuch as his desiccated flesh turned a deeper shade of yellow; I saw he was terrified, his eyes halfway out of his head, his lower lip trembling and his whole body shaking. He was looking at a fixed spot behind me and as I turned quickly round and nothing was there that could explain his fright, I asked him why he was so terrified and whether Satan was so bold as to get up to his old tricks among so many soldiers.

'She's already vanished,' he said faintly and dropped his arms listlessly.

'So then, she's been here again?'

'Yes, in that group where the soldiers are dancing… can you see there are some girls there from San Esteban?'

'I certainly can; but either I have forgotten what Señora Inés looks like, or she's not one of them,' I replied, unable to repress a smile. 'If she was there, one could give her a piece of one's mind for dancing with soldiers.'

'Well, my dear sir, you may have doubts whether it's daytime now,' he declared still not recovered from his excitement, 'but you cannot doubt that she was there. I see that the Devil is making his temptations worse and increasing the strength of his attacks on the redoubts of my fortress, and he's doing that because I am sinning…'

'Sinning now, sinning for speaking with an old friend?'

'Yes, sir, since it is sinning to surrender the spirit freely to the delights of conversation with laypeople. In addition, I have been resting here for more than an hour and a half, something I have not done for three years, and I have enjoyed the refreshing shade of these trees. My soul,' he added with intense fervour, 'up you get, no sleeping, be on constant watch for the enemy who besets you, do not surrender to the corrupting pleasure of friendship, do not falter for a single moment nor enjoy the sweetness of rest. Be alert, always alert.'

'Are you going already?' I said, seeing him untying the good donkey. 'Come on, don't refuse this bit of bread for the journey.'

He took it and, putting it into the mouth of the placid donkey, which was clearly not in favour of monastic abstinence, he picked for himself a bunch of grass and held it to his breast.

'Either he's a fraud,' I said to myself, 'or he is the purest and most innocent saint wearing a monk's girdle.'

'Good afternoon, Señor Don Gabriel,' he said in a humble voice. 'I am going to Béjar and then carrying on tomorrow to Candelario where we have a hospital. And you, where are you going to?'

'Me? Wherever they take me; perhaps to conquer Salamanca which is held by Marmont.'

'Farewell, my dear sir and brother,' he replied. 'Thank you, thank you very much for so much kindness.'

And pulling the cord, he left with the donkey after him. When his spare, blackish figure grew fainter as he descended a hill, I thought I was looking at a body in a melancholy search for its lost grave and unable to find it.

VI

Two days later, beyond Dios le Guarde,[185] a momentous event broke the monotony of our march. Round about dawn our troops in the vanguard broke out in cries of jubilation; orders were given to form up, so that the companies should have the martial order and fine appearance necessary for presentation to an intelligent military man; by command of the general some of the men hurried to cut branches from the groves of oaks nearby, to make some sort of crowns, trimmings or triumphal arches. When we reached the Ciudad Rodrigo road, we saw a large phalanx of men dressed in scarlet and horsemen on the swiftest steeds. As soon as they came into sight, everyone shouted out joyfully as one: 'Long live the *lord*!'

'It is Cotton's cavalry of General Graham's division,'[186] said Carlos España. 'Gentlemen, take care that we do not do something silly. The English are very ceremonious and pay great attention to form. If there are enough branches we will make a small triumphal arch for the conqueror of Ciudad Rodrigo to pass under, and I will deliver a speech to him which I have prepared, praising him for his skill in the art of war and eulogising the Constitution of Cádiz,[187] both excellent things and to which we will owe our eventual triumph when all is said and done.'

'The *lord* is no great friend of the Constitution of Cádiz,' said Don Julián Sánchez who was on Don Carlos's right. 'But what does that matter to us? If we can defeat Marmont, then good luck to all the *milords*.'

The red cavalrymen came up to us and their commander, who spoke a Spanish that God would have wished for, paid his compliments to our general, telling him that His Excellency the Duke of Ciudad Rodrigo would not be long in arriving at Sancti-Spíritus. We at once began to erect our arch of branches and sticks at the entrance of that village and you should have seen a local schoolmaster who appeared carrying some large canvas placards each one with inscriptions and verses he had thought up himself. His poetical compositions lauded to the skies the virtues of the modern Fabius, in other words, Sir Arthur Wellesley, Viscount Wellington of Talavera, Duke of Ciudad

Rodrigo, Grandee of Spain and Peer of England.[188]

Numerous divisions of the army kept arriving one after the other, spreading out into the surrounding area and occupying the adjoining villages, and at last, among the most brilliant of the Scottish, English and Spanish soldiers, appeared a post-chaise, greeted with acclamations and cheers by the troops on each side of the road. Inside it I saw a long, red nose, below which gleamed some very white teeth. With the rapidity of the march, that was pretty much all I could make out, other than a benevolent and courteous smile greeting the troops from the depths of the carriage.

I should not fail to mention, although it is hardly in keeping with serious history, that as the coach was passing under the triumphal arch, since this had not been built by Roman craftsmen or engineers, the arch was hit and shaken by one of the wheels, it seemed on the verge of tumbling down and it finally did so, falling in a jumble of branches and canvases onto the head of the schoolmaster who had played such an important part in its ill-fated construction. As no one was hurt, this singular collapse was celebrated with laughter. The boys immediately grabbed the large placards which were about three spans in diameter, and after making a hole in the middle and putting their heads through it, strolled around with these Walloon or Flemish ruffs in front of Wellington.

Meanwhile, Don Carlos España disgorged his speech before the *lord*, and no sooner had he concluded than the schoolmaster presented himself with the ominous plan of speaking as well. The General consented, concealing his weariness with the utmost politeness, and listened to the pedantries of the orator, with nods of his head and with that special English smile which makes one believe in the existence of some intermandibular cord, which can be pulled to make the mouth fold like a curtain.

'Sir,' my orderly said to me joyfully after I had left the generals to see about my lodging. 'Has your Excellency seen the other army behind them?'

'It must be the Portuguese.'

'Portuguese my foot! They are women, an army of women. This is what I call living well. Instead of a baggage train the English take along a train of baggages. That's a nice way to wage war.'

I looked and saw twenty, what do I mean twenty? Forty, up to fifty wagons, coaches and vehicles of all sorts, all full of women. Some seemed to be upper-class, others lower-class, and of varying degrees of beauty and age, although in general, if truth be told, most were ugly. The moment the vehicles stopped amid clouds of dust you should have seen the travelling ladies get out with alacrity and heard one of the most discordant hullabaloos possible. On one side the women shrieked, calling out for their consorts, the latter in turn forced their way into the throng of femininity, shouting *Anna, Fanny, Matilda, Elizabeth*. Happy couples formed in an instant and the air was filled with a tumultuous concerto of guttural voices, sharp inflexions and flowing talk.

As it was not possible for the entire allied division which had just arrived to spend the night in that village, a section of it followed the road onwards to Aldehuela de Yeltes.[189] Many of the women got back into their carriages, forming part of the convoy of supplies and munitions, and the others remained in Sancti-Spíritus. The day passed, all of us being occupied in finding the best lodgings possible, but as we were so many, the question had not been solved by nightfall. As for me, I thought I would be obliged to sleep out in the open. Tribaldos informed me that the local schoolmaster would have the greatest pleasure in letting me have his room. After paying a visit to my worthy host, I went out to attend to various military duties and I was just going back to the house when I heard shouts and cries of alarm near the road. I ran towards where the sounds were coming from and there, approaching along the road ahead, was a small carriage whose horse was pulling it with so much jolting and leaping that it looked as if it would shatter into a thousand pieces at any moment. As it swept by us at breakneck speed, a woman's cry reached my ears.

'There's a woman in that coach, Tribaldos!' I shouted to my orderly who had joined me.

'It's an Englishwoman, sir, who's been left behind by the others.'

'Poor woman… and is there not even one among so many men brave enough to stop the horse and save that unfortunate woman? It seems it's slowing down… it's stopped… quickly, let's go over there.'

'The coach has come off the road,' said Tribaldos in dismay, 'and stopped in a very dangerous place.'

I saw in an instant that the coach was on the point of falling over a cliff. The horse had got entangled in some thickets and fallen, exhausted from the severe shock it had suffered. But because the slope was steep, gravity was pulling it towards the depths of the ravine.

It was impossible for me to see the terrible situation of the unfortunate traveller without immediately going to her help. The coach had fallen over, but had not broken up; the danger lay in its position. I ran towards it on my own, at every leap loosening stones, which rolled down with an ominous sound, and finally got to where the vehicle had stopped. A woman was calling pitifully from inside.

'Señora!' I shouted. 'I'm coming. Don't be alarmed. You won't fall into the ravine.'

The horse was kicking out as it struggled to get up and in its distress and desperation it was dragging the coach towards the abyss. A moment more and all would be lost.

I braced myself against a large rock and with both hands held back the leaning coach.

'Señora!' I shouted eagerly. 'Try to get out. Hold on round my neck... don't be afraid. If you can jump onto the ground, there's nothing to fear.'

'I can't, I can't, sir!' she cried in distress.

'Have you broken any bones?'

'No, sir... I'll see if I can get out.'

'Try your best... if we lose a moment both of us will fall over the edge.'

I cannot describe the prodigies of mechanics we both performed. The fact is that in such critical cases, the human body, through a marvellous instinct, stamps its limbs with a strength it does not have in ordinary times and performs a series of wonderful feats which cannot be recalled or repeated afterwards. All I know is that with God's help, and not without some risk to myself, I rescued the unknown woman from the grave predicament she was in and saw her safe on the ground. Making use of the stones, I held her up and I had no choice but to carry her in my arms to the road.

Miss Fly.

'Hey, Tribaldos, you lazy coward!' I shouted to my orderly who had come to my aid. 'Help me up out of here.'

Tribaldos and some other soldiers who had not given me any assistance up to then, helped me up; there are certain people whose character is never to come close to danger that threatens until the danger is overcome, something that makes for an easy and profitable life.

Once up on the road, the unknown woman took a few steps.

'Sir, I owe you my life,' she said recovering her lost colour and the brilliance of her eyes.

VII

She was about twenty-three years old, tall and slim. Her graceful bearing, her gentle voice, her beautiful face, the ceremonious way she addressed me,[190] no doubt due to her not knowing Spanish well, made a deep and lasting impression on me.

She leant on me and tried a few steps, but immediately her weak legs could not support her. Without a word, I picked her up in my arms and called to Tribaldos,

'Help me, we'll take her to our lodgings.'

Luckily, these were not far off and we were soon there. In the doorway, the Englishwoman turned her head, opened her eyes and said to me,

'I do not want to trouble you further, sir. I can go upstairs on my own. Give me your arm.'

At the same moment a hot and bothered English officer, called Sir Thomas Parr whom I knew from Cádiz, came up in a hurry. Once he had been briefly told about the unfortunate incident, he spoke in English with his compatriot.

'But is there a *comfortable* room here for the lady?' he then asked me.

'She can rest in my own room,' said the schoolmaster who had come down to help on hearing the noise.

'Very well,' said the Englishman. 'This young lady stayed in Ciudad Rodrigo longer than she should have and tried to catch up with us. Her rashness has already given us a lot of trouble. Let's get her upstairs. I will have the chief surgeon of the army come and see her.'

'I do not need any surgeons,' said the unknown woman. 'I am not badly hurt, just a slight bruise on the forehead and another on my left arm.'

She said this while going upstairs leaning on my arm. Once upstairs she sank into a chair in the first room and drew a long breath.

'I owe my life to this gentleman,' she said, pointing to me. 'It was a miraculous escape.'

'I am very glad to see you, my dear Señor Araceli,' the Englishman said to me. 'We haven't seen each other since last year. You remember me… from Cádiz?'

'I remember perfectly.'

'You went with Blake's expedition.[191] We did not see each other because you went into hiding after the duel in which you killed Lord Gray.'[192]

The Englishwoman looked at me with deep interest and curiosity.

'Is this the gentleman…?' she said.

'The same one I told you about a few days ago,' Parr answered.

'If only the libertine who brought misfortune to so many families in England and Spain had always run up against men like you… according to what I have heard, Lord Gray dared to look at someone who loved you… the energy, the severity and the nobility of your conduct have been superior to these times.'

'In order to fully understand that event,' I said, certainly with no great pride in what I had done, 'it would be necessary for me to explain some of the background…'

'I can assure you that before making your acquaintance, before you had rendered to me the service I have just received from you, I felt a great admiration for you.'

I then said all that modesty and courtesy required.

'So then, this lady is to lodge here?' Parr said to me. 'It is impossible where I am. There are seven of us sleeping in a single room.'

'I have said that I will give her mine, which is fit for Sir Arthur himself,' said Forfolleda, this being the schoolmaster's name.

'In that case, she will do very well here.'

Sir Thomas Parr spoke at some length in English with the lovely unknown woman and then left. It caused me no little surprise that her compatriots would abandon such a beautiful woman who no doubt had a husband or brothers in the army, but I said to myself, 'This must be the English custom for arranging these matters.'

Meanwhile, Forfolleda's wife (since Forfolleda had a wife) put a poultice onto the unknown woman's arm and staunched the blood from the graze she had suffered on her head. With this operation we considered that surgical care had been concluded and we turned our thoughts to tidying up the room and the bed in which the lady would spend the night.

A moment later the precious body of the English lady was resting on a bed slightly softer than a rock, to which I had had to take her in my arms, because she was overcome once more by that earlier fainting fit which had made all bodily movement impossible. She thanked me in silence, turning towards me her beautiful blue eyes which, sweetly and with that enchanting vagueness and wandering look that follows fainting fits, gazed

Forfolleda.

first at me and then at the walls of the room. The more I looked at her, she seemed to me to be more lovely with every instant. I can give no idea of the extreme beauty of her blue eyes. Every feature of her face was distinguished by the purest regularity and refinement. Her blonde hair was like the image of the golden tresses so much used by poets and her mouth was companion to the most delicate and whitest teeth that could be seen. Her body, tortured beneath the stays of a tight bodice, from which hung a riding skirt, was extremely slender, but did not lack the curves and elegant shapes and irregularities that distinguish a woman from a stick turned on a lathe.

'Thank you, sir,' she said to me in a melancholy voice and still using the ceremonial form of *you* to address me, 'If I did not fear to trouble you, I would ask you to give me something to eat.'

'Would the lady like a piece of leg of lamb?' said Forfolleda who was rearranging the furniture in the room. 'Some garlic soup, chocolate or perhaps a little *salmorejo*[193] with chili? I also have dried cod. They say that Sir Arthur is particularly fond of dried cod.'

'Thank you,' the Englishwoman replied bad-temperedly, 'I cannot eat that. May I have a little tea?'

I went to the kitchen where Forfolleda's wife told me that they didn't have any tea there nor anything like it, adding that if she tried just a drop of that mouth rinse of tripe, she would throw up along with her guts the first milk she had sucked. Then she began to reproach her husband for having admitted into the house Lutheran and Calvinist heretics, which is what the English were, but her husband victoriously refuted the attack, asserting that, thanks to the help of the Lutheran and Calvinist heretics, Catholic Spain would triumph over Napoleon, which meant nothing more than that God makes use of the bad to produce the good.

'Go off to one of the houses where there are English,' I said to Tribaldos, 'and bring some tea. Do you know what it is?'

'Some shrivelled-up black leaves. I know what it is... the captain's wife drank it

215

every evening.'

I returned to the side of the Englishwoman who told me that she couldn't eat any of our food, and having asked me for bread, I gave her some until the longed-for tea arrived.

After a short time Tribaldos came in carrying a wide cup that gave off a strange smell.

'What is this?' said the lady in dismay when the vapours of the damned liquid reached her nose.

'What is this concoction you have made up, you devil?' I exclaimed, threatening the confused fellow.

'Sir, I haven't made up anything, nothing more than the shrivelled leaves with a little cinnamon and some cloves. Señora Forfolleda said this was how you did it and she had done it this way many times for the English who went to Salamanca to see the old cathedral.'

The Englishwoman burst out laughing.

'Señora, please forgive this animal who does not know what he is doing. I myself will go to the kitchen and you will drink tea.'

Shortly afterwards, I returned with my handiwork, which must have satisfied the interested party, as she accepted it with pleasure.

'I will now withdraw, señora, so that you can rest,' I said to her. 'I am at your command tomorrow, or even tonight. If you want word sent to your husband… or perhaps he is in Picton's division[194] which is not in this village…'

'Sir,' she said, solemnly drinking her tea, 'I do not have a husband; I am unmarried.'

This put the finishing touch to my surprise, and hesitant at first in my thoughts, I could only stammer a few half-formed words in answer to her.

'A fine specimen this one, that's been hanging on my arm!' I said to myself. 'The French take women of doubtful virtue with them, but I didn't know that the English…'

'Unmarried, yes,' she added with aplomb and took the cup from her lips. 'You are astonished to see a young lady like me on a battlefield in a foreign land and away, far away from her family and her homeland. You must know that I came to Spain with my brother, an officer in the engineers in Hill's division[195] and who perished in the bloody Battle of Albuera.[196] Grief and despair made me ill and for a few days brought me close to death, but awareness of the duties I had to perform in that difficult situation revived me and I devoted myself to finding the body of the poor soldier for burial in England, in our family vault. It did not take me long to carry out this sad mission and, being on my own, I was about to return to my country. But I found myself at the same time so captivated by the history, traditions, customs, literature, art, ruins, popular music, dances, and costumes of this nation, so great in olden days and even greater again in present times, that I decided to stay here and study everything, and having obtained the permission of my parents, this is what I have done.'

'God only knows what kind of bird you are,' I said to myself, and then looking fixedly in her sky-blue eyes, I said out loud, 'And your parents consented, without reflecting on the continuous and grave danger to which a delicate girl on her own and without support is exposed in a foreign country, in the middle of an army! Señora, for the love of God...'

'Ah, you are no doubt unaware that we, the daughters of England, are protected by the law in such a way and with such rigour that no man dares to show us any discourtesy.'

'Yes, they say that is the case in England. I understand that over there young ladies go out alone to walk and travel alone or accompanied by some handsome young man.'

'It might even be their lover, it makes no difference.'

'But we are in Spain, señora, in Spain! You don't know what country you have got involved with.'

'But I am following the allied army and I am under the protection of English laws,' she said, smiling. 'Sir, if you were to forget your sense of decency and attempt to woo me in a less decorous way than that you followed in your love of the Dulcinea who was the cause of the death of Lord Gray, Lord Wellington would have you shot if you did not marry me.'

'I would marry you, señora.'

'Sir, I see that, perhaps without intending it, you are beginning to behave improperly.'

'Then I would not marry you... please permit me to withdraw.'

'You may do so,' she said to me, rising with difficulty to close the door from the inside.

'I will thank you to have my case brought in the morning. Happily, I do not take it with me. It is in the convoy.'

'The case will be brought. Goodnight, señora.'

VIII

Once I was outside the room I heard the sound of the bolts, which the beautiful Englishwoman drew inside and I retired to my lodging which was the corner of a dark corridor where Tribaldos had arranged a bed of blankets and greatcoats for me. I stretched out on these rough things but for a good part of the night I was unable to sleep, so much had the strange English lady intruded into my brain, with her fall, her fainting, her tea and her perfect beauty. But finally, overcome by great weariness, I slept peacefully. In the morning Forfolleda's wife told me that the young, blonde lady was better; she had asked for water, tea and bread, offering plenty of money for any service one might do for her. As I showed signs of going in to greet her, Señora Forfolleda added that it would not be convenient, as the young lady was getting ready and putting on make-up, despite the slight wounds to her arm.

When I went out to attend to my duties, which were very many and which occupied me for most of the day, I met Sir Thomas Parr, to whom I entrusted the matter of the case.

I returned to the Forfolledas' house in the evening, having worked so much during the day that I had almost forgotten the interesting lady, and I saw a large number of Englishmen going in and coming out, like faithful friends going to inquire about the health of their fellow countrywoman. I went in to pay my respects and the small room was full of red coats belonging to as many blond men talking merrily. The young Englishwoman was laughing and joking and had made herself so pretty, without a change of dress, that she did not seem the same ailing, melancholic and nervous person of the night before. The bruise on her arm slowed her gracious movements somewhat.

After we had greeted each other, and the gentlemen present and I had exchanged bows with distant courtesy, one of them invited the young woman to go out for a stroll; another one spoke warmly of the beauty of the peaceful evening and there was not one of them who did not say something to persuade her to leave her sad bedroom. She, however, declared that she would not go out until the next day and then, with one conversation after another during which she paid not the damnedest bit of notice to her rescuer, night came and with the night lamps were brought into the room and after the lamps the English servants brought in a couple of teapots. All faces then lit up with joy and the pouring out began with such eagerness that the one who drank the least must have swallowed a river of the liquor of China, all without the conversation stopping even for a moment. They then brought in bottles of sherry, which in a jiffy were left as dead men with no soul since they had passed on to fortify the souls of those illustrious men, although not one lost his dignity. We drank to England, to Spain and at about nine o'clock we all withdrew. The beautiful nymph affably bade us goodnight, without singling me out from the others by so much as a single word, gesture or glance.

I retired to my hiding place and heard the unknown woman draw the bolt. Persistent insomnia tormented me that night as on the previous one, but I was on the point of overcoming it when the squeaking of the bolt used to secure her room made me sit up in bed. I looked towards the door and saw the Englishwoman come out and walk to a gallery or sun lounge situated at the other end of the corridor and the house. As she had left the door open, the light from her room was sufficient to illuminate what was happening in the house.

She reached the dilapidated gallery, opened a window and looked out over the countryside. As I was dressed, it was easy for me to get up in a moment and walk towards her with a soft step so as not to startle her. When I was close, she turned to me and, to my great surprise, did not turn a hair at seeing me. On the contrary, with imperturbable calm, she said to me,

'Are you taking a walk around here? The heat in that room is intolerable.'

'It's the same in mine, señora,' I said. 'When I saw you, I was thinking I would go out into the country to breathe the cool night air.'

'I was thinking exactly the same... The night is beautiful... You were thinking of going out, then?'

'Yes, señora, but if you will allow me, I will have the honour of accompanying you and together we can enjoy these sweet surroundings, the pleasant aroma of those pine groves...'

'No... you leave, go on down, I'll come, too,' she said with lively determination and as if it was the most natural thing in the world.

Going quickly into her room to fetch a strangely shaped cloak and throwing it over her shoulders, she asked me to wrap it carefully around her as she had no movement in her wounded arm. Once I had covered her up well, we went out together, without her taking my arm, like two friends going out for a stroll. The sound of soldiers could be heard everywhere, and the bright moon made it possible to see everything and recognise people.

Suddenly, and without heeding some commonplace remark I had made, the Englishwoman said to me,

'I am sure you are a noble, sir. Which family do you belong to? The Pachecos, the Vargas, the Enríquez, the Acuñas, the Toledos or the Dávilas?'

'None of those, señora,' I replied, hiding with my cloak the smile I could not repress, 'but the Aracelis of Andalusia who are descended, as you are no doubt aware, from Hercules himself.'[197]

'From Hercules? No, I certainly did not know that,' she replied simply. 'Have you been on campaign for a long time?'

'From when it started, señora.'

'You are brave and generous, without doubt,' she said, looking fixedly at my face. 'It is easy to see in your countenance that there flows in your veins the blood of those famous noblemen who were the astonishment and envy of Europe over so many centuries.'

'Señora, you are too kind.'

'Tell me, can you fire arms, break in a colt, throw a bull to the ground, play the guitar and compose verses?'

'I cannot deny that I have a little ability in one, but not all, of those skills.'

After a short pause, she stopped and asked me brusquely,

'And are you in love?'

For a moment I did not know what to say, so strange did those words seem to me.

'How could I not be, being Spanish, young and a soldier?' I replied, deciding to let the conversation go wherever the fantasy of my unknown friend wanted to take it.

'I see that you are surprised at my manner of talking to you,' she added. 'Accustomed to hearing only mincing words, banalities and hypocritical phrases from the mouths of your prudish Spanish ladies, this freedom of expression of mine surprises you, these unusual questions I direct at you... perhaps you think badly of me...'

'Oh, no, señora.'

'But my honour does not depend on what you think. You would be a fool if you believed this were anything other than the curiosity of an Englishwoman, I might almost say, of an artist, of a traveller. The customs and characters of this country are worthy of profound study.'

'So, what she wants is to study me,' I muttered to myself. 'Let us resign ourselves to being a textbook.'

'The man who killed Lord Gray, who carried out that great masterstroke of justice, who was the arm of God and avenger of outraged morals, excites my curiosity to an extraordinary degree... People have spoken to me about you with admiration and told me about things you did which are worthy of great respect... Forgive my curiosity, which would shock a Spanish woman and no doubt shocks you... Having killed Gray out of jealousy, you must clearly be in love.'

'And your lady' (her use of '*your lady*' made me laugh again), 'does she live in a castle in the vicinity or in some palace in Andalusia? Is she noble like you?'

When I heard this, I realised that I had to contend with an excited and romantic imagination, and a spirit of mischief immediately took hold of me. I had no intention of making fun of the Englishwoman, who, despite her extraordinary sentimentality, was not ridiculous; but my nature prompted me to follow up the joke, so to speak, and lend myself to the fancies of that ideal, as enchanting as it was false. All of us have something of the poet in ourselves, and it is very sweet to embellish one's life even when knowing that the transformation is our own handiwork. So it was with a certain romantic passion, too, but not completely seriously, that I replied to the damsel,

'She is indeed noble, señora, and very beautiful and illustrious; but, what use is it to me if I have in her a model of perfection, when an evil destiny constantly separates me from her? What would you think, señora, if I tell you that sometime ago a wicked enchanter transformed her into a cheap and common actress who goes around villages as a member of a company of small-town players?'

This was, no doubt, going a bit far.

'Come now, sir,' the Englishwoman said in amazement, 'are there still enchantments in Spain?'

'Not exactly enchantments,' I said, trying to bring this flight down to earth, 'but there are devilish arts, or, if not devilish arts, the malicious tricks and wiles of wicked men.'

'I see that you read books of chivalry.'

'Well, who can doubt that they are the most beautiful books of all that have ever been written? They fill the mind with wonder, awaken sensibility, arouse valour, encourage enthusiasm for great deeds, extol glory and scorn fear in all moments of life.'[198]

'Extol glory and scorn fear!' she exclaimed and paused. 'If what you have said is true, you are worthy to have been born in other times... but I am still not sure I fully understand how your lady has been transformed into a common actress...'

'That's how it is, señora. If I could tell you everything that happened before this transformation, I have no doubt that you would pity me.'

'And where are the enchanted one and the enchanter? I give them these names because I see you believe in enchantments.'

'They are in Salamanca.'

'They might as well be in the other world. Salamanca is in the hands of the French.'

'But we will take it.'

'You say that as if it was the easiest thing in the world.'

'And it is. Do not laugh at my presumption, but if all the allied army had disappeared and I alone remained...'

'You would go and conquer the city on your own, you mean to say.'

'Ah, señora!' I exclaimed emphatically. 'A man in love does not know what he is saying. I can see it is absurd.'

'Relatively absurd,' she replied. 'But now I realise that you are making fun of me. You have fallen in love with an actress and want to have her pass as a grand lady.'

'When we enter Salamanca I will be able to convince you that I am not joking.'

'I do not doubt there are actors in the country, still less pretty actresses,' she said, laughing. 'Two days ago a company passed by me which reminded me of the cart of The Assembly of Death.[199] There were seven or eight actors and, in fact, they said they were going to Salamanca.'

'They had two or three carts. In one of them were two women, one of them very beautiful. They were coming from Plasencia.'

'I think so.'

'And in the other cart they were carrying some painted canvases.'

'You have seen them then, but you do not know what I know. When they passed by in front of me, surprising me with their strange appearance that reminded me of one of the most amusing adventures in the *Book*,[200] someone next to me from Puerto de Baños[201] said to me: 'Those are not actors but villainous freemasons who disguise themselves like that to go among Spaniards who would tear them apart if they knew who they were."

'You have told me nothing I do not already know,' I replied. 'Señora, have you heard it said when Lord Wellington will throw our troops upon Salamanca?'

'You are impatient... There is another thing I want to know. Do you love your Dulcinea in an ideal and sublime manner, making her more beautiful in your thoughts than she really is, attributing to her every sort of perfection you can imagine and dedicating to her all the sweet ecstasy of a heart always inflamed by love?'

'Absolutely, the same way, señora,' I said with an enthusiasm that was not entirely false, and wanting to see how far this mysterious woman would go and whose character I was beginning to grasp. 'It seems you can read my soul like a book.'

Once she heard this, she remained silent for a long time and then started the conversation again with a sudden change of subject, the third one in that strange talk.

'Sir, do you have a mother?' she said to me.

'No, señora.'

'Or sisters?'

'None either. No mother, no father, no brothers, no relatives at all.'

'I can see that the Hercules lineage is in a very poor state. So you are alone in the world,' she added compassionately. 'Unfortunate knight! And that grand lady, actress or freemason, does she love you?'

'I think so.'

'And have you made sacrifices for her, faced dangers and overcome obstacles?'

'Very many, but they are nothing compared to what I still have to do.'

'What is that?'

'A dangerous action, an act of madness; the ultimate in daring. I expect to die or achieve my objective.'

'Are you afraid of the dangers that await you?'

'I have never known fear,' I replied with a conceit, whose memory has made me laugh many times.

'There's no need to worry, as the allies will enter Salamanca, and then you can easily…'

'By the time the allies enter it, my enemy and his victim will have fled towards France. He is no fool... I must go to Salamanca before then...'

'Before it is taken!' she exclaimed in amazement.

'Why not?'

'Sir,' she said, suddenly stopping. 'I can see that you are making fun of me.'

'Me, señora!' I replied somewhat alarmed.

'Yes, you describe to me a chivalric adventure which is pure invention and fable. You paint yourself as a superior character, like one of those spirits who become exalted by danger and you have adorned your tales with beautiful figures of Dulcinea and enchanters who do not exist except in your imagination.'

'My dear señora, you...'

'Have the goodness to accompany me to my lodging. The smell of these pine trees is making me feel sick.'

'As you wish.'

I confess, and why not confess it, that I felt somewhat abashed.

The elegant Englishwoman did not say a further word to me all the way back, and when we went into the Forfolledas' house and I took her to her room, which I was already beginning to picture to myself as a royal boudoir, hung with satins and organdies, she shut herself into her poky little room, like a fairy in her cave, and, sharply wishing me goodnight, she drew the bolts of gold... or iron, and I was left alone.

Gabriel.

IX

Settling down in my bed, I spoke to myself as follows:

'Could this Englishwoman be one of those women of doubtful virtue who are wont to follow armies? They do come in different types, but in reality I have never seen one in the train of soldiers of any country who is so beautiful or of such a noble and aristocratic bearing. I have heard that there are birds of a different plumage following the French Army. Bah! Don't they say that Masséna had such bad luck in Portugal because of the corruption of his officers and soldiers, and even more because of his own mistakes with some dolled-up amazons who went around the camps as much at their ease as in Paris?...'[202]

Then, with my thoughts turning in another direction, at the point when the sweet drowsiness that precedes sleep was beginning to overpower me, I said,

'Perhaps I am wrong. Having known Lord Gray, I am in no doubt that the peculiarities and eccentricities of the English are practically limitless. Perhaps my fellow guest is as proper as virginity itself would seem at the side of a prostitute, and I am insulting her. Tomorrow I will ask the English officers I know… might she not be one of those impressionable and passionate natures who are born by chance in the North and who, like swallows, seek out warmer climes and land, full of anxiety, in the South, demanding light, sun, passion, poetry, food for the heart and imagination which they do not always find, or only partly find. With frantic desire they chase after originality, after strange customs and adore impassioned characters, even though they are almost savages; they seek out a life of adventure, chivalric gallantry, ruins, legends, popular music and even the swear words of the common people as long as they are witty.'

Talking or thinking in this way and entwining these with other thoughts that preoccupied me more deeply, I fell into the most profound and restorative sleep. I got up very early the following morning, and without giving a thought to the beautiful Englishwoman, as if the night had swept away all the cobwebs constructed and spread out the day before in my brain, I left my lodgings.

'We are marching towards San Muñoz,'[203] said Figueroa, a Portuguese officer who was a friend of mine serving with General Picton.

'And the *lord*?'

'He's going, but I don't know where. Graham's division is above Tamames.[204] We are going to form the left wing of Carlos España's division and the *partida*[205] of Julián Sánchez.'

As we were walking together to the general's lodging, I asked him about the English lady whose character and strange ways I have set out and he replied,

'She is Miss Fly, or, which is the same thing, Miss Warbler, Butterfly, Little Bird or something like that. Her name is Athenais. Her father is Lord Fly, one of the most important nobles in Great Britain. She has been following us since Albuera,[206] painting churches, castles and ruins in some big book she carries around with her and writing down everything that happens. The *lord* and the other English generals hold her in high esteem, and if you want to get something good and proper, just dare to show any lack of respect to Miss Fly. And in English they say 'Flai', since as you know in that language they write words in one way and then pronounce them in another, which is a delight for anyone wanting to learn it.'

I then told my friend about the events of the previous night and the walk in the solitude of the night that Miss Fly and I took in the neighbourhood, which, when he heard about it, caused Figueroa much surprise.

'It's the first time,' he said, 'that the young blonde has been so familiar with a Spanish or Portuguese officer, since up to now she has regarded all of them with disdain…'

'I took her as being a person of somewhat free and easy ways.'

'One might do so, as she goes by herself, rides horseback, passes in and out of the army, speaks with everyone, visits the positions of the vanguard before a battle and the bloody hospitals afterwards… sometimes she takes herself away from the army to roam about nearby villages on her own, particularly if they have abbeys, cathedrals or castles, and in her spare time she does nothing but read old Spanish ballads.'

Speaking about this and other matters, we passed the morning and at around midday we went to the lodgings of Carlos España, who was not there.

'España,' the guerrilla Sánchez told us, 'is at headquarters.'

'Isn't Lord Wellington going?'

'It appears he is staying here, but we are leaving for San Muñoz in an hour.'

'Let's go to the duke's lodgings,' said Figueroa. 'We'll get some definite information there.'

Lord Wellington was in the town hall, the only building sufficiently large and decent for such a distinguished person. The small square, the portico, the entrance hall and the staircase were filled by a multitude of officers of every rank, Spanish, English and Portuguese, who were going in and coming out, forming small groups, debating and joking with each other in friendly intimacy as if everyone belonged to the same family. Figueroa and I went in, and after a wait of over an hour and a half in the anteroom, España came out and said to us,

'The commander-in-chief is asking whether there is a Spanish officer who dares to enter Salamanca in disguise to inspect the strong points and temporary works the enemy has done on the walls, observe the artillery and find out whether the garrison is large or small, and the supplies plentiful or scarce.'

'I will go,' I said boldly without waiting for the general to finish.

'You,' said España with that scornful familiarity he used when speaking to his officers. 'You dare to undertake such a risky mission? Bear in mind that you have to go and come back.'

'I assume that is the case.'

'It will be necessary to cross the enemy lines and the French occupy all the villages this side of the Tormes.'

'I will get in the best way I can, General.'

'Then you will have to cross the walls, the strong points, penetrate the city, visit the cantonments, draw up plans…'

'All that is just child's play for me, General. Going in, getting out, observing…

a mere diversion. If your Excellency would do me the favour of presenting me to the duke, informing him that I await his orders whatever they are.'

'You are a scatterbrain and won't do at all,' Don Carlos replied. 'We'll find someone else. You don't know a thing about geometry or fortification.'

'I would not be so sure about that,' I answered, getting angry.

'Well, someone has to go, someone has to,' my superior added. 'The lord has still not made his plan for battle. He has not decided whether to assault Salamanca or to blockade it; he has not decided whether he will cross the Tormes and pursue Marmont, leaving Salamanca in the rear, or whether… You say that you are ready to go?'

'Why would I not be? I will dress as a peasant, go into Salamanca selling vegetables or coal. I will observe the strong points, the garrison, the provisions; I will draw up a sketch and return to the camp… General,' I added with passion, 'either your Excellency will present me to the duke, or I will present myself.'

'All right, come on, come on right now,' España said, leading me into the room.

Next to a table placed in the middle was the Duke of Ciudad Rodrigo with three other generals examining a map of the country and so absorbed were they in the lines, points and letters with which the geographer had delineated the ruggedness of the terrain that they did not raise their heads to look at us. Don Carlos España motioned to me that we would have to wait, and in the meantime, as was my custom, I looked around the room to investigate where I was. Other officers were speaking in low voices away from the centre, and among them, to my surprise, was Miss Fly, having a lively conversation with a colonel in the Artillery called Simpson.

Finally, Lord Wellington lifted his eyes from the map and looked at us. He bowed affably and then the Englishman looked at me closely, from head to toe. I in turn observed him at my ease, delighted to have before me a person so beloved then by all Spaniards, and who so inspired my admiration. Wellesley was quite tall, with blond hair and a ruddy complexion, although not for the reasons to which the common herd attributes the reddened skin of the English. One knows of course that it is proverbial in England that the only great man who has never lost his dignity after dessert is the conqueror of Tipoo Sahib[207] and Bonaparte.

Lord Wellington.

X

Wellington looked forty-five years old, and this was his age, exactly the same as Napoleon, both being born in 1769, one in May and the other in August. The sun of India and Spain had changed the paleness of his Saxon colouring. His nose, as I have already said, was long and slightly reddish; his forehead, sheltered from the rays of the sun by his hat, had kept its whiteness and was handsome and serene like that of a Greek statue, suggesting a mind never excited or febrile, a well-controlled imagination and a great power of reflection and calculation. A tuft of hair or a toupee adorned his head, certainly not something seen on Greek statues, but which did not look too bad in its role at the apex of the crown of an English head. The general's large blue eyes had a cold gaze, vaguely resting on the object under observation, and observing without apparent interest. His voice was sonorous, measured, moderate, unchanging in tone and without any irritation or harsh accents, and his whole manner of expressing himself, with gesture, voice and eyes, produced a gratifying impression of respect and affection.

His Excellency observed me, as I have said, and then Don Carlos España said,

'General, this young man wishes to carry out the mission that your Excellency spoke to me about just now. I will answer for his bravery and loyalty, but I have tried to dissuade him from his undertaking as he does not have the necessary knowledge.'

This statement embarrassed me, mainly because Miss Fly was present and because, in actual fact, I had not studied at any military academy.

'For this commission,' said Wellington in fairly good Spanish, 'a certain amount of technical knowledge is necessary.'

His eyes were fixed once more on the map. I looked at España and España looked at me. But humiliated as I was, I nevertheless made a sudden resolution and without commending myself to God or the Devil, I said,

'General. It is true that I have not attended any academy, but long experience in war, in battles and above all in sieges, has perhaps given me the knowledge that your Excellency requires for this commission. I know how to draw up a plan.'

The Duke of Ciudad Rodrigo, raising his eyes once more, said,

'There are many professional officers on my staff, but no Englishman could go into Salamanca, as he would immediately be discovered by his face and his language. It is necessary that a Spaniard goes.'

'General,' España said fatuously, 'there is no lack of professional officers in my division. I brought in this man because he insisted on parading his fearlessness before your Excellency.'

I gave an indignant glance at Don Carlos, then exclaimed, with great vehemence,

'General, even though this enterprise is full of dangers, and all the difficulties imaginable, I will enter Salamanca and return with the information your Excellency may desire!'

With the utmost calmness Lord Wellington asked me,

'Officer, where did you begin your military career?'

'At Trafalgar,' I replied.

When this historic and glorious word was heard in the general silence in the room, the heads of everyone present turned as if they belonged to a single body and all eyes were fixed on me with the keenest interest.

'So you have been a sailor?' inquired the duke.

'I was fourteen years old when I was in the battle. I was a friend of an officer on board the *Trinidad*. The losses in the crew obliged me to take part in the battle.'

'And when did you start to serve in the campaign against the French?'

'On 2nd May 1808, General. The French shot me at the Moncloa. I escaped by a miracle, but my body carries the marks of the horrors of that day.'[208]

'And then did you enlist?'

'I enlisted in the regiment of Andalusian volunteers, and I was in the Battle of Bailén.'[209]

'In the Battle of Bailén as well!' said Wellington in astonishment.

'Yes, General, on 19th July 1808. Would your Excellency care to see my record of service, which starts on that date?'

'No, I am satisfied,' Wellington replied. 'And then?'

'I returned to Madrid and took part in the engagement of 3rd December.[210] I was

D. Carlos España.

taken prisoner and they were going to take me to France.'

'Did they take you to France?'

'No, General, as I escaped in Lerma, and ended up in Zaragoza, happily in time to catch the second siege of that immortal city.'

'For the whole siege?' said Wellington with growing interest in me.

'All of it, from 19th December until 12th February 1809. I can give your Excellency detailed information about all the vicissitudes of that great feat of arms, the glory and pride of so many of us who were there.'[211]

'And then which army did you join?'

'The Centre, and I served quite some time under the orders of the Duque de Parque.[212] I was in the Battle of Tamames and in Extremadura.'

'Were you in any other siege?'

'The siege of Cádiz, General. For three days I defended the castle of San Lorenzo de Puntales.'[213]

'And then you must have been in General Blake's expedition to Valencia?'

'Yes, General, but they assigned me to the second corps commanded by O'Donnell and for four months I served under *El Empecinado* in that guerrilla warfare in which one learns so much.'

'So you have been a guerrilla as well?' said Wellington, smiling. 'I see you have fully earned your promotions. You will go to Salamanca if that is what you want.'

'General, I dearly want to.'

Everyone there was still observing me closely, none more so than Miss Fly.

'Very well,' added the hero of Talavera,[214] fixing his gaze alternately on me and the map. 'You are to do as follows: you will make your way in disguise this very day to Salamanca, making a circuit to enter by Cabrerizos. This will inevitably mean you have to pass through Marmont's troops who are guarding the roads from Ledesma and Toro. There is a strong possibility that you will be shot as a spy; but God protects the brave and perhaps… perhaps you will succeed in entering the city. Once inside you will draw a sketch of the fortifications, paying great attention to the monasteries which have been converted into strong points, the buildings that have been demolished, the artillery that defends the approaches to the city, the state of the walls, the earthworks and fascines, absolutely everything, without forgetting the supplies the enemy has in stores.'

'General,' I replied, 'I understand what is wanted and I hope to satisfy your Excellency. When must I leave?'

'At once. We are twelve leagues from Salamanca. After the march which we will make today, I hope that we shall be spending the night at Castroverde, close to Valmuza. But by going ahead on horseback you can get into the city the day after tomorrow, Tuesday. During the whole of Tuesday you will have to complete this mission, leaving on Wednesday morning so as to reach headquarters, which will certainly be in Bernuy on that day. So, I will expect you at noon precisely on Wednesday. I am not accustomed to waiting.'

'Understood and accepted, General. At noon on Wednesday I shall be in Bernuy on my return from the expedition.'

'Take all precautions. Make your way to the Ledesma highway, but taking care always to go away from the roadway. Disguise yourself well, as the French let villagers carrying supplies enter the city, and when doing your sketches avoid people watching you as much as possible. Take arms but hide them well. Do not provoke any of the enemy, pretend you are friendly with them, in a word, bring into play all your talent, your bravery and all the knowledge of men and war that you have acquired over so many years of active military service. The quartermaster will provide you with the money you need for the expedition.'

'General,' I said, 'does your Excellency have any further command for me?'

'Nothing more,' he replied with a kind smile, 'except that I worship punctuality and consider that the careful calculation and distribution of time is the origin of success in war.'

'Which means that if I have not returned by noon on Wednesday I will displease your Excellency.'

'Very much so. You can do what I have entrusted to you within the time assigned.

Two hours to do the sketch, two to visit the strong points, under the guise of selling things to the soldiers, four for going round the whole town and taking note of the demolished buildings, two for overcoming unforeseen obstacles, half an hour for resting. That makes ten and a half hours during daylight on Tuesday. The first half of the night is for studying the spirit of the city, what the garrison and the inhabitants think of this campaign, an hour to sleep and the rest of the night for leaving and getting out of reach and sight of the enemy. If you do not delay in any way you can report to me in Bernuy at the appointed time.'

'I am at your orders, General,' I said, preparing to withdraw.

Lord Wellington, the greatest man of Great Britain, the rival of Bonaparte, the hope of Europe, the victor of Talavera, Albuera, Arroyo Molinos[215] and Ciudad Rodrigo, got up from his chair, and with grave courtesy and cordiality, which filled my soul with pride and happiness, gave me his hand, which I shook with gratitude.

I left to prepare for my journey.

An hour later I was in the house of some farm labourers bargaining for the clothes I had to wear, when I felt a light tap on my shoulder, produced, it seemed, by a whip held by delicate hands. I turned and Miss Fly, for it was none other than she who had struck me, said,

'Sir, I have been looking for you for an hour.'

'Señora, the preparations for my journey have prevented me from placing myself at your orders.'

Miss Fly did not hear my last words as all her attention was fixed on a peasant woman who was there and who, for her part, while suckling a new baby, did not take her eyes off the Englishwoman.

'Señora,' said the latter, 'could you provide me with some clothing like that you are wearing?'

The peasant woman did not understand the Englishwoman's imperfect Spanish, and continued looking at her, absorbed, and made no reply.

'Señorita Fly,' I said, 'are you going to dress up as a peasant woman?'

'Yes,' she replied, smiling mischievously. 'I want to go with you.'

'With me!' I exclaimed in utter surprise.

'With you, yes. I want to go in disguise with you to Salamanca,' she added calmly, taking some coins out of her purse so that the peasant woman would understand her better.

'Señora, I can only believe you must have gone mad,' I said. 'Go with me to Salamanca, go with me on this risky expedition, from which no one knows if I will come back alive?'

'And why not? Can I not go because there is danger? Sir, what makes you think that I am acquainted with fear?'

'It is impossible, señora, simply impossible for you to accompany me,' I stated emphatically.

'Well, I did not think you would be so rude. You are one of those who reject everything outside the ordinary limits of life. Can you not understand that a woman has sufficient courage to confront danger and to perform difficult services in a holy cause?'

'On the contrary, señora, I understand that a woman like you is capable of wonderful exploits and at this moment Miss Fly inspires in me the greatest admiration; but the commission which takes me to Salamanca is very delicate and requires that no one goes at my side, least of all a lady who cannot disguise herself and conceal her foreign speech and noble bearing.'

'Why can't I disguise myself?'

'Well, señora,' I said, unable to restrain a smile, 'you can start by taking off your riding habit and putting on this full skirt, in other words, a long piece of cloth which you wrap around the body like swaddling-clothes on a child.'

Miss Fly looked at the strange and picturesque clothing of the peasant woman with amazement.

'Then,' I added, 'loosen those beautiful golden tresses and tie them at the top of your head into a topknot with ribbons hanging from it, and at the temples make your curls into two wagon wheels with silver hairpins. Next fasten the velvet bodice around your waist, and then cover your beautiful shoulders with that most graceful garment, but most difficult to wear, the *dengue* or *rebociño*.'[216]

Athenais looked displeased as she watched the peasant woman take these singular garments out of a chest.

'And then you must wear little shoes over openwork silk stockings, put on the black goat hair jacket edged with sequins and, the final stone of this handsome edifice, the semicircular mantilla worn over the shoulders.'

Miss Butterfly looked at me with indignation, having realised the impossibility of disguising herself as a peasant woman.

'Well,' she declared, looking scornfully at me, 'I shall go without disguise. In reality I do not need to since I know Colonel Desmarets who will let me enter. I saved his life at Albuera… and don't you think that my acquaintance with Colonel Desmarets could be useful to you…'

'Señora,' I said, becoming serious, 'the honour you give me and the pleasure I feel at being accompanied by you are so great that I do not know how to express them. But I am not going to a party, señora, I am going into danger. Besides, if this does not scare a person such as you, does the harm that may be caused to the reputation of a noble lady from travelling with an unknown man over rough tracks and wild places mean nothing?'

'A poor idea of honour you have, sir,' she said with pride and disdain. 'Either your deeds are a lie, or your thoughts are very much inferior to them. For God's sake, don't drag yourself down to the level of the common herd, or you will make me hate you. I shall go with you to Salamanca.'

Having decided not to answer my reasonable objections, she went to headquarters, while I went in the direction of my lodgings to transform myself from an officer in the army into the most rustic peasant ever seen in the Salamancan countryside.

With my tight breeches of dark grey cloth, my black stockings and leather shoes; with my chequered waistcoat, my jerkin with a small skirt at the waist and slashed at the inner angle of the elbow, and the hat with broad wings and ribbons hanging down which I fitted onto my head, I looked a treat. My outfit was completed for now by a wallet which I sewed into the inside of the jerkin with what was needed to draw a few lines and, the heart of the expedition, in other words the money, which I put into an inside pouch on my belt.

XI

'Well, then, señor Araceli, you're off on your campaign now,' I said to myself. 'On Wednesday at noon I have to return to Bernuy... a fine little adventure I've got myself into! If that Englishwoman achieves her objective of accompanying me, I am a lost man... but I will resist with all my strength and if she doesn't listen to reason I will report this caprice of his bold countrywoman to the commander-in-chief so that he can clip the wings of this roving and headstrong sylph.'

I was not so immodest as to suppose that Athenais was driven purely by some fancy or affection for me personally. But still believing myself unworthy of affectionate persecution by a beautiful lady, I resolved to put into practice an effective means to free myself from that annoying, although adorable and tempting, distraction. So, craftily and without a word to anyone, like Don Quixote on his first outing, I hurried away from Sancti-Spíritus ahead of the vanguard of the army, which at that moment was beginning to depart for San Muñoz.

But, dear readers, imagine my surprise when shortly after having left, spurring on my mount whose pace was like that of Rocinante,[217] I heard behind me the squeal of rough wheels, the galloping of a steed and the crack of a whip, accompanied by strange sounds as used in every language to buck up a lazy brute! Imagine my surprise when I turned round and saw Miss Fly herself in an indescribable little carriage, as decrepit and old as the one of the famous disaster, which she was driving herself, accompanied by a boy from Sancti-Spíritus.

When she drew up alongside me, the Englishwoman gave a shout of triumph. Her face was excited and wreathed in smiles, like someone who has won a prize in a race, her eyes shone with the bright light of unbounded delight; stray locks of her golden hair floated in the wind, giving her the unreal look of some sort of flying goddess of the type that runs round the friezes of classical architecture and her hand waved the whip with as much dash as a centaur his lethal dart. If I may use words which I do not think properly apply to the human form, but which are commonly used in descriptions, I

would say that she was *radiant*.

'I have caught up with you,' she exclaimed in great triumph. 'If Mrs. Mitchell had not lent me her wreck of a carriage, I would have come on a gun carriage, Señor Araceli.'

And when I once more explained to her the difficulties caused by her decision, she said to me,

'What great pleasure this gives me! This is the life for me: freedom, independence, enterprise, daring. We will go to Salamanca… I suspect you have something more to do there in addition to Lord Wellington's commission… but your affairs do not concern me. Sir, you should know that I despise you.'

'And what have I done to deserve that?' I said, slowing my mount's pace to that of her horse and slackening off, which pleased both animals greatly.

'What? Calling this plan of mine crazy. Men have no other word to express our inclination for unknown impressions, for grand themes that the soul has glimpsed without being able to state them precisely, for fanciful forms with which chance seduces us, for sweet emotions produced by anticipated danger and wished-for success.'

'I understand completely the greatness of your vigorous spirit, but what is there to be found in Salamanca that would justify the exercise of such notable talents? I am going as a spy, and there is nothing sublime about spying.'

'Do you expect me to believe,' she said mischievously, 'that you are going to Salamanca on Lord Wellington's commission?'

'Certainly.'

'One does not ask to serve one's country with such eagerness. Remember what you told me about the person you are in love with, the one who is imprisoned, enchanted or possessed by the Devil (which is what you said), who is in the city we are going to.'

A smile rose to my lips, but I suppressed it, saying, 'It's true, but perhaps there won't be enough time for me to be concerned with my own affairs.'

'On the contrary,' she said with great amusement. 'You will be concerned with nothing else. Might one know, Señor Araceli, who is a certain countess that writes to you from Madrid?'

'How do you know?' I asked in amazement.

'Because shortly before I left Forfolleda's house, an officer arrived with a letter he had received for you. I looked at the outside and saw a coat of arms with a crown. Your orderly said, 'Now we have another little letter from my lady the countess.''

'And I left without getting that letter!' I exclaimed, annoyed. 'I will return immediately to Sancti-Spíritus.'

But Miss Fly detained me with a charming gesture, saying with inimitable gracefulness,

'Do not be so impetuous, young soldier. Here is your letter.'

She then gave it to me and I opened it immediately and read it. In it the countess simply told me, apart from some pleasant things and flattering words, that she had just learnt through Marchena that our enemy was preparing to leave Plasencia for Salamanca.

'It seems that it has some important news for you, judging by how much you are reflecting on it,' Athenais said to me.

'It does not tell me anything I do not already know. The unfortunate mother, overwhelmed with grief and impatience, ceaselessly urges me to restore to her the treasure that has been taken from her.'

'That letter is from the mother of the enchanted girl,' said Miss Butterfly in disbelief. 'You invent some very fine stories, sir, but they will not fool shrewd people like me.'

I glanced quickly through the letter, and having assured myself that it did not contain anything that should not be disclosed to strangers, given that the countess herself had made public the secret that she was the unfortunate mother, I gave it to Miss Fly to read. She, with intense curiosity, read it in a moment, repeatedly raising her eyes from the paper to fix them onto me and accompanying her reading by expressions of tenderness and questions.

'I know this signature,' she said first. 'The Countess of ***. I got to know her in el Puerto de Santa María.'[218]

'In January '10, Señora.'

'Exactly... and she says you are her guardian angel, that her happiness depends on you... that she owes her life to you...that she would exchange all the honours of her house for your bravery, for the nobility of your heart and the honesty of your fine sentiments.'

'Is that what she says? I only read what was important.'

'And also that she has complete confidence in you, because she believes you will succeed in the great enterprise that you are undertaking... that Inés (so her name is Inés, then?), for all her beauty and worth, seems a poor reward for your constancy...'

Miss Fly returned the letter to me. She was inflamed by a sweet confusion, I would almost say an ecstatic enthusiasm, and her sparkling fantasy, suddenly awakened with dashing strength, no doubt magnified the adventure I had before me to fabulous limits.

'Sir!' she exclaimed without hiding the great and magnificent exaltation in her poetic soul. 'This is most splendid, so splendid that it hardly appears real. What I suspected and is now completely revealed to me is as beautiful as any invention of the novels and ballads. So then you will be going to Salamanca to attempt...'

'The impossible.'

'Better to say two impossibles,' Athenais declared excitedly, 'because the commission from Wellington... Such a sublime event, such incomparable bravery, señor Araceli! Colonel Simpson said a short time ago that the chances of you being shot were ninety-nine to one.'

'God will protect me, señora.'

'Certainly. If there were not men like you in the world, there would be no history, or it would be very boring. God will protect you. You are behaving very nobly... I approve of your conduct. I will help you.'

'Do you still insist on that?'

'An extraordinary occurrence!' she said, ignoring my question. 'And how it seduces and captivates me! It's in Spain, only in Spain, that one can find something like this which inflames the heart, inspires fantasy and gives life the allure of passion that it needs. A young woman abducted, a faithful knight who, scorning all dangers, goes in her pursuit and with a brave spirit penetrates into the enemy city and with only the valour of his heart and the stratagems of his wits, aspires to snatch the subject of his love from the barbarous hands that hold her prisoner... oh, what a lovely adventure! What a delightful ballad!'

'Are you fond of adventures and ballads,[219] señora?'

'Am I fond of them? I am enchanted by them, I love them, I am captivated by them more than by all the books that the geniuses of the world have ever written,' she replied enthusiastically. 'Ballads! Is there nothing more beautiful, or that speaks to our souls with such sweet and magnificent eloquence? I have read and know them all, the Moorish ones, the historical ones, the tales of chivalry, the love stories, the tales of devotion, the popular ones, those about captives and those sentenced to the galleys and the satirical ones. I read them passionately and I have translated many of them into English, in verse or in prose.'

'Ah, my dear lady and worthy scholar!' I said, confirming to myself that Miss Fly's psychological affliction was an obsession with literature. 'How much is owed to you by Spanish letters!'

'I read them passionately,' she continued without taking any notice of me, 'but, alas, I search for them in real life but I can never find them, never.'

'Of course, because those days have gone, and there are no more Lindarajas, or Tarfes, or Bravonels, or Melisendra'[220] I stated, acknowledging that I had been mistaken in my previous opinion about the Little Bird's affliction. 'But have you really been intent on finding the ballads in real life? For example, those Moorish maidens dressed in green who lean through silver grilles to say farewell to their gallants as they left for war, those young men who entered the arena with their ribbons of yellow or purple, those bearded kings of Jaén or Antequera who...'

'Sir,' she said seriously, interrupting me. 'Have you read the ballads of Bernardo del Carpio?'

'Señora,' I replied, bewildered. 'I must confess my ignorance. I do not know them. I think I have heard them being hawked for sale by the blind, but I never bought any. I have not paid much attention to my education, Miss Fly.'

'Well, I know them all by heart, from

> *In the Kingdoms of León*
> *Alfonso the fifth reigned*
> *He had a beautiful sister*
> *Doña Jimena she was called*

to the death of the hero, where it says

> *At the foot of a black tumulus*
> *There lies Bernardo del Carpio.*

Incomparable poetry! Nothing better has been written since the Iliad. Well, then. You must know even by hearsay about the ballad in which *Bernardo frees from the Moors his lover Estela, and Carpio whom they surrounded?*'

'It must be good.'

'It seems that the olden days return,' said Miss Fly with an expression of unfathomable vagueness, like the look of a prophetess. 'It seems that men emerge from their tombs, taking on their previous forms, or it is time and the world taking a step backwards to ease their sadness, reviving for a moment their marvellous deeds... Nature, bored with the vulgarity of the present day, adorns herself with the finery of her youth, like an old woman who no longer wishes to be one... History draws back, tired of doing foolish things, and with childish enthusiasm leafs through the pages of her own diary and then looks for the sword in the box of forgotten and noble toys... But don't you see this, Araceli, don't you see this?'

'Señora, what is it you want me to see?'

'The ballad of Bernardo and the beautiful Estela, which for the second time...'

On saying this, the horse, which was wearily dragging along the decrepit carriage of the poetic Athenais, began to limp, no doubt because, unlike History, it could not bring the sprightly robustness and agility of its youth to life again. But the Englishwoman paid no attention to this and with the utmost seriousness continued. 'Also to the point is the ballad of Don Galván, which has not been written down, but which can be collected from the  common people as I have done. In it, however, Don Galván would not have been able to rescue the princess from the tower without the help of a fairy or an unknown woman who appeared before him…'

Then the horse, which could stand it no more, stumbled and fell to its knees.

'My dearest fairy, here you have the reality of life,' I said to her. 'This horse cannot carry on.'

'What?!' the Englishwoman exclaimed angrily. 'It will go on. If not, harness yours to the carriage and we will go in it together.'

'Impossible, señora, impossible.'

'What a pity! Mrs. Mitchell was right to tell me this animal was good for nothing. But I thought, though, it was fit to draw Phaeton's chariot.'

We got the animal up and it took a few paces before falling again after a short distance.

'Impossible, impossible,' I exclaimed. 'Señora, I shall be compelled, much to my sorrow, to leave you.'

'Leave me!' said the Englishwoman.

In her beautiful eyes there was a flash of that imperious anger which the poets attribute to the goddesses of antiquity.

'Yes, señora, I am very sorry. Night is falling. It is ten leagues from here to Salamanca and by noon on Wednesday I have to be back in Bernuy. I need say no more.'

'Very well, sir,' she said, her lips trembling and with a bitter reproach in her glance. 'Proceed. I have not the slightest need of you.'

'Duty forbids me to remain an hour longer,' I said, turning to mount my horse, and then, with the assistance of the village boy, I got Miss Fly's horse back on its feet. 'The allied army will not delay. Ah, there they are already! The vanguard is appearing on that hill… Simpson is in command of them, your friend Colonel Simpson… Therefore, with your permission… do not say, my dear señora, that I am leaving you on your own… here comes a rider. It is Simpson himself.'

Miss Fly looked back in despair and sadness.

'Goodbye, my fair señora,' I cried, spurring my horse. 'I cannot stay. If I live, I will tell you what happened to me.'

Driven by my duty, I left at full speed.

XII

I kept going that afternoon and for part of the night, and after a few hours' sleep in Castrejón, I left the horse there. Having acquired a large amount of vegetables, together with the skinniest and saddest of donkeys, I had something to eat and took up my journey again along a path which led directly, so I was told, to the Vitigudino road.

Ciperez.

I reached this at noon on Monday, but left it once I had recognised it and, using shortcuts and rough tracks, I reached the Tormes, which I crossed to take the Ledesma road into the village of Villamayor. From various peasants whom I met in an inn playing *calva*[221] and pitch-and-toss I learnt that the French were not letting anyone enter without a safe conduct issued by them, and that they even stopped pedlars in the city from going where they could see the forts.

'I haven't got any desire to go back to Salamanca, my lad,' said the well-built and stout peasant who gave me this gratifying information having invited me to have a drink with him at the door of the inn.

'It's only by a miracle of God and the Holy Virgin that Señor Baltasar Cipérez – in other words me – is alive.'

'Why is that?'

'Because… I'll tell you. As you know, they have ordered all the inhabitants of these villages to go and work on the fortifications. Places that don't send any of their people are punished by being sacked and sometimes by being put to the sword… It's well said that the Devil is cunning. What happens is that while the villagers are working, the soldiers are peaceful, chatting and smoking, but at intervals sergeants come along with whips in their hands, keeping their eyes sharply open for anyone who relaxes or looks up to the sky or talks with his neighbour… It's a true saying that the Devil never sleeps and meddles in everything… and the moment you are a bit careless… smack!'

'They get the measure of your shoulders.'

'I am hot-blooded,' Cipérez continued, 'and I do not consider I was born to be a slave. I am a rich man of the village, I am used to giving orders and not to be given whippings. You can't teach an old dog… so when that Lucifer started on me…'

'If I was being whipped, I would do the same.'

'I shut my eyes, my blood was up and I went at them all, because… Baltasar Cipérez whipped by a Frenchman! I was throwing punches everywhere… if you can't hit the donkey, you hit the pack. Well, we had a right old ding-dong for quarter of an hour… look at the results.'

The rich peasant, opening his loose coat, worn inside out, as was the custom in the region, showed me his bandaged arm held with a shawl in a sling.

'Is that all? Well, I would have thought they would have hanged you!'

'No, stupid, they didn't hang me. Did you really think so? They would have done if a French soldier hadn't taken my part. He's called Molichard, a good man and quite fond of his drink. As we were friends and often had a few glasses together, he contrived to get me out of prison and got me safe, if not sound, to the Zamora gate. Poor Molichard, such a drinker and such a good fellow! Cipérez the rich won't forget his generous conduct.'

'Señor Cipérez,' I said to the loyal Salamancan, 'I am going to Salamanca but I don't have a safe conduct. If you could provide me with one…'

'And why are you going there?'

'To sell these vegetables,' I replied, pointing at my donkey.

'You'll do good business. They'll give you a high price for them. Have you got what they call roses of Jericho?'

'Kidney beans? Yes, they're from Castrejón.'[222]

The peasant looked at me somewhat suspiciously.

'Do you know where the English Army is headed for?' he asked, his eyes fixed on me. 'The lion can be recognised by his claw…'

'It is nearby, Señor Cipérez. But are you going to give me the safe conduct?'

'You are not what you seem,' the peasant said slyly. 'Long live all good patriots and death to the French, all the French, except Molichard, who is the apple of my eye!'

'No matter who I am… will you give me the safe conduct?'

'Baltasarillo!' Cipérez shouted. 'Come here.'

A lively and cheerful young man of about twenty left the group of players.

'This is my son,' the Salamancan said. 'He's a brave lad... Baltasarillo, give me your safe conduct.'

'But...'

'No, you're not going to Salamanca tomorrow. You'll go back with me to Escuernavacas.[223] Didn't you say that your mother was very sad?'

'Even flies frighten my mother, but not me.'

'They don't?'

'No one stops scattering seed for fear of sparrows,' the young man replied. 'I want to go to Salamanca.'

'No, you're going home. I'll send you tomorrow with a little present for Señor Molichard... Give me your letter.'

The young man got his document out and his father gave it to me, saying,

'With this paper your name is Baltasarillo Cipérez, a native of Escuernavacas, district of Vitigudino. You two youngsters look pretty alike. The paper is in order, I obtained it myself two months ago, the last time my son was in Salamanca with his sister María for the birthday festival of King Cups.'[224]

'I will pay for the services you have done for me,' I said, putting my hand in my purse, after young Baltasar had moved away from me.

'Cipérez the rich does not take money for a favour,' he said proudly. 'I believe you are serving the country, eh? In spite of your dress, well, a man without a cape is as good as the King or the Pope... we're all one together. Me as well...'

'How will these villages receive the *lord* when he comes?'

'Will they be receiving him? Have you seen him? Is he near?' he asked eagerly.

'If you want to see him, go to Bernuy on Wednesday.'

'Bernuy! Being in Bernuy is being in Salamanca!' he exclaimed in great delight. The saying is, 'Here Samson will fall,' but I say, 'Here Marmont will fall and all his men with him.' Have you seen the students and the lads in Villamayor?'[225]

'No, I haven't seen anything, señor.'

'We have arms,' he said mysteriously. 'Let them grab our feet to shoe us and they'll see what they've got hold of... when the *lord* sees us...'

Then, taking me quietly to one side, he added,

'You are going to Salamanca on the *lord's* orders, eh? I was sure of it. Don't be afraid. The man whose father is the judge need not worry about the trial. Well, my friend... you must know that we are ready in all these villages, even though it doesn't seem so. Even the women will come out to fight... the French want us to help them, but give to the cat what you were going to give to the mouse and save yourself some trouble. I served some time with Julián Sánchez and I went into the city many times as a spy... a nasty job... but the tambourine is in hands that know how to play it.'

'Señor Cipérez,' I said. 'Long live good patriots!'

'We're only waiting for the Englishman before turning out, all of us, with our muskets, sickles, pikes, swords and whatever else we've collected and stored away.'

'And I'm off to Salamanca. Will they let me work on the fortifications?'

'That's a tricky business. And what about the whip? The ones that clipped me still have the shears in their hands... Anyway, the villagers do not work on the forts any longer.'

'Who does, then?'

'The city residents.'

'And the villagers?'

'They hang them if they suspect they are spies. Let them hang. You only know an egg is bad when it's broken and Martinmas comes to every pig[226]... But I'm not afraid of anything now as he who rings the alarm bell is safe.'

'But what about me?'

'Courage, young man... God is in Heaven... and now I'm going to Valverdón[227] where two hundred students and more than four hundred villagers are waiting for me. Long live our country and Fernando VII! Ah, if it will help you, you can say in Salamanca that you're going to fetch some old iron for your father, Cipérez the rich... Goodbye...'

'Goodbye, noble gentleman.'

'Me, a gentleman? Little is the difference between Peter and Peter... although I wear the shoes I don't make them dirty... Goodbye, lad, good luck. Do you know the way? Straight on from here and keep straight on. You'll soon meet the French, but keep going straight on. The fox knows much, but he who catches him knows more.'

The worthy Cipérez and I shook hands heartily in farewell and I hurried on my way.

XIII

I stayed in Cabrerizos for a rest late into the night of Monday to Tuesday and at dawn on the following day when I was about to enter the city, the noble teacher of Spain and of the world's civilisation, the French, who up to then had not bothered me, appeared in the road ahead of me. It was a detachment of dragoons escorting a convoy that had been sent by Marmont from Fuentesaúco.[228] Although I had no reason to think that they would trouble me, I was afraid of some misfortune. But I concealed my anxiety and suspicion, urging on the donkey and pretending to alleviate the tedium of the journey with cheerful songs.

My heart did not deceive me as our country's invaders (may they be devoured by wolves now, sooner or later), without meaning deliberately to do me any harm, in fact by apparently helping me, seriously upset my plans.

'Nice vegetables,' said a corporal in French, slowing his horse to my donkey's pace.

I said nothing and did not even look at him.

'Hey, idiot!' he shouted in bastardised Spanish, hitting me on the shoulder with the flat of his sabre. 'Are you taking those greens to Salamanca?'

'Yes, sir,' I replied, trying to seem as stupid as possible.

An officer stopped and ordered the corporal to buy all my merchandise.

'Everything, we'll buy all of it,' said the corporal, taking out a greasy canvas purse. '*Combien?*'[2]

I shook my head.

'Aren't you taking this to sell in Salamanca?'

'No, sir, it's a present.'

'Damn your presents! We'll buy the lot, so then, you great idiot, you'll be able to return to your village.'

I realised that refusing to sell would raise suspicions and I asked them a fortune for

---

2   'How much?'

the greens, which were very scarce thereabouts at that time. Then the enraged soldier threatened to split me neatly in two; the offer then went up from the original one, I lowered my price a little bit and we made a deal. I got my money, my donkey had no load, and now I had no obvious reason to justify me going into the city, as those who went without any provisions had the gates shut in their faces. Nevertheless, I continued on my way and the corporal called out to me,

'Hey, fellow! Aren't you going back to your village? I've never seen anyone so stupid.'

'Sir,' I replied, 'I'm going to get a load of old iron for my donkey.'

'Have you got a safe conduct?'

'Of course I have one! I got it when I was in Salamanca two months ago to see the King's birthday celebration... but now that I don't have any load they might not let me go in to collect the old iron. If Señor Corporal would permit me to go with him and tell them that he bought my greens, why, then I can get the old iron.'

'All right then, *sac du papier!*[3] Keep your donkey at my horse's pace and follow me, but I don't know if they'll let you enter as there are very strict orders to prevent spying.'

We arrived at the Zamora gate and I was stopped there by the sentry and treated with every rudeness.

'Let him through,' said my corporal. 'I bought his greens and he's going to load up his donkey with some iron.'

The chief of the guards looked at me suspiciously and, seeing portrayed on my face that beatific stupidity peculiar to those peasants who have lived a long time in the most impenetrable woods and wastelands, said,

'These yokels are very cunning. Hey, *monsieur le badaud,*[4] we hanged three spies this week.'

I pretended not to understand and he continued,

'You can enter if you have a safe conduct.'

I showed the document and they then let me through.

I went down a long street, Zamora, which led me straight into a large and handsome square with arcades, filled at that time with a great crowd of salesmen. I looked for somewhere nearby where I could leave my donkey so that I could devote myself freely to the purpose of my visit and when I had found an inn, the best in the city, and had stabled my peaceful companion there with a good feed of straw and barley, I went out

---

3   nitwit!
4   Mister gawper

to the street. It was Calle de la Rúa, as I was told by a girl that I asked. I wanted to get to the walled area so that I could survey it all. All of a sudden I saw a crowd of people of all types marching in confusion, each one carrying a mattock or pick on his shoulder. They were being escorted by French soldiers and they certainly didn't look at all happy.

'They must be the city residents going to work on the fortifications,' I said to myself. 'The French are taking them by force.'

I moved away for fear that my curiosity would give rise to suspicion, and going in no particular direction and without any knowledge of the streets I arrived at a monastery, through whose doors some pieces of artillery were in the course of being taken in. Suddenly, I felt a heavy hand on my shoulder and heard a voice in bad Spanish saying to me,

'Aren't you carrying a hoe, you idler? Come with me to police headquarters.'

'I'm from the country,' I replied. 'I've come with my little donkey…'

'Come along and we'll find out who you are,' he continued, looking at me closely. 'If, *par exemple*, you were an *espion*…'[5]

My first impulse was to refuse to follow him, but resistance would have given me away and it seemed more prudent to yield. Putting on an air of extreme meekness I followed my strange captor. He was a short and sprightly soldier, black-eyed, swarthy and officious, whose manner and behaviour did not amuse me at all. In the turnings made by a tortuous and dark street I tried to trick him by hanging back for a moment so as to beat it with my characteristic speed, but the wretch, guessing my intention, grabbed my arm and said to me sarcastically,

'Think I'm not as smart as you? Forwards and no kicking, or I'll take off the lid of your brainbox, you yokel. I'm sure you are an *espion*. You were observing the artillery in the Bernardine monastery. You were measuring the walls. Let me tell you that there are some very clever officials who spy on the spies and I am one of them. Have you never danced at the end of a rope?'

Once more I felt the urge to free myself from that man by force, but luckily I had time to reflect, stifling my anger and trusting my salvation to cunning and craftiness. The fiendish little Frenchman took me to a vast building in whose courtyard I saw many troops. He stopped with me in front of a group of four robust and tough soldiers in brilliant uniforms with twirled moustaches and impressively elegant airs, and pointed at me with an expression of triumph.

---

5   If, for instance, you were a spy.…

'What have you brought, *Tourlourou?*' the oldest of them drawled.

'A *crapaud* [6] that I've just caught.'

I took off my hat, and with a show of contrition and utmost humility I made many bows to those fine gentlemen.

'A *crapaud*!' the old officer repeated, looking at me fiercely. 'Who are you?'

'Sir,' I said, clasping my hands, 'this soldier thinks I am a spy. I've come from Escuernavacas to fetch some old iron, my donkey is at the inn of a woman by the name of Fabiana, and I am called Baltasar Cipérez, if your honour pleases. If you want to hang me, hang me...' and then, sobbing in the most lamentable manner and uttering cries of grief that would have moved a very statue of bronze, I exclaimed, 'Farewell, my dear mother, farewell, father of my heart, you will never see your little son again, farewell, my beloved Escuernavacas, farewell, farewell! But, what have I done, what have I done, sirs?'

The old officer said with impassive calmness,

'Molichard, Sergeant Molichard, have him shut up in jail. We'll interrogate him later. I'm very busy now. I'm going to see the *Maréchal des Logis*[229], as I've heard we're leaving Salamanca this evening.'

Another Frenchman appeared, as tall as a tree, as straight as a ramrod, thin, hard and flexible like an Indian cane, with a tanned and sardonic face, sharp eyes, straight and black moustaches and feet and hands of an uncommonly large size. When I saw this fine figure of a soldier, whose uniform hung on his frame as if on a clothes-hanger, when I heard his name, a life-saving idea suddenly flashed into my brain, and moving from thought to execution with the speed of human willpower in emergencies, I gave a shout in which I combined at the same time affected surprise and joy; I ran towards him and embraced him round his knees with passionate warmth, and weeping, said,

'Oh, my precious Señor Molichard, dearest and most revered Señor Molichard! I've found you at last. How long I've been looking for you with none of these rascals giving me any information about you! Let me embrace you, let me kiss your knees and revere you, worship and venerate you... Oh, Holy Mother of God, what wonderful joy!'

'I think you must be mad, my good fellow,' said the Frenchman, shaking his legs.

'But don't you recognise me?' I added. 'But then, why would you recognise me if you have never seen me? Give me this hand which I kiss and may the good Señor Molichard who saved my father from death live for a thousand years. I am Baltasar

---

6   toad

Cipérez, look at the safe conduct, I am the son of the Baltasar they call Cipérez the rich, from Escuernavacas. May Señor Molichard be blessed. I am in Salamanca because my father sent me with a present for your honour.'

'A present!' exclaimed the sergeant, looking excited.

'Yes, sir, a trifling present, since my father cannot repay what you did with the poor fruits of his kitchen garden.'

'Greens! Where are they, then?' said Molichard looking all around.

'A corporal of the dragoons took them from me on the way. I don't know his name but he must be here somewhere and he can vouch for what I say. In truth, he didn't really like them much. The old woman liked amaranth so much, she didn't leave any, green or dry.'[230]

'Oh, a plague on dragoons!' my father's protector exclaimed in fury. 'I'll tear their guts out!'

'He forced me to sell them,' I continued, 'but I can give you the money he gave me and, in addition, the next trip that I take to Salamanca I will bring not one, but two loads, for Señor Molichard. But that is not the only present I was bringing for your honour. My father did not know what to do, since he who gives quickly gives twice; my mother, who did not come in person to throw herself at your feet because they're putting new ribbons into her mantilla, wanted my father to pull out all the stops in giving a present to his protector, and when I set out the two of them thought that the greens were a present unworthy of his grateful heart, his liberality and his great wealth, for which reason they gave me three gold doubloons so that I could buy you a half-barrel of Nava wine in Salamanca, which is good here, whereas the wine from the village messes up your liver.'

'Señor Cipérez is a generous man,' said the Frenchman, showing off in front of his friends, who were no less engrossed and delighted as him.

'The first thing I did this morning in Salamanca was to order the half-barrel in Fabiana's inn. So let's go for it...'

'Fabiana's wine can't be any better than the wine in the Zángana bar. You can buy some there.'

'I'll give you the money now so that your honour can buy it as he likes. It's well said that he whom God loves has food brought to him at home. How much work it cost me to find Señor Molichard! I was asking everyone and no one could give me any information until this good friend took me for a spy and brought me here... Every cloud has a silver lining... Finally I have had the pleasure of embracing the friend of my father's! What a coincidence! Eyes that love each other see each other from afar... Señor Molichard, when your honour has put me in jail, where the officer ordered me to be taken, you can go and choose the wine you like best. Thanks be to God that He made my good father rich enough to be able to pay off his debts generously! My father is very fond of Señor Molichard. He who gives you a bone does not want you dead.'

'One can recognise the blood of Señor Cipérez from the way you rattle off all these proverbs,' said Molichard.

'If the priest sings well, the altar boy is not far behind.'

Molichard seemed uncertain and after consulting with his companions by signs and some monosyllables I couldn't understand, he said to me,

'I would really rather not shut you up in jail, because, in truth, when one receives such a present from Señor Cipérez... but...'

'No, please don't put yourself out on my account, Señor Molichard,' I said with all the ease in the world. 'I don't want you to get into trouble with the officer because of me. I'm happy to go to jail as I'm sure the officer and any other officer in the world will be convinced I'm not a bad sort.'

'You won't have a nice time in jail, lad,' the Frenchman said. 'Let's see what we can do. I'll tell the officer that...'

'The officer will already have forgotten what he had ordered,' stated Tourlourou who, miraculously, had overcome his bad feelings towards me.

'Hey, Jean-Jean,' Molichard shouted at a soldier who was passing nearby. I recognised in his pompous figure the corporal of the dragoons who had bought my greens on the road.

Jean-Jean approached and recognised me immediately.

'My good friend,' I said to him, 'I think it was your honour who bought the greens from me that I was bringing for this gentleman.'

'For Molichard?'

'Didn't I say they were a present?'

'If I had known they were for this *chauve-souris*[7],' Jean-Jean said, 'I wouldn't have given you a cent for them.'

'Jean-Jean,' said Molichard in French. 'Do you like Nava wine?'

'I don't see any. Where is it?'

'Look, Jean-Jean. This youngster has given me some as a present. But we have to put him in jail...'

'In jail!'

'Yes, *mon vieux*[8], they think he's a spy but he isn't one.'

'Let's go all four of us to the bar,' Tourlourou said, 'and then this gentleman can go to jail.'

'I would not want your honours to get into trouble with your superiors because of me,' I said with meek diffidence. 'Take me to prison and lock me up... every wolf has

---

7   flitter-mouse
8   old chap

its track and every cock has its dung heap.'

'What's all this about locking up?' cried Molichard cheerfully and now the life and soul of the party. 'To the Zángana, *messieurs*. Cipérez, we'll answer for you.'

XIV

'But what if the officer gets angry? I'll stay here.'

'A Frenchman, a soldier of Napoleon,' said Tourlourou with a gesture like Bonaparte pointing at the Pyramids, 'does not have a quiet drink while his Spanish friend is dying of thirst in a dungeon. Bravo, Cipérez,' he added, embracing me, 'you're my finest comrade. Let's embrace… there, that's how it should be… friends until death. Gentlemen, you see here together *l'aigle de l'Empire et le lion de l'Espagne*[9].'

Frankly, as for me, the lion of Spain, I was none too happy to be in the arms of the eagle of the Empire.

And with this and various other verbal excesses from the three servants of the great empire, they took me from the headquarters and we went in procession to a small inn close to the fortifications of San Vicente.

'Señor Molichard, apart from the half-barrel of Nava, which is a present from my

---

9   the eagle of the Empire and the lion of Spain

father, I'll pay for everything,' I said when we entered.

In a short while, Tourlourou, Molichard and Jean-Jean had indulged their venerable bodies with the best that was to be had in the inn, and here they were gradually losing their serenity, although the corporal of the dragoons seemed to have more resistance to alcohol than his illustrious companions in arms and wine.

'Has your father got a lot of property?' Molichard asked me.

'Enough to get along with,' I replied modestly.

'They call him Cipérez the rich.'

'Certainly, and he is... I realise my present seems small... but that's just the beginning. We all know that it's a laying hen that sits on an egg.'

'I didn't mean that. Here's to the health of *monsieurrrrr* Cipérez!'

'What I brought today is because I was coming to buy some old iron... but my father and mother, and the whole family, will come in a *soalem* procession with something better. Señor Molichard, my sister would like to meet Señor Molichard...'

'She's a pretty girl, according to what Cipérez said. Here's to the health of María Cipérez!'

'A beauty. She's a lovely girl and everyone who sees her thinks she's a princess.'

'And with a good dowry... if one were finally to settle down in Spain. We can say like Louis XIV, 'There are no more *Pyrrrenees*.[231] Have another drink, Baltasarico.'

'My head is swimming. With the three half-glasses of wine I've drunk, I feel as if I've got the whole of Salamanca between my temples,' I said simulating the unsteadiness of drunkenness.

Jean-Jean was singing:

"*Le crocodile en partant pour la guerre*
disait adieux à ses petits enfants.
Le malheureux
traînant sa queue
dans la poussière..."[232]

Tourlourou, having crawled around on all fours, got to his feet and with a sweeping gesture exclaimed, 'Comrades, from the height of this bottle *quarrrrante siècles vous contemplent.*'[233]

I said to Molichard,

'Señor sergeant, as I'm not used to drinking, I'm feeling slightly drunk... I'm going outside for a moment to get some air. Have you chosen your Nava wine?'

Without waiting for an answer I paid the bill at Zángana.

'Fine. Let's go outside for a moment,' said Molichard, taking me by the arm.

Once outside, I found myself in a place that was neither a square, nor a courtyard nor a street, but all three things combined. On two sides could be seen high walls, some half-demolished, others still standing and supporting the wrecked roofs. Between them one could make out the open interiors of what had been churches, whose altars remained in the open air and the daylight, illuminating from afar the pictures and gilding, giving them a look of old pieces of junk that antique dealers at fairs piled up on the street. Soldiers and peasants were at work, taking away rubble, digging ditches, dragging cannons, piling up earth in mounds, finishing off the demolition of what had been half-demolished or repairing what had been demolished in excess. I saw all this and, remembering the words of Lord Wellington, concentrated on looking hard. I wished I could have taken in everything I saw in one glance and keep it in my memory, stone by stone, weapon by weapon, man by man.

'What are they doing here, señor Molichard?' I asked innocently.

'Fortifications, stupid,' said the sergeant, who was beginning to lose his respect for me now that he had filled himself with my wine.

'Oh, yes, I see,' I replied, feigning insight. 'For the war. And what's this place called?'

'Where we are is in the fort of San Vicente. There was a Benedictine monastery here, which was demolished. A nest of reactionaries, my little friend.'

'And what are they going to do with so many cannons?' I asked in amazement.

'You really are pretty dumb. What are they for, then? For firing!'

'Firing!' I said fearfully. 'All at the same time?'

'You're looking pale, coward.'

'One, two, three, four... they're bringing another one over there. That makes five. And this earth, sergeant, what's that for?'

'I've never met anyone so stupid. Can't you see that they're making escarpments and counter-escarpments?'

'And what about that large house in ruins you can see over there?'

'That's the Romano Arabic castle. *Foudre et tonnerre!*[10] You are an ignoramus... Give me your hand, San Cayetano is dancing before my eyes.'

'San Cayetano?'

'Can't you see it, nitwit? That large monastery on the right. We're fortifying it as well.'

---

10   Thunder and lightning!

'This is all very nice, señor Molichard. It will be fun to see it when the firing starts. And those large walls they are demolishing?'

'The Colegio Trilingüe[234].... *triquis linguis* in Latin, that is, *of three languages.* They still haven't finished the covered way going down to La Alberca.'

'But they've demolished whole streets here, señor Molichard,' I said, going ahead and giving him my arm so that he didn't fall over.

'You must have come out of the madhouse, *ventre de boeuf.*[11] Don't you see that we've levelled the main street so as to get raking fire from San Vicente?'

'And there's a square there...'

'A bastion.'

'Two, four, six, eight cannons at least. They are frightening.'

'Just toys... the good ones are those four, the ones in the ravelin.'

'And there's a ditch going along...'

'From the gate up to Los Milagros, idiot.'

'And behind it? Jesus, Mary and Joseph, how frightening!'

'Behind the parapet is where the mortars are.'

'Let's go that way now.'

'By San Cayetano? Ah, I see you are an inquisitive one, a little inquisitor... *Saperlotte*[12]. I warn you that if you carry on asking questions like that and looking at everything with those bulging eyes... you'll make me believe that you really are a spy... and, in truth, my little friend, I suspect...'

The sergeant looked at me with blatant disdain. Just then, Tourlourou came up in a lamentable state, poorly supported by his friend Jean-Jean, who was singing a warlike song.

'*Espion,* yes, *espion!*' said Tourlourou, pointing at me. 'I maintain that you are an *espion*! To jail!'

'Frankly, señor Cipérez,' said Molichard, 'I don't want to disobey orders or have the commanding officer put me into the glasshouse for you.'

'This young man here,' declared Jean-Jean, hitting me firmly on the shoulder so that I nearly fell over, 'has the face of a rogue.'

'The moment I saw him I suspected there was something wrong about him,' said Molichard. 'You can't be sure of anyone in this cursed Spain. Spies crawl out from under the very stones…'

I shrugged my shoulders, pretending not to understand anything.

'I told you he was observing the Bernardine monastery when they were making loopholes in it, didn't I?' Tourlourou said.

I realised I was lost, but forced myself to keep calm. Suddenly a ray of hope came into my heart when I heard Jean-Jean say the following words in bad Spanish,

'You are idiots. Leave Señor Cipérez to me, as he's my friend.'

He put an arm around my shoulder with affectionate familiarity, although with a good grip.

'Let's go back to headquarters,' said Molichard. 'I go on guard at ten.'

And seizing me by the arm, he added,

'*Peste, mille pestes!*[13]… Planning to escape, are you?'

'He'll be searched at headquarters!' Tourlourou exclaimed.

'Clear off, *goguenards*[14],' Jean-Jean said forcefully. 'Señor Cipérez is my friend and I'm taking him under my protection. The Devil take you and leave him here with me.'

Tourlourou laughed, but Molichard looked at me fiercely and insisted on taking me with him. But my impromptu protector gave him such a strong thump on the shoulder that he finally decided to leave with his companion. Both made off, describing S's and other letters of the alphabet with their swaying bodies.

I have written in some detail about the deeds and words of those barbarians whose abominable figures will take a long time to be erased from my memory. In recalling the former I have kept as close to the truth as possible. As for the words, it would be impossible for even the most retentive memory to retain them as they came out of those drunken mouths, in a horrible gibberish that was neither French nor Spanish. I have put most of it into Spanish, but without omitting those foreign expressions which imprinted themselves most on my memory and keeping the formal address of *vos* with

---

13   Damn and double damn!
14   jokers

which the French, who knew little of how we spoke, addressed us.[235]

Was Jean-Jean's protection disinterested or did it mean a new danger, greater than the earlier ones? We will see now whether my friends have the patience to hear a detailed account of my adventures in Salamanca on the day of 16th June 1812, which, had I myself not been the protagonist and principal actor, I would have considered to be the dishonest creations of fantasy or a novelist's inventions to entertain the common herd.

XV

Jean-Jean took me by the arm and leading me on through those sad ruins, said to me,

'Friend Cipérez, I like you, let's take a stroll together… When are you planning to leave Salamanca? I swear I'll miss you.'

Such affected expressions caused me the darkest foreboding and I commended my soul to God. In my concern, I did not even take heed of the weapon I had at my side and I forgot, sweet Jesus, about Lord Wellington, England and Spain.

'I'm delighted to be in your company,' I said with a brave air. 'Let's go wherever you want.'

I felt the Frenchman's arm, like an iron vice, gripping mine tightly. That grip meant 'no, you can't escape from me.' As we went along I noticed that there were fewer people and the places we were slowly wandering through were becoming more and more lonely. I only had a clasp-knife with me as a weapon. Jean-Jean, who was a very strong man and of good height, carried a large sabre. With a rapid glance I looked at the man and the weapon to weigh them up and compare them with the forces I could muster in any fight.

'Where are you taking me?' I asked, getting free at last, ready for anything.

'Follow me, my good friend,' he said with a mocking expression. 'We'll stroll by the banks of the Tormes.'

'I'm a bit tired.'

He stopped, and fixing his little eyes on me, said,

'Don't you care to follow the man who saved you from the gallows?'

With that flame of intuition that suddenly illuminates us in moments of danger, with the insight we acquire at the critical point when will and thought are trying with desperate strength to overcome terrible obstacles, I read in that man's look the idea that was occupying his mind. Without doubt Jean-Jean had concluded that I had more money on me than I had shown at the inn and, whether he believed I was a spy or really Baltasar Cipérez, my gold excited his greed and the fierce dragoon was devising an easy way to get hold of it for himself. That shifty look of his, the lonely spot he led me to, indicated his criminal plan, be it to kill me and then throw my body into the river, or be it to rob me and then denounce me as a spy.

For an instant I felt myself a coward and my spirit vanquished, my body trembling and cold; all my blood welled up in my heart and I saw death, a horrible and dark end, whose prospect afflicted my spirit much more than a thousand deaths on the glorious field of battle... I looked around and everywhere was deserted and lonely. My executioner and I were the only people in that sad, abandoned and desolate place. To our side, disfigured ruins illuminated by the brightness of a sun that seemed terrifying to me; ahead, the sad river where the stagnant and calm water produced, it seemed, neither any flow nor any sound, and beyond, the green bank on the other side. No human voice could be heard, nor the step of man or beast, nor any sound other than the song of the birds who were gaily crossing the Tormes, fleeing from this place of desolation in search of the freshness and greenery of the other bank. There was no one to ask help from other than God.

But suddenly I sensed the illumination of a wonderful idea, yes, wonderful, that came into my mind, cast like an invisible ray from the immortal and sublime source of thought; I heard some sweet voices; I felt some hopeful beating of my heart, an inexplicable verve, a hope which filled me completely and sensing this, thinking of it and formulating a plan became all one. And this is how.

Brusquely and disguising my fear so much that I might be the criminal and he the victim, I stopped Jean-Jean and assumed a severe, determined and serious attitude. I looked at him as someone might look at a wretch who is going to perform a service for us and in a very haughty tone I said to him,

'Jean-Jean, this seems to me to be a very good place to have a word with you alone.'

The man was stunned.

'From the moment I first saw you and spoke with you, I took you to be a man of understanding and action, and it is exactly this sort of man I need now.'

He hesitated a moment, and then said stupidly,

'So then...'

'No, I'm not who I seem. Those imbeciles Tourlourou and Molichard can be taken in, but not you.'

'I had figured it out,' he stated. 'You are a spy.'

'No. Strange that someone as intelligent as you could have made so banal a mistake,' I said, unabashedly using *tú* to address him.[236] 'You know very well that spies are always peasants who risk their lives for money. Now, look at me closely. Apart from the clothes, do I have the look of a peasant?'

'No, by my faith. You are a gentleman.'

'Yes, a gentleman, a gentleman, and you are one, too, since poverty does not stop one being a gentleman.'

'Certainly not.'

'Have you ever heard of the Marquis of Rioponce?'

'No, that is, yes, I think I have heard of that name.'

'Well, that's me. Now am I correct in thinking that on this ill-fated day for me, I have met a sympathetic man who could serve me, for which I can show my gratitude by rewarding him beyond his wildest dreams? Because, being a soldier, you're poor, aren't you?'

'I am poor,' he said, not hiding the greed that showed through the open windows of his eyes.

'I am not carrying much on me, but for the enterprise which I have in hand today, I have brought a tidy amount cunningly concealed within the stuffing of my donkey's saddlebag.'

'Where did you leave your donkey?' he asked.

'That's something for later.'

'If you are a spy, don't count on me for anything, señor marquis,' he said in some embarrassment. 'I won't be a traitor to my flag.'

'I've already said I'm not a spy.'

'*C'est drôle*[15]. So what the devil brings you to Salamanca dressed like this, selling greens and passing yourself off as a peasant from Escuernavacas?'

'What brings me here? A love affair.'

I said this and what I had said earlier with such assurance and with such composure and self-possession that I saw conviction join greed in the eyes of the man who had planned to be my murderer.

'A love affair!' he said, once more assailed by doubt, after some brief reflection. 'But why have you not come as you really are? Why hide yourself like this from all Salamanca?'

'What a question! Really, there are moments when I think you are an innocent child. You would be right if the love affair were one of those that come about in the ordinary way but the one I am involved in is dangerous and so difficult that it is essential that I completely disguise my identity.'

'Is it a Frenchman who has stolen your sweetheart?' asked the dragoon, smiling for the first time in our conversation.

'Well, something like that... you're close. In Salamanca there's someone I love and whom I'll take with me if I can, and there's another I hate and whom I will kill if I can!'

'And is that second person one of our dear generals, perhaps?' he said drily. 'Señor marquis, don't count on me for any help.'

'No, that person is no general, nor even French. He's a Spaniard.'

'Well, if he's a Spaniard, *le diable m'emporte*[16]... you can do whatever you like with him. No Frenchman will stop you.'

'No, because this man is powerful and, although a Spaniard, he's served the French cause for a long time. He's as clever as nobody else, and if I had turned up here under my own name, I would have found it impossible to escape immediate and terrible persecution, perhaps death.'

'In a word, my dear sir,' he said impatiently, 'what is it you want me to do for you?'

'First, not to hand me over, stupid,' I said haughtily so as the better to establish my superiority. 'Then, to help me to find where my enemy is living.'

'Don't you know?'

---

15   That's strange
16   the devil take me

'No. This is the first time I've been to Salamanca, and as your loutish comrades wanted to have me arrested, I haven't had any time to do anything.'

'Now that you mention my comrades...' Jean-Jean said very suspiciously, 'I remember... you played the role of a peasant very carefully. I haven't forgotten the proverbs. If now as well you're ...'

'Do you suspect me?!' I shouted scornfully.

'Don't get so high and mighty, my little marquis,' he replied insolently. 'I can hand you over, remember.'

'If you hand me over, I will simply have the annoyance of failing in my plan, but you will lose what I could have given you.'

'There's no need to quarrel,' he said in a kindly tone. 'Tell me some more about your love affair as so far you've only told me vaguely about it.'

'A despicable son of Salamanca, a libertine, a *sans-culotte*,[237] abducted from her paternal home a certain noble maiden, of the highest rank of nobility of Spain, an angel of beauty and of virtue...'

'Abducted her! Come now, are maidens abducted like that?'

'He abducted her to take revenge, as revenge is the only pleasure of his perverted soul; to keep in his power a pledge that allows him to threaten the most honourable and illustrious family of Andalusia, as kidnappers keep the rich man hostage so that they can demand the ransom from his family. For a long time all my hard work and that of the unfortunate girl's parents to find where her treacherous kidnapper is keeping her has been in vain, but by chance a seemingly insignificant event, but which was no doubt a sign from God, informed me that both are in Salamanca. He only stays in cities occupied by the French, because he fears the anger of his countrymen, because he is a wretched man, a traitor to his country, irreligious, cruel, a bad Spaniard and a bad son, Jean-Jean, who, devoured by an ungodly bitterness against his native land, harms it as much as he can. His dark life, like that of moles, is occupied with the founding and propagating of masonic societies, with sowing discord, with raising from the depths of society the corrupted sediment that is always sleeping in it and with scattering the seed of unrest among peoples. You protect him because you protect everything that divides, destroys and disarms Spaniards. He passes from village to village, and during his travels he hides his true name, nature and occupation to avoid provoking the anger of the natives. When he can't travel in the company of French troops, he hides himself with the most contemptible disguises. He's recently come from Plasencia to Salamanca pretending to be an actor, and his band imitated a group of travelling actors so perfectly that few suspected the trick as they passed through…'

'Now I know who it is,' Jean-Jean said suddenly with a smile. 'It's Santorcaz.'

'The very same, Don Luis de Santorcaz.'

'Whom some Spaniards regard as a sorcerer, enchanter and necromancer. And so as to have it out with this wrong'un,' the Frenchman added, 'you've disguised yourself like this. Who told you that Santorcaz had power with us? He might have been powerful in Madrid, but not here. The authorities tolerate him, but they don't protect him. He's been out of favour for some time.'

'Do you know him well?'

'Well, yes; we were friends in Madrid. I was his escort when he went to Toledo to confer with the Junta[238] and we met again in Salamanca. He's been here three months and after a short absence, he's returned… Señor marquis, or whatever you are, you don't need to wear this rough costume or disguise your nobility to fight such a man; you can do whatever you like with him, kill him even, without any interference from the French government. Obscure, forgotten and unpopular, Santorcaz consoles himself with freemasonry, and in the lodge in the Calle de Tentenecios a few incorrigible Spaniards and Frenchmen, no doubt the worst of both nations, amuse themselves in exterminating the human race, turning the world upside down, abolishing the aristocracy and making the King and Queen sweep the streets with a broom in their hands. You can see that this is ridiculous. I've been there a few times instead of going to the theatre, and in truth they needn't have disguised themselves as comedians as they really are ones.'

'I can see you are a man of the greatest talent.'

'What I am,' the soldier said in an alarmingly suspicious tone, 'is a man who wasn't born yesterday. How can it be that your sole enemy is a man so little liked and you, being such a grand marquis, have to come here selling vegetables and deceiving everybody, as if you did not have to fight against a low-class intriguer, but against all of us, our power, our police and even the governor of the city himself, General Thiébaut-Tibo?'[239]

Jean-Jean's reasoning was logical and for a brief time I did not know how to answer him.

'*Connu, connu*[17]… enough of this farce. You are a spy!'

---

17   It's obvious, obvious…

he exclaimed fiercely. 'If after coming here as an enemy of France, you are making fun of me, I swear...'

'Calm down, calm down, my friend Jean-Jean,' I said, trying to avoid the great danger threatening me, after thinking I had warded it off. 'I've told you it is a love affair... Haven't you noticed that Santorcaz has a young lady with him?'

'Yes, so what? They say she's his daughter...'

'His daughter!' I exclaimed, pretending to be absolutely furious. 'That wretch dares to say she's his daughter? I don't believe it.'

'That's what they say, and she does actually look quite like him,' Jean-Jean replied calmly.

'Oh, for God's sake, my friend, by all the saints, by all that you most love in the world, take me to the house of that man and if he dares to say in front of me that Inés is his daughter, I'll rip out his tongue.'

'What I can tell you is that I have seen her strolling around the city and its surroundings, giving her arm to Santorcaz, who is very ill, and the girl, very pretty certainly, didn't look as though she was unhappy being at the mason's side, since she leads him lovingly through the streets and makes a great fuss of him and keeps him amused... And now, *mon petit*, so you're saying then that she is your sweetheart, and an enchanted woman or *princesse d'Araucanía*, as you have given to understand... So, what then?'

'I have come to Salamanca to take possession of her and restore her to her family, an enterprise I hope you will help me in.'

'If she had been abducted, why didn't that family, which is so powerful, not complain to King Joseph?'

'Because that family did not want to ask for anything from King Joseph. You're more inquisitive than a tax inspector, and I have just about had it with you,' I cried, unable to contain my impatience. 'Will you serve me, or not?'

Jean-Jean, seeing my determined attitude, hesitated a moment and then said to me,

'What have I got to do? Take you to the Calle del Cáliz, where Santorcaz lives, go in, knock him down and carry off the enchanted princess in my arms?'

'That would be very dangerous. I can't do this without getting her agreement first so that I can prepare her escape carefully and without any uproar. Can you get into the house?'

'Not very easily, because Señor Santorcaz has the habits of an anchorite and does not like visits, but I know Ramoncilla, one of the two servants that are in his service, and I could manage to get in in an absolute emergency.'

'Very well, I will write a couple of words which you will see get to the hands of Señorita Inés, and once she is alerted…'

'Now I see what you're up to, you rascal,' he said, sly as a fox and mocking me. 'You want me to leave you on your own so that you can escape.'

'Do you still doubt me? Take note of what I write in pencil on this paper.'

Resting a piece of paper against the wall, I wrote the following while Jean-Jean read it over my shoulder,

'Trust in the bearer of this document, who is a friend of mine and of your mother's, the Countess of ***, and inform him of the place and hour when I can see you, as I have come to Salamanca determined to save you and I will not leave here without you. *Gabriel.*'

'Nothing more than that?' he said, taking the paper and examining it with the profound attention of an antiquary trying to decipher an obscure inscription.

'Let's finish this. You take this paper, get it delivered to Señorita Inés and if you bring it back to me endorsed with just one letter by her, even if it's traced with her nail, I will hand you the six doubloons I have here, leaving what I left in the inn as a reward for more important services.'

'Aha, a nice little business!' the Frenchman said scornfully. 'I go to the Calle del Cáliz and once I'm far away, you, who want nothing more than to get out of my sight, start running off and…'

'We'll go together and I'll wait for you at the door.'

'That's just the same, because if I go in and leave you outside…'

'Do you doubt my word, scoundrel!?' I exclaimed, inflamed by indignation which displayed itself terribly in my voice and gestures.

'Yes, I do… Well then, I will suggest something that will give me security over you. While I go to the Calle del Cáliz, I will leave you locked up somewhere very secure, which is impossible to escape from. When I return from my mission I will let you out and you will give me the money.'

I was beside myself with rage, but seeing that it was impossible to escape from the clutches of such a villainous enemy, I accepted what he proposed, recognising that it was not hard to choose between dying and being locked up for a period of time which could not be long or between being handed over as a spy and being briefly detained.

'Let's go,' I said to him with contempt. 'Take me where you please.'

Without another word, Jean-Jean walked by my side and we turned back into that maze of ruins, half-demolished buildings and jumbled debris where the fortifications began. At first I saw a few people on our path, then many more coming and going and working on the parapets, piling up earth and stones, in other words, making war with the remains of religion. The two of us arrived in silence at a vast portico that seemed to belong to a monastery or college, and we went into a cloister where I saw two dozen or so soldiers who lay on the ground, playing games and laughing uproariously, happy people in the midst of that destroyed nationality, poor, simple young men, ignorant of the reasons that had moved them to turn the work of centuries into dust.

'This is the Monastery of Merced Calzada,' Jean-Jean told me. 'We couldn't demolish it completely as there was too much to do on the other side. Two hundred of us are bivouacked in what remains. Nice lodgings! The monks be blessed! *Charles le Téméraire!*[240] he shouted, calling to someone in the knot of soldiers.

'What's the matter?' said a short and podgy soldier coming forward. 'Who've you got with you?'

'Where's my cousin?'

'He's over there. *Pied-de-mouton!*'[241]

Shortly after there appeared a sergeant somewhat similar to my disagreeable companion, who said to him,

'*Pied-de mouton*, give me the key to the tower.'

A moment later, Jean-Jean led me into a room, which was neither dark nor damp, as those for holding prisoners usually are.

'Allow me, little Señor Marquis,' he said to me with mocking courtesy, 'to lock you up in here while I go to the Calle del Cáliz. If you give me the doubloons you promised before I leave, I'll let you go free.'

'No,' I replied scornfully. 'If you want your reward without performing any service, you'll have to kill me, villain. Try it and I will defend myself as best I can.'

'Well, stay here, then. I'll be back shortly.'

He left, locking the extremely heavy door from the outside.

XVI

Finding myself alone, I felt the walls whose thickness of six feet showed a solidity of construction proof against earthquakes… what a wretched situation I was in! It was about midday and before I had been able to obtain the information my general wanted, I was a prisoner, prevented from surveying the city on my own and at my ease. Speaking bluntly, God had done me no favours and with the hours passing, I knew little and had achieved nothing.

I felt tired but lifted my head to explore what was above me and I saw some stairs which, starting from the ground, continued with turns in the corners, winding their way upwards until they were lost high above where I could not see clearly. The flights of black wood rose up the inner angle of the walls, joining up in the corners like the joints of a snake, and the final turns lost themselves in the upper region where the bells were. A very bright light, entering by the wide, unglazed windows, illuminated that long, vertical tube in whose lower part I found myself. A powerful attraction called me upwards and I ran up. In fact, rather than running upwards, my rapid dash was more as if I had thrown myself into an upside-down well.

Leaping up the stairs two-by-two, I came to a level where various wrecked pieces of apparatus told me that there had once been a clock there. On the outside a black hand that had been turning for three centuries now pointed with ironic immobility to an hour that would run no more. Ropes were hanging on all sides but there were no bells. It was the corpse of a Christian tower, dumb and inert like all corpses. The clock had ceased to beat out the oscillation of life and the tongues of bronze had been torn out of those throats of stone, which over so much time had sounded forth at set intervals, saluting the new dawn, praising the Lord on His high days and requesting prayers for the dead. I carried on going upwards and right at the top, two windows, two enormous eyes looked in astonishment at the vast sky, the city and the open country, like the terrified eyes of the dead, without radiance and without light. I leant out of those cavities and gave a cry of joy.

Before my eyes there was laid out a map of the greater part of the city and its environs, the river and the surrounding countryside.

A gentle wind soughed in the dome of the lonely tower, making mysterious whistling sounds in that empty skull. I fancied that the edifice was swaying like a palm tree, threatening to fall down before the pickaxes of the French had destroyed it stone by stone. At times it seemed to me that it rose taller, taller and taller and that the noble city, the famous *Roma la chica*,[242] vanished far below, losing itself in the mists on the ground. I saw other towers, roofs, streets, the majestic mass of the two cathedrals, a multitude of churches of different types which had been granted the privilege of survival, countless ruins where hundreds of men, like ants dragging grains of wheat, were running about and mingling. I saw the Tormes, which disappeared to the west in broad curves, leaving the city to its right and skirting the green fields of El Zurguén on the other bank. I saw the platforms, the escarpments and counter-escarpments, the ravelins, the curtains, the embrasures, the cannons, the walls with loopholes, the parapets made with colonnades from churches, the entrenchments made from piles of dust and earth which had been the flesh and bones of venerable nuns and monks. I saw the cannons lined up in rows pointing outwards, the mortars, the fosse, the ditches, the bags of earth, the mountains of cannon balls, the artillery parks in the open air... Oh, Almighty God, you have given me more than I asked for! I was wandering through the city, prevented from completing my task, threatened with death, exposed to thousands of dangers, betrayed, lost, condemned, without any ability to see, to observe, to listen, to get any exact idea, or even a rough idea, of my surroundings until an arm of stone picked me up from the ruins on the ground and lifted me up aloft so that I could see everything.

'Blessed be the mighty and merciful God,' I exclaimed. 'All I need now is a pair of eyes, and luckily I have them.'

The tower of La Merced was high enough to be able to see everything from it. Almost at its feet was the Colégio del Rey;[243] then came San Cayetano and after that, further to the west, the Colegio Mayor de Cuenca,[244] and finally the Benedictines.[245] On the high ground opposite I saw a mass of ruined buildings whose names I did not know, but whose walls could be easily distinguished from the pieces of artillery stationed there. Turning round to look in the opposite direction I saw what was known as the Teso de San Nicolás,[246] the Premonstratensians[247] and Monte Olivete,[248] and between these positions and others, the fosse and the covered ways descending to the bridge.

From the San Vicente gate, where there was the ravelin with the four revolving cannons that Molichard had spoken about, a fosse ran to connect with Los Milagros.[249] Along the front and upper parts of the fosse was a line of loopholes supported by a strong stockade. The whole building of San Vicente was full of loopholes from which fire could be directed both into the city and to the countryside. San Cayetano was impressive. Almost completely demolished, they had made it into a spacious earthwork with batteries of all calibres, whose fire could sweep the Plazuela del Rey, the bridge and the Hospicio esplanade.

Although I was afraid that my jailer would return soon and therefore did my drawing in great haste, it did not turn out badly. I captured, imperfectly but very clearly, pretty much everything I saw. I did it while hiding behind the parapet of the tower, and, although the geometric projection left something to be desired as a scientific work, I did not omit any detail, indicating the number of cannons with scrupulous accuracy. Once I had finished my work, I carefully hid it and descended to the entrance of the tower. Throwing myself down on the bottom stair, I waited for Jean-Jean, intending to pretend I was asleep when he arrived.

A long time passed, making me anxious and worried but at last he appeared and I acted as if he had aroused me from a long and pleasant sleep. The expression on his face seemed to me to augur well. God had begun to protect me and it would have been extraordinarily cruel to cut off my road at that moment when it seemed to stretch before me so easy and passable, leading me directly to good fortune.

'You can come with me,' Jean-Jean said. 'I have seen your loved one.'

'And what happened?' I asked with great anxiety.

'I think she loves you, señor marquis,' he said in a flattering tone and smiling with the servility of one who does everything for money. 'When I gave her your note, she went whiter than the paper on which it was written… Señor Santorcaz, who is very ill, was sleeping. I called Ramoncilla and promised her a doubloon if she got the girl to come to me so that I could give her the note, but she said that would be impossible since the girl is locked up and when the master is asleep he keeps the key under his pillow… I insisted, promising two doubloons… The serving girl went in, made signs, and at a little window an extremely beautiful face appeared and a hand stretched out… I got up on a barrel… it wasn't high enough and I put a chair on the barrel… Oh, señor marquis, after reading the paper she told me you should come at once and then when I told her you needed to see two letters of hers to make you believe me, she wrote what you see now with a piece of charcoal… and if I have done well enough to earn my six doubloons,' he added flatteringly with one of those courtesies that only Frenchmen know how to do, 'your Excellency will no doubt say.'

The rogue had completely changed his attitude and behaviour to me. I took the paper on which was written '*Come at once*' in writing I recognised immediately. The scribbles with which the angels are meant to write the names of the chosen in the book of admission to Heaven could not have made me happier.

I paid Jean-Jean without making him have to repeat his indirect request.

We hurriedly left the tower, the observation point for my spying, and then the cloister and the ruined monastery, directing our steps along streets and lanes we passed in front of the cathedral, and then we plunged once more into various narrow alleys until at last Jean-Jean stopped and said,

'Here it is. We must go in quietly, although there's nothing to be afraid of and no one will stop us getting to the courtyard. Ramoncilla will let us through. After that it's up to God.'

We crossed the dark hall and pushing open a door we made out a narrow and damp courtyard where Ramoncilla appeared before us. She solemnly made signs that we should not make any noise and then leant her head onto the palm of her hand to indicate that her master was no doubt still asleep. We went forward step by step and Jean-Jean, still wearing his flattering smile, pointed out to me a narrow window, which was in one of the walls of the courtyard. I looked but no one appeared at it. My emotions were running so high that I was short of breath, and looked wildly to every side like someone who is seeing ghosts.

I heard a strange noise, a sound like the wings of an insect hovering by one's ear or like some pieces of fine fabric being rubbed together. I looked up and saw Inés at the window, holding the curtain aside with her left hand and putting the index finger of her right hand to her mouth to impose silence on me. Her face wore an expression of fear similar to that which overcomes us when we find ourselves at the edge of a deep precipice without being able to stop the force of gravity, which is propelling us towards it. She was as pale as death and her frightened look was driving me mad.

I saw a staircase to my right and rushed towards it, but the serving girl and the Frenchman told me, more with signs than with words, that I could not get in by that way. I held out my arms, ordering Inés to come down, but she made signs to say no, which made me more desperate.

'Where do I get up?' I asked.

The unfortunate girl put her hands to her head, cried and again signalled no. Then she seemed to want me to wait.

'I'm going up,' I said to the Frenchman, looking for something that would shorten the distance between us.

But Jean-Jean, officious and attentive, as someone who has received six doubloons, had already rolled over the barrel from where it was in a corner of the courtyard and placed it under the window. That was some help, but there was still a large gap without anything to support me or to hold onto. I was staring at the wall, or not so much wall, but inaccessible mountain, when Jean-Jean, swift, diligent and smiling, climbed onto the barrel and pointed me to his broad shoulders. Understanding his idea and following it was the work of a moment and climbing up that staircase of French flesh, my trembling hands were on the window ledge. I was up.

XVII

I found myself face to face with Inés who was looking at me, and in her eyes were mingled two very different feelings: joy and terror. She did not dare to speak to me and quickly put her hand to my mouth when I tried to say the first word, and wept burning tears onto my breast. Then, indicating to me with anxious gestures that I should not be there, she said to me,

'What about my mother?'

'Fine... why do I say fine? She's half-dead because of your absence... Come immediately... I have you at last... Are you crying with joy?'

I caught her in my arms in a rush of affection and said again,

'Come away with me now... poor little one! You're suffocating here... So long looking for you... Let's fly, my heart and life!'

The news of my imminent death would not have made me so sad as the words of Inés when, trembling in my arms, she said to me,

'You go. I cannot.'

I moved away from her and looked at her as one looks at something mysterious and shocking.

'What about my mother?' she repeated.

'Your mother is waiting for you. Do you see this letter? It's from her.'

She snatched the letter from my hands, covered it with kisses and tears and hid it in her bosom. Then, with the utmost swiftness, she withdrew from me, vehemently waving me towards the courtyard.

The soul that goes complacently to Heaven and at the gates meets Saint Peter who says to him, 'Good friend, this is not your destiny, take that path to the left,' that soul who has taken the wrong path because he had mistaken his destiny could not be as stunned as I was.

Two distinct emotions struggled with each other in my heart: first, immense joy, then anxiety, but all these gave way to fury and rage when I saw that lovely creature, whom I wanted to restore to liberty, sending me away without giving any reason. It was enough to make you mad! To find her after so much hard work, glimpse the possibility of taking away from there to return her to her anguished mother, to society, to life; to recover the lost treasure of my heart, to take her by the hand and to find that hand rejected!

'You're coming with me out of here right now!' I said, not keeping my voice down and pulling her arm so strongly that, because of the pain, she could not repress a small cry.

She threw herself at my feet and three times, three times, I tell you, in a voice that froze the blood in my veins she repeated,

'I cannot.'

'Didn't you order me to come?' I said, remembering the words she had written in charcoal on the paper.

She took a long document, recently written, from the table and gave it to me, saying,

'Take this letter, leave and do what I tell you in it. I will see you some other time at this window.'

'I will not,' I cried, tearing the paper into pieces. 'I won't leave without you.'

I looked out of the window and saw that Jean-Jean and Ramoncilla had disappeared. Inés went on her knees before me once more.

'The key, quickly go and fetch the key!' I said roughly. 'Get up off the floor, do you hear?'

'I cannot go,' she murmured. 'Leave immediately.'

Her large eyes, wide open with terror, were expelling me from the house.

'You're mad!' I exclaimed. 'Tell me to 'die', but don't tell me to 'leave'. That man is stopping you from going with me. He has so much power over you that he makes you forget your mother and me, your brother, your husband, me who has covered half of Spain looking for you and who has asked God a hundred times to take me in return for your liberty! Do you refuse to follow me? Tell me where that tyrant is, I want to kill him. That's the very thing I've come to do.'

Her distress made the words stick in my throat. She pressed my hand tenderly and in an anguished voice, so faint that it was hardly audible, she said to me,

'If you still love me, go away.'

I was on the point of giving way again to even greater fury when a distant voice, an echo, weakened by the distance from us, called many times,

'Inés, Inés.'

At the same time a little bell rang with a discordant note.

She got up, horrified, tried to compose her face and hair, dried the tears from her eyes and came towards me, her look imploring me with all her soul to be silent, to be calm, to obey her and then, moving away from me, she quickly left through a long corridor opening from the rear of the room.

Without a moment's hesitation I followed her. In the dark, I was guided by her white form which slipped between the two dark walls and the noise of her dress as it brushed against each one while she rushed along. She went into a spacious and well-lit room, which I also entered. It was her bedroom and with my first glance I noticed the pleasant modesty and tidiness of the room, artistically and elegantly furnished. The bed, the chairs, the chest of drawers, the pictures, the fine-coloured matting, the flower vases, the dressing table were all pretty and carefully chosen.

Because she was going much more quickly than me, by the time I had set foot in the bedroom, she had already passed into the adjoining room through a glass door, whose window was covered by white curtains of printed calico with blue bunches of flowers. I stopped there and saw her go to the far end of a vast room in semi-darkness which echoed with the voice of Santorcaz. Bitterness made me recognise him in the shadows of the large room and I made out the person of the wretch, reclining painfully in an armchair with his legs extended over a stool and surrounded by cushions and rugs.

I could also see the white form of Inés approaching the armchair; for a short time the indistinct shapes of both were blurred and joined together and I heard the smack of loving kisses which the man's lips planted on the woman's cheeks.

'Open up those shutters, open them up as it's very dark in the room,' Santorcaz said. 'I can't see you properly.'

Inés did so and the full, rich light of midday lit up the room. My eyes scanned it in a second, observing everything, the people and the scene. Santorcaz with a full and almost entirely white beard, a yellow face, his fiery eyes sunken, the handsome and wide forehead furrowed with wrinkles, bony hands, laboured breathing; no one but me would have recognised him because the features of that hated face were engraved in my mind. He was old, very old. The room had displays of fine collections of arms, some old furniture worn and marked, many books, various wardrobes, large chests, a bed whose canopy was supported by turned pillars and a wide pedestal table covered with a confused jumble of papers.

Inés moved close to the man who, because he was prematurely aged, I could call an old man.

'Why were you so long in coming?' Santorcaz said in a gentle and affectionate

voice, which surprised me greatly.

'I was reading that book… you know, that book,' the girl said in confusion.

The old man took the hand of Inés to his lips and kissed it with ineffable love.

'When my pains,' he continued, 'allow me some rest and I sleep, my daughter, an agonising worry torments me in my dreams: I think you are going away and leaving me alone, fleeing from me. I want to call you, but I can make no sound; I want to get up to follow you, but my body which has turned into a statue of iron does not obey me…'

Falling silent for a moment to rest his strained voice, he then continued as follows,

'A moment ago I was sleeping fitfully. I thought I was awake. I heard voices in the room leading to the courtyard; I saw you ready to flee, I wanted to cry out, but a horrendous weight, a mountain, was pressing down on my breast… The cold sweat of that anguish still moistens my brow… When I woke up I noticed that everything was a repetition of the same dream that torments me every night. Tell me, are you going to abandon me? Are you going to abandon this poor, sick man, this man, once young, now old, almost dying, who has done you some harm, that I admit, but who loves you, adores you, not as men love their fellow beings, but as they adore God or the angels? Are you going to abandon me and leave me on my own?'

'No,' Inés said.

That single word hardly reached me.

'And will you forgive me for the wrong that I have done to you, the freedom I have taken away from you? Can you forget the empty and deceptive grandeurs that you have lost on my account?'

'Yes,' the girl replied.

'But you will never love me as I love you. You will never be able to wipe from your heart the prejudice and horror I inspired in you and that makes me lose hope. All my efforts to please you, my determination to make your life pleasant, the quiet comfort that I have provided for you, all is useless… Instead of the venerable face of a father you will always see in me the hateful image of a thief. Are you still not convinced that I am a good, honourable, loyal, loving man, and not an abominable monster as some fools believe?'

Inés did not answer. I saw her glancing anxiously at the glass windows, which I was hiding behind.

'If I fear death for anything, it is for you,' the old man continued. 'Ah, if only I could take you with me without taking your life! But who would make sure I died? No, my illness is not mortal. I will live many years at your side, gazing at you and blessing you, because you have filled the emptiness of my existence. Blessed be the Supreme Being![250] I will live, we will live, I promise you that you will be happy. But you're not now? What's the matter? Why aren't you answering me? You're terrified, I'm making you afraid...'

The old man fell silent for a moment, and for a short while the only sound to be heard in the room was the beating of the thin wings of a fly bumping into the window panes, deceived by their transparency.

'My God!' he exclaimed bitterly. 'Am I the criminal they say I am? Is that what you think? Do you consider me to be a villain? You know I have done some strange things in my life, my daughter, but everything is explicable and justifiable in this world... Why should your mother have you when she abandoned you for so long while being able to come for you, and why should I not have you, I who love you at least as much as she? No, I love you more, much more, because she always took more pride in being a countess than being a mother and never called you daughter. She kept you by her side like a precious toy or trivial plaything. My daughter, the idleness, corruption and vanity of those grandees, so demeaning for their character, know no limits. Abandon those people, convince yourself of your superiority over them because of the nobility of your soul and do not give them the honour of filling your thoughts with anything to do with their rotten pride. Take pleasure in their torments and look forward with joy to the day when all of them fall into the mire. Nourish your imagination with the spectacle of redress and the justice of that great fall which awaits them and accustom yourself to feeling no pity for the exploiters of mankind who have done everything possible to make the people dance on their bodies after they have been killed.... But are you crying, Inés? You always say you do not understand this. I cannot wipe the memory of those days from your soul...'

Inés said nothing.

'I see then,' Santorcaz said with bitter irony after a brief pause. 'The young lady cannot live without a carriage, without a palace, without lackeys, without parties and without strutting around like the corrupted courtiers in the royal palaces... A man of the *Third Estate*[251] cannot give that to a young lady and the young lady looks down on her father.'

Santorcaz's voice assumed a harsh and scolding tone.

'Perhaps you hope to go back there,' he added. 'Perhaps you are hatching some plot against me... Ah, you ungrateful child, if you abandon me, if you let your heart be suborned by other loves, if you scorn the immense, infinite love of this unfortunate man… Inés, give me your hand, why are you crying? There, there, that's enough cant… Women are pampered and capricious… Come, daughter, you know I don't like tears. Inés, I want a happy face, quiet consent, contentment…'

The old man kissed his daughter on the forehead and then said,

'Bring up a table, I want to write.'

I could not contain myself anymore, and pushing open the glass door, I went into the room.

'A man, a thief!' Santorcaz shouted.

'You're the thief,' I said, moving forward boldly.

'Ah, I know you, I know you,' the old man exclaimed, lifting himself not without difficulty from his seat and flinging cushions and rugs to one side.

On seeing me Inés gave a piercing shriek and clutching her father, said,

'Don't hurt him, he's leaving.'

'Fool,' he cried. 'What do you want here? How did you get in?'

'What do I want? You ask me what do I want, villain?' I exclaimed, putting all my hatred into the words. 'I have come to take what is not yours from you. Have no fear for your miserable life because I will not vent my anger on that wretched body to which God has given a deserved piece of Hell in advance. But don't provoke me or hold on for a moment longer to what does not belong to you, reptile, or I'll flatten you.'

When he looked at me Santorcaz's eyes burnt with poison. There was so much venom and so much fire in them!

'I was expecting you!' he shouted. 'You are in the service of my enemies. A son of the people that eats the leftovers from the table of the great, I despise you. I may be sick and an invalid, but I'm not afraid of you. Your wretched condition and the brutalisation caused by servitude drive you to strike me with the hand with which you carry the litter of the nobles. I scorn your words. Your tongue, which worships the powerful and insults the weak, is fit only to sweep the dust in palaces. You can insult me or kill me, but my adored daughter, my daughter in whose veins flows the blood of a martyr of despotism, will not follow you out of here.'

'Let's go!' I shouted to Inés, ordering her imperiously to follow me, disdaining that garrulous revolutionary style of speaking which was so fashionable at that time among *afrancesados* and freemasons. 'Let's get out of here.'

XVIII

Inés did not move. She seemed a statue of indecision. Santorcaz, proud of his triumph, exclaimed,

'Lackey, lackey! Tell your contemptible masters that you're of no use to them.'

When I heard this a cloud of blood covered my eyes, I felt flames burning in my breast and I sprang forward towards the man. A lightning flash, when it strikes, must feel like I felt. He stretched out his arm to grab a pistol that was on a nearby table and when he pointed it at my breast, Inés rushed between us so violently that if he had fired, he would surely have killed her.

'Don't kill him, Father!' she screamed.

That scream, the appearance of that sick old man who threw the weapon far away from himself, refusing to defend himself, surprised me so much that I stood dumb, frozen and motionless.

'Tell him to leave us in peace,' the old man murmured, embracing his daughter. 'I know that you have known this unfortunate young man for a long time.'

The girl hid her tear-filled face in her father's breast.

'Heartless youth,' Santorcaz said to me in a trembling voice, 'leave; you inspire in me neither hatred nor affection. If my daughter wants to abandon me and follow you, take her with you.'

He fixed his burning eyes on his daughter and gripped the unhappy young girl's arm with his bony hand, no less hard and strong than a claw.

'Do you want to leave my side and go away with this young man?' he added, letting her go and pushing her gently away from himself.

I went forward a few steps and took Inés's arm.

'Let's go,' I said to her. 'Your mother is waiting for you. You are free, my darling, and your imprisonment and the torments of this house, which is a tomb inhabited by a madman, are over.'

'No, I cannot leave,' Inés said to me, running to the side of the old man who put his arms around her neck and kissed her tenderly.

'Very well, señora,' I said with so much anger that I felt impelled to all sorts of execrable violence, 'I will go. You will never see me again. You will never see your mother again.'

'I knew very well that you were incapable of the disgrace of abandoning me,' the old man exclaimed, weeping tears of joy.

Inés gave me an impassioned and profound look in which, through the tears, her black eyes told me all sorts of mysteries, revealed to me all sorts of enigmatic thoughts which, in the turbulence of that moment, I was unable to comprehend. No doubt she wanted to tell me much, but I understood nothing. Anger was suffocating me.

'Gabriel,' the old man said, recovering his calmness, 'you're not wanted here. You've heard already that you should go. I suppose you brought a rope ladder but so that you can leave more safely, take the key that is on the table, open the door that's in the corridor and take the staircase you'll see down to the courtyard. I would ask you to leave the key in the door.'

Observing my indecision and confusion, he added with caustic and cruel irony,

'If I can be of any use to you in Salamanca, don't hesitate to ask me. Do you need anything? You look as if you haven't had anything to eat today, my poor fellow. Your face suggests a lack of sleep, deprivation, hard work, hunger... The house of a man of the *Third Estate* does not lack for a piece of bread for the poor who come to its door. Does the same thing happen in the house of a nobleman?'

Inés looked at me with so much pity, and I felt the same for her as she did not hide her horrible suffering from me.

'Thank you,' I replied drily, 'I don't need anything. The piece of bread that I came looking for did not come into my hands, but I will return for it… Farewell.'

And taking the key, I hurriedly went from the room, the staircase, the courtyard, the horrible house; but father, daughter, room, courtyard and house, I carried them all inside me.

When I found myself in the street, I tried to think things over so that reason, numbed by my suffocating anger, could help me understand this unexpected event a little, but I was ruled only by passion, a wild irritation that made me stupid. Away now from the stage, far now from the characters, I tried to remember word by word what had been said there. I also tried to recall the expressions on their faces so that I could inquire into the background, find out causes and secrets. These things cannot rise up from the depths of souls to the surface of impassioned speeches in a lively dialogue between people who deeply love or hate each other.

Sometimes I regretted not having strangled that man made old by his passions, and at other times I felt an inexplicable pity for him. Inés's conduct, so unflattering to my amour propre, filled me at times with violent rage, the rage of a scorned lover, and at times with secret astonishment mixed with some of that instinctive sense of wonder produced by the grandeurs of Nature when one is close to them, when one knows one is about to see them, but has not yet done so.

My brain was full with the earlier meeting. Time passed and I went mechanically from one place to the other and I could still see them before me: she heartbroken and frightened, wanting to be kind to me and to her father; Santorcaz, furious, sarcastic, defiant and insulting with me, tender and loving with her. Looking closely at Inés, sinking deeper into her sorrow and into that pathetic sympathy of hers for human misery, there was really nothing new. But with him there was, a lot.

I drew out the past and set it before me; I went through all of that part of my life where I had had dealings with both of those persons. Finally, I arrived at a reason for my thoughts and feelings, which enlightened my mind a little.

'For a long time, and even today when I found myself face to face with him,' I said, 'I have always considered that man a villain, and I have never considered that he was a father.'

I had no doubt become accustomed to seeing this matter from a point of view that was not the most advisable.

With these thoughts and feelings, my brain full, my heart full, projecting my inner turmoil all around me, which made me look strangely at my surroundings, living only for myself, having completely forgotten what had brought me to Salamanca, I wandered through unknown streets.

Suddenly, a face appeared before me. I looked at it with as much indifference as one might look at a painted fop and it took me a long time to arrive at the conviction that I knew that face. When the soul is deep in abstractions, waking up takes time and is preceded by a series of mental processes where it argues with the senses about whether it recognises what is before it or not. I reasoned it out in the end and said to myself,

'I know those rat-like eyes I see in front of me.'

Gradually recovering my perception I spoke to myself as follows,

'I have seen that insolent nose somewhere and that hellish mouth that opens as wide as the ears in shameless and brazen laughter.'

Two heavy hands fell onto my shoulders.

'Let go of me, drunkard,' I exclaimed, pushing away at the intruder, who was none other than Tourlourou.

'*Satané farceur!*[18]' shouted Molichard who, unfortunately for me, was with him. 'You're coming to the barracks.'

'*Drôle de pistolet*[19]... come,' Tourlourou said, laughing diabolically. 'Chevalier Cipérez, Colonel Desmarets awaits you...'

'*Ventre de biche!*[20]... running off when you were going to be locked up.'

'And pulling out a knife to murder us.'

'Monseigneur Cipérez, *vous serez coffré et niché*[21].'

I tried to defend myself against those savages but it was impossible since, although drunk, the two of them together had more strength than me. At the same time, because the events in Santorcaz's house were paralysing my mental powers in a pitiful manner, I did not think of any ruse or trick that could get me out of this new difficulty, more serious no doubt than those overcome earlier.

They took me, or rather dragged me, to the barracks where in the morning I had had the honour of meeting Molichard. Tourlourou stopped at the gate, looking to the end of the street.

'*Dame!*[22]' he yelled. 'Here comes Colonel Desmarets.'

When my tormentors announced that the colonel in charge of police in the city was nearby, I commended my soul to God, certain that if by any chance they searched me and found the plan of the fortifications on me, it would take no more than a quarter of an hour before I was dancing at the end of a rope, as they would say. I looked anxiously all around me and asked,

---

18	Blasted trickster!
19	An awkward customer
20	Ruddy hell!
21	You will be thrown into jug and tucked up nicely.
22	Yes!

'Isn't Señor Jean-Jean here?'

Although the dragoon was no saint, I thought he was the only person who could save me.

Colonel Desmarets came up behind me. When I turned round... oh, wonder of wonders! I saw upon his arm a lady, I tell you, a lady who was none other than the very same Miss Fly herself, the very same Athenais, the very same Little Bird.

I stood amazed and she promptly greeted me with a vainglorious smile that showed her great pleasure in the surprise she had given me.

Molichard and his villainous companion went up to the colonel, a grave man of rather more than middle age, and with all the respect that their unsavoury drunkenness allowed, told him that I was a spy for the English.

'You insolent liars!' Miss Fly exclaimed with indignation in French. 'Do you dare to say that my servant is a spy? Colonel, pay no attention to these wretches whose eyes are overflowing with wine. This boy is the one who brought my luggage and the one I've been looking for with your help throughout the city in vain up to now... Tell me, fool, where have you put my case?'

'At the Fabiana inn, señora,' I replied humbly.

'At last! A fine walk I've had to take the colonel on, helping me to look for you... two hours scouring streets and squares...'

'It wasn't at all wasted, señora,' Desmarets said to her with gallantry. 'In this way you were able to see the most notable sights of this very interesting city.'

'Yes, but I needed to get some things from my case and this idiot... He is an idiot, colonel.'

'Señora,' I said, pointing to my two cruel enemies, 'when I was looking for your Excellency, these drunkards tricked me in to going into a tavern, drank at my expense, and then left me without a penny and said that I was a spy and planned to hang me.'

Miss Fly looked at the colonel with anger and haughtiness and Desmarets, who no doubt wanted to please the beautiful Amazon, gathered up all that feminine outrage to hurl it in a military way onto the two brave Frenchies who, seeing themselves changed from accusers to accuseds, seemed drunker than before and more incapable of keeping upright on their wobbly legs.

'To the barracks, you rabble!' their chief shouted in fury. 'I will deal with you shortly.'

Molichard and Tourlourou, arm in arm, confused and in mental and physical distress, stumbled into the building, each one blaming the other.

'I promise you I will lay a heavy hand on those scoundrels,' the brave officer said. 'But now that you have found your case, I will conduct you to your lodging.'

'Yes, I will thank you to do so,' Miss Fly said, setting off and ordering me to follow her.

'And then,' Desmarets added, 'I will issue an order allowing you to visit the hospital. I believe that there is no English officer left there. Those that were there recovered and were exchanged for the Frenchmen who were in Fuenteguinaldo.'[252]

'Oh, dear God! Then he must have died!' Miss Fly exclaimed with affected anguish. 'Unfortunate youth! He was a relation of my uncle, Viscount Marley... But won't you accompany me to the hospital?'

'Señora, it is not possible for me to do so. You already know that Marmont has given an order that we are to leave Salamanca this very day.'

'Are you evacuating the city?'

'That's what the general has ordered. We are threatened with a close siege. We are short of supplies and, as the fortifications we have created are excellent, we are leaving eight hundred picked men here who will be enough to defend them. We are leaving for Toro[253] to wait for them to send us reinforcements from the north or Madrid.'

'And are you leaving soon?'

'Within an hour. I can be at your service for only an hour.'

'Thanks... I'm sorry you can't help me find that brave young man, my countryman, whose whereabouts are unknown and who is the cause of my ill-timed and tiresome journey to Salamanca. He was wounded and was taken prisoner at Arroyomolinos. Since then nothing has been heard of him... They told me he might be in one of the French hospitals in this city.'

'I will give you a safe conduct so that you can visit the hospital and with that you will have no need of me.'

'Thank you very much. I believe we have arrived at my lodging.'

'Yes indeed, this is it.'

We were at the door of the Lechuga inn, no more than twenty paces from the one I had left my donkey at. Desmarets took his leave of Miss Fly, repeating his courteous and gentlemanly offers.

'So you see,' Athenais said to me after we had gone up to her room, 'you made a mistake when you didn't let me accompany you. No doubt you have had thousands of setbacks and difficulties. I, who know the brave Desmarets of old, would have spared you them.'

'Señora de Fly, I still haven't recovered from my amazement and I believe that what I have before me is not the true and real image of the beautiful English lady but a deceptive ghost that has come to increase the confusions of this day. How did you come to Salamanca? How were you able to enter the city? How did you manage to get that old prig, that Desmarets…'

'All this which seems so strange to you is the easiest thing in the world! Coming to Salamanca! Haven't you heard of roads? When you abandoned me with such rudeness and boorishness, I decided to come on my own. And here I am. I wanted to see how you would carry out your difficult commission and I hoped I could be of some service to you, although after your ingratitude you do not deserve any of my attention.'

'Oh, a thousand thanks, señora! When I left you I did so to spare you the dangers of this expedition. God knows how much pain it has caused me to sacrifice the pleasure and honour of being accompanied by you.'

'Well, then, señor peasant, when I got to the gates of the city, I remembered Colonel Desmarets whom I had rescued from the battlefield after Albuera, tending his wounds and saving his life. I asked for him and he came out to meet me, and since then I have had no difficulty in either coming in here or finding lodging. I told him I had been drawn by the desire to know the whereabouts of an English officer, a relative of mine, lost at Arroyomolinos, and because I wanted to find you, I pretended that one of my servants whom I had brought with me, carrying my case, had disappeared into the gates of the city. Wishing to help me, Desmarets took me to various places. Walking about for two hours! I was desperate… I was looking from one side to the other saying, 'Where can that idiot be? He must have been struck dumb by the forts… he's such a fool…'

'And the young boy who accompanied you?'

'He came in with me. Didn't you make fun of Mrs. Mitchell's carriage? It's a great vehicle and drawn by the horse that Simpson gave me, it was like Apollo's chariot… Now let's see, señor officer, how you have employed your time and if you have done anything to justify the duke's confidence in you.'

'Señora, I have hidden on me a plan of the fortifications… In addition, I have a lot of information which will be very useful to the commander-in-chief. I have encountered thousands of difficulties but in the end, as far as my military commission is concerned, everything has turned out well for me.'

'And you did it without me!' the Butterfly said spitefully.

'If I had time to tell you about the tragedies and comedies I have been acting in these last few hours… but I'm so tired that I can hardly even speak. The shocks, the joys, the emotions, the anger of today would have overcome a stronger spirit and a more vigorous body, all the more my spirit and body, one being stunned and sad, the other so empty of any solid sustenance, like someone who has not eaten for sixteen hours.'

'Actually, you do look almost dead,' she said, going into her room. 'I'll get you something to eat.'

'An excellent idea,' I replied, 'and since we have miraculously met here, which proves our common destiny, it is best we set ourselves up under the same roof. I will go and fetch my donkey in whose saddlebag I left something worth eating. I'll be back immediately. Ask the landlady what she has… but be quick, very quick.'

I went to the inn where I had left my donkey and when I entered the large room I heard the voice of the innkeeper deep in dispute with another one which I recognised to be that of the worthy Jean-Jean.

'Young man,' the innkeeper said to me as I went in, 'this French gentleman wants to take away your donkey.'

'Excellency!' Jean-Jean said politely although very embarrassed. 'I didn't want to take away the animal… I was asking for you.'

I remembered the promise I had made to the dragoon and the little fib I had made about the saddlebag to get out of an awkward spot.

'Jean-Jean,' I said to the Frenchman. 'I still need your help. The French are leaving today, isn't that the case?'

'Yes, sir, but I'm staying. Twenty of us dragoons are staying to escort the governor.'

'I'm glad to hear it,' I said preparing to take the donkey with me. 'Now, Jean-Jean, my friend, I need to know whether this head of the masons is also planning to leave Salamanca today. It's probable that he will.'

'I will find out, sir.'

'I'm at the inn next door, understood?'

'The *Lechuga*, yes.'

'I will expect you there. We have much to do today, Jean-Jean, my friend.'

'I desire nothing more than to serve your Excellency.'

'I pay well those who serve me well.'

Miss Fly, using the excuse that the inn's serving girl should not hear what we were talking about, served me with the frugal meal herself, something which, if it did not conform with the canons of English etiquette, suited the circumstances perfectly.

XIX

'Your sadness,' the Englishwoman said, 'proves to me that even if you have succeeded in your military commission, the same thing has not happened in the other matter that you undertook.'

'That is the case, señora,' I replied, 'and I swear to you that I have never been as grief-stricken or disheartened in my life.'

'Isn't your princess in Salamanca?'

'She is, señora,' I replied, 'but under such circumstances that it would be better if she were not here or within a hundred leagues of here. Because, what good is it finding her if it turns out she…'

'Is enchanted,' the Englishwoman said, interrupting me with painful jollity, 'and transformed, like Dulcinea, from the finest lady into a rustic and ugly peasant girl?'

'It amounts to much the same thing,' I said, 'because if my princess has lost none of the gracefulness of her presence, nor any of the unequalled beauty of her face, she has on the other hand suffered a great transformation in her soul, because she did not wish to accept the freedom I offered her and, preferring the company of her barbarous jailer, neatly showed me the door to the street.'

'There's a very simple explanation for that,' the lady told me, laughing with true delight, 'and that is that your imprisoned archduchess no longer loves you. Didn't you think how awkward it would be to appear before her in those clothes? The long time with her kidnapper will have led her to fall in love with him. Do not laugh, sir. There are many cases of ladies having been snatched by bandits in Italy or Bohemia who have ended up falling madly in love with their kidnappers. I myself knew a young Englishwoman who was seized near Rome and in a short time became the wife of the chief of the band. In Spain, where thieves are so poetic, so chivalrous that they are almost the only gentlemen in the country, the same thing is sure to happen. There's nothing absurd in what you have told me, sir, and it fits perfectly with the ideas I have formed about this country.'

'Your lively imagination,' I said to her, 'deceives itself perhaps when it encounters certain things outside books. But, whatever the case may be, señora, what has happened to me is very sad… because…'

'Because you love your child even more since she now adores that pasha with three tails, that Fra Diavolo, whom I fancy is a great thief, but a handsome one like the handsomest ones in Calabria and Andalusia, braver than the Cid[254], a great horseman, a sublime swordsman, a bit of a magician, generous to the poor, cruel to the rich and the wicked, as rich as the Grand Turk and owner of an immense number of jewels which always seem to him to be too few for his lover. I also imagine him to be like Carlos Moor,[255] the most poetic and interesting of the highwaymen.'

'Oh, Miss Fly, I see that you have read a lot! My enemy is not as you paint him, he is a sick old man.'

'Well, then, Señor Araceli,' Athenais said in disgust, 'don't try and deceive me by describing this young woman as a worthy person since if she has formed a relationship with a sick old man, it must have been out of greed, a characteristic quality of seamstresses, maidservants, actresses or other lowly types, to whose respectable class I shall from now on believe the highly lauded lady you adore belongs.'

'I have not deceived you by elevating the class she belongs to. As for the affection she might have for her kidnapper, there is nothing reprehensible about that, since he is her father.'

'Her father!' she exclaimed in surprise. 'That's certainly not something I have read in my books. And you call a father that keeps his daughter by his side a thief? That really is something strange. There's no country like Spain for odd happenings and where everything is so different from what is natural and common in other countries. Explain this to me, sir.'

'You believe that all episodes of love and adventure have to happen in the world in accordance with what you have read in novels, ballads and the works of great poets and writers. You are not aware that strange and dramatic events are usually seen in real life before appearing in books, full of conventional stories and each one reproducing another one. The poets copy their predecessors, who copied earlier ones, and while they invent this imaginary world, they do not notice that hidden away from the public and the printing house, nature and society are creating thousands of new things which amaze or delight.'

I used all my powers of ingenuity to sustain in some way the conversation with Miss Fly, who had the advantage of me with her ardent poetic feeling and at my every word her vivid imagination became more inflamed in its flight in pursuit of strange, unknown, romantic events, sources of passion and idealism. I cannot deny that Athenais surprised me, as in my ignorance, I was unaware of the sentimentalism which was fashionable among the people of the North, invading literature and society to an extraordinary extent.

'Tell me all about this,' she said to me impatiently.

Without fear of committing any indiscretion I told my beautiful companion point by point everything the reader knows. She listened to me so attentively and with such an appearance of delight that I did not omit any detail. At times I thought I saw in her signs more of manly enthusiasm than of feminine emotion, and when I came to the end of my tale, she stood up and with a determined look and in a spirited tone said to me,

'And you live calmly like that, sir, and recount those dramas from your life as if they were pages from a book you had read the night before? You are not a Spaniard, you do not have in your veins that sublime fire that drives a man to fight against the impossible. There you are twiddling your thumbs looking at an Englishwoman and nothing occurs to you; it doesn't occur to you to enter that house, snatch that unhappy woman from the power keeping her prisoner, throw a rope round the neck of that man and take him off to the madhouse. It doesn't occur to you to buy an old sword and fight with half the world if half the world opposes your desire, break the doors of the house, set it on fire if necessary, grab the girl without trying to persuade her to follow you and take her where you think best, kill all the constables that get in your way and open a path through the French Army if the French Army en masse prevents you from leaving Salamanca. I confess that I thought you were capable of this.'

'Señora,' I replied warmly, 'tell me in which book you read that fine thing you have just told me. I want to read it, too, and then I will test whether such deeds are possible.'

'In which book, you silly man?' she replied with admirable elation. 'In the book of my heart, the one of my fantasy, the one of my soul. Do you want me to teach you some more from it?'

'Señora,' I said in confusion, 'your soul is more elevated than mine.'

'Let's go immediately to that house,' she said, picking up a riding whip and preparing to leave.

I looked at Miss Fly with admiration, but an admiration that was not entirely serious in that something inside me was laughing.

'Where, señora, where do you want us to go?'

'What a question!' Athenais exclaimed. 'Sir, if I had thought you capable of asking that question which reveals the hesitation in your soul, I would never have come to Salamanca.'

'No, but I understand perfectly,' I replied, not wishing to appear inferior to her. 'I understand… we're going to… well… do an extraordinary thing, one that will be famous… I dare to do it, and greater things, too.'

'So…'

'That was precisely what I was thinking of doing. I don't know fear.'

'Nor the obstacles, nor the danger, nor anything. Yes, yes, that, sir, is the answer,' she cried out with enthusiasm.

Her glowing face, her brilliant eyes, the timbre of her moving voice exercised a strange power over me and awoke in me some sort of vague sensations of glory, asleep in the depths of my heart, so asleep that I did not believe they existed. Without knowing what I was doing, I got up from my chair, crying out to her,

'Let's go, let's go there!'

'Are you ready?'

'Now I remember that I need a sword... an old one...'

'Or a new one... it would do no harm to see Desmarets.'

'I don't need anybody, I'm enough on my own, more than enough,' I exclaimed with determination and pride.

'Sir,' she said enthusiastically, 'that's really what I should have said so that I'm like Medea.'

'I said that we couldn't go in there with Desmarets,' I suggested, thinking a bit on the bright side, 'because he's leaving Salamanca today.'

At that moment we heard some noise outside. It was the French Army leaving. A deafening sound of drums filled the street. Then their booming sounds were drowned out by the passing cavalry squadrons and finally the tremendous rumble of the gun carriages made the walls shake as if in an earthquake. For a long time troops continued to pass by.

'I hope I will be the first to bring Lord Wellington the news that the French have left Salamanca,' I said in a low voice to Miss Fly, watching the troops march past from our window.

'There goes Desmarets,' the Englishwoman replied, fixing her eyes on the troops.

Desmarets was indeed passing by on horseback in front of his regiment and he saluted Miss Fly gallantly.

'We have lost a protector in the city,' she said to me, 'but it doesn't matter, we won't need him.'

At this point there were some light knocks on the door. I opened it and there before us stood Jean-Jean, hat in hand, making a series of elaborate bows.

'Excellency, the innkeeper told me you were here and I have come to tell you...'

'What?'

Jean-Jean looked suspiciously at Miss Fly, but I immediately reassured him, saying,

'You can speak, Jean-Jean, my friend.'

'Well, I came to tell you,' the soldier continued, 'that this Señor Santorcaz is leaving the city. As Salamanca is going to be besieged, many families are fleeing tonight, and the mason won't be one of the last, according to what Ramoncilla has told me. He left his house a moment ago, no doubt to fetch some carriages and horses.'

'That means he's going to escape us,' Miss Fly said sharply.

'They won't leave until after midnight,' he replied.

'Jean-Jean, my friend, I'd like you to get me a sabre and two pistols.'

'Nothing easier, Excellency,' he answered.

'And also a cape… then when it's night get the coach ready…'

'There's not one to be found in the city.'

'We have one below. Harness the horse which is also below and take it to the gate nearest to the Calle del Cáliz.'

'That's the Santi-Spíritus gate… I would advise you that Santorcaz has returned to his house. I saw him accompanied by five well-built friends, terrifying men who are capable of anything…'

'Five men!'

'Who don't like games being played with them. They meet there every night and are well armed.'

'Have you got some friend who'd like to earn himself a few doubloons and who is besides brave, calm and discreet?'

'My cousin *Pied-de-Mouton* would be good for the job, but he's a bit sick. I don't know if *Charles le Téméraire* wants to get involved in such a rough house. I'll ask him.'

'We don't need your friends,' Miss Fly said. 'We don't want any ruffians at our side. We'll go entirely on our own.'

'You will have the weapons in a moment,' Jean-Jean stated. 'Aren't you going to tell me anything about your donkey?'

'I will give him to you, with saddlebag and all… but don't go looking for anything in it yet. I'll give you what you deserve once we are safe outside the city gates.'

Jean-Jean gave me a suspicious look, but either trust was reborn in his breast or he was able to disguise his mistrust and he left. When he returned at nightfall and brought me the weapons, I ordered him to wait for me in the Calle del Cáliz. And with that the Englishwoman and I considered preparations complete for that stupendous and unheard-of event, which the reader will learn about in the following chapters.

XX

Coming to this part of my story I am compelled to pause by a certain serious doubt that I cannot get rid of, however much I try. Despite the accuracy and truthfulness of my memory, which preserves so precisely the most distant events, it is the case that I doubt whether it was really me that performed the rash act in question, pressed into it by the poetic and wilful power of a beautiful Englishwoman, or whether, dreaming that I had done it, I believed that I did it, because as often happens in life, it is not easy to untangle what is dreamt of from what is real, or if instead of it being my own person who threw himself into such undertakings, it was another me who knew how to interpret the fiery sentiments and noble ideas of the bewitching Athenais. The thing is, considering myself to be sane today, as I was then, I find it hard to state conclusively that it was me who was responsible for such madness, even though all the facts, all the information and every tradition agree that it could not have been anyone else. I bow my head to the evidence and continue my tale.

So then, night came, wrapping the whole of *Roma la chica* into its shadows. Miss Fly and I left and, crossing the Rúa, we penetrated the dark and twisting streets that would lead us to the place of our mysterious adventure. Very soon we got lost, both of us being ignorant of the city's layout, and we wandered at random, trying to guess where we were by the buildings we had seen during the day, but in the darkness we were unable to make out clearly the forms of those blocks which emerged as we passed. Suddenly we found ourselves barred by a gigantic wall whose top was lost way up in the heavens. Then one could almost believe that the enormous mass moved to one side to let us go down an alley lit in the distance by small devotional lamps, burning before an image.

We went on ahead believing we would find the street we were looking for, and we stumbled onto a portico and a tower where in the darkness of the night everyone was coming together from different directions and getting in our way. Finally we recognised the cathedral among those mountains of darkness which surrounded us. We could make out perfectly its vast, irregular shape, its towers which began in one artistic period and finished in another, its pointed arches, its crenellations, its round cupola and behind the new building, the old cathedral, huddled up next to it as if seeking shelter. We could get our bearings there and going in the direction we believed was best, we quickly ran up against the twin porticos of the university in whose façade the large heads of the Catholic Monarchs[256] gazed at us with their absorbed eyes of stone. Slipping down a side of the vast edifice, we found ourselves surrounded on all sides by walls with no way out to be found.

'This is a labyrinth, Miss Fly,' I said, with some bad temper, 'let's look for this blessed street towards the back of the cathedral. Otherwise, we'll spend the night going up and down streets.'

'Why are you in such a hurry? Better to wait till later.'

'Señora, Lord Wellington is expecting me tomorrow at noon in Bernuy. I think I have said enough… let's see if there's a passer-by who can show us the way.'

But there was no living soul to be seen in that lonely place.

'What a beautiful city!' Miss Fly said in contemplative bliss. 'Everything here exudes the greatness of an illustrious and glorious age. How sublime, how powerful must have been the feelings that required so much stone, so very much, to express them! Don't they say anything to you, those high towers, those long arched windows, those roofs, those giants raising their hands to Heaven, those two cathedrals, the one ancient and on its knees, lined, an invalid, crouching on the ground and protected by its daughter, the other one, superb and upright, beautiful, immense, vigorous, exuding life in its robust bulk? Don't they say anything to you, those hundred colleges and monasteries, works of science and stone combined? And those palaces of the great lords, those walls full of shields and grilles, emblems of pride and caution? Happy that age when the soul could always find something to feed its insatiable hunger! For religious souls the monastery, for heroic ones war, for passionate ones love, the more beautiful the more it was thwarted, for everyone gallantry, grand emotions, sublime sacrifices, glorious deaths… calculation had still not been invented. Passion ruled the world and put its seal of fire on it. A man overcomes everything to possess his beloved or dies fighting before the gates of the home she is imprisoned in… For the sake of a woman wars break out and two nations destroy each other for a kiss… The force that seemingly holds sway is not the brutal drive of the moderns, but a powerful breath, the heavy breathing of the two lungs of society, honour and love…'

'That little speech wouldn't sell at all badly,' I murmured, 'if we could only find…'

When she said this we had already lost sight of the cathedral and we were in the depths of narrow and dark streets, looking in vain for Calle del Cáliz. We saw an old woman leaning on a stick and walking slowly close to a wall and I asked her,

'Señora, can you tell me where Calle del Cáliz is?'

'You're asking for Calle del Cáliz when you're already in it?' the old woman replied sharply. 'Are you going to the masons' house or to the lodge in Calle de Tentenecios? If you are, carry on straight ahead and don't trouble a poor old woman who wants nothing to do with the devil.'

'And which is the masons' house, señora?'

'Asking for it when it's here in your hand!' the old woman answered. 'The large doorway behind you is the entrance to the dwelling of those rascals. That's where they commit their foul heresies against religion, that's where they say awful things about our beloved monarchs… Wretches! How I'd like to go and see them burn on the Plaza Mayor! May God rid us of the French who allow such filthy goings-on… Masons and the French are all the same, the left and right claws of Satan.'

The old woman left, talking to herself. When we were alone I recognised from the large doorway that we were close to Santorcaz's house.

'How many times we must have passed here without you recognising the house!' Miss Fly said. 'If I had seen it just once… you seem a bit slow-witted, Araceli.'

The door was a very ancient Byzantine arch composed of six or eight concentric curves on which ran mysterious vegetal forms, worn away by time, snakes and intertwined fillets, and on the impost were some little devils, monkeys or some other impudent animals prancing about and blending their scrawny little legs with the sprigs of the dead leaves of stone. Unintelligible letters which no doubt dated from the time of its construction had left their grotesque and twisted traces as if an unsteady finger had traced them as a form of spell. The door was reinforced with iron hooks as rusty as the badly joined boards were worm-eaten and broken, and a massive knocker in the figure of a coiled serpent hung in the centre waiting for an impatient hand to move it.

I gave Miss Fly a quizzical look and saw her hand approach the large door knocker.

'So soon, señora?' I asked, restraining her.

'Well, what are you waiting for?'

'It's best to reconnoitre the enemy first... the house is well built... Jean-Jean said that inside there were... how many men?'

'Fifty, if I remember correctly... but even if there were a thousand...'

'That's right, even if there were a million.'

We saw a man approaching and I immediately recognised Jean-Jean.

'Reinforcements are arriving, señora,' I said. 'You will see how quickly I'll polish them off.'

Miss Fly, seizing the door knocker, struck it hard.

I felt for my weapons and finding that I had not forgotten them, I could not avoid a feeling, I did not know which, of self-mockery or self-admiration, because in truth, dear readers, what I was about to do, what I was trying to do at that moment was either something foolish or a deed like one performed in ballads and books of chivalry. I remember having read somewhere that a helpless lover arrives, neatly and with no help other than the strength of his arm, or the protection of some powerful necromancer or other, at the gates of a castle where the coarsest and biggest bearded Moor or giant of those wild and remote parts is holding prisoner the most delicate maiden, princess or empress who has combed threads of gold and wept liquid diamonds, and this helpless lover cries from down below, 'Cruel caliph, or barbaric sultan, I have come to snatch from you that royal queen whom you hold captive and I call upon you to yield her to me this instant if you do not want your body to be split in two by this my sword and do not laugh or threaten me, as even if you had more armies than the Parthian had for the conquest of Greece, not one of your men would remain alive.'

And this, dear readers, this, nothing more or less, is what I was about to undertake.

When I touched my pistols and the sword belt from which hung the sharp sword and flung the top of the cape from me and the brim of my wide hat over my eyebrow, I confess that of the feelings that were struggling in my heart it was ridiculousness that prevailed and I laughed in the darkness. I had the appearance of a bragging, flashy and tricky character who would strike fear into the bravest soul, if he didn't scoff and laugh instead. But Miss Fly had no doubt read of the deeds of Don Rodulfo de Pedrajas, Pedro Cadenas, Lampuga, Gardoncha and Perotudo,[257] and my appearance must have seemed to her more inclined to inspire love than laughter.

Seeing there was no reply, I grabbed the door knocker and rapped several times. I had not weighed up the extent of the danger I was about to face, nor was it possible to reflect on it, even though a flash of light from my brain would have been enough to enlighten me about the horrendous fight I was about to get involved in... I did not think of that, because I felt the inexplicable delight that young men in love have in everything mysterious and unknown, the more beautiful and attractive the more dangerous it is, because I felt in me a desire to commit some nameless act of brutality, that I might stake my strength and courage in the service of the person I loved most in the world.

It should not be forgotten that my despair and anger from the morning still remained. The memory of those scenes that I have described earlier completed my blindness and to attain through violence what I could not achieve by other means was no doubt a great attraction for my excited mind. In the street fantasy spurred me on, and from inside, the heart, all my past life and what I could dream of the future called me... Who would not break down a wall, even though with one's head, when driven to it by two women, one from inside and one from outside?

XXI

I should not deny that the beautiful Englishwoman had acquired a great hold over me. I cannot express her domination and my enslavement without using a word much used in novels, and I do not know if it will clearly indicate my thoughts, but not having any other word to hand, I will use it. Miss Fly fascinated me. That greatness of spirit, that refined sentiment untainted by egoism in her words, that character which possessed, with an unequalled abundance, all the material, let us call it that, about the great deeds, found a secret affection in a corner of my being. I laughed at her and I admired her; her words of advice seemed foolish remarks to me, but I followed them. That greatness of mind, so distant from reality, seduced me and sooner than admitting to being a coward in following the flight of her powerful will, I would have died of shame.

I knocked repeatedly with more force, but nothing was to be heard from inside the house. Darkness and silence as in the tomb reigned in it. The little animal, lizard or serpent which formed the door knocker raised (or so it seemed) its head full of rust, and fixing its green eyes on me, opened its horrible mouth to laugh at me.

'They don't want to open,' Jean-Jean said to me. 'Nevertheless, they are inside. I saw them go in… They are the most *afrancesado* in the whole city, greater masons than the Grand Copt and greater atheists than Judas… a bad lot. My opinion, Señor Marquis, is that you should leave. The coach is waiting for you at the Santi-Spíritus gate.'

'Are you afraid, Jean-Jean?'

'Besides, Señor Marquis,' he continued, 'I have to warn you that the patrol will be passing here soon… You and the señora look highly suspicious… There are still some who believe you are a spy and the señora as well.'

'I, a spy?' Miss Fly said scornfully. 'I am an English lady.'

'You leave, Jean-Jean, if you are afraid.'

'What you're doing is mad, sir,' the dragoon replied. 'Those men are going to come out and beat us all up.'

I thought I heard the sound of wooden shutters opening high up and I shouted,

'Hey there in the house! Open up immediately.'

'This is madness, Señor Marquis,' the dragoon said brusquely. 'Let's get away from here…'

At that point I noticed an obvious change in the sullen and gloomy face of Jean-Jean, which was certainly not caused by fear.

'I'm telling you again I'm leaving you on your own, Señor Marquis… The night watch is about to come… let's go to Sancti-Spíritus, or I will not be responsible for the consequences.'

His insistence and the desire to get us outside the city aroused a terrible suspicion in me.

Miss Fly redoubled the hammering, saying,

'We'll have to break the door down if they don't open.'

The iron hooks which reinforced the door tightened, making horrible faces, mocking symbols in shapes which I did not know if they were strange smiles or grimaces, or wry expressions on mysterious faces.

I was starting to lose my patience and my calm. I was anxious about Jean-Jean and feared treachery, not because of the suspicion of spying, as he had told us, but because of the temptation to rob us. This was nothing new and the soldiers who garrisoned the villages of the poor conquered country committed a whole range of excesses with impunity. Also, the adventure was taking on a grotesque character since nobody was answering to our knocking, nor did any human face appear at the window up above.

'There's certainly not a trace of anyone here. The masons have left and this villain has brought us here to plunder us at his leisure.'

Suddenly I saw someone appear at a bend in the street. Two people were standing there as if lying in wait. I turned to the dragoon, but he suddenly abandoned us without waiting for me to say anything to him and joined the others.

'This wretch has betrayed us!' I bellowed in rage. 'Señora, we are lost! We didn't reckon with such treachery.'

'Treachery!' said Miss Fly in confusion. 'It can't be.'

We had no time for discussion because the two who were watching us and Jean-Jean were on top of us.

'What are you doing here?' one of them asked me, an artilleryman without any regimental markings.

'I don't have to give an account to you,' I replied. 'Let us pass.'

'Is this the English camp follower?' the other one said, looking insolently at Miss Fly.

'Villain!' I shouted, drawing my sword. 'I will teach you how to speak to ladies.'

'The little marquis has got his roasting spit out,' the first one said. 'Come along with us, youngsters, to the guardhouse and you, *milady sauterelle*[23], give your arm to *Charles le Téméraire* so that he can conduct you to the palace of the public stocks.'

'Araceli,' Miss Fly said to me, 'take my whip and drive them away.'

'*Pied-de-mouton*, run him through,' the artilleryman shouted.

Pied-de-mouton, as a sergeant in the dragoons, was armed with a sabre. *Charles the Bold* was an artilleryman and carried a short machete, a weapon of little use on this occasion. In a flash, while Jean-Jean was hesitating between going for the Englishwoman or me, I slashed at *Pied-de-mouton* with such good fortune, violence and steadiness that I laid him out on the ground. Letting out a hoarse yell he fell, covered in blood… I got close to the wall to guard against any attack from behind and waited for Jean-Jean who, seeing his companion fall, left Miss Fly while Charles the Bold was leaning over to help the wounded man. Swift as thought, Athenais bent down and picked up the latter's sabre. Without waiting for Jean-Jean to attack me and seeing he was somewhat disconcerted, I fell upon him, but he took a few steps backwards, startled, and roared,

'*Corne du Diable! Mille millions de bombardes!*[24] Do you think I'm afraid of you?'

---

23   my lady grasshopper
24   The Devil's horn! Blistering bombards!

With these words he broke into a run down the street and Charles the Bold followed him, as quick as the wind. Both of them shouted,

'Police, police!'

'There are some police nearby, señora. Let's be off. The ballad has come to an end here.'

We ran in the opposite direction to the one they had taken, but we had not gone a few paces when we heard in the distance the sound of footsteps and we could see a detachment of soldiers coming towards us at top speed.

'They're cutting off our retreat, señora,' I said, turning round. 'Let's go another way.'

We looked for a junction that would let us go in another direction but we didn't find one. The patrol was getting closer. We ran to the other end and heard our two enemies still shouting,

'Police!'

'They have caught us,' Miss Fly said with incomparable calmness, which took my breath away. 'Never mind. Let's surrender.'

Just then, as we were passing by the doorway whose door knocker we had hammered at so uselessly, I saw that the door was open and someone was looking out curiously, having no doubt been unable to overcome his desire to know the outcome of the fight... Heaven opened up before us. The patrol was nearby, but since the street turned at a sharp angle there they could not see us. I pushed at the door and the man who was looking out in curiosity with an ironic smile on his face, and, although at first neither of us wanted to give way, I used so much force that Miss Fly and I were quickly inside and with incredible alacrity I drew the heavy bolts.

'What are you doing?' asked in amazement a man I saw in front of me, and who was lighting up the narrow doorway with a lantern.

'Save me and save this lady,' I replied, listening closely to the footsteps which could be heard in the street, outside the door, shortly after our entry. 'The patrol is stopping...'

'Now they are examining the body...'

'They didn't see us come in...'

'But, either I'm an idiot, or it's Araceli I have before me,' said the man, who was none other than Santorcaz.

'The very same, Don Luis. If it's your intention to denounce me, you can do so by handing me over to the patrol, but keep this lady in a safe place until she can leave Salamanca freely... They're still there,' I continued in great anxiety. 'What a lot of grunting! They must be recovering the body. Is he dead or just wounded?'

'They are going,' Athenais said. 'They didn't see us enter... They'll think it was just a fight between soldiers, as long as those villains don't start talking…'

'Go on in, señores,' Santorcaz said irritably. 'The first duty of a son of the people is hospitality and his home receives as many of his fellow men that need shelter. Señora, you have nothing to fear.'

'And who told you that I was afraid of something?' Miss Fly said arrogantly.

'Araceli, was it you that was demolishing my door a moment ago?'

I hesitated an instant in answering and had the words in my mouth when Miss Fly jumped in, saying,

'It was I.'

After making a bow to the English lady, Santorcaz remained silent, waiting to hear the reasons why the lady had knocked so loudly.

'Why are you looking at me with your mouth open?' Miss Fly said brusquely. 'Go on and light the way for us.'

Santorcaz looked at me in amazement. Which of us surprised him more, her or me? For my part, I was surprised, too, and greatly, on finding that the head of the masons was receiving us with such courtesy.

We went slowly up the stairs. From it could be heard loud voices of men in the interior of the house. When we came to a bare and dark room, weakly lit by Santorcaz's lantern, he said to us,

'Might I know what you are looking for in my house?'

'We entered here looking for refuge from some villains who wanted to murder us. I would like you to hide this lady in case they persist in pursuing her into the house.'

'And what about you?' he asked me sarcastically.

'I value my life,' I replied, 'and I would prefer not to fall into the hands of Jean-Jean. But I ask you no favours and I will go out into the street right now if you promise me to keep this lady safe.'

'I do not abandon my friends,' Santorcaz said with his habitual charm and smoothness. 'The lady and her gallant can breathe freely. No one will harm them.

XXII

Miss Fly had sat down in an uncomfortable leather armchair, the only piece of furniture in that untidy room, and without paying attention to our conversation, was looking at the two or three worm-eaten paintings hanging on the walls, when the maid entered, carrying a light.

'Is this your daughter?' the Englishwoman asked excitedly, fixing her eyes on the girl.

'It's Ramoncilla, my maid,' Santorcaz replied.

'I passionately want to see your daughter, sir,' the Englishwoman said. 'She has the reputation of being very beautiful.'

'Present company excepted,' the mason said gallantly, 'I don't believe there is anyone more beautiful... but reverting to our business, señora, if you and your husband wish...'

'This gentleman is not my husband,' Miss Fly declared without looking at Santorcaz.

'Very well, I meant your friend.'

'He is not my friend either, he is my servant,' the lady said, annoyed. 'You are indeed impertinent.'

Santorcaz looked at me, and in his look I could see that he did not believe the lady's declaration.

'Very well... are you and your servant intending to stay in Salamanca?'

'No, we just want to leave without anyone troubling us. I cannot achieve the objective which brought me to Salamanca and therefore I'm going...'

'Then I will get both of you out of the city before daybreak,' Santorcaz said, 'because I'm making all preparations for leaving at dawn.'

'And are you taking your daughter?' Miss Fly asked with great interest.

'My daughter loves me so much,' the mason replied with great pride, 'that she will never leave me.'

'And where are you going now?'

'To France. I don't intend to set foot in Spain again.'

'You are a poor patriot...'

'Señora, tell me your title so that I can address you with it. Although I am a son of the people and a defender of liberty, I know how to pay respect to the hierarchies established by the monarchy and history.'

'Just call me *señora*, that's enough.'

'Well, then, given that the señora wants to meet my daughter, I will introduce her,' Santorcaz said. 'If the señora would be so good as to follow me.'

We followed him and he took us to a room, which was better furnished than the one we had left and was lit by an oil lamp with four wicks. The old man offered a chair to the Englishwoman and then disappeared, returning shortly afterwards with his daughter on his arm. When the unhappy woman saw me, she turned as pale as death and could not stop herself from uttering a cry of surprise which, in its intensity, seemed one of fear.

'My daughter, this is the lady who has just arrived here requesting my hospitality for her and the young man accompanying her.'

Inés looked like someone who had seen a ghost. She looked first at Miss Fly then at me, trying to convince herself that the persons she saw before her were real and tangible. I smiled, trying to dispel her confusion with the language of eyes and plays of expression, but the poor girl became more and more amazed.

'She is certainly beautiful,' Miss Fly said gravely. 'But don't take your eyes off this young man who accompanies me. No doubt you find him similar to the other one you know. My child, he is the one you think he is, the same one.'

'Except that this rascal,' Santorcaz said, shaking me by the arm with impertinent familiarity, 'has changed so much. When he was an officer, he didn't look too bad, but since he was discharged from the Army for cowardice and bad conduct and has placed himself at the service of…'

Such a bad joke did not deserve an answer and I remained silent, leaving Inés more confused.

'Sir,' Miss Fly said angrily, turning to Santorcaz, 'if I had known you intended to insult my companion I would have preferred to stay out on the street. I told you he was my servant, but that is not correct. This gentleman is my friend.'

'Your friend,' Don Luis added. 'Precisely. That's what I said.'

'A loyal friend and an irreproachable gentleman to whom I shall be grateful all my life for the service he performed for me tonight, risking his life for me.'

Fresh confusion on the part of Inés. Her anguished face was changing colour every second and she was engrossed in watching the Englishwoman and me as if, by looking at us, reading us, devouring us with her eyes, she could resolve this highly mysterious enigma that was before her.

Revenge is a wicked pleasure, but so enjoyable that on some occasions one has to be a saint or an archangel to suppress this particle, to extinguish this ember, of hell that exists in our heart. So it was that, feeling inside me the burning of this diabolical fire that sometimes leads us to mortify those we love most, I said with the utmost seriousness,

'My dear lady, ordinary actions which are a duty for persons of honour do not require thanks. Anyway, if we are talking about thanks, what can I say when I recall the attention you showed me in the allied headquarters and before we both came to Salamanca?'

Miss Fly seemed to exult at my words and in her look appeared a glow of satisfaction which she did not bother to hide. Inés looked at the Englishwoman, trying to read in her face the words she had not said.

'Señor Santorcaz,' the Warbler said after a pause, 'have you not thought of marrying off your daughter?'

'Señora, my daughter seems up to now to be very happy with her estate and the company of her father. However, in time… she will not get married to a nobleman, nor to a soldier because both of us loathe those torturers and butchers of the people.'

'We could take offence at what you say about these two very respectable classes,' Miss Fly replied benevolently. 'I am noble and this gentleman is a soldier. So then…'

'I was speaking in general, señora. In any event, my daughter does not want to get married.'

'It's impossible that someone so pretty does not have thousands of suitors,' Miss Fly said, looking at her. 'Is it possible that this beautiful child is in love with nobody?'

Inés could not conceal her anger at this point.

'She is not in love with anyone nor has she ever been,' her father replied officiously.

'That's not true, Señor Santorcaz,' the Englishwoman said. 'Don't try to deceive me, because I know the history of your adored daughter inside out, up to when you seized her in Cifuentes.'

Inés went as red as a cherry and looked at me with scorn or terror, I could not tell which. I remained silent and, gauging her feelings by my own ones, I said to myself in all innocence, 'The poor girl will get really angry.'

'Childhood cuddles and silliness,' Santorcaz said, clearly annoyed by what he had just heard.

'That may be so,' the Englishwoman said, then pointing in turn at Inés and me, she continued, 'but both are now adults and their ideas as well as their feelings have clearly taken the right road. I do not know the character and thoughts of your enchanting daughter, but I do know the generous spirit and the noble mind of the young man who is listening to us and I can assure you that I can read his soul like a book.'

Inés could scarcely contain herself. It was obvious from her eyes that her soul was prey to a form of affliction, of despair, to some powerful feeling as yet unknown to her.

'For some time,' the Englishwoman continued, 'we have been united in a noble, frank and pure friendship. This gentleman has a lofty spirit. His heart, superior to the common sentiments of ordinary life, burns with the ardent desire for a life of greatness, of struggle, of danger. He has no wish to tie his existence to the mean mediocrity of a peaceful home, but rather to throw it into the tumults of war, and society where he hopes to find a mate worthy of his great soul.'

I could not stop myself smiling, but luckily nobody noticed my indiscretion, unless Inés did so as she watched me.

'What do you say to that?' Athenais asked my sweetheart.

'It all seems to me very fine,' she replied as best she could, falteringly and boldly at the same time. 'If one has such a great soul, it seems proper to confront the dangers of a patrol instead of calling at the first door that appears.'

'You can see, señora,' Don Luis said, 'that my daughter is not a fool.'

'Yes, but you are,' Miss Fly replied sharply.

As she said this, the house resounded with knocking as loud as ours had been shortly before.

'The patrol!' I exclaimed.

'No doubt,' Santorcaz said. 'But have no fear. I promised to hide you both. If it's Cerizy, who's a friend of mine, leading the patrol there is nothing to fear. Inés, hide the señora in the library, and I will file this character away somewhere else.'

While Inés and Miss Fly disappeared through a side door, I let myself be led by my old friend who took me to the room where I had seen him that morning and where now this evening there were five men seated round the wide table. On it I saw a confusion of books, bottles and papers and one could easily say that all of them were engaged in equal measures with the three types of objects. They were reading, writing and drinking hard, talking and laughing all the while. I also noticed that there were weapons of all sorts in the room.

On seeing us enter, the youngest, liveliest and most vivacious of those present said, 'They are thundering away at your door again, Papa Santorcaz.'

'It's the watch,' the mason replied. 'Let's see where we can hide this young man. Monsalud, do you know who's commanding the watch tonight?'

'Cerizy,' replied a tall, thin and dark young man who greatly resembled a spider.

'In that case we needn't worry,' he said to me. 'You can go into this room and hide there, if by any chance he comes up for a drink.'

I stayed some time, hidden, but not locked up, in the room he had shown me, long enough for Santorcaz to go down to the door and converse for a short time with the watch and for its captain to come up and do the honours to the bottles which had been politely offered to him.

'Gentlemen,' exclaimed the French officer who entered with Santorcaz, 'good evening… what, working? A fine life you lead.'

'Cerizy,' replied the one called Monsalud filling a glass, 'here's to the health of France and Spain united.'

'To the health of the great Franco-Spanish Empire,' Cerizy said, downing a glass. 'To the health of good Spaniards.'

'Any news, Cerizy my friend?' asked one of the others, a grim and ugly old man.

'That the lord is nearby… but we will defend ourselves well. Have you seen the fortifications? They don't have any siege artillery… the Allied army is one *pour rire…*'

'Poor things!' exclaimed the old man whose name was Bartolomé Canencia. 'To think that so many men are going to die… that so much blood will be shed…'

'Señor philosopher,' the Frenchman said. 'It's because they want it so… persuade the Spanish that they should submit…'

'Rest a moment, Cerizy my friend.'

'I can't stay… a sergeant of dragoons has been wounded in this street…'

'Some quarrel…'

'Nobody knows… the attackers have fled… they say they are spies.'

'English spies! Salamanca is certainly full of spies.'

'They say it's a Spaniard and an Englishwoman, or an Englishman accompanied by a Spanish woman, I don't know which… but I can't stay. I was ordered to check the houses… Tell me, isn't there a meeting of the lodge tonight?'

'A meeting? But we are leaving.'

'Leaving?' the Frenchman said. 'And here I was hurrying to finish my *Memorial on the Various Forms of Tyranny.*'

'Read it to yourself,' said the philosopher Canencia. 'It's the same for me with my *Treatise on Individual Liberty* and my translation of Diderot.'

'But what's all this about leaving?'

'Because the English are coming into Salamanca,' Santorcaz said, 'and we don't want them to catch us here.'

'I wouldn't give twopence for my neck after the Allies enter,' said the youngest and most vivacious of them.

'The English will not enter Salamanca, gentlemen,' the officer stated smugly.

Santorcaz shook his head sadly in an expression of doubt.

'Well, Señor Santorcaz, since you have all decided to run, now that we are in a tight spot,' Cerizy added, his smugness now laced with a slight tone of disapproval, 'you should know that freemasons are not as safe in Marmont's headquarters as they are here.'

'Are they not?'

'No, they are not to the liking of the general-in-chief who has never been fond of secret societies. He tolerated them because it was necessary to encourage the Spanish who did not follow the insurgents' cause, but you already know that Marmont is something of a *bigot*.'

Marmont.

'Yes…'

'But what you don't know is that urgent orders have come from Madrid to separate the French cause from everything that smacks of freemasonry, atheism, irreligion and philosophy.'

'I expected that as Joseph is also something of a…'

'*Bigot*… so have a safe journey and don't trust too much in the general-in-chief.'

'As I have no intention of stopping before I get to France, my dear Señor Cerizy,' Santorcaz said, 'I am not worried.'

'It's impossible to live in this abominable country,' the old philosopher stated. 'I will publish my *Treatise on Individual Liberty* and my translation of Diderot in Paris or Bordeaux.'

'Goodnight, Señor Santorcaz, gentlemen all.'

'Goodnight and good luck against the lord, señor Cerizy.'

'We'll meet again in France,' the Frenchman said as he left. 'What a shame about the lodge… it was going so well… Señor Canencia, I'm sorry that you won't get to hear my *Memorial on Tyrannies*.'

While the captain of the watch was going down the stairs, Santorcaz brought me from my hiding place and, introducing me to his friends, said sarcastically,

'Gentlemen, may I introduce to you an English spy.'

I said nothing in response.

'We know each other well, but we won't quarrel,' the mason added, offering me a seat and putting a cup before me, which he filled. 'Have a drink.'

'I won't have anything.'

'Friend Ciruelo,' Don Luis said to the youngest one present, 'you will remain in Salamanca until tomorrow morning as this young man will leave in your place.'

'Yes, that's right,' Ciruelo objected, looking at me angrily. 'And if the allies come and hang me… I'm not an English spy.'

'English, French!' exclaimed the philosopher Canencia in a sibylline voice. 'Men fighting over territory, not ideas. Why should I care about a change of tyrants? For those like me who fight for philosophy, for the great principles of Voltaire and Rousseau, it's a matter of indifference whether the red coats or the blue cloaks rule in Spain.'

'And what do you think?' Monsalud asked me, eyeing me curiously. 'Will the allies enter Salamanca?'

'Yes, sir, we will enter,' I replied coolly.

'We will enter… so you belong to the allied army.'

'I belong to the allied army.'

'And how did you get here?' asked another one of those present, a man as strong and robust as a bull, in a tone and attitude of the utmost ferocity.

'I'm here because I came here.'

I had to make a great effort to control my indignation.

'This young man is making fun of us,' Ciruelo said.

'Well, I maintain that the allies won't enter Salamanca,' Monsalud added. 'They haven't brought any siege artillery.'

'They'll bring some…'

'They don't know what type of fortifications they have to deal with.'

'There is nothing the Duke of Ciudad Rodrigo does not know.'

'Well, let them enter,' Santorcaz said, 'seeing that Marmont is abandoning us…'

'That's what I say,' the philosopher commented. 'Red coats or blue cloaks… what does it matter?'

'But it's outrageous that we're helping Wellington's spies!' the rough Monsalud exclaimed angrily, getting up from his chair.

I said to myself, 'There's no bolt-hole in this damned house that I can escape through on my own with her.'

'Sit down and be quiet, Monsalud,' Santorcaz said. 'It's of little importance to me whether *Nostrils*[258] enters Salamanca or not. Let me just set foot in my beloved France… Here is no place to live.'

'If the French would take my advice,' the young Ciruelo said with the air of someone certain that he was imparting a great idea, 'rather than handing over this historic city to the allies, they should blow it up. They would just have to put six hundredweight of powder in the cathedral, another six in the university, the same dose in the Estudios

Menores,[259] in the Compañía,[260] in San Esteban,[261] in Santo Tomás[262] and the other main buildings. The allies turn up: would you like to come in? Fire! What a beautiful pile of ruins! In this way you achieve two objects: make an end of them, and destroy one of the most terrible testaments of the tyranny, barbarism and fanaticism of those dreadful times, gentlemen...'

'Orator Ciruelo, you're a great one for revolutions,' Canencia said with majestic self-righteousness.

'What I say,' growled Monsalud, 'is that whether the allies come or not, I'm not leaving Spain.'

'Me neither,' the bull bellowed.

'I prefer to join the insurgents,' said the fifth one who had not opened his mouth up to then.

'I am leaving Spain for ever,' Santorcaz stated. 'I think the French cause is in a bad way. Within two years Fernando VII will be back in Madrid.'

'Nonsense, lunacy!'

'If this campaign ends badly for the French, as I believe...'

'Badly? Why?'

'Marmont does not have the forces.'

'They will send him some. King Joseph will come to his help with troops from New Castile.'

'And the Estève[263] division which is in Segovia.'

'And Bonnet's army[264] is already nearby.'

'And also Caffarelli[265] with the Army of the North.'

'But they still haven't come,' Santorcaz said sadly. 'Well, if those troops come and the French give it their all...'

'They will win.'

'What do you think, Araceli?'

'That Marmont, Bonnet, Estève, Caffarelli and King Joseph won't find anywhere to run to if they come up against the allies,' I said with great coolness.

'We will see, sir.'

'That's right, you will see,' I replied. 'We will all see.'

'Do you really know what it's like, the allied army that has taken Ciudad Rodrigo and Badajoz? Do you know what those Portuguese and Spanish battalions and the English cavalry are like? Imagine an immense force, an admirable discipline, a wild enthusiasm and you will have an idea of this wave which is coming and which will roll up and destroy everything in its path.'

The six men looked at me amazed.

'Let's suppose the French are defeated, what would the Emperor do then?'

'Send more troops.'

'Not possible. What about the Russian campaign?'[266]

'Which they say is going very badly,' I noted.

'On the contrary, it's going very well,' Monsalud exclaimed with a threatening gesture.

'The latest notices,' said the fifth person, who had a military appearance and was a strong, burly and imposing man, cross-eyed and with a disagreeable face, 'are as follows… I read them in the papers they sent us from Madrid. The Emperor is expected in Warsaw. The first corps is crossing the Piegel.[267] Marshal Duke of Reggio,[268] who is commanding the second corps, is in Wehlau.[269] Marshal Duke of Elchingen,[270] in Soldass. The King of Westphalia[271] in Warsaw…'

'That's all a long way away and is of no importance to us,' Santorcaz said with disdain. 'Even if the Emperor survives that rash campaign, he won't be able to send troops to Spain for a long time… and it seems that Soult is in a difficult situation in Andalusia and Suchet in Valencia.'

'You always look on the black side,' Monsalud shouted angrily.

'I see the war for the colour that it is now… in any event, I'm off to France, come what may.'

'It's a sad business to live like this,' the philosopher said. 'We are sheep moving from pasture to pasture. It is true that wherever we go we leave the seed of the *Social Contract* which will soon germinate and populate the earth with true citizens… But it is also sad and shameful that we have to pass as travelling players.'

'Wild horses wouldn't make me dress up as a clown anymore,' Monsalud declared.

'As for me, rather than letting myself be cut into pieces as an *afrancesado*, I'll join the insurgents,' said the one who had the figure and heavy build of a bull.

'We lose nothing by using our disguise,' Don Luis said. 'Dressed like that and with the cart full of equipment following us, we can avoid coming to any harm in those savage villages… So gentlemen, let's get going. Araceli, give me your weapons as we don't carry any… if you don't, I won't run the risk of taking you out of the city.'

I gave them to him, hiding the rage that filled my soul, and they immediately began preparing to leave. Some of them ran to close their portmanteaus, more full of papers than clothes. Ramoncilla sorted out the luggage of her master and soon the house was deafened by the sounds of horses and carts in the courtyard. When I went to the room where Inés and Miss Fly were, I was surprised to find them in easy conversation, although apparently not a cordial one, and upon the former's face I noticed an enchantingly wry and ironic expression, mixed with profound sadness. I concealed and suppressed a storm of indignation, of anguish deep in my breast. Even there, surrounded by so many people I was anxiously looking in every corner, trying to find some opening, some opportunity to escape with her on my own. I believed myself capable of the deeds dreamt of by the noble spirit of Miss Fly.

But there was no human way to realise my thoughts. I was in the power of Santorcaz, or as we might say, in the power of the Devil. I tried to get close to Inés to speak to her on her own, hoping to find in her a loving accomplice in my desire, but Santorcaz, clearly by design, and Miss Fly, perhaps unintentionally, prevented me from doing so. Inés herself seemed determined not to honour me with even a glance from her loving eyes.

Athenais, still wearing her riding skirt, had undergone a transfiguration, graciously concealing her bust and head under the folds of a Spanish cloak.

'How do I look in this?' she asked me, laughing, in a moment when we were alone.

'Good,' I replied coldly, preoccupied by another image that attracted my mind's eye.

'Nothing more than good?'

'Wonderful. You look very beautiful.'

'Your fiancée, Señor Araceli,' she said with a merry expression and somewhat patronisingly, 'is pretty simple.'

'A little bit, Señora.'

'She's good enough for a poor man... But are you sure that you love... that thing?'

'Oh, heavens above,' I said to myself without paying attention to Miss Fly, 'isn't there some way I can escape alone with her?'

The Englishwoman was about to repeat her question when Santorcaz called out to us to hurry downstairs. He and his companions had kitted themselves out in wretched old clothes.

'The two ladies in the coach driven by Juan,' Don Luis said. 'Three on horseback and the rest in the cart. Araceli, get into the cart with Monsalud and Canencia.'

'Father, don't go on horseback,' Inés said. 'You are very ill.'

'Ill? I'm stronger than ever... Come on, let's go, it's very late.'

The travellers distributed themselves as instructed and in a comic procession we soon left the house, the street and then Salamanca. Almighty God! It seemed as if I had spent a century inside the city. When I found myself outside the terrible gates, having met no obstacles in the streets or at the encircling walls, I felt as if I had come back to life.

In accordance with Santorcaz's orders the little coach with the two ladies went in front, the riders followed and then the two carts, in one of which it was my lot to ride with the two interesting persons mentioned. Although my anxiety about the dangers I had faced in *Roma la chica* had calmed once I was in the open country, I was in great distress for reasons that can be readily understood. I was under a duty to go at all speed to headquarters, abandoning that strange convoy with which went the loves of my whole life, the soul of my existence, my lost treasure, found but lost once more with no hope of recovering it again. Although I myself had been taken and carried away by that gang of devils, it was still impossible for me to follow her as duty compelled me to leave her halfway along the road. Despair took hold of me, when in the darkness of the night, I could no longer see the two women who were travelling ahead of me. I jumped to the ground and running at an incredible speed, my intensely deep anguish seeming to give me wings, I shouted with all the force of my lungs,

'Inés, Miss Fly! Here I am, stop, stop…!'

Santorcaz galloped up behind and stopped me.

'Gabriel!' he shouted. 'I have got you out of the city and now you can go and leave us in peace. The Aldeatejada road is to your right.'

'Bandit!' I exclaimed angrily. 'Do you think I would leave on my own if you hadn't taken away my weapons?'

'You're a wild one! A fine way to repay the favour I've just done for you. Now, be off with you. I swear to you that if you come before me again and dare to threaten me, I will deal with you as you deserve.'

'Villain!' I cried, springing onto the saddle tree of his horse and sinking my fingers into his flaccid muscles. 'Even though I am unarmed, I can take care of you!'

The horse reared and threw me some distance.

'Give me what's mine, thief!' I exclaimed, turning to face my enemy. 'Do you think I'm afraid of you? Get down from that horse, give me back my sword and we'll see.'

Santorcaz made a disdainful gesture and the silence of the night was broken by the sound of his ironic laugh. Then the other horseman, who was the one like a bull, joined him instantly.

'Either you leave right now,' Don Luis said, 'or we'll stretch you out on the road.'

'The English lady has to come with me. Make her stop,' I said, concealing the intense anger that was suffocating me because of my evident disadvantage.

'That lady can go where she cares to.'

'Miss Fly, Miss Fly!' I shouted, putting both hands to my mouth.

There was no response and I could not even hear the wheels of the coach. I ran for a long stretch by the side of the horses, tired, breathless, covered in sweat and with deep anguish in my soul. I then shouted again,

'Inés, Inés! Wait a moment… I'm coming!'

My strength was failing. The horsemen threatened to ride me down, but I used my last remnant of energy to escape them by leaping off the road. The horses went on ahead and the laughter of Santorcaz and the man-bull echoed in my ears like the croaking of carnivorous birds wheeling near me, describing terrifying circles around my head. Even though my body was faint and almost lifeless, I still had a powerful voice and I cried out for as long as I thought I could be heard,

'Wretches! I will get my hands on you yet. Hey, Santorcaz, keep watching out! I'll be there after you, I'll be there!'

XXIII

Very soon the sound of hooves and wheels died away in the distance. I was alone on the road. When I reflected that Inés had been in my hands and that I had been unable to keep hold of her, I felt an urge to run onwards, believing that rage alone would make the powerful wings of a condor sprout from my body... In my desperate impotence I threw myself to the ground, bit the earth, uttering shrieks to Heaven that would have terrified any passers-by, if any living soul had happened to cross that desolate plain at that hour... 'She has escaped from me, perhaps for ever!' I surveyed the horizon all around me – everything I saw was black, but images of the two armies of the world's two most powerful nations appeared in my disturbed imagination. There were the French... there were the English! One more step and the smoke and shouts of a bloody battle rose to the skies; one more step, and this earth, which was supporting me, will shake with the weight of so many bodies falling onto it. 'Oh, God of battles, war and extermination is what I want!' I exclaimed. 'May not a single man remain between here and France... Araceli, off to headquarters now... Wellington is expecting you.'

This idea calmed me somewhat and I got up from the ground where I had been lying. When I took my first steps, I experienced that intake of breath, that indefinable fear we feel when we realise that something we have been carrying is missing or lost.

'What about Miss Fly?' I said, stopping, thunderstruck. 'I don't know... onwards.'

Certain that the French had gone in the direction of Toro, I took the road south in search of the Valmuza, a little stream that ran about four or five leagues from Salamanca. I walked as fast as my physical exhaustion and mental fatigue allowed and at eight in the morning I came into Aldeatejada[272] after wading across the Tormes and crossing some rough and uneven terrain beyond Tejares.[273] Before I got there some villagers told me there were no French in the village or its surroundings and in the village I heard that very many English had been seen the previous night in Siete Carreras and Tornadizos.[274]

'My friends are not far off,' I said to myself and after having something to keep me going, I continued onwards.

Nothing of note happened to me until Tornadizos where I came across the English vanguard and various *partidas* of Julián Sánchez. It was ten in the morning.

'A horse, gentlemen, lend me a horse,' I said to them. 'If you don't, you'll have to answer to the duke… where are headquarters? I think they are in Bernuy. A horse, quick.'

Finally they gave me one and galloping at full speed first along the road and then down narrow lanes and paths, I was at headquarters at a quarter to twelve. I hurriedly put on my uniform, at the same time finding out where Lord Wellington was lodging so that I could report to him immediately.

'The duke came by here a moment ago,' Tribaldos told me. 'He's surveying the village on foot.'

A moment later, I met the duke in the square returning from his walk. He recognised me at once and I approached him and said to him,

'I have the honour to report to Your Excellency that I have been in Salamanca and have brought with me all the information and news Your Excellency desires.'

'All?' Wellington said without showing any sign of pleasure or discontent.

'All, General.'

'Are they determined to defend themselves?'

'The French Army evacuated the city yesterday evening, leaving only eight hundred men.'

Wellington turned to the Portuguese General Troncoso who had come to his side. Without understanding the English words of their exchange, it seemed to me that the latter was confirming this,

'This is what Your Excellency expected.'

'Here is the plan of the fortifications defending the way in over the bridge,' I said, handing him the sketch I had made.

Wellington took it and, after examining it with the closest attention, asked,

'Are you sure that there are swivel guns in the ravelin and eight ordinary pieces in the bastion?'

'I counted them, General. The drawing may not be perfect but there is not one line in it that is not a representation of an enemy work.'

'Ah, ha! A fosse from San Vicente to the Milagro!' he exclaimed in surprise.

'And a parapet on San Vicente.'

'San Cayetano seems to be strongly fortified.'

'Terribly so, General.'

'And these other ones at the head of the bridge…'

'Which are connected to the forts by zigzag stockades.'

'Very good,' he said contentedly, keeping the sketch. 'You have performed your mission satisfactorily, it would seem.'

'I am at your command, General.'

Then, glancing round with his penetrating look, he added,

'They tell me that Miss Fly was rash enough to go into Salamanca as well, to look at buildings. I don't see her.'

'She has not returned,' said one of the English staff officers.

I felt some embarrassment as everyone interrogated me with an alarming look. I would have given anything for Miss Fly to have appeared at that moment.

'She hasn't returned?' the duke said with an expression of alarm and fixing me with his eyes. 'Where is she?'

'General, I don't know,' I replied quite put out. 'Miss Fly did not go with me to Salamanca. I met her there and then… we separated when we left the city as I had to be in Bernuy before noon.'

'Very well,' Lord Wellington said as if he thought he had given too much attention to something that did not of itself merit it. 'Come up now to my lodgings to complete your report.'

I had not taken more than two steps, humbly bringing up the rear of the duke's staff officers, when I was stopped by an English officer, an oldish man, with a small face, no less red than his uniform, and whose lined and diminutive face displayed an expression of impertinent excitement, emphasised by his sharp nose and gold-rimmed spectacles. Accustomed as we Spaniards were to regard the military profession as having some characteristic types of person, we were surprised and even amused to come across Artillery or general staff officers who seemed like professors, notaries, Customs officers or lawyers.

Colonel Simpson, for it was none other than he, looked at me haughtily and I looked at him in the same way and once we had both had enough of looking at each other, he said,

'Sir, where is Miss Fly?'

'Sir, why should I know? Has the duke made me the guardian of that beautiful woman?'

'It was expected that Miss Fly would return with you from her visit to the architectural monuments of Salamanca.'

'Well, she hasn't returned, Mr. Simpson. I had understood that Miss Fly could come and go and leave and return when she wanted.'

'That is how it should be and what she has always done,' the Englishman said. 'But we are in a country where men do not respect ladies, and it is possible that Athenais, despite her noble lineage, may not have the absolute assurance of being properly respected.'

'Miss Fly is mistress of her own actions,' I replied. 'As for her delay or detour, only she can inform you when she appears.'

It was clearly absurd to require me to be responsible for the good or bad behaviour of the capricious and restless Englishwoman when she recognised no restraint on her liberty nor had any safeguard for her honour than her own honour itself.

'These explanations do not satisfy me, Señor Araceli,' Simpson said to me, honouring me with an angry look that was magnified through the lenses of his spectacles. 'The distinguished Lord Fly, Earl of Chichester,[275] charged me with looking after his daughter…'

'Looking after his daughter! And is this the way you do it? I did not see you at her side when she was on the point of losing her life in Sancti-Spíritus. Looking after her! Is that how you look after young ladies in England? By leaving it to Spaniards to offer them lodgings and accompany them on visits to abbeys and castles?'

'This young lady has always been accompanied by worthy gentlemen who did not abuse her trust. There are no fears of any weaknesses on the part of Miss Fly whose own sense of decorum is the best guardian. But what one does fear, Señor Araceli, is the outrages and crimes which are common among the passionate natures of this land. In short, I am not satisfied by the explanations you have given me.'

'I have no further word to add to what I have had the honour to report to Lord Wellington in respect of Miss Fly's whereabouts.'

'Enough, sir,' replied Simpson, turning as red as a pepper. 'We will speak further on a more opportune occasion. I have informed Don Carlos España of my concerns and he told me that you were someone who could not be relied upon… Goodbye.'

He left me in lively fashion to rejoin the staff officers who were now some way off, and I have to say the studious old officer made me think. Shortly afterwards, Don Carlos España laughingly said to me in that free and somewhat crude manner which was characteristic of him,

'You sly rascal, where in the devil's name have you put the Amazon? What have you done with her? I always thought you were a fine one. When Colonel Simpson told me that he was on tenterhooks, I replied to him, 'Do not worry, my friend, the Spanish see all women as their own property."

I tried to convince the general of my innocence in this delicate affair, but he just laughed, more for reasons of esteem than of reproach, because that is how we Spaniards are. Then I told him how, needing the help of the freemasons to leave Salamanca, we accompanied them until we had gone a fair distance from the city, but when I said that Miss Fly had followed them, neither España nor any of those listening believed me.

When I went to the lodgings of the commander-in-chief to inform him about the thousands of details he wanted to know about the destroyed monasteries, the munitions, the supplies, the morale of the garrison and the residents, I found the duke, with whom I conferred for over an hour and a half, so cold and so severe with me that my spirit was filled with sadness. He received my news, so precious for the allied army, without giving me any clear or heartfelt sign, which I was expecting, that my service had been appreciated, or, if appreciating the deed, he despised the one who did it. He praised the sketch, but it seemed to me he was not confident, even to the point of doubting, that the minute drawing could be accurate.

I was dismayed but, full of respect for that grave personage, whom we Spanish regarded at the time as little short of a god, I did not dare open my lips except in answer to his questions, and when the hero of Talavera dismissed me with a rigid and cold bow like a statue bending at the waist, I left in great confusion and dejection, but also in anger because I realised that some suspicion as serious as it was unjust had tarnished my reputation. After the many labours and hardships I had endured to perform a great service to the allied army I was being treated as no more than a common and mercenary spy! I did not want promotion or money as payment for my services! I wanted respect, appreciation and for the lord to call me his friend, or for some affectionate and touching phrase to fall from the height of his fame and genius onto the trifle that I was, like a pat given to a loyal dog, but I achieved none of this. When at the same time and in a confusing jumble I remembered what I had suffered the day before, my sketch, my services, and my hardships, the horrendous dangers and then the severe and almost frowning face of Lord Wellington, spite led me to say to myself such phrases as,

'Perhaps you would like to have been in the hands of Jean-Jean and Tourlourou before putting on a face like that... it's one thing to issue orders from the campaign tent and another to obey them on the ramparts... An order is one thing, danger is another... You risk death a hundred times for a...'

XXIV

I said this and worse things which I won't mention as we left that afternoon for Salamanca, reaching the outskirts before nightfall and then bearing away from the city to cross the Tormes by the Canto and San Martín fords. Everywhere I kept hearing,

'Tomorrow we'll attack the forts.'

Having seen them and examined them, I knew this could not be the case.

'You're mistaken if you think those forts are toys like the ones built in Madrid on 3rd December!'[276] I said to my friends, with an air of self-importance. 'You're mistaken if you think the guns defending them are just pots and pans!'

And then I would embark on pompous descriptions which I would always conclude with the following,

'It's only when you have seen the things, when you have measured them inch by inch, when you have drawn them with some skill that you can get a complete idea of them.'

'Tell me, have you also seen Miss Fly, measured her inch by inch and drawn her with some skill?' they would ask me.

This brought me back to my feelings of sadness and *saudades* (to use a Portuguese term)[277] caused by the disfavour of Lord Wellington and the injustice and lack of justification for his coldness and harshness towards a loyal servant and obedient soldier.

Lord Wellington ordered an assault on the forts merely for the sake of morale and to encourage the troops who had not fought since Arroyo Molinos.[278] The duke knew very well that those works built on the extremely thick walls of the monasteries could fall only before a powerful siege train, and to this end he had ordered heavy guns to be brought from Almeida.[279] Waiting, then, for support and carrying out feint attacks, two or three days passed during which nothing of historical or personal import occurred, neither did Lord Wellington acquire any new titles of nobility, nor did Miss Fly appear, nor did I get any information about the direction taken by the wretched and thrice-damned masons.

So the only things which happened that deserve a place, and indeed very much a preferred place, in this true account are the looks given to me from time to time by Colonel Simpson and his harsh words which I always returned with even greater vehemence. Frankly, dear readers, I was anxious, almost as anxious as the learned Colonel Simpson, since the eclipse of Miss Fly had continued for days now. I was given to believe that detailed investigations were being conducted and that, heavens above, I was facing a severe interrogation following which harsh criminal measures would be taken against me, but God, no doubt to save me from punishments I did not deserve, brought into view very early on the 20th on the hills to the north... not the ballad-loving and interesting Englishwoman, but Marshal Marmont with 40,000 men.

The very day the French appeared before us on the same road to Toro, the assault on the forts was broken off and we made various manoeuvres to take up positions in case the enemy intended to bring us to battle. But it was soon clear that Marmont had no desire to throw his army against us, his intention being to shadow us, distract the besieging forces and perhaps reinforce the forts. However, Wellington, although the Artillery had not yet arrived from Almeida, persisted with Saxon tenacity in trying to take San Vicente and San Cayetano, the two formidable monasteries turned into castles by an absurdity of history. I felt I was still watching them from the tower of La Merced!

Tenacity, which can sometimes be a virtue in war, is often also a mistake, which the assault on the monasteries clearly was, a rare thing for Wellington who was not accustomed to making mistakes. The Spanish division was in Castellanos de Moriscos, observing the French who were moving now to the right, now to the left, when we were told that in the unsuccessful assault on San Cayetano 120 English had been killed as well as General Rowes, highly distinguished in the allied army.

'Now we can see that even great men make mistakes,' I said to my friends. 'Anyone could see that San Vicente and San Cayetano were no chicken coops, but let us respect the errors of our superiors.'

'There she is! She's over there... great news! Now we've got her, over there!' exclaimed Don Carlos España who had appeared suddenly and unexpectedly.

'Who, Miss Fly?' I asked in great delight.

'The artillery, gentlemen, the heavy artillery that was ordered to be brought from Almeida. It's arrived in Pericalbo, it'll be in the parallels by this evening, mounted tomorrow, and then we'll see how good those forts that used to be monasteries are.'

'Ah, and welcome it is! I thought you were talking about Miss Fly, for whose appearance I would give my right arm...'

In fact it was not the arrival of Miss Fly, about whom no living soul had heard a word, but of the siege artillery and Marmont, who had guessed it, made to cross the river to draw off forces to the left of the Tormes. We saw him move quickly to our right, towards Huerta, and we immediately received orders to occupy Aldealengua.[280] As the French crossed the Tormes, General Graham did so, too, and they showed a clean pair of heels when they saw this. Marmont, who did not have enough forces, lacking cavalry above all, did not dare to engage in any serious action.

As to San Vicente and San Cayetano, they did not offer much resistance to the siege artillery. The English (and I say this from reports as I did not see anything) opened a breach on the 27th and set fire to the storehouses of San Vicente with hot cannon balls. The besieged asked for terms of surrender, but Wellington, not wanting to agree terms advantageous to them, ordered an assault on La Merced and San Cayetano, scaling the one and entering the other one through breaches. The garrison was taken prisoner.

This event filled the whole army with delight, particularly when we saw Marmont moving away at a good pace towards the north. We did not know whether in the direction of Toro or Tordesillas, as our patrols could not tell because of the darkness of the night. But we were soon to find out because the Spanish division and the guerrillas of Don Julián Sánchez received orders to pursue the French rearguard while the whole allied army, once Salamanca had been secured, also marched towards the lines of the Duero.

On the morning of 28th June we were close to San Morales,[281] on the road from Valladolid to Tordesillas. We were told that the enemy's rearguard and baggage train had left that place a few hours earlier, taking with them, in accordance with well-established and certain custom, everything they could grab. Count España and Don Julián Sánchez with his fearless guerrillas who knew the country like their own house went ahead of the division and gave the order for a forced march to try and get something from the Frenchies' slow-moving convoy. Without waiting to recover their strength after the night's long march, our vanguard pushed on to Babilafuente[282] while the rest of us gleaned whatever was left in San Morales after the enemy's recent clean-up and pillage. Having at last had something to sustain us, we continued as well in that direction. After an arduous two hours' forced march, when we reckoned we had scarcely another two to go before reaching Babilafuente, we could make the place out in the distance, but this was not because of a sight of far-off houses, or any ancient tower or castle, or even a hill or a copse, but because of a column of thick, black smoke which rose up in coils from a point on the horizon before mingling with the white mass of clouds.

'The French have set fire to Babilafuente,' a guerrilla shouted.

'Hurry... forward march... poor Babilafuente!'

'They're burning it to stop us... they think we're bothered by a bit of soot... forward!'

'But Don Carlos and Sánchez must have reached them,' someone else said. 'I think I hear shooting.'

'Forward, friends. How long will it take us to get there?'

'Just over an hour.'

Then another column of black smoke could be seen rising from a more distant spot and it seemed to embrace the first one in the heights of the sky.

'Villorio's[283] burning as well,' they said. 'Those thieves are setting fire to the granaries once they've taken the grain.'

And closer to us, we saw red flames flickering above the rooftops and a crowd of terrified women, old men and children fleeing across the fields in fear of that curse of men, more terrible than those of Heaven. From what those unfortunate people could tell us between their tears and cries of anguish, we learnt that España's and Sánchez's men had arrived just when the French were leaving, having set fire to the village, that some shots had been exchanged between them, but without any result, as our men were concerned only with putting out the fires.

We were about two hundred paces from the first houses of the unfortunate village, when a strange figure, beautiful, a true and graceful creation of fantasy, an elegant person, as different from normal earthly images as are the admirable creations of the poetry of the North from everyday life, an ideal woman carried by a proud and swift horse, passed before us in the distance, like those splendid riders that cross the rosy spaces of an artist's dream, not touching the earth, giving the wind manes and tresses and altering their majestic course according to the changes in light. It was the figure of a horsewoman, dressed in black or white, I did not know, but just like those galloping women with whose good looks and swift impulses are represented air and fire, things that fly and things that burn, and who truly fly along, urging on their steeds with vehement cries. The elegant person was going off the road, in the opposite direction to ours, over an extensive plain full of ditches and pools, which the steed jumped over with a graceful leap, associating its drive and resolution with the will of the rider in such a way that rider and horse seemed one person. The unreal figure no sooner moved away than came back closer, but despite its course and the distance, immediately I saw it, my heart gave a leap, the blood went suddenly to my brain and I trembled with surprise and joy. Need I say who it was?

Launching my horse off the road, I shouted,

'Miss Fly, Miss Butterfly… Mistress Little Bird… Mistress Warbler, dearest Athenais… Athenais!'

But the Little Bird did not hear me and kept racing on, or rather, flying about, going away, coming back, leaving again, then returning, tracing capricious circles, angles, curves and spirals over the ground and in the brightness of space.

'Miss Fly, Miss Fly!'

The wind prevented my voice from reaching her.

XXV

I quickened my pace, without taking my eyes off that beautiful apparition, which made one believe it was about to disappear like a capricious creation of the light or the wind, but no, it was the very same Miss Fly, trying to find a path through that treacherous plain, furrowed with ditches and pools of greenish still water.

'Ah, Mistress Warbler! Here I am! Here, over here.'

Finally, I got close to her, and she heard me and then saw me, something which seemed to please her greatly and dispelled her confusion and bewilderment. She hurried towards me, laughing and greeting me with expressions of triumph and when I saw her close up I could not help noticing the difference that exists between images transfigured and embellished by the mind and sad reality, since the steed the intrepid Athenais was riding, incidentally side saddle, was very far from the flying Pegasus I thought it was shortly before, neither was her hair free in the wind, like a tongue of flame symbolising thought, nor did her black costume have that undulating transparency I thought I could discern at first, nor did the pony, since pony it was, have much by way of fetlocks than half a dozen strands of withered and yellowing hair, nor was Miss Fly as interesting as usual, although just as beautiful, even if somewhat pale, with her plaits poorly interwoven with the skill of the fingers, without that orderly nonchalance of the

Muses' coiffure, and lastly with her costume in inharmonious disorder on account of the dust, creases and tears it had in various places.

'Thank God I've found you,' she exclaimed, extending her hand to me. 'Don Carlos España told me you were in the rearguard.'

I rejoiced to see her safe and free, something that was tantamount to a precious proof of my integrity, and I was tempted to try and embrace her in the middle of the open field, from horse to horse, and I would have carried out my impudent intention if she, somewhat astonished and shocked, had not stopped me from doing so.

'A fine position you put me in,' I said to her.

'I thought as much,' she replied, laughing. 'But it is your fault. Why did you leave me in the hands of those people?'

'I did not leave you in the hands of those people – a thousand curses on them! I lost sight of you and the freemason stopped me from following. And what about our travelling companions?'

'Do you mean young Inés? You will find her in Babilafuente,' she said, becoming serious.

'In that village! For goodness' sake! Let's hurry there now. But did you suffer any mishap? Did they put you in any danger? Did those barbarians torment you?'

'No, I was bored, nothing more. An hour and a half after leaving Salamanca we ran into the French who seized the masons, saying that they had been spying for the allies in Salamanca. Marmont has an order from the King not to make common cause with those scoundrels who are so hated in the country. Santorcaz defended himself but an officer called him a fraud and a liar and ordered all of us in the procession to be made prisoner. Thanks to Desmarets, they treated me with great consideration.'

'Prisoners!'

'Yes, and after that they kept us in that horrible Babilafuente while the lord took Salamanca. And I saw nothing! Did the forts surrender? What a great service you did with your visit to Salamanca! What did his lordship say to you?'

'Don't talk to me of his lordship! His Excellency is satisfied with his loyal servant... I would have you know, Miss Fly, that far from the duke being pleased me, he detests me and is preparing to bring me before a court martial as a common criminal.'

'Why, my friend? What did you do?'

'What did I do? Well nothing, Mistress Little Bird, nothing more than seducing an honest daughter of Great Britain, taking her with me to Salamanca, insulting her with I know not what sort of outrages, and then, as a finishing touch, knavishly abandoning her, or concealing her, or killing her for, on this blackest part of my savage crimes, Lord Wellington and Colonel Simpson have not yet come to an agreement.'

Miss Fly burst into laughter so open, so spontaneous and so merry that I began laughing, too. We both rode briskly towards Babilafuente.

'What you have told me, Señor Araceli,' she said with an enchanting blush, 'is a fine tale. It's a long time since I heard of such a dramatic event, or such a nice imbroglio. If life didn't have these romances, how boring it would be!'

'You can dispel the doubts of the general and restore my honour to me, Miss Fly, since I believe that neither his lordship nor Sir Abraham Simpson have any doubts about the purity of your feelings. It is me who is the accused, the thief, the ogre of fairy tales, the great giant of legend, the brutal Moor of the ballads.'

'And didn't Simpson challenge you?' she asked, showing me how much pleasure this strange affair aroused in her soul.

'He looked at me with disdain and said words to me for which I cannot forgive him.'

'You should kill him, or at least seriously wound him, as you did with that shameless and insolent Lord Gray,' she said, an extraordinary light in her eyes. 'I want you to fight someone for my sake. You should undertake the riskiest of enterprises because of the liking great hearts have for great dangers. You have given proof of that deep and serene courage which springs from the roots of the soul. A man of such a nature will not allow his worth to be doubted and he will persuade those who do doubt it with the sword in the twinkling of an eye.'

'A more convincing proof, Athenais, must be you yourself... Now let's turn our minds to the rescue of those unfortunate people in Babilafuente. Is Inés in any danger? I must be mad, why am I so calm?! Is she well? Is she in any danger?'

'I do not know,' the Englishwoman replied indifferently. 'The house they were in caught fire.'

'And you can say that with the utmost tranquility!'

'As soon as they told us the Spanish had come and I found myself free I went in search of the commander. Don Carlos España received me affably and did not mind giving me a horse so that I could go back to headquarters.'

'Did Santorcaz, Monsalud, Inés and the rest of the masonic company escape as well?'

'No, not all of them. The great captain of this roving lodge has been prostrate on his bed for three days, unable to move. How could he escape?'

'This is God's handiwork,' I said joyfully and quickening my pace. 'He won't get away from me now. With or without his consent we'll take Inés from his side and send her safely under guard to Madrid.'

'It depends whether she wants to leave her father. Your enchanted lady is a young girl with a limited outlook, faint of heart; she lacks imagination and… and impulsiveness. She only sees what's in front of her. She is what I call a domestic fowl. No, Señor Araceli, don't ask the chicken to fly like the eagle. You will speak to her in the language of passion and she will reply to you by clucking in her enclosure.'

'A hen, Señorita Athenais,' I said to her as we entered the village, 'is a useful animal, affectionate, amiable, sensitive, born to and living for sacrifice, since she gives man her children, her feathers and finally her life, whereas an eagle… But this is awful, Miss Fly, the whole village is burning…'

'The sight of Babilafuente from the plain is truly incomparable. I'm sorry I didn't bring my sketch book.'

The fragile houses were falling to the ground with a tremendous din. The afflicted residents were rushing out onto the street, carrying with difficulty mattresses, furniture, clothes, as much as they could save from the fire and in various places the crowd was pointing in horror at the ruins and burnt wood, indicating that some unfortunate ones had met their end under them. Everywhere only wailing and cursing could be heard, the voices of a mother asking for her son or of young children deserted and alone looking for their parents. Many residents and some soldiers and guerrillas were engaged in getting people who were in danger of being stuck out of their dwellings, and it was necessary to break grilles, tear down partitions, smash doors and windows to go in, defying the flames, while others were involved in putting out the fire, a difficult task as water was scarce. In the middle of the square, Don Carlos España was giving orders for one thing after another, completely ignoring the pursuit of the French, from whom only a few carts had been taken. The general was shouting at the top of his voice and his posture and features were those of a raging madman.

Miss Fly and I dismounted in the square, and the first thing we saw was an unfortunate man in manacles who was being cruelly shoved along by four guerrillas who would drag him roughly from time to time when he refused to follow. No sooner had they got him into the terrifying presence of Don Carlos España, the latter clenched his fists, knitted his black and stormy eyebrows and shouted, 'Why have you brought him here to me!? Shoot him on the spot. These *afrancesado* dogs who work for the enemy must be crushed when they're caught, nothing else will do.'

Looking closely at the features of the man, I recognised Señor Monsalud. Before recounting what I did next, I will say a few words about how he came to such a sad state and disastrous misfortune. It happened that the poor masons, equally disliked by the French, who were leaving, and the Spanish who were entering, Babilafuente, chose nevertheless to try and follow the former. Apart from Santorcaz, who was still in a lamentable state, all of them fled, but the rascally Monsalud had such bad luck that when he jumped over a garden wall in search of the Villorio road, he was seized by the guerrillas and as they unfortunately knew him from some villainies, neither saintly nor masonic, that he had committed in Béjar, they instantly intended him for sacrifice in expiation of the faults of all the masons and *afrancesados* in the Peninsula.

'General,' I said to the count, making my way through the crowd of soldiers and guerrillas. 'This wretched man is very much a rogue and I have no doubt he worked for our enemies, but I owe him a favour as much as life itself, for without his help I would not have been able to leave Salamanca.'

'What's the point of this sermon?' said España with fierce impatience.

'To ask Your Excellency to pardon him, commuting the death penalty for something else.'

Poor Monsalud, who was already half-dead, revived and with a powerful expression of gratitude, looked at me from the depths of his soul.

'You come here with your absurdities, good God, Araceli, I'll have you arrested!' the count exclaimed, gesturing wildly. 'You cannot stop this, young meddler. Get this wretch out of my sight and shoot him right now. Somebody has to be punished! Somebody!'

Despite this obvious cruelty, which sometimes showed itself in a terrible way, España had not yet reached that extreme level which years later would make his name as famous as it was dreadful.[284] He looked first at the victim, then at me and Miss Fly and then, after he had given vent to his anger with a bout of swearing and accusations directed at everybody around, he said,

'Very well, he'll not be shot. Give him two hundred strokes... but two hundred strokes well laid on. Boys, I'm turning him over to you... over there, behind the church.'

'Two hundred strokes!' the victim muttered sadly. 'I'd rather they gave me four bullets. At least I would die in one go.'

Just then the uproar increased and a guerrilla appeared, saying,

'All the seed fields and threshing floors towards Villorio are burning and Villoruela is burning, as well as Riolobos and Huerta.'

The horrible sight could be seen from the square, one side of which was open to the countryside. Wandering and erratic flames sprang up here and there from the dry ground, running over the cornfields, like a floating head of hair, whose topmost locks were lost to view in the sky. Further off, the columns of smoke were more numerous, each one indicating the barn or granary that had fallen victim to the fleeing army's scheme of fire.

XXVI

I had never seen such desolation. In their retreat the enemy soldiers were burning, laying waste, pulling up young trees in orchards, making illuminations out of the straw on the threshing floors. With every step they crushed a cottage, laid waste to a cornfield and their bitter breath of death was as destructive as the anger of God. A lightning flash, a hailstorm, a simoom[285], rain and an earthquake working with one accord would not have done so much destruction in such a short time. But the lightning flash and the simoom all the furies of Heaven combined, what are they compared to the efficiency of an army in retreat? A wounded wild animal, it will not allow anything to live after it has gone by.

Don Carlos España took a rapid decision.

'To Villorio, to Villorio, and no resting!' he shouted, mounting his horse. 'Let's see if we can catch them, Don Julián Sánchez. Anyway, we must also help those other villages.'

Orders were given immediately and some of the guerrillas with two regiments of the line made ready to follow Don Carlos.

'Araceli,' the latter said to me, 'stay here and carry out my orders. If the English get here today, you are to follow on to Villorio, but if not remain here. Put out as much of the fire as you can, rescue as many people as you can, and if you find any supplies…'

'Very good, General.'

'And as for this rogue we've caught, mind you don't let him off even one of his strokes. Two hundred exactly and well laid on. Goodbye. Keep good order, and… not one less than two hundred.'

Once I was master of the village and at the head of the troops and guerrillas at work there, I quickly began giving out orders. It goes without saying that the first was to free Monsalud from the horrible torment and excessive punishment of his beating, but when I arrived at the place of the sad scene, they had already given him twenty-three poultices of ash wood and the unhappy man was on the point of surrendering his soul to the Lord from their burning pain. I stopped the torture and, although he seemed more dead than alive, they assured me he wouldn't die from it as freemasons have seven lives, like cats.

Miss Fly lost no time in pointing out to me the house which served as a shelter for Santorcaz, one of the few that had hardly been touched by the flames. At the door were some women and villagers, accompanied by two or three soldiers, reinforcing the former in demonstrating with all the eloquence of their sex that the greatest scoundrel they had seen for many years in Babilafuente had taken refuge inside.

'The one they took to the square,' said an old woman, 'is a saint in Heaven compared to the one hiding away here, the captain general of all those devils.'

'And even the French themselves disregard them. Tell me, Frasquita, why do they call these people masons? Upon my honour, I do not understand the *epithet*.'

'Me neither, but it's enough to know that they are very wicked and that they are in cahoots with the French, getting rid of religion and closing churches.'

'And these people, when they come into town, they seize every virgin they come across. Well, I say, you've got to take care of the children as well, because they snatch them to bring them up in accordance with their notion, which is the faith of Mohammed.'

The soldiers had started to break down the door and the women were encouraging them, so great was the deep aversion in the village against masons. We had already seen what had happened to Monsalud. Santorcaz, being the Pontifex Maximus of the wandering sect, would certainly not have ended up any better on this occasion if I had not arrived. When the door gave way to the strong blows and axe strokes, I ordered that no one should go in, charged the soldiers, guarding the entrance, to hold back and clear away the screaming and abusive women, and went in. I crossed two or three rooms where the furniture in disorder was evidence of the confused escape. All the doors were open, and I could move freely from room to room until I came to a small and dark one where I saw Santorcaz and Inés, he laid out on a miserable bed, she at his side, the two in so close an embrace that their figures merged in the shadows of the room. Father and daughter were terrified, quivering like someone expecting death at any moment, and they had embraced each other to await the terrible last moments together. On recognising me, Inés gave a cry of joy,

'Father,' she exclaimed, 'we aren't going to die. Look who's here!'

Santorcaz stared at me, his eyes shining like two embers in a deathly pale face, and in a hollow voice, whose timbre froze my blood, he said,

'Are you coming for me, Araceli? Has that tiger of a butcher who commands you sent you to get me because the journeymen in the slaughterhouse have nothing to do already? They've already dispatched Monsalud, now it's my turn…'

'We're not killing anyone,' I said, moving closer.

'They are not going to kill us,' Inés exclaimed, shedding tears of joy. 'Father, when those barbarians were knocking down the door, when we expected to see them come in armed with axes, swords, guns and guillotines to cut off our heads, as you say they do in Paris, didn't I tell you that I thought I heard Araceli's voice? We owe him our lives.'

The mason fixed his eyes on me, looking at me as if he was not sure that it was really me. His physiognomy was extremely distorted, his eyes sunk into their sockets, his beard long and his forehead shiny and yellow. It seemed he had aged ten years since the scenes in Salamanca.

'They spare my life,' he said with disdain. 'They spare my life when they find me sick and ailing, unable to move from this bed where I am stuck fast by my sickness. The Count of España, is he coming here?'

'The Count of España has left Babilafuente.'

When I said this, the old man let out a breath as if a great weight had been lifted from him. He sat up, helped by his daughter, and his features, contracted by fear, relaxed a little.

'That executioner has gone away… to Villorio? So we can escape by way of… of… and the English, where are they?'

'Escape is impossible, everywhere is guarded. The journeys through the villages are over.'

'So that means I am a prisoner,' he exclaimed in astonishment. 'I am your prisoner, prisoner of…! You have caught me like a mouse in a trap and I have to obey you and follow you perhaps!'

'Yes, you are my prisoner for as long as I wish.'

'And you can do what takes your fancy with me, like a little boy who pitilessly torments the lion in his cage because he knows it can do him no harm.'

'I will do what I have to, and first of all…'

Santorcaz, seeing my eyes fixed on his daughter, took her in his arms once more, shouting,

'You will not part her from me without killing her, you despicable and miserable executioner! Is this how you repay the favour I did you in Salamanca? Order your barbaric soldiers to shoot us, but do not separate us.'

I looked at Inés and saw in her such love, such open attachment to the old man, such truth in her demonstration of filial affection, that I could do nothing other than put an end to my violent intention.

'Here I have found a feeling whose existence I did not suspect,' I said to myself. 'A grand, immense feeling which has suddenly been shown to me and which astonishes me, holds me and makes me draw back. I thought I was travelling along a continuous and sure path, but I have arrived at a point where the path stops and the sea begins. I cannot continue… what is this immensity before me? This man may be a villain, may be the jailer of this unfortunate girl, may be an enemy of society, an agitator, a madman who deserves to be exterminated, but here there is something more. Between these two beings, the one so good, the other so odious and hated, there is a link that I should not and cannot break, because it is the work of God. What shall I do?'

Other reflections similar to these followed, but did not bring me to a definite decision on my conduct so I expressed myself as follows, as this seemed the most appropriate under the circumstances,

'If you change your behaviour, you might perhaps be able to live nearby, if not at your daughter's side and see her and have dealings with her.'

'Change my behaviour! And who are you, ignorant youth, to tell me to change my behaviour, and where have you learnt to judge my actions? You are full of pride because despotism has disguised you in that uniform and put on those epaulettes whose only purpose is to show the hierarchy of the various oppressors of the people. What do you know about behaviour, fool!? You've been listening to the monks and Don Carlos España and think you have all the knowledge of the world.'

'I don't possess any knowledge,' I replied in exasperation. 'But can one allow innocent, honourable and worthy creatures to live with such parents?'

'And you, a stranger to her, a stranger to me, why is it a concern for you and what it's got to do with you?' he exclaimed, waving his arms and hitting the bedclothes of the disordered bed.

'Señor Santorcaz, let's bring this to a close. I will leave you in liberty to go wherever you please. I undertake to guarantee your safety until you leave the area occupied by the allied army. But this young woman is my prisoner and will go nowhere except to Madrid to her mother's side. If by good fortune tender feelings have been born in you that you did not know before, I assure you that you will be able to see your daughter in Madrid whenever you ask.'

As I said this, I looked at Inés who glanced alternately at me and her father as if in a trance.

'You're mad,' Don Luis said. 'My daughter and I will not part. Talk to her about it and you will see how she feels… Well, then, Araceli, are you going to let us escape or not?'

'I cannot stay for a debate. I have said all I need to say. In the meantime you will stay here in the house and nobody will dare to do you any harm.'

'A prisoner, caught, my God!' Santorcaz exclaimed, more heartbroken than angry, and crying in despair. 'A prisoner, caught by this mercenary soldiery that I hate; caught before being able to do anything useful, before being able to land a few good blows! This is terrible! I am a wretch… useful for nothing… I have left everything to the end… I've busied myself with foolish trifles… the important thing, the serious thing, is to destroy everything possible, since there is certainly nothing worthy of being preserved.'

'Keep calm, as the state of your body is not suitable for reforming mankind.'

'Do you think I'm weak, that I can't get up?' he shouted, trying to sit up with a pitiable effort. 'I can still do something… this will pass, it's nothing… I've still got a pulse… Ah, in future I'll forgive no one. Anyone who comes into my hands will perish for certain.'

Inés put her hands on his shoulders to quieten him and she gathered up the bedclothes which the sick man had thrown everywhere.

'A prisoner, caught like a rat!' he continued. 'It's enough to make one mad. After I had founded thirty-four lodges which the bravest and the most rebellious had joined, that is to say, the best and the worst of all the land! Oh, those contemptible French have betrayed me! I have served them, and this is how they pay me… Araceli, are you saying I'm a prisoner, that I'll be taken to prison in Madrid, to Ceuta[286] perhaps? I curse the vile livery of despotism you are wearing! Ceuta! Well, I'll escape like the last time… my daughter and I will escape. I've still got agility, strength, spirit, I am still young... To fall into the hands of those executioners with epaulettes when I thought I was free for ever and would enjoy the fruits of my work over so many years! Because yes, you are nothing more than executioners with epaulettes, false ranks and fake honours. Women of the earth, bear sons for the nobles to scourge, for the monks to excommunicate and for these henchmen to kill! This is what I've always said! Freemasonry should have no feelings, it must be cruel, cold, hard, crushing like the executioner's axe. Who says that I am ill, that I am weak, that I am going to die, that I cannot get up anymore? It's a lie, a hundred times a lie. I will get up and woe to anyone who stands in my way! Watch out, Araceli, watch out, you apprentice executioner... I can still...'

He carried on talking for some time more, but gradually his strength failed and his words became confused and unintelligible. Finally we could hear only broken muttering and guttural sounds which were meaningless. His breathing was laboured and he had closed his eyes, although he opened them from time to time with sudden attacks of the fever. I touched his hands and they were burning.

'This man is very ill,' I said to Inés, who was looking at me in perplexity.

'I know, but we have nothing in this house, no medicine, no food, in short, nothing.'

Summoning my orderly who was outside, I ordered him to give Inés whatever she needed that was available in the place.

'My orderly will not move from here while you need him,' I said to my friend. 'The door will be secured. You can relax. We shall be here all day. Goodbye, I am going to the square, but I will return soon, as we have to talk, we have a lot to talk about.'

When I returned she was sitting at the bedside of the sick man and staring at him. Turning her head she made a sign to me not to make any noise. She then got up, leant over Santorcaz's face and after making sure he was having a complete and beneficial rest, left the room. Both of us went to the next door room, leaving the door fully open so that we could keep an eye on the unfortunate sleeping man, and sat down facing each other. We were on our own, almost on our own.

XXVII

'Have you had any news from my mother?' she asked me, with great emotion.

'No, but we will see her soon…'

'Here, good God! Such happiness is not for me.'

'I will write to her today and say I have found you and that you will not escape from me. I will tell her to come immediately to Salamanca.'

'Oh Gabriel! You are doing exactly what I wanted, what I have wanted for so long. If you had been a bit more patient in Salamanca and listened to me before…'

'My darling, there are lots of things you'll have to explain to me that I don't understand,' I said lovingly.

'And you to me? You certainly need to explain yourself well. Until you do so, don't expect a word from me, not a single one.'

'I've been looking for you for six months, my love, six months of troubles, hardships, anxiety, despair. How much has God made me work before granting me what was meant for me! How much I have suffered for you, how much have I cried for you! God knows that I have won you well!'

'And during all that time,' she asked with charming mischievousness, 'were you not accompanied by that English lady, who calls you her knight and who has driven me mad with her questions?'

'With questions?'

'Yes, she wants to know everything and to keep her quiet I've had to tell her how and when we met. She cares little for me; it's your life she's interested in. She was wearing me out so much with her desire to know all the mad and sublime things you have done for unhappy me that I was forced to amuse myself at her expense...'

'Well done, my darling.'

'How proud she is! She laughs whenever I speak and, according to her, I only open my mouth to say stupid things. But I have punished her... since she insisted on knowing your amorous exploits, I told her that after the Battle of Bailén twenty-five armed men were about to rob me, but you killed them all on your own.'

Inés smiled sadly and I stifled a laugh.

'I also told her that in the Pardo,[287] in order to speak to me, you disguised yourself as a duke and that your clothing was so good that it deceived all the court and they presented you to Emperor Napoleon, who shut himself up with you in his study and confided to you his plan of campaign against Austria.'

'Thus you avenged yourself,' I said delighted by my poor sweetheart's mischief. 'Embrace me, little one, an embrace or I'll die.'

'Thus I avenged myself. I also told her that when I was in Aranjuez you swam the Tagus every night to see me; that in Córdoba you entered the convent and handcuffed all the nuns to abduct me; that another time you rode eighty leagues on horseback to bring me a flower; that you fought with six French generals because they had looked at me, and thousands of other heroic deeds, attacks and amorous feats that came to mind as she was asking me questions. Hey, my little knight, don't say that I don't look after your reputation! I praised you to the skies. You can imagine that the Englishwoman was amazed. She looked at me with her pretty mouth wide open. What do you think? She takes you for a Cid, and thinks she is no less than Doña Jimena[288] herself.'

'What fun you have had with her!' I exclaimed, moving my chair closer to hers. 'But were you jealous? Tell me that you were indeed jealous so that I can laugh for the next three days...'

'Señor Araceli,' she said, with a charming frown, 'yes, I was and I am still...'

'Jealous of that crazy woman! Yes, she is crazy,' I replied, laughing, my soul full of gratitude. 'Inés, my darling, embrace me.'

She snatched her pretty little hands away from me and slapped my face as I moved nearer. I caught them in mid-air and kissed them.

'Inesilla, my love, embrace me... or I'll eat you up.'

'You're certainly starving.'

'Starving for your love, my wife. Just think of it, loving a shadow for six months. And you?'

I did not know what to say. I was deeply moved. My unfortunate friend tried to hide her emotion but she could not hold back the tears struggling to fall from her eyes.

'Don't think any more of that woman, if you don't want to annoy me. It is impossible that you, with the nobility of your soul, your admirable insight, could have...'

'No, I am not crying because of that, my dear,' she said to me, looking at me with deep tenderness. 'I am crying... I don't know why. I think for happiness.'

'Ah, if only Miss Fly were here, if she could see us together, if she could see how we loved each other with the special blessing of God, if she could see this love of ours, overcoming the world's obstacles, she would realise how different her poetic fantasies are from this inexhaustible fountain from the heart, from this heavenly light which our souls enjoy, which they will enjoy for ever and ever.'

'Don't mention Miss Fly to me... if knowing her did cause me pain for a moment, she doesn't bother me anymore,' she said, drying her tears. 'Initially, to be honest, I felt doubtful, more than doubtful, jealous, but once I got to know her better, that feeling vanished. Nevertheless, she is beautiful, more beautiful than me.'

'The very idea of comparing her to you. She's a real tomboy.'

'She's also very rich, according to her. She's a noble... Anyway, despite all her qualities Miss Fly made me laugh, I don't know why. I reflected and said to myself, "It's impossible. Good heavens, it cannot be... I can take every misfortune except that one." I really would not have been able to bear that.'

'How well you thought it through! I thank you, Inés. I thank your great soul. It doubts the whole world, it doubts what you see before you, but you do not doubt me, who adores you.'

'My heart is bursting,' she exclaimed, clutching her breast with a hand that had escaped from mine. 'I have been wanting to cry like this – before you – for a long time. God be blessed for having started to listen to me!'

'Inés, I, too, have been jealous, darling, jealous in another way but worse than yours.'

'Why?' she asked, looking at me sternly.

'Alas, I remember your mother, and I said to myself as I looked at you, 'This naughty girl does not love us anymore."

'Does not love you?'

'My darling, now I'm going to question you like they do children. Who do you love?'

'Everybody,' she replied resolutely.

This reply, as concise as it was eloquent, left me confused.

'Everybody,' she repeated. 'If I didn't think you were capable of understanding this, I would think very poorly of you.'

'Inés, you are a superior being,' I stated with true admiration. 'You have a larger share of the spirit of Heaven in your soul than others. You love your enemies, your cruellest enemies.'

'I love my father,' she said firmly.

'Yes, but your father...'

'You are going to say he's a villain and it's not true. You don't know him.'

'Very well, dear, I believe what you tell me, but the circumstances under which you came into this man's power are not ones most likely to inspire great love for him...'

'You are talking of things you do not understand. If I were to tell you something...'

'Wait... let me finish... I know what you're going to say. You found in him the least you expected, a noble and deep fatherly affection.'

'Yes, but I found something more.'

'What?'

'Misfortune. He is the unhappiest and most unfortunate man in the world.'

'It's true, the nobility of your soul is limitless... but, tell me, surely you have no sympathy for the feelings of hatred and fanaticism of this wretched man.'

'I hope to reconcile him,' she said simply, 'with those he hates or seems to hate, since with certain people his anger does not rise up from the heart.'

'Reconcile him!' I repeated, truly astonished. 'Oh, Inés, if you could accomplish such a great feat with just the strength of your sweetness and love, I would think you were the most wonderful person in the world. But a lot must have happened between him and you which I don't know about, my darling. When you were snatched from the arms of your sick mother by that man, didn't you feel...?'

'Horrified, terrified... don't remind me of that, dearest, it makes me shudder... what a night, what agony! I thought I was dying, and in truth I was pleading for death... Those men... they all seemed to be in black, with bristly skin and hands like hooks... Those men shut me up in a coach. It would be impossible to exaggerate my fear, my entreaties, how I cried continuously for I don't know how many days. Sometimes I was so desperate and crazy that I cursed them again and again or begged on my knees for freedom. For a long time I refused to eat any food and also tried to escape... impossible as I was closely guarded. After a few days' journey they all went away and I was alone with him in a place called Cuéllar.'[289]

'And did he mistreat you?'

'Never; at first he treated me harshly, but later as my self-confidence grew, he became gentler. In Cuéllar he told me that I would never see my mother again, which made me so desperate and distressed that I tried to throw myself that night from a window onto the ground. Suicide, which is such a great sin, did not hold me back. He took me next to Salamanca and there he told me once more that I would never see my mother again. Then I noticed that my tears had a big effect on him. One day, after we had both been arguing and shouting, he went onto his knees in front of me, and kissing my hands he told me he was not a bad man.'

'Did you suspect you might be related to him?'

'You'll see... I replied that I thought he was the wickedest and most abominable being in the world, and that was when he told me he was my father. This revelation left me so bewildered, so astonished, that I lost consciousness for a moment. He took me in his arms and for a long time lavished me with the most affectionate caresses. I did not want to believe it. In the depths of my soul I denounced God for having made me be born from that monster. Then, observing my doubt, he showed me a portrait of my mother and some letters which he had chosen from the many he had. I was half-dead. I thought I was dreaming. In the anguish and distress of this sad scene, I stared at his face and a cry escaped my lips.'

'Hadn't you looked closely at him before?'

'Yes, I had noticed some incomprehensible mystery in his features, but up till then I hadn't seen... I hadn't seen that his forehead was my forehead, that his eyes were my eyes. I found it impossible to sleep that night, I had a terrible fever and I tossed and turned in bed, thinking I was surrounded by shadows or demons who were tormenting me. When I opened my eyes I found him seated at my feet, his penetrating gaze fixed on me, which made me tremble. I sat up and asked him, 'Why do you hate my dear mother?' He kissed my hands and replied, 'I do not hate her. It is she who hates me. For having loved her, I am the unhappiest of men; for having loved her, I am this obscure and scorned crony of the French you see before you; for having adored her, I provoke fear in you instead of love.' Then I said to him, 'You must have done some very wicked things to my mother for her to hate you.' He did not reply. He tried hard to calm my agitation and from that night onwards until I had recovered from my illness he did not leave my side for a moment. Whatever could be invented to entertain a sad and sick creature, he invented; he told me stories, some happy, some terrible, all from his own life, and finally he told me the thing I most wanted to know about it… I was trembling at every word. He had begun to inspire in me so much compassion that sometimes I asked him to be silent and not say anything more. I was gradually losing my fear of him, I had a definite respect for him, but loving him – that was impossible! I kept stating that I could not live away from my mother, and this, if it made him furious initially, then prompted him to redouble his shows of affection and esteem towards me. His aim was always to persuade me that no one else in the world loved me more than him. One day, when I was impatient and distressed at my long imprisonment, I spoke to him very sharply and he threw himself at my feet, asking forgiveness for the great hurt he had caused me and cried so much…'

'That man shed a tear?' I said in surprise. 'Are you sure? I never would have believed it.'

'He shed so many and such bitter ones that I now felt not just compassion but I was moved to pity. My heart was not born to hate, it was born to respond to all generous feelings, to forgive and to reconcile. I had before me an unfortunate man, my own father, alone, destitute, forgotten; I remembered some dark and vague words of my mother about him which I thought were a bit unfair. Deep sorrow oppressed me. The adoration, the crazy idolatry which that unhappy man felt towards me, could not make me indifferent, no, not at all, despite the harm suffered. So I said some words of consolation to him that came to me, and the poor man thanked me so much for them, so very much… He was happy for the first time in his life.'

'You heavenly angel,' I exclaimed with great emotion, 'say no more! I understand and admire you.'

'He then begged me to treat him with more intimacy, that I should call him *padre* and *tú* in the fashion of France, which would give him great comfort, so that is what I did. That terrible man, who frightens everyone who listens to him and who talks of nothing but extermination and destruction, trembled like a child when he heard my voice and, forgetting the guillotine, the nobles and what he called the *third estate*, he spent whole hours in my presence in ecstasy. Then I formed my plan, although I told him nothing, hoping that the power I had over him would achieve the ultimate goal.'

'What plan?'

'To bring that corpse back to life, to bring him back into the world, to his family, to untie that heart from the wheel on which he was suffering torture, to bring that

unhappy reprobate out of Hell and destroy the hatred in his soul that was devouring him. For some time I did not speak any more of returning to my mother's side, nor did I complain of the long and sad periods of loneliness, but I appeared resigned and even content. Then we began those horrible journeys to establish lodges, those hateful men began to be our companions and I could not hide my repugnance. When we were speaking together on our own, he laughed at the masonic practices, saying they were simple and foolish, even though necessary to gain control over peoples. His hatred of nobles, monks and kings was still very much alive, but when he spoke of my mother, he always mentioned her with respect and also with feeling. This was a gratifying sign and a start to the fulfilment of my dearest wish. I was grateful to him and rewarded him by being more affectionate to him, but I was still reserved. The numerous journeys, the lodges and our masonic companions filled me with disgust, loathing and fear. I did not hide these feelings and he told me, 'This will soon be at an end. I can win over stupid people only with this masquerade, and if the French establish themselves in Spain, you'll see what I'll stir up...' 'Father,' I said to him, 'I do not want you to stir up any bad things or to kill anyone, nor to avenge yourself. Revenge and cruelty are typical of low persons.' He spoke warmly to me of the injustices and villainies of today's society, assuring me that it was essential to turn everything upside down, and that one had to begin by destroying everything. How we spoke about this! Finally, I stopped being shocked by all these horrors. I am convinced that my poor father is not as cruel or as bloodthirsty as he seems...'

'If you say so, that must be true.'

'We were in Valladolid when he fell ill, very ill. A famous doctor in that city told me that he would not live much longer. However, whenever he felt a bit better he believed he had recovered completely. In one of his most serious attacks, when we were in Salamanca, he said to me: 'I kidnapped you, my daughter, to make you an instrument of the horrible rage that was devouring me. But God, who undoubtedly did not permit my soul to be lost, filled me with a deep and heavenly love that I did not know before. You have been for me a guardian angel, the living image of divine goodness, and you have not only consoled me, but you have also converted me. Bless you a thousand times for this new vitality you have given to my sad life. But I have committed a crime; you do not belong to me, I entered like a thief into another's garden and stole this flower... No, I cannot keep you a moment longer at my side against your will.' The unfortunate man said this to me with such sincerity that I felt drawn to love him more. Then he continued. 'If you have pity for me, if your generous soul can resist leaving me in my loneliness, sick and hated, be my companion and help me, but only if it is your wish and not because of my violence. Let me kiss you a thousand times, and then you can leave if you do not want to be at my side.' My only answer was to embrace him with all my strength and weep with him. What could I have done, what should I have done?'

'Stay.'

'This occasion was the best opportunity to talk confidentially to him about my wishes. After saying again that I would not leave him, I told him that he should become reconciled with my mother. At first he took my advice very badly, but I begged and implored him so much that he eventually agreed to write a letter. I started it, and as I put in it some words I can't remember now about asking for forgiveness, he became very angry and said, 'Ask for forgiveness, ask for her forgiveness! I'd rather die.' Finally, by taking out and putting in wording, I finished the epistle, but the following day I found him quite changed from his conciliatory disposition, and, what do you think, my friend? Well, he tore up the letter, telling me, 'Later, we'll write it later. Let's wait a bit.' I waited with holy resignation and when we were in Plasencia, I made a new attempt. He wrote the letter himself, taking no less than four hours, and we were just about to send it when one of those hateful men who accompanied him came in and told him that the French police were looking for him and pursuing him because of the actions of a noble lady in Madrid. Oh, Gabriel! When he heard that, his anger flared up once more and he made threats against all mankind. I don't have to tell you that we did not send the letter, nor did he speak about the matter for several days. But I persisted in my plan. When we returned to Salamanca I stated to him that reconciliation was necessary; he got cross with me, I told him I would go away to Madrid, he embraced me, wept, wailed, threw himself at my feet like a fool, and in the end, my boy, in the end we wrote a third letter, I wrote it myself. Finally, my adored mother would have some news of her poor daughter. Ah, that evening my father and I chatted happily, we made fresh plans, together we cursed all the freemasons of the earth, revolutions and guillotines present and future; we went to bed thinking of the supposed happiness that awaited us, we told each other of all the sorrows of our past lives... but on the following day...'

'I turned up... isn't that right?'

'That's right... you know his character... when he saw you and learnt that you had been sent by my mother, when you insulted him... his anger was so great that day that it made me afraid. 'There you are,' he said, 'I'm prepared to be good to her, and she sends the French police against me to torment me and a thief to deprive me of your company. Now you can see, she's implacable... To France, we'll go to France, you'll come with me. That woman has finished with me and I with her...' You know the rest which I don't need to tell you. This morning we thought we were going to die here! How much have I suffered here in this horrible Babilafuente seeing him sick, so sick that he'll never recover again, seeing us threatened by the mob wanting to come in and finish us off! And it's all for what? For freemasonry, for that nonsense that leads to nothing.'

'It leads to something, my dear, and the seed that your father and others have sown will one day give its fruit. God knows what it will be.'

'But he is not an atheist, like the others, and he does not mock God either. It's true that he is in the habit of giving him a strange name, like the *Supreme Being* or something similar.'

'Whether he's called God or the Supreme Being,' I exclaimed, imprisoning the hands of my lover between mine once more, 'what he has done is to create consummate and perfect masterpieces, and one of them is you, who puts me to shame and makes me feel small and overwhelms me the more I know you, speak to you and look at you.'

'You really are a silly thing, since what have I done that isn't natural?' she asked, smiling.

'It is natural for angels to exist unblemished, to inspire good deeds, to praise God, to raise beings to Heaven, to spread good through the sinful world. What is it that you have done? You have done what I never expected or guessed, even though I always thought you were goodness itself; you have loved this unhappy man, the unhappiest of men, and this marvel, now that it has been done, seems to me to be so natural, whereas before I thought it was an aberration and an impossibility. You have an instinct for the divine; I do not. You achieve the greatest things with the simplicity peculiar to God and I have no other role than to admire them once they have been done, amazing myself at my stupidity in not having understood them... Inesilla, you do not love me, you cannot love me!'

'Why do you say that?' she asked innocently.

'Because it's impossible for you to love me, because I don't deserve you.'

When I said this, I was so convinced of my inferiority that I did not even try to embrace her when, dropping her defences by uncrossing her arms, she seemed to leave me with the field open for such an amorous excess.

'Really, it seems to me you are very silly.'

'But if your heart knows only how to love, if it can do nothing else, even though the world may teach it the opposite in thousands of ways, perhaps there may be a little corner in it for me.'

'A little corner? What size?'

'How happy I am! But I'm telling you the truth, I do wish I were an unfortunate man.'
She said nothing in reply, but just laughed, making fun of me.

'I want to be unfortunate so that you'll love me like you have loved your father, so that you'll long for me, so that you'll be crazy for me, so that... But you're laughing, you're still laughing? Perhaps I'm talking nonsense?'

'Greater than this house.'

'But I am truly dumbfounded. Tell me, you who know everything, if there is some extraordinary way to love, a new way, an unknown...'

'Don't keep going on, that will do now... and there's no need for you to be unfortunate either. No, let's not dwell on misfortunes, we've had enough of them. Let's ask God for there to be no more battles you could die in.'

'I want to die!' I exclaimed, sensing that pure and extreme emotion was drawing my mind into a myriad of rare subtleties and affected courtesies, and my heart into incomprehensible and perhaps ridiculous fancies.

'Die!' she cried in distress. 'What makes you say that? May one know why, my dear sir?'

'I want to die so that I can see you weeping for me... but actually that's absurd, because if I died, how could I see you? Tell me you love me, tell me.'

'Of course I do. No more of that old story...'

'But you have never told me you do... perhaps you maintain that you have told me.'

'Didn't I?' she exclaimed with charming mirth. 'Well, then, I didn't.'

I did not know what more she was going to say, but she was certainly about to say something, sweeter to me than the words of angels, when a husky voice came from the next room.

'No, don't go, my dove, without embracing your husband,' I exclaimed, squeezing her lovely body as she escaped from my arms to fly to the side of the sick man.

XXVIII

I went nearer to the door of the gloomy bedroom. Santorcaz did not see me because his eyes were tired and slow from his illness and the living room was half in darkness.

'There was someone there,' the sick man said kissing his daughter's hands. 'I thought I heard the voice of that rogue Gabriel.'

'Father, don't speak badly of those that have done us a favour, don't tempt God, don't provoke Him.'

'I've done him some favours, too, and now you see how he repays me – by arresting me.'

'Araceli is a good lad.'

'God knows what those tyrants will do with me,' the old man exclaimed, letting out a sigh. 'It's over, my daughter.'

'Yes, the madness, the journeys, the lodges which only cause trouble, they're over,' Inés said, embracing her father. 'But in their place is the love of your daughter, and the hope that we can all live together, happy and peaceful.'

'You live on sweet hopes,' he said, 'I live on sad or unfortunate memories. Life is opening up for you, for me, it's the opposite. It has been so horrible that now I want that black and sombre door to close, shutting me outside in one go... you talk of hopes; what if those despots shut me up in a prison, if they send me to die in one of those dung heaps of Africa?'

'They won't take you, I will see that they don't take you, dear Father.'

'But whatever my fate will be, it will be a sad one, dearest child... I will live in prison, and you, what will you do? You will be forced to leave me... or what, shut yourself up in a prison cell?'

'Yes, I will shut myself up with you. Wherever you are, I will be there,' the young woman said lovingly. 'I won't go away from you, I will never leave you, nor go... no, I will not go anywhere you can't go, too.'

I did not hear any sound but the sobs of the poor, sick man.

'But in exchange, dear Father,' she continued in a tone of affectionate admonishment, 'you need to be good, you must not have any bad thoughts, you must not hate anyone, you must not talk of killing people, since God has a knack for doing that; you must stop all that nonsense which has driven you crazy and not get upset or lose your health because there's one king more or one less in the world, nor worry about monks and nobles who, dear Father, won't be suppressed or wiped out just because you want it, nor because the bad-tempered Señor Canencia, Señor Monsalud and Señor Ciruelo want that, too... These are just three men who speak badly of nobles, the powerful and kings because until now no king, nor any lord has thought to throw them a bit of bread to keep them quiet or to shout out in their cause... So will you be good? Will you do what I told you? Will you forget this nonsense? Will you love me and all those who love me?'

While saying this, she adjusted the bedclothes, made the venerable and handsome head of Santorcaz comfortable in the pillows, smoothed out the folds and creases that could inconvenience him, all with such love, solicitude, kindness and gentleness that I was charmed by what I was witnessing. Santorcaz was silent and sighed, letting himself be treated like a child. In this the daughter seemed to be less a daughter than a tender mother who pretends to be annoyed with a lovely child who does not want to take his medicine.

'You'll turn me into a little boy, dear,' the sick man said. 'I am so touched... I could weep. Put your hand on my forehead so that the divine light I have in my brain does not escape... put your hand on my heart and press down. I'm hurting from feeling so much. Did you say that you wouldn't leave me?'

'No, I won't leave you.'

'And if they take me to Ceuta?'

'I will go with you.'

'You'll go with me!'

'But you need to be good and meek.'

'Well? Do you doubt me? I adore you, my daughter. Tell me that I am good, tell me that I am not wicked and I will thank you more than if you had come to summon me on behalf of the Supreme... on behalf of God, as we Christians say. If you tell me that I am a good man, that I am not bad, I will think that those who see fit to call me wicked are liars.'

'Who doubts that you are good? I think you are at least.'

'But I have done you some harm.'

'I forgive you, because you love me and above all because you are sacrificing your passions for my sake, because you are letting me be the one to take out those thorns which have been stuck fast in your heart for so long.'

'And how they sting!' the unhappy mason exclaimed in deep anguish. 'Yes, take them out, take them all out with your angelic hands, take them out one by one, and the bloody wounds will staunch themselves... So, I am good?'

'Well, yes, that's what I will tell anyone who thinks the opposite and I hope they will be convinced when I tell them. I should hope so... the truth is the first thing. You'll see how much everyone will love you and what good things they will say about you. You have suffered; I will tell them about all that you have suffered.'

'Come,' Santorcaz murmured in a tremulous voice, opening out his arms to take the head of his daughter into his quivering hands. 'Bring your dear head which I adore here. It is not the head of a woman but of an angel. God looks at the earth and men through your eyes and is happy with His work.'

The old man covered the beautiful forehead with kisses and I for my part will not conceal that I wanted to do the same. At that moment I took a few steps and Santorcaz saw me. I noticed a sudden change in his expression and he looked at me with annoyance.

'It is Gabriel, our friend who is defending and protecting us,' Inés said. 'Why are you alarmed?'

'My jailer,' Santorcaz murmured sadly. 'I had forgotten I was a prisoner.'

'I am not a jailer, but a friend,' I said, moving forwards.

'Señor Araceli,' he continued in a grave voice, 'where are they taking me to? Oh, wretch that I am! It's a bad thing to fall into the claws of the lackeys of despotism... no, no, daughter, I haven't said anything, I meant that the soldiers... I cannot deny that I hate soldiers just a little, because without them, you see, without them kings could not... Damn all kings! No, no, I don't care if there are kings, daughter, they can sort themselves out. It's just that… frankly speaking, I can't help hating this servant who wanted to take you away from me a little. Now it's clear, his masters ordered him… these military types are a servile bunch used by the great to oppress the sons of the people… I can't look at him, nor can you, isn't that so?'

'Not only can I look at him, but I have the highest regard for him.'

'Well, let him come in… Araceli… I had a high regard for you once. Inés says that you are a good lad… I have to believe it… Given that she holds you in high regard, do you know what I'll do? Make an exception just for you, just for little you, put you to one side and send the rest of them to the guillot… No, no, I did not say that… If others want to set one up, let them do so at the right time; I won't be doing anything other than watching and cheering… no, no, I won't be cheering either, guillotines can go to the Devil!'

'Father,' said Inés, 'give your hand to Araceli who has to go off to his duties and ask him to return to see us afterwards. Oh, they say there's going to be a battle: don't you feel that something bad will happen to him?'

'Yes, certainly,' Santorcaz said, extending his hand to me. 'Poor young man! The battle will be very bloody, and it's more than likely you'll die in it.'

'What are you saying, Father?' Inés asked, terrified.

'The best battle in the world, my daughter, will be the one in which all the soldiers of the two opposing armies perish.'

'But not him, not him! You are scaring me.'

'Well, well, let him live… let Araceli live. Young man, my daughter has a regard for you, and I… I, too… I have a regard for you, too. So God would be doing very much good if He saved your precious life. But you must no longer serve the hangmen of mankind, the oppressors of the people, those that grow fat on the blood of the people, those knavish monks and…'

'Good heavens! You're sounding just like Canencia.'

'I didn't say anything, but this Araceli… whom I hold in high regard… hates us, my dear, he wants to separate us, he's the agent and servant of a person…'

'Whom you also hold in high regard, Father.'

'Of a person,' the mason continued, turning as pale as a corpse.

'Whom you love, Father,' the young woman continued, putting her arms around the head of the poor, sick man, 'from whom you will ask for forgiveness… for…'

Santorcaz's face suddenly became flushed, bright flashes shot from his eyes. He sat up in the bed and stretching out his arms and clenching his fists and with a terrible frown, shouted,

'Me! Ask her for forgiveness… ask her for forgiveness, me… never! Never!'

Saying this he fell back onto the bed like a body from which life has suddenly and terrifyingly fled.

Inés and I hastened to help him. He babbled fiery phrases… called out for Inés thinking she was not there, looked at her absently, dismissed me with shouts and threats and finally quietened down, becoming very drowsy.

'Next time will be the last,' Inés said to me, her eyes full of tears. 'I am certain. Do what we said. Write to her this very afternoon.'

'I will write to her and she will come immediately to Salamanca. Get ready to leave for there with your sick father.'

Making a lot of noise, loudly calling my name and striking the doors and furniture with her whip, Miss Fly entered the house. I met her in the living room and when she saw me she smiled with a matchless grace that was not in truth free of coquettishness. My attention was struck by how smartly she had made herself up, something quite surprising in that place and at that time. Her face shone with beauty and freshness. She had done her hair as if she had had to hand the most delicate equipment of the dressing table and her costume, now clean of dust and mud, concealed its tears and wrinkles with an art unknown to me and revealed only to women. Why not say it? I hate priggishness and hypocrisy. Yes, I will say it: Athenais was enchanting, bewitching and very pretty.

When I expressed to her my surprise at this restoration of her attractive person, she answered,

'Señor Araceli, after your soldiers had put out the fire, there was a little water left for me. They provided what I needed to do my hair in one of the houses in the village… But, Major, is this how you do your duty? Wouldn't you be better at the head of your troops? Leith[290] arrived sometime ago with his division and he was asking for you.'

When I heard this news I could not stay. I took my leave of Inés and having safely secured the entrance to the house and ordered Tribaldos to look after the two prisoners, I went to the square, where Miss Fly left me for no apparent reason. The English troops were starting to arrive. General Leith, to whom I said that España had ordered me to follow when the English had arrived, ordered me to wait until nightfall.

'It is impossible to pursue the French closely,' he said. 'They are a long way ahead and it will be difficult for us to inflict any damage. Our troops are tired.'

I was not entirely displeased at this and I did what was necessary for the transfer of Santorcaz and his daughter to Salamanca. Luckily, my closest and dear friend, Buenaventura Figueroa, was going back there that evening for garrison duty, and I gave him exhaustive instructions about what he was to do with my prisoners in the city and during the journey. The latter was in a convoy which was going overnight to *Roma la chica*, and with some difficulty I managed to get a reasonably comfortable covered wagon, in whose interior I put father and daughter, accompanied by Tribaldos and a good supply of provisions for the journey. I wanted to give them some money as well, but Inés refused, and in truth, they did not need any, because Señor Santorcaz (I don't know if I have mentioned this) had come into his full inheritance the year before and owned a middling country estate, more than enough for his modest needs.

I also gave instructions to Inés to help her stop her unfortunate father making more sallies into the countryside of Montiel[291] with his masonic adventures, and she promised me unequivocally that she would keep him suitably imprisoned without tormenting him, whereupon with much anguish the two of us said farewell to each other, me with this new separation whose end I did not know, and she with foreboding for the danger I was exposed to in the terrible campaign that was under way. With this, and with writing a letter to the countess about what the reader can readily imagine, I spent most of the final hours of the day.

We left at dawn on the following day in pursuit of the French who did not stop until they had crossed the Duero at Tordesillas, from where their lines stretched out to Simancas. There Marmont reinforced his army with Bonnet's division and we waited for him on the left bank, keeping an eye on his movements. The question was where the Frenchman intended to cross the river to meet the allied army whose headquarters were in La Seca.

Marmont, as may be readily supposed, did not want to do as we wanted and suddenly, without any warning, he set off towards Toro. Left wheel, everyone, English, Spanish, Portuguese, on the march again towards the Guareña[292] and the luckless villages of Babilafuente and Villorio!

'And this is what they call waging war!' someone said. 'The English have got such good legs from all the exercise they do. It will end up with Marmont not giving battle at the Guareña either and we'll have to chase him to the Pisuerga,[293] the Adaja[294] or even to the Manzanares[295] or the Abroñigal[296] at the gates of Madrid.'

The only result of two weeks of marches and countermarches was that we found ourselves once again on the outskirts of Salamanca. But the funniest thing was that when we danced the minuet, as the Spanish called it, both armies marched a whole day in parallel, they on the left, we on the right, only half a cannon shot apart, yet not one cartridge was fired. This took place not far from Salamanca and when we stopped in San Cristóbal, you should have heard the mocking remarks about such a manoeuvre and the strategic march, which the common soldiers called a quadrille.

I wanted to go from San Cristóbal to Salamanca but I could not do so as no passes or leave were being granted. However, I had the comfort of learning that it had all been quiet in the house on the Calle del Cáliz during my absence and the marches and minuets of the allied army. As for Miss Fly (I hasten to mention her as I hear the same question on the lips of those that care to listen to me), she had honoured me a number of times with her enchanting conversation during our journeys to Tordesillas, la Nava and the Guareña, but the meetings had always been short and furtive, as if there were some unknown obstacle, some mysterious impediment to her hitherto unbounded familiarity. In these brief meetings I always noticed in her an incomparable gentleness and melancholic resignation and also an unjustified admiration for all my actions, even though they were the most commonplace and insignificant.

Otherwise, if the meetings had been too short, they were very frequent. No sooner had we stopped somewhere than Athenais appeared before me like my own shadow and spoke demurely with me, generally talking to me of refined and delicate things, if not mellifluous and passionate ones. My answers were inspired by the most refined courtesy and good-humoured jesting. She entertained me at every moment with thousands of trifles, titbits and scraps of little value that she had learnt in the various villages on the way.

In the meantime (I beg my readers to pay close attention to this, as it was an unfortunate antecedent to one of the most important setbacks of my life), I noticed that the unfounded suspicion among my English and Spanish colleagues aroused by Athenais's journey to Salamanca had not dissipated. In short, the Little Bird had returned to headquarters and my reputation and standing as a gentleman still continued to be as problematical as they were on the day I had arrived in Bernuy. On two occasions when I had the great honour of speaking with the Duke, I was deeply embarrassed, as he was not only disdainful but also extremely severe and sharp with me. Colonel Simpson's spectacles shot Olympian rays at me and in general all my acquaintances in the English ranks showed in their different ways little or no liking for my worthy person.

'Señor Araceli, Señor Araceli,' Athenais said to me when she appeared suddenly on 21ˢᵗ July when we had just occupied the hill commonly called Arapil Chico, 'come here. Simpson still hasn't left Salamanca. Has something happened to you since we saw each other yesterday?'

'Nothing, señora, nothing has happened to me. And to you?'

'To me, yes, but I'll tell you about that later. Why are you looking at me like that? You also seem to believe, like the rest, that I am sad and pallid, that I have changed a lot...'

'In fact, Miss Fly, I do think that you don't look the same.'

'I don't feel well,' she said with a graceful smile. 'I don't know what's the matter with me... Oh, don't you know? They say there's going to be a great battle.'

'I have no doubt of that. The French are there towards Cavarrasa. When will it be?'

'Tomorrow... you seem happy,' she said, showing a womanly fear that surprised me, knowing as I did her manly daring.

'And you, too, will be happy, señora. A soul like yours needs these grand shows, where immense danger is followed by colossal glory, to sustain itself at its proper level. We will fight, señora, we will fight the Empire, the common enemy, as they say, in England, and we will defeat it.'

Athenais did not respond, as I expected, with any fit of enthusiasm and the poetry of the ballads seemed to have subsided with fear, and shame perhaps, into the hidden depths of her soul.

'There will be a great battle and we will win,' she said dejectedly, 'but... many people will die. Does it not occur to you that you could die?'

'Me? And what does that matter? What does the life of one miserable soldier matter if the flag triumphs?'

'That's true, but you should not expose yourself,' she said with some feeling. 'They say that the Spanish division will not fight.'

'I don't recognise you, señora, you are not Miss Fly.'

'I am coming to think you are right,' she stated, staring at me with her gentle blue eyes. 'I am coming to think I am not Miss Fly... Listen carefully to what I'm going to tell you, Araceli. If you do not come under fire tomorrow, as I hope you won't, let me know... Goodbye, goodbye.'

'But wait a moment, Miss Fly,' I said, trying to stop her.

'No, I can't. You are very indiscreet... If you knew what they were saying... Goodbye, goodbye.'

XXIX

Going a few steps towards her, I called her many times but in the same instant I saw a coach or carriage stop in front of me in the middle of the road. I saw a face, a hand, an arm appear at the door. It was indeed the countess. Almighty God, what immense joy! It was the countess who had stopped her coach in front of me, who was looking around for me, beckoning me elegantly, who was undoubtedly going to say the sweetest things. I ran towards her, mad with joy.

Before talking about what we said, I should say something about the place and the moment these things occurred, because these things concern both history and the tale of the events in my life that I am relating. In the afternoon of the 21st we crossed the Tormes, some by the bridge in Salamanca, others by nearby fords. The French, according to all conjectures, had crossed the same river at Alba de Tormes and were apparently in the woods beyond Calvarrasa de Arriba.[297] We were formed into a not very extensive line, whose left rested on the ford of Santa Marta and the right on the Arapil Chico, next to the Madrid road. A small English division with some lightly armed troops occupied the spot of Calvarrasa de Abajo,[298] the most advanced point of the Anglo-Hispano-Portuguese line.

It was on the slope of the Arapil Chico, by the side of the road, where I met Athenais when she was riding back from Calvarrasa, and a few minutes later, the countess, my beloved protector and friend. I ran towards her, as I have said, and with the deepest emotion kissed her beautiful hands which were still showing at the door. The immense pleasure that I felt hardly let me articulate any sounds other than 'mother and my lady', sounds with which my soul, with supreme spontaneity and confidence, expected similar loving expressions from her. But I was shocked and distressed to see in the countess's eyes scorn, annoyance, anger and, what can I say, an inexplicable severity that left me completely dumbfounded.

'And my daughter?' she asked drily.

'In Salamanca, señora,' I replied. 'You could not have come at a better time. Tribaldos, my orderly, will accompany you. It was fortunate that we met here.'

'I already knew that you were at this place they call the Arapil Chico,' she said to me in the same severe tone, without a smile, without an affectionate look, without a handshake. 'In Calvarrasa de Abajo, where I stopped for a moment, I met Sir Thomas Parr who told me where you were, together with other things about your conduct which have caused me as much shock as indignation.'

'About my conduct, señora!' I cried in pain as sharp as if a steel blade had penetrated my heart. 'I believed there was nothing in my conduct that could have displeased you.'

'I knew Sir Thomas Parr in Madrid and he is a gentleman incapable of lying,' she continued, an indescribable blaze of anger in her eyes which in other times had showed so much tenderness towards me. 'You have seduced a young Englishwoman, you have committed an iniquity, an outrage, a villainous deed.'

'Me, señora, me! This man of honour that has given so many proofs of his loyalty? This man has done such wicked things?'

'Everyone says you have. It's not just Sir Thomas Parr, but many others. Wellesley will also tell me the same.'

'Well, if Wellesley were to confirm it, 'I replied in desperation, 'if Wellesley were to confirm it, I would tell him...'

'That he's lying...'

'No, the first gentleman in England, the first general of Europe, cannot lie. It's impossible that the Duke would say such a thing.'

'There are deeds which cannot be excused,' she continued, 'which cannot be misrepresented. They say that the wronged woman is disposed to ask that you be obliged to comply with the laws of England on marriage.'

When I heard this, a wild hilarity and a terrible indignation cut across my heart with their different impacts, like two bolts of lightning which come together to strike the same place and for an instant they contended with each other. I laughed and I was on the point of weeping with rage.

'Señora, I have been slandered, it's a falsehood, a lie that I...' I cried, putting first my head and then my upper body through the door of the coach. 'I will go mad if you, this person I respect and love and whom I could never lie to, gave credence to such a vile slander.'

'So it's a slander?' she said with great sadness. 'I never should have believed it of you… we live only to see horrible things… But tell me, can I see my daughter right away?'

'I say again that it's false. Señora, you are killing me, you will drive me to the edge of madness, of desperation.'

'Nobody will stop me collecting her and taking her with me?' she asked eagerly, paying no attention to the frenzy that gripped me. 'Have your orderly come with me. I cannot stay. Didn't you say in your letter that everything had been arranged? Is that tyrant dead? Is my daughter alone? Is she expecting me? Can I take her with me? Answer me.'

'I don't know, señora, I don't know anything, don't ask me anything,' I said, confused and lost in thought. 'From the moment you mistrust me…'

'And I mistrust you greatly. In whom can one have confidence? Let me continue… you are no longer what you were to me.'

'Señora, señora, don't say that to me or I'll die,' I cried with immense sorrow.

'Well, if you are innocent, you have time enough to prove it to me.'

'No, no… tomorrow there's going to be a great battle. I could die. I will die angry and I will blame myself… Tomorrow! God knows where I will be tomorrow! You are going to Salamanca, you will see and speak to your daughter; the two of you will concoct a web of suspicions and false assumptions in which there will be tangled up for ever the memory of the unhappy soldier, who perhaps will breathe his last on this very spot where we are now. It's possible that we'll never see each other again. We are on a battlefield. Can you see those holm oak woods down there? Well, the French are behind them. Forty-seven thousand men, señora! Tomorrow this place will be covered with corpses. Cast your eyes over the surrounding area. Do you see those young men of three nations? How many of them will be alive tomorrow? I believe I am destined to perish, to perish in great pain because the idea of having lost the love of the two people to whom I have dedicated my life will precipitate my death.'

My words, passionate with the voice of truth, had some effect on the countess and I saw she was bewildered and moved. She looked round the field which was occupied by so many troops and then covered her face with her hands, falling back into the depths of the coach.

'How horrible!' she said. 'A battle! Aren't you afraid?'

'I am more afraid of slander.'

'If you prove your innocence, I will believe that I have regained a lost son.'

'Yes, yes, you will regain him,' I stated. 'But isn't it enough that I have told you, isn't my word sufficient? Did we meet only yesterday? Oh, if I told Inés what you have said, she would not believe it. Her generous soul would have absolved me without a word from me.'

A voice shouted,

'Get that coach out of the way!'

'Goodbye,' said the countess. 'They are throwing me out of here.'

'Goodbye, señora,' I replied in deep sorrow. 'If we don't see each other again, ever again, please know that on the last day of my life I will still have all, absolutely all of the feelings that I have gloried in at every moment of my life for you and for the one who is very dear to both of us. I thank you, today as in the past, for the love you have shown me, the trust you have had in me, the self-respect you have instilled in me, the raising of my conscience... I don't want these doubts... if we never see other again...'

The coach left, forced to move on by a battery. When I had my last sight of the countess, she had a handkerchief at her eyes to hide her tears.

Upset and absorbed by the distressing sorrow that filled my heart, I did not notice that the general staff were coming along the road in the direction of the Arapil Chico. The duke and some of his suite dismounted at the bottom of the hill and surveyed the country towards Calvarrasa de Arriba. The duke summoned officers from the Irish Regiment, one of those in position there, and as I was the first to appear, he said to me,

'Ah, it is you, Señor Araceli...'

'It is, General,' I replied, 'and if Your Excellency will permit me to speak of a private matter on this occasion, I would beg you to throw light immediately on the slanders that have weighed on me since my trip to Salamanca. I cannot endure people jumping to conclusions about me based on malicious gossip.'

Lord Wellington, no doubt occupied with something more important, hardly paid me any attention. After quickly scanning the whole horizon with his spyglass, he said, almost without a glance at me,

'Señor Araceli, my only answer to you is that I am determined that Great Britain shall be respected.'

As I had never failed to respect Great Britain, or any of the other European powers, those words, which were no doubt a veiled threat, disconcerted me somewhat. The staff officers who surrounded him were having a very important discussion with him about the battle plan. My complaints then seemed to me to be inopportune and even ridiculous, so somewhat perturbed I replied as follows,

'Great Britain! I have no wish other than to die for her.'

'Brigadier Pack,'[299] Wellington said in lively fashion to one of those accompanying him, 'there is a vacancy among the aides of the 23rd Line. Put this young Spaniard, who wants to die for Great Britain, into it.'

'For the glory and honour of Great Britain,' I added.

Brigadier Pack honoured me with the kindly look of a protector.

'Desperation,' Wellington then said to me, 'is not the principal source of bravery, but I will be happy to see Señor Araceli tomorrow on the summit of the Arapil Grande. Mr. O'Lawlor,'[300] he continued turning to his close friend who was accompanying him, 'I believe the French are preparing to occupy the Arapil Grande before us tomorrow.'

The duke appeared slightly uneasy and for a long time his spyglass surveyed the distant oak woods and hills to the east. Little could now be seen as night was falling. The army corps continued to move to the positions ordered by the commander-in-chief and I said farewell to my companions in the Irish Regiment and the Spanish Division.

'We're going to Torres, at the extreme right of the line,' España told me, 'more to observe the enemy than to attack him. An admirable plan! It seems that General Picton and D'Urban's Portuguese[301] have been charged with guarding the crossing of the Tormes, so the situation of the French could not be more disadvantageous. The only thing needed is to occupy the Arapil Grande.'

'That is planned for, General. Pack's brigade, which I have just been attached to, will, God willing, be at the hermitage of Santa María de la Peña at dawn and after that… whatever the honour of Great Britain requires…'

'Farewell, my dear Araceli, behave well.'

'Farewell, dear general. I will salute my companions from the summit of the Arapil Grande.'

XXX

The Arapil Grande! It was the larger of those two rocky sphinxes, raised up one against the other, looking at each other and looking over us. Between the two of them on the following day there was to take place one of the bloodiest dramas of the century, a true prelude to Waterloo, where the horns of the Iliad of the Empire sounded for the last time. On each side of the place called Arapiles the two famous hills rose up, one small, the other one large. The first belonged to us, the second belonged to nobody on the night of the 21st. It belonged to no one for the same reason that it was the most coveted prize; the leopard on the one side and the eagle on the other looked at it, eagerly wanting to take it, but fearing to take it. Each one feared meeting his opponent there at the very moment of raising his standard on the precious heights.

Further to the right of the Arapil Grande and closer to our lines was Huerta and to the left at a forward point, forming the apex of the wedge, was Calvarrasa de Arriba. Calvarrasa de Abajo, much further away and on the shoulders of the larger Arapil, was in the hands of the French.

It was a July night, calm and clear. Pack's brigade set up camp on a plain and waited for daybreak. As it was not permitted to light any fires, the poor English had to eat cold meat, but the women, who in this matter were important auxiliaries to the British soldiery, had brought some very tasty cold cuts from Aldeatejada and even Salamanca, which, with the abundant rum, restored the souls of those weary bodies. The women (and I saw no fewer than twenty in the brigade) talked fondly with their husbands and as far as I could understand, prayed or kept their spirits up with memories of Green Erin or Bonny Scotland. It was a great hardship for the Highlanders who were not allowed to play the pipes there, intoning the melancholy songs of their country, but they formed animated little groups, which I surreptitiously joined to have the strange pleasure of listening to them without understanding them. I greatly enjoyed seeing the resilience and happiness of those people, transported so far from their country, sustained in their duty and led towards sacrifice by loyalty to that same country. I listened with delight to their words and, although I understood very few of them, I believed I recognised the spirit of their lively conversations. A well-built, tall and handsome Scotsman, with golden blond hair and rosy cheeks like those of a maiden, got up when he saw me approaching the little group and, in a mixed-up language, half-Spanish, half-Portuguese, said to me,

'Mister Spanish officer, please be so good as to honour us by accepting this piece of meat and this glass of rum, and let's drink to the health of Spain and Old Scotland.'

'Here's to King George III!' I exclaimed, accepting without hesitation the gift of those brave men.

Loud 'hurrahs' answered me.

'Man dies and nations live,' said another Scotsman, turning to me, who had the enormous swollen skin of some bagpipes under his arm. 'Hurrah for England! What does dying matter? A grain of sand that the wind carries here and there means nothing on the world's surface. God is watching us, friends, through the beautiful eyes of our mother England.'

I could not help embracing the valiant Scotsman who hugged me, saying,

'Long live Spain!'

'Long live Lord Wellington!' I cried.

The women were crying and talking quietly. Their language, incomprehensible to me, seemed to me to be like a chorus of birds chattering around the nest.

The Scots stood out with their picturesque costume of red and black checks, bare legs, handsome Ossianic heads covered with a fur hat and a belt decorated with some long hair that seemed like the head of hair snatched from the skull of the vanquished in the savage wars of the north. The English mingled among them, their red coats making them very visible despite the darkness. The officers, wrapped in white cloaks and wearing their pointed hats with plumes, not at all elegant, seemed like long-legged birds with broad wings and mobile crests.

At the first light of day the brigade set out for the Arapil Grande. The closer we got, the more we were sure that the French had beaten us to it, they having had the easier operation because their line was closer. The brigadier deployed his forces and the guerrillas spread out. The eyes of all were fixed on the hermitage located roughly halfway up the hill and on the few scattered houses, the only buildings that intruded here and there into the lonely and bare landscape.

Some columns ascended without meeting any obstacle and when we got to within a hundred yards of Santa María de la Peña, the ground fell away as we advanced and we could see first a line of heads, next a line of shoulders, and then full figures. It was the French. The rising sun, which shone from behind the backs of our enemies, was dazzling us so that we could not see them clearly. A distant murmuring reached our ears, and the Scots close by also uttered some words; nothing more was needed to set off the electric spark. A volley broke out. The guerrillas gave supporting fire, while some ran to occupy the hermitage.

In front of it was a courtyard, something like a cemetery. The English went into it, but the Imperialists, who had taken up positions in the apse, quickly took control of the main part of the building and the outbuildings at the back so that even before our men could force the door, they were being fired upon from the belfry and the open skylight above the portico.

Brigadier Pack, one of the bravest, calmest and most gallant men I have known, harangued the Highlanders. The colonel who commanded the 3rd Light Infantry harangued his men, and in short all the officers gave a harangue, including me, speaking, in Spanish, language most appropriate to the occasion. I am sure they understood me. The 23rd Line had not entered the courtyard but was on the left flank of the hermitage, watching to see if more French forces were coming. If they didn't the game was ours, for the simple reason that there were more of us at that point. But another enemy column soon appeared. To wait for it, to give it breathing space, in other words, to give the appearance for a moment that we were afraid of it, would mean we had given up any advantage in advance.

'At them!' I shouted to the colonel.

'*All right!*' he exclaimed.[302]

And the 23rd Line fell like an avalanche onto the French column. A sharp hand-to-hand fight ensued; our Englishmen wavered a bit because the enemy's drive in the first moments was terrible, but assuming once more that imperturbable constancy, which, if it is not heroism, is the next thing to it, all the advantage was soon ours. The Imperialists retired in disorder, or rather, they changed tactics, dispersing in small groups to wait for reinforcements to join them. Each side had suffered almost equal losses, and several bodies were lying on the ground, but this was still nothing, just child's play, an innocent preface that was almost laughable.

The real disadvantage in our position was that we did not know how many forces the French could send against us. We could see the thick Calvarrasa wood opposite us, but nobody knew what was hiding under that blanket of greenery. Were there many, were there few? When the intuition, inspiration or clairvoyance of great captains cannot answer these questions, military science runs the risk of becoming as vain and fruitless as the jargon of pedants. We looked at the wood but the dark foliage of the oaks said nothing to us. We could not read that dark green surface which displayed mysterious changes in colour and light, moving bands and oscillating signs in its vast extent. It was an enormous mass of greenery, a squat and horrible monster that lay flat over the ground with drooping head and stretched-out wings, under which it was perhaps brooding innumerable warriors.

When he saw the second French column retreating, Pack ordered a renewed attempt on the hermitage and the Highlanders were about to attack it from various points, which would have been easy had not something strange happened over by the wood when the first shots sounded. It seemed the monster was moving, lifting one of its wings, discharging a swarm of homunculi, who could be made out at that distance at their mother's side, as small as ants. Then they were growing, coming closer... they turned from pygmies into giants, their helmets shone, their swords seemed flashes of lightning; column after column, man after man came on in a threatening movement.

The colonel looked at me and all of us officers looked at each other without a word. With the quickness of the good tactician, Pack, without abandoning the assault on the hermitage, sent us more men and we waited quietly. The wood continued to disgorge men.

'We shall have to fight on the defensive,' the colonel said.

'Yes, on the defensive. Long live England!'

'Long live the Emperor!' the distant echoes repeated.

'Englishmen, England is watching you!'

The shouts of 'Long live the Emperor!' which had answered us from afar sounded louder. The animal was coming closer and its fierce bellowing was spreading a sense of foreboding.

XXXI

Some old houses and tile workshops about 60 yards each side of the hermitage were immediately occupied, establishing an imaginary line of defence where the only material assistance was a depression in the ground, a sort of shallow ditch that seemed to mark the boundary between two properties. If I had had all the forces at Brigadier Pack's command, I would have tried to go for broke and disrupt the enemy before he could attack us. But the English never attempt such strokes of madness which fail twenty times for each time they succeed. On the contrary, Pack arranged his forces defensively: with an admirable and swift eye he noted and took advantage of every accident of the ground, the slight hollows in the hill on that side, the isolated outcrop of rock, the solitary tree, the ruined wall, all of them.

The French arrived. They looked at us from a distance with suspicion, smelling us out, listening to us.

Have you seen a stork stretch its neck from one side to the other so that you don't know whether it is looking or listening, standing on one foot and holding up the other one until it finds some solid ground to step on? Well, that is how the French advanced. Some of our men were laughing.

I cannot give an idea of the silence that reigned in the ranks at that moment. Were they soldiers on watch or monks at prayer? But in a moment the stork put both feet on the ground. It was on firm terrain. A thousand shots sounded as one and over us came a human wave composed of bayonets, shouts, stamping, and unbounded ferocity.

"Fire! Death! Blood! Swine!" were just some of the words with which I can indicate, from what little I understood, the din of English anger, which roared around me, a concert of guttural speech, a shriek both discordant and sublime at the same time as if thousands of heavenly parrots and cockatoos were chattering all together.

I had seen wonderful things done by Spanish and French soldiers when attacking but I had never seen anything comparable to the English when defending. I had never seen columns letting themselves be slashed. The motionless old tree trunk does not receive the blow of the axe cutting it with as much patience as those men did the bayonet that was lacerating them. They repulsed the French many times, forcing them to run far beyond the hermitage. There were men for everything: to die resisting and to kill pushing forward. At moments it seemed we had repulsed them for good, but the wood, sending forth new broods of men from under its plumage, kept us at a numerical disadvantage, and, even though some companies came to help us from the Arapil Chico, we were still outnumbered.

The slaughter was great on each side, but more on ours, and it got to the point where we found ourselves in great difficulties in removing the many dead and wounded who were making it impossible for us to move. The fight stopped and started for short intervals. We did not withdraw an inch, but neither did we advance, and we had abandoned the courtyard in front of the hermitage as it was impossible to remain there. But the farmhouses and tile workshops were still ours and the Highlanders showed no signs of letting themselves be removed from them. However, this series of advantages and setbacks which balanced the two enemy forces, this fearlessly maintained equilibrium, could not last for long. If the French sent more men, or, on the other hand, if the Duke of Wellington sent some, the question would soon be decided, but if they both sent more at the same time… well, only God knew the outcome.

Brigadier Pack summoned me and said,

'Make haste to headquarters and tell the duke what is happening.'

I mounted and rode at top speed to headquarters. When I was going down the slope towards the lines of the Allied armies, I could easily make out the masses of the French Army in constant motion, but not one shot was fired between the centres of each army. All interest was on that isolated theatre of Arapil Grande, that place that seemed an insignificant detail, a caprice of the military genius who was then planning a great battle.

As I passed by the various sections of the allied line, I was struck by how calm and quiet they were, idly waiting for orders. There was no battle, indeed it did not seem there was going to be a battle, just an exercise. But the commanders, all standing on the higher points of ground, on the ammunition wagons and even on the gun carriages, were observing, with the aid of their telescopes, the vicissitudes of the Arapil Grande, near the hermitage.

'Why are all these people not hurrying to help Brigadier Pack?' I said to myself, full of confusion.

The fact was that neither Wellington nor Marmont wanted to make a show of wishing to occupy the Arapil Grande, for the very reason that each of them considered that position was the key to the battle. Marmont feigned various movements to disconcert Wellington: he threatened to strike for the Tormes so that the imperturbable Englishman would take his eye off the Arapil; then he would pretend to retire as if he did not want to give battle. But all this time Wellington, calm, immutable, serene, attentive, vigilant, remained at his post observing the Frenchman's manoeuvres and holding in his powerful hand the thousand reins of that army that wanted to hurl itself forward prematurely.

Marmont wanted to deceive Wellington, but Wellington did not only want to deceive Marmont, he was actually deceiving him. The latter was manoeuvring to deceive his enemy, but the Englishman paid close attention to the other man's forays, waiting for the slightest mistake by the Frenchman to fall upon him. At the same time he pretended not to care about the Arapil Grande and positioned enough troops on the right bank of the Tormes to make it seem that he thought the critical point of the battle was there. Meanwhile, he had an enormous force at his disposal in case of an emergency on the hill. But this state of emergency, in his view, had not yet occurred, nor would it occur as long as any of the men in Santa María de la Peña were alive. It was ten o'clock in the morning and apart from the brief action I have described, the two armies had not fired a shot.

As I went through the ranks, many officers at various points asked me questions which were impossible to answer and when I arrived at headquarters I saw Wellington on horseback, surrounded by a multitude of generals.

Even before I reached him, my expressive gestures and looks had already said,

'It can't be done.'

'What can't be done?' he exclaimed calmly after I had told him what was happening there.

'Occupy the Arapil Grande.'

'I did not order Pack to occupy the Arapil Grande, because that is impossible,' he replied. 'The French are very close to it and since yesterday they have made numerous preparations to dispute that position with us, even though they conceal it.'

'So...'

'I did not order Pack to occupy the hill completely, but to prevent the French from establishing themselves there. Will they establish themselves? The 23rd Line, the 3rd Light Infantry and the 7th Highlanders are still there, are they not?'

'A few of them are still there, General.'

'With the reinforcements that have gone there since, there are enough for the purpose, which is to hold out, nothing more than holding out. It will be sufficient if no Frenchman sets foot on this side of the hill. Even if they cannot occupy the hermitage, I believe there are enough men to keep the enemy engaged for a few hours.'

'Yes, indeed, General,' I said. 'However quickly they may die, eight hundred men will give a good account of themselves. We can keep what we hold until noon.'

While I was saying this, he was paying more attention to the distant enemy lines than to me and I saw him make a sudden movement, turn to General Álava[303] who was beside him and say,

'Things are suddenly changing. The French are extending their lines too much. Their right intends to encircle me...'

A formidable mass of Frenchmen was moving towards the Tormes, leaving quite a significant gap between it and Calvarrasa. One would have needed to be blind not to see that through this gap the genius of the allied army was about to thrust his terrible sword up to the hilt.

The general staff retired, orders were given, officers hurried from one side to the other, an eloquent murmuring resounded through the entire army, cannons advanced, horses pawed the ground. Without waiting for more, I raced back to the Arapil to announce that everything was changing. The lines of the regiments could be seen oscillating and the reflections on the bayonets appeared to be moving like luminous waves; the army's units were shuddering, affected by the intimate palpitations of that exceptional fear which always precedes heroism. The breath and emotion of so many men gave off a certain strange warmth into the atmosphere. The burning and heavy air was not enough to go round.

The orders delivered with overwhelming speed carried with them the thought of the commander-in-chief. We all guessed it, by virtue of that strange solidarity which at given times is established between the will and the body, between the brain that thinks and the hands that execute. The plan was to throw the centre into the gap in the enemy line and at the same time hurl upon the Arapil the full force of the right, which up to then had remained expectantly on the plain.

XXXII

I had not gone far when a horrendous noise hurt my ears. It was the artillery of the enemy's left which was firing at the larger hill. They were attacking it with colossal force. Our right, composed of the bravest brigades of the army, was at the same instant ascending to rescue the incomparable Highlanders, the 23rd Line and the 3rd Light Infantry, of whose prowess I have already told, from the spot they were in.

I passed through the Fifth Division under the command of General Leith that was marching from the village of Arapiles to the hill. I passed through the Third Division, commanded by Major General Pakenham,[304] the cavalry of General d'Urban and the dragoons of the 14th Regiment, which were advancing in four columns to encircle the enemy's left on the famous heights, and I saw from afar the brigade of General Bradford[305] and that of Cole,[306] and the cavalry of Stapleton Cotton which were marching in the opposite direction against the enemy's centre. At the same time I could make out in the distance my comrades of the Spanish Division forming part of the reserve commanded by Hope.[307]

The hermitage referred to earlier was not on the summit of the Arapil Grande as there were further heights above it. This eminence in fact was regular and terraced and if from afar it did not seem so, once you were on it, you found large hollows, ups and downs, slopes, some gentle, some steep, and rather stony soil.

The French, from the moment they had decided it was no longer worth concealing their intentions, appeared at several points and occupied the highest ground and hillocks, and from them threatened the meagre forces that had been operating there since the morning. The first division to open fire on the enemy was Pakenham's, which as planned went up the slope overlooking the village. The Portuguese cavalry of d'Urban was in support, but they did not make great progress because the French, having just come out of the wood, had taken positions higher up and, although the slope was gentle, it gave them a considerable advantage.

When I reached the neighbourhood of the hermitage, Brigadier Pack had not lost one line of his earlier positions, but his brave regiments had been reduced to less than half their number. General Leith had just arrived with the Fifth Division and the outlook had changed completely, because if the enemy had many forces on the crest of the hill, we were in no way inferior in numbers or bravery.

But there was no time to lose. We had to throw men and yet more men at that heap of earth, scorning the fire of the French artillery, which was bombarding us from the wood, although without doing us much damage. We had to drive the French out of Santa María de la Peña and then continue upwards, right up until we had planted the English standards on the peak of the Arapil Grande.

'Reinforcements have come almost before I have with the answer,' I said to Brigadier Pack. 'What am I to do?'

'Take command of the 23rd Line, which has no officers. Upwards, keep going upwards! I see now what we have to do – hold this position and engage as many of the enemy's troops as we can so that Cole and Bradford meet less resistance at the centre. This is the key to the battle. Upwards, keep going upwards!'

The French no longer seemed to give much importance to Santa María de la Peña and crowned the summit. Their columns, skilfully arranged in echelon, awaited us steadfastly. It was not possible to destroy them there with cavalry, nor to do them much damage with our distant guns. It was necessary to march squarely up there and throw them off as best we could with God's help. The problem was difficult, the task immense, the danger horrendous.

It fell to the 23rd Line to have the glory of being the first to advance against the immovable French columns that occupied the heights. A dreadful moment! The stairway, readers, was a terrible one to mount, and at each one of its fateful steps, the soldier was astonished to find himself still alive. If, instead of going up, it went down, it would be the stairway to Hell. Yet the troops of Pack and Leith went upwards. How did they do it? I do not know. It was an inexplicable wonder. Those Englishmen were unlike any men I had seen. They were ordered to do something absurd, impossible, yet they did it, or at least attempted to.

In recounting what happened there, it is not possible for me to give details of the movements of each battalion or the orders given by each officer, nor what everyone did in their own area. Imagination retains what is important in indelible and terrifying characters, but not what is incidental, and the important thing is that we then climbed upwards driven by an irresistible force, by some powerful hands that gripped our shoulders. We saw death ahead of us and above us, but our own death drew us on. Ah, someone who has only gone up the staircase in his own home will never understand this!

As the ground was uneven, there were places where it did not slope. On these ledges scattered combats of unheard-of bitterness and ferocity took place. The brave men of the South, who seldom display the passive heroism of letting themselves be killed before breaking ranks and scattering, will not understand that kind of imperturbable fury to which desperation converted into power had led us. It is easy for the lofty hilltop to break loose and swoop down, its speed increasing as it moves, and fall upon the plain, crushing and overcoming it, but we were the plain, set on reaching the summit and wanting to overwhelm it, destroy it and wreck it. In war as in nature, height rules and triumphs, it is material superiority and a symbolic form of victory, because victory really is something that descends with lightning speed, driving along and running over, cracking open and destroying. The one who is above has real and moral force and as a result has a conception of the struggle, which he can direct as he pleases. Like the head in the human body, he can make use of feelings and ideas… We were poor, creeping forces who, scratching along the ground, were at the mercy of those above, but yet we wanted to dethrone them. Imagine the feet being set on knocking the head off the shoulders so that they could go on top, stupid things that only know how to walk!

The first steps did not offer any great difficulty. Many men died, but we went on. It was very different later. It seemed as if the French had allowed us to come up so that they could take us at closer quarters.

The dispositions that Pack had made so that we would suffer as little as possible were admirable. It goes without saying that all the commanders had dismounted and, some at the rear, some at the head of the lines, led the obedient soldiers by the hand, so to speak. Our good order in the middle of the dead, a steady step, and an unequalled coolness in executing manoeuvres prevented the ravages from being as bad as they could have been. With modern arms, this feat would have been impossible.

It was vital for us to take advantage of the intervals when the enemy was reloading and charge with fixed bayonets. However, our tiredness did not help and even if in some place the gradient was little more than a ramp, in some it was a proper slope. The French, fresh, confident and sure of their position, raked us with accurate fire and received us with bare bayonet. Sometimes one of our columns succeeded, by its daunting steadfastness, in making an opening by climbing over the enemy's dead, but this meant doubling and tripling the attacks, doubling and tripling the dead, and the results did not match the enormous effort.

What a frightening ascent! During any pauses, when they were engaged in separate fights, the shouts, the tumult, the throngs in those craters were incomparable to anything that the anger of man had invented to match the ferocity of wild beasts. With a thousand deaths, the ground was conquered hand by hand, and once it had been taken, the piece of earth large enough to plant one's feet on was ferociously held. England would not yield the space on which it had fixed the soles of its shoes. To remove them and defeat that marvel of endurance, the French would have to use all their courage and the advantage of height. Even so they failed to drive the British down the slope. Woe to him who turned first! Knowing the danger of a momentary faltering, a retreat, a look backwards, the feet of those men became rooted. Even after they had been killed, it seemed that their long legs became embedded into the ground up to their knees, like stakes marking for ever the conquest by the mighty spirit of England.

But finally a terrible moment arrived, a moment when the columns were going up and dying, when the many men who threw themselves up that bank, destroyed, burnt up, depleted, feeling cut down at every step, realised that their great efforts were making no headway. Behind the crushed French columns appeared others. Like the terrifying wood of Macbeth, on the crest of the Arapil Grande, every branch was a man. We got closer to the top and the uppermost crater was spitting soldiers. No one knew where so many soldiers could come from, but the plateau on the summit had space for an army. Then came the moment when the English saw the crest of the hill itself come upon them, a horrible monstrosity that wielded thousands of bayonets and fired thousands of guns. Panic seized everyone, not that nervous panic that makes men flee, but a supreme and profound anguish which removes all hope and brings resignation. It was impossible, completely impossible, to carry on going upwards.

But going down was a trickier issue. Nothing easier if you just let yourself be cut down by the French, resigning yourself to rolling down dead or alive. A retreat downhill step by step, and giving the enemy each inch of ground with as much tenacity as the enemy had shown when it was taken, is the height of difficulty. Pack roared with rage and it seemed as if the flood of blood in the purple flesh of his face was about to burst from every pore. He was a man to have made it to the top of the hill on his own. He was giving orders in a hoarse voice, but his orders could no longer be heard. He wielded his sword, cutting at the sky, since it was no doubt the fault of Heaven that the English could not advance further.

The time had come when one soldier would die stoically to protect with his body the man taking a step backwards behind him. In this way half of the meat was saved. A bad retreat throws everything on the spit onto the grille. The columns kept their order with admirable skill. The fire became fiercer and each time one of those heavy waves broke up during the descent it seemed as if it was all over. But the momentary confusion disappeared in an instant and the masses of English appeared once more compact and formidable, and death had to be satisfied with just the half. In this way part of the ground was being slowly surrendered until the Imperialists stopped attacking us. They had got to a point where the English cannon was doing much damage to them and the progress of Pakenham on the flank of the Arapil Grande was causing them concern. They regrouped and waited.

Meanwhile, elsewhere wonderful and glorious events were occurring. Everything was going well everywhere apart from on our ill-starred hill. General Cole destroyed the French centre. The cavalry of Stapleton Cotton, going right through the broken ranks, made one of the most brilliant, most sublime and, at the same time, one of the most dreadful charges ever seen. From the position where we had stopped, not ashamed but very humiliated, we could make out in the distance that wonderful display that made us envious. The columns of dragoons, the phalanxes of horses, the lightest, quickest and most warlike to be seen, wound like immense serpents among the French infantry. The sabre blows showed as a constant sprinkling of little flashes, a shower of steel that was shattering breasts, annihilating men, sweeping them aside and routing them like a hurricane. The shouts of the horsemen, the gleam of their helmets, the snorting of the horses, whose brutal and coarse souls rejoiced in such a bloody feast, offered a terrifying spectacle. Indifferent, as is natural, to the misfortunes of the enemy, warlike hearts became absorbed in this spectacle. Confidence flees from battles, a shocked and weeping deity, led by fear. Nothing is left except warlike anger which forgives nothing, and the barbaric instinct of force, which by some mysterious enigma of the mind is turned into an admired virtue.

Stapleton Cotton's squadrons, as I have said, were performing the great wonder of this battle. It was in vain that the French had won some advantage elsewhere. It was in vain that they had managed to seize some houses in the village of Arapiles. Believing that it was important to occupy the village, they took the first buildings with spirit and defended them bravely. They clung to the earthen walls and stuck to them like mussels on a stone;

they would rather be squashed against the walls than abandon them, swept by English shrapnel. It was precisely when the French thought they had gained a great advantage by occupying the village and when we were coming down the Arapil Grande, that Cotton's cavalry thrust into the heart of the Imperial army like a huge dagger. The mighty body could be seen split in two, cracking and shattering at the violent contact with the powerful wedge. Everything yielded to it, force, foresight, skill, valour, daring, because it was a wonderful power, an overwhelming unity, composed of thousands of pieces that worked in harmony without any discordance. The thousands of cuirasses suggested a Roman *testudo*, but this immense tortoise, with its shell of steel had all the nimbleness of a reptile with thousands of feet and thousands of mouths to roar and bite. It enlarged the hole it had made with its bites; everything fell before it. The enemy battalions wailed in terror. Marmont hurried to restore order and a cannon ball took off his right arm. Bonnet then hurried over to replace him and he fell, too. Ferey,[308] Thomières[309] and Desgraviers,[310] illustrious generals, perished along with thousands of soldiers.

Firing had ceased at the foot of our hill. An officer who had fallen at my side during the withdrawal downhill was being carried by two soldiers. I saw him go by and, close to death, he called me over with a sign. It was Sir Thomas Parr. When he was laid onto the ground, the surgeon, examining his shattered chest, implied there was nothing to be done. Other English officers, most of them wounded also, surrounded him. Poor Parr turned his eyes, from which the last glimmers of life were slowly fading, towards me and said in a feeble voice,

'They told me before the battle that you felt some bitterness towards me and that you were ready to demand satisfaction from me for some insults I have no idea about.'

'My friend,' I exclaimed, much-affected, 'no trace of anger can remain in my breast at this time! I forgive and forget everything. The slander that you repeated, surely without malice, cannot harm my honour. It is one of those flippant remarks we all make.'

'Who does not say one sometimes, Señor Araceli?' he said gravely. 'Acknowledge, nevertheless, that I could not have offended you. I die without the worry of being hated... Do you say that I slandered you? Are you referring to the matter of Miss Fly? Is that what you call slander? I repeated what I had heard.'

'Miss Fly?'

'As it is said you have no choice but to marry her, I have nothing to hold against you. Will you acknowledge that I have not offended you?'

'I acknowledge it,' I replied, not knowing what I was saying.

Parr, turning to his compatriots, said,

'It seems we are losing the battle.'

'The battle will be won,' they replied.

'Let England know that I die for her. May my name not be forgotten!' he murmured, his voice fading away gradually.

He mentioned his wife, his children, said some affectionate words, shaking the hands of his friends.

'The battle will be won... I die for England!' he said, closing his eyes.

Some slight movements and a gentle quivering of his lips were the final signs of life in the body of that valiant and generous soldier. A moment later another number was added to the frightening total of dead soaked up by the Arapil Grande.

XXXIII

The tremendous charge of Stapleton Cotton had changed the situation. Leith appeared once more among us, accompanied by Brigadier Spry.[311] From their faces, their gestures and the shouting of Pack I realised that a new attack on the hill was being prepared. The situation of the enemy was already much less favourable than before, because the advantage won in our centre by the advance of the cavalry and the progress of General Cole had completely changed the aspect of the battle. Pakenham, having ejected them from the village, was applying considerable pressure on them at the eastern foot of the hill so that they were exposed to the risks of an encircling movement. But they still had powerful forces on the vast hill and also a safe line of retreat through the woodlands of Calvarrasa. Spry's brigade which had been operating earlier on the outskirts of the village, hurried to the right to support Pakenham. Leith's division and Pack's brigade with the 23rd Line and the 3rd and 5th Light Infantry went once more into battle.

The French, who had reconcentrated themselves in their positions from the hermitage upwards, waited in an imposing position. Shots sounded from various points; the columns marched in silence. We already knew the terrain, the enemy and the pitfalls of that ascent. As before, the French seemed ready to let us advance, the better to receive us with a hail of bullets. But this did not happen, because they suddenly unleashed themselves in a menacing rush onto Pakenham and Leith with such courage that only

Englishmen could resist them. The columns on both sides had lost their alignment, and irregular and broken groups faced each other, bristling with sharp points, if I may use that expression, and set upon each other. The two armies sank their claws into each other and ripped away. Streams of blood furrowed the ground. The bodies of those that had fallen were often the principal obstacle to an advance. Sometimes these sorts of death lock would be broken off and each side retired a short way to gather new strength for a new onslaught. We saw the open patches of ground covered with blood and full of corpses, but far from being dismayed at that terrible sight, we renewed our attacks with redoubled fury. Covered in blood, which I did not know if it had come from my veins or those of others, I flung myself into the same delirium that I saw in the others, forgetting everything, feeling (and this is obvious) like a second, or rather, a new soul who existed only for the purpose of rejoicing in that boundless ferocity, where all memory of the past, any idea other than that of the frenzy it was involved in, had been erased from its inflamed faculties. I roared like the Highlanders and – an extraordinary thing – I was speaking English! I have never been able to speak that language before or since but on that occasion I am sure that when I yelled in the battle they understood me and I in turn understood them.

The powerful efforts of the Scots disconcerted the Imperial lines slightly, precisely at the moment when Clinton's[312] division arrived in our camp, having been in reserve up till then. Fresh and eager troops joined the action and from that moment we could see that the horrible ranks of Frenchman ceased to be active but still held their ground firmly. Shortly afterwards we saw them fall back, but still keeping up a lively fire. Despite this, the English did not launch themselves upon them. More time passed and then we saw that the troops occupying the crest of the hill were slowly abandoning it, protected by the rearguard that continued firing.

I do not know if they were ordered to do so, but what I do know is that the English regiments, who had occupied various points of the slope, suddenly advanced upwards, calmly and without hurrying. The top of the Arapil Grande was an irregular and vast area, composed of other little hills and small valleys. It could hold an immense number of soldiers, but night was falling, and the centre of the enemy's army had been defeated, as well as its left in the direction of the Tormes, so that it was impossible for them to defend the contested heights. France began to retreat and the battle was won.

However, it was not easy to break the French, who still occupied some of the high ground, with the bayonet, much as some would have liked to, because they defended themselves with spirit and covered their retreat with skill. It was on our side that more damage was done to them. We laboured hard to break their ranks, to destroy and rout that wall which protected the rest of them in their flight to the woods, but it was not easy at first. The sight of the considerable number of troops retreating quietly and almost unharmed drove us to charge at them with increased zeal, and finally, after so much pounding and beating of the unfortunate French line, we saw it crack, break and crumble and the victor's fist and claw thrust through the innumerable gaps, leaving nothing alive. How terrible is the hour when a beaten army has to organise a retreat before the menacing and implacable rage of the victor, who will destroy it if it flees and also destroy it if it stays!

Evening was falling and the landscape was slowly growing darker. The scattered groups of the enemy army, fleeting lines winding along the ground in the distance, disappeared, absorbed by the earth and the woods, accompanied by the sad sound of the raucous drums. These, the din nearby and the sound of the cannons which were still singing the final mournful verses of the poem, produced a crazy racket that numbed the brain. You couldn't even hear the voice of your friend shouting next to you. The moment had come when expressions and gestures said everything – it was pointless to give orders as you couldn't be heard. For the soldier, the occasion had come for individual exploits, no commanders were needed for this and everything was already reduced to seeing who could kill more fleeing enemy soldiers, who took more prisoners, who could get their hands on a general, who could seize one of those venerated eagles that had strutted proudly over all Europe, from Berlin to Lisbon.

The roar that thundered through the air when the victor, full of rage and thirsting for vengeance, fell upon the vanquished to crush him is impossible to describe. Anyone who has not heard the thunderbolt crash in the heart of the storms of men will never know what these scenes are like. Blind and crazy, with no thought of danger or death, hearing nothing but the whirring of the whirlwind, we threw ourselves into that volcano of fury. We became mixed up with them: some were unarmed, others threw themselves at the feet of the brave man that wanted to take them prisoner, some died while killing, some let themselves be taken stoically. Many English were sacrificed in the final kicks of the wounded and desperate beast; they bayoneted pitilessly, thousands of hands meted out death in all directions and victors and vanquished fell entwined together in confusion, mixing their burning blood.

There is no hatred in history comparable to that of the English and the French at that time. Guelphs and Ghibellines, Carthaginians and Romans, Arabs and Spaniards forgave each other sometimes, but England and France at the time of the Empire hated each other like Satan. The mutual jealousy of those two peoples, one of whom dominated the world's seas, the other the land, exploded horribly on fields of battle. From Talavera to Waterloo the duels of these two rivals laid a million bodies out on the earth. At Salamanca, one of the bloodiest affrays, both reached the peak of ferocity.

In order to take prisoners, everything in the life of the enemy that could be was crushed. With some Portuguese and English I pushed on perhaps further than advisable into the core of the disorganised and fleeing infantry of the enemy. I saw insane struggles on every side and heard the most insulting words of those two languages which fought with their curses as did the men with their weapons. I was carried along in the vortex of the whirlwind, not knowing what I did, the only thing in my soul was a burning desire to kill something. In that confusion of shouts, raised arms, hellish faces, eyes disfigured by passion, I saw a golden eagle on the end of a pole, around which was wrapped a filthy

rag, a colourless piece of cloth that looked as if it had been used to clean all the plates on the tables of all the kings of Europe. My eyes devoured that scrap which unfurled in the wind in one of the surges of the throng and displayed an N which had been in gold and showed against three bands whose hue was a pastel of earth, blood, mud and powder. Bonaparte's whole army had wiped off the sweat from a thousand battles with that handkerchief full of holes and now without any shape or colour.

I saw that glorious emblem of war only some five yards away. I do not know what happened; I do not know if the flag came towards me or if I ran towards the flag. If I believed in miracles, I would believe that my right arm stretched out five yards, since without knowing how, I grabbed the pole with the flag and did so with such strength that my hand stuck to it and I shook it, trying to snatch it away. Moments like that are beyond the understanding of the senses. I found myself surrounded by people, falling, stumbling, some dying, others defending themselves. I redoubled my efforts to snatch the flagstaff and a voice shouted in French,

'Take that!'

At the same instant a pistol was fired at me. A bayonet went into my body, I did not know where, but I knew that it had. Before me was a livid figure, a face covered in blood, eyes flashing fire, hands gripping the flagstaff and a contorted mouth that looked as if it was going to swallow eagle, rag and pole, and me, too. To say how much I hated that monster is impossible. We looked at each other for a moment and then we struggled together. He fell to his knees; one of his legs wasn't a leg, but just a piece of flesh. I fought to tear the banner from his hands. Somebody came to my assistance and someone helped him. I was wounded again and I got even angrier and crushed the brute against the earth with my knees. With both hands I was grasping both the flagstaff and my sword. But this could not last and soon I just had my sword in my right hand. I thought I had lost the flag, but the steel blade I was thrusting buried itself deeper and deeper into something soft, and a thread of blood shot straight up like a needle into my face. I now had the flag, but from that body writhing beneath me there sprang some claws, like feelers or some sort of rabid and sticky tentacles, and a mouth buried its sharp teeth into my arm with such force that I let out a cry of pain.

I fell, tightly held by that dragon, for dragon he seemed to me. I felt him pressing on me and we rolled down I don't know how many slopes, among thousands of bodies, some dead and inert, others alive and running. I could see nothing anymore; I just sensed that, as we rolled swiftly about, I was clutching the eagle firmly in my arms. The monster's terrible mouth was fastened ever more tightly on my arm and he carried me with him, the two of us wrapped together, mixed up, one on top of the other and against each other, beneath thousands of feet which trod on us, in the dust that blinded us, in a sinister darkness, in a buzzing sound so loud that it seemed everyone was just one bumblebee, without any idea of what was above or below, with all the confused and vague indications that I had turned into a constellation, into some sort of creature that flies around where all its limbs, all its entrails, all its flesh, blood and nerves make infinite and vertiginous loops around the burning brain.

I don't know how long I was rolling about; it must have been a short time but it seemed like centuries to me. I do not know when I stopped, what I do know is that the monster did not cease forming one person with me, nor did his ferocious mouth stop biting me. Finally, not content with eating into my arm, it seemed as if he was sinking his poisoned tooth into my heart. What I also knew was that the eagle still lay on my chest, as I felt it there. I felt as if the pole was thrust into my entrails. My mind, aware of all this, was in a wayward delirium because it was itself a burning light which was falling from I knew not where, and in the inconceivable speed of its course it described a stripe of fire, a line without end, that… I had no idea where it was going either. I had never experienced such torment! This ended when I lost all notion of existence. The Battle of Salamanca was over, at least for me.

XXXIV

Let me rest a moment and then I will answer your questions. I did not recover consciousness immediately, but I was entering little by little the mysterious clarity of understanding, I was reviving little by little with vague perceptions, I was recovering the use of some of my senses and inside me there was some sort of dawn, but a very slow, extremely slow and painful one. My new life hurt me; it tormented me like the blind man tormented by the light he has not seen for so long. But everything was in turmoil. I saw things but did not know what they were. I heard voices and did not know what they were either. It seemed I had completely lost my memory.

I was in a room (because it was undoubtedly a room located on this terrestrial globe). I could see shapes all round me, but I did not know that the walls were walls or that the ceiling was a ceiling. I heard wailing but I did not recognise those whining vibrations that hurt my ears. Before me, very close, right opposite me, I saw a face. On seeing it, my mind tried hard to understand what it was looking at, but it could not do so. I did not know whose face it was; I had no knowledge of it as one has no knowledge of another person's thoughts. But the face had two very beautiful eyes that were looking at me lovingly. All this came to me through feeling, because – understanding? I understood nothing. So it was through feeling that I guessed that in the person in front of me there was a compassionate, tender and loving affection for me.

But the strangest thing was that the love which hung over me and protected me like a guardian angel also had a voice and that voice vibrated in space, agitating all the particles of air, and with the particles of air all the atoms of my being from the centre of my heart to the tips of my hair. I heard the voice saying,

'You're alive, you're alive... and you will be well soon.'

The beautiful countenance became so happy that I became happy, too.

'Do you recognise me?' the voice said.

I did not have to answer because the voice repeated the question. My sensitivity was so great that every word pierced my breast like a blade of steel. Pain and weakness overcame me once more, no doubt because my efforts to pay attention had been too much for my condition and I fell back into unconsciousness. Shutting my eyes, I stopped hearing the voice. I then felt something physical bothering me. A foreign object was brushing my forehead, falling over my eyes. As if the protecting angel had guessed it, I noticed immediately that the nuisance had disappeared. It was my unkempt hair that had fallen over my forehead and eyebrows. I felt a cool, affectionate gentleness that must have been a hand removing the annoying thing from my forehead.

A little later (I still had my eyes closed) I thought a butterfly was hovering over my head and after making some swoops and turns as a sign of indecision, it settled on my forehead. I felt its two wings resting on my skin, but the wings were warm, heavy and fleshy. They pressed down on me for some time, then they went away, producing a strange sound, a gentle explosion which made me open my eyes.

But as swiftly as I opened them, the winged insect flew off more swiftly. But the same face from before was so close to mine, so close that its warmth made me feel a bit uncomfortable. It was somewhat flushed. On seeing it, my mind made an effort, a great effort and said to itself, 'Whose face is this? I think I know this face.'

But finding no answer, it resigned itself to not knowing. The voice spoke once more, saying with feeling,

'Live, live, for God's sake! Do you recognise me? How are you feeling? You are not badly wounded… you have had a brain haemorrhage, but the fever has gone down… you will live, you must live, because I want you to… What use is human willpower if it cannot revive the dead?'

In the depths of my being, deep down, some faculty, I did not know which, emerging numb from its profound stupor, uttered mysterious sounds of agreement.

'Can't you see me?' she continued (I repeat that I did not know who she was). 'Why don't you speak to me? Are you angry with me? That can't be so, because I have not offended you. If I didn't see you, if I didn't speak with you more often in the last few days, it was because I wasn't allowed to. They almost sent me back home to my country in a cage… but they can't stop me looking after the wounded, and here I am watching over you. How much have I been suffering in hoping you'll open your eyes!'

I felt my hand being shaken vigorously. The face moved away from me.

'Are you thirsty?' said the voice.

I wanted to reply with my tongue, but the gift of speech was still denied to me. Nevertheless, I somehow made it clear that I was thirsty, because the guardian angel put a cup to my lips. This gave me immense comfort. While I was drinking another figure appeared before me. I did not know exactly who it was either, but within me, deep within, a restless spark of memory stirred, trying to explain to me with its flickering brightness the enigma of that other person, lean, scraggy, bony, sad and from whose skeleton hung a black costume cut like a shroud. Crossing his hands he looked at me with deep sadness. The woman then said,

'Brother, you can go back to looking after the other wounded and sick. I will watch over him tonight.'

From within that black covering that enveloped the living bones of a man came another voice, which said,

'Poor Don Gabriel de Araceli! What an unfortunate condition he is in!'

When I heard this, my mind felt greatly uplifted. Everything rejoiced, everything was moved as the mind of Columbus must have been moved at discovering the New World. Relishing its great conquest, my mind thought as follows,

'So my name is Gabriel Araceli? Then I'm a man who was at the Battle of Trafalgar and at the Second of May… then I'm the one who…'

This effort, the greatest I had made up to then, weakened me once more. I felt drowsy. It was growing darker; night was approaching. A reddish light coming from a miserable lantern illuminated the alcove I was in. The man had disappeared and only the beautiful woman remained. For a long time she looked at me without saying anything. Her silent, sad and steady image, as if painted on canvas, gradually faded away and vanished as I sank once more into that dark night in my soul, from whose bottomless core I had emerged shortly before. I do not know how long I slept, but when I came to my senses again, I had made little progress in clarifying my thoughts. My stupor continued, although it was not as dense. The thaw was going very slowly.

My angelic protector had not left me and after giving me something to drink that gave me great relief and revived me, she made my head comfortable on the pillow and asked me,

'Are you feeling better?'

A murmur ran from my brain to my lips which articulated, 'Yes.'

'You are conscious at last,' the voice added. 'Your face has changed. I think the fever is going.'

I replied yes for a second time. In the stupidity which overwhelmed me I did not know how to say anything else, and I was delighted to use constantly the only treasure I had acquired up to then from the vast domain of speech. *Yes* is the entire vocabulary of idiots. To reply yes to everything, to assent to whatever exists, does not require any reasoning or comparison, or any judgment whatever. In contrast, to say *no* it is necessary to set out a new argument against that of the person asking the question and this requires a certain degree of intelligence. As I was in the twilight of reason, to have replied in the negative would have been a prodigy of genius, precocity, inspiration.

'You slept very peacefully last night,' said the voice of my nurse. 'You will be well soon. Give me your hands which are a bit cold. I will warm them for you.'

As she did so, a flash went through my mind, but it was so weak, so quick, that I still had no certainty, but just a presentiment, a hope of knowing, an advance notice. In

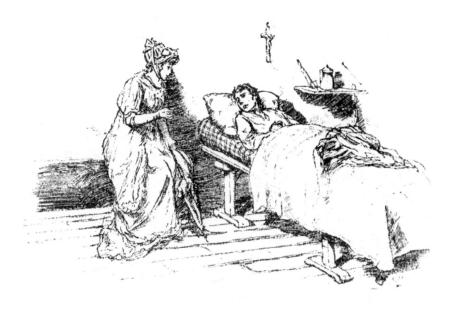

my brain the skein was untangling, but so slowly, so slowly...

'You owe your life to me...' continued the voice of the person whose hands were pressing and warming mine. 'You owe your life to me.'

The skein in my brain shook its threads, using so much force to unravel them that they almost snapped.

'When you were delirious,' she continued, 'you let slip some words which were very pleasing to me. The soul, when it finds itself free from the rule of reason, stands naked and unmuzzled; it shows all its beauties and says everything it knows. That was how yours hid nothing from me. Why are you looking at me with those staring eyes, black and sad as night? If you are asking me with them to say it to you, I will, although it is contrary to the rules of propriety. You should know that I love you.'

The skein then pulled so strongly on its threads that it was on the point of breaking, which it then did irretrievably.

'It should not be necessary to tell you that as you know it already,' she continued after a long pause. 'What you don't know is that I loved you before meeting you. I had a twin sister, more beautiful and purer than an angel. I bet that you do not know anything of this... Well, then, a libertine deceived her, seduced her, stole her from God and her family, and my poor little thing, my darling, my idolised Lillian had a moment of desperation and abandoned herself to death. The elder of my brothers pursued the malefactor, the author of our shame. One night both of them were on the seashore; they fought and my poor Charles fell, never to rise again. Shortly after, my mother, unhinged by grief, was slowly letting go of the world and one morning in May she said farewell to us and fled to Heaven. I'm sure you knew nothing of this.'

I continued being an idiot and replied yes.

'After these events, a man more loathed than Satan existed on the face of the earth. His name alone was an abomination to me. I hated him so much that if I had seen him repentant and on the path to Heaven, my lips would not have pronounced one word of forgiveness for him. Imagining him as a corpse, I trampled on him...'

The skein gave a few twists and turns and got into such a tangle and mess that my brain was in acute pain. Inside was a taut and rigid thread which, hurting me more than the other ones, made me say to myself,

'I am Araceli, the very same that was at Trafalgar and was wrecked on the *Rayo* and lived in Cádiz... In Cádiz there is a tavern whose owner is Señor Poenco.'[313]

'One day,' she continued, 'being in Spain where I had come following my second brother, they told me that that man had been killed by another one in a duel of honour. I inquired about the name of the victor with such eagerness and profound curiosity that I almost knew it before they revealed it to me. I was told your name and they gave me some details of the case and from that moment – why should I hide it? – I adored you.'

My mind performed an inexplicable balancing act between two grotesque images where two large figures called Poenco and Don Pedro del Congosto[314] were placed in some scales, and while one went up the other went down. At that moment I had to say something more substantial than the previous *yeses*, because she (I still did not know who she was) put her hand on my forehead and said,

'You foresaw me, I'm sure, you saw me from afar with the eyes of the heart. I spent many months looking for you. You took so long to appear that I thought you didn't really exist. I read the ballads and all of them applied to you. You were el Cid, Bernardo del Carpio, Zaide,[315] Abenámar,[316] Celindos,[317] Lancelot of the Lake, Fernán González[318] and Pedro Ansúrez[319]... You took shape in my imagination and I took care that you grew in it, but as much as my eyes searched the land they could not find you. When I did find you, I thought you were going to demean yourself but I quickly saw you reach the great heights that I thought you were capable of. Until then all the men I had dealings with either laughed at me or did not understand me. It was only you that looked at me face to face and who could cope with the exalted boldness of my thoughts without being frightened. I saw that you were naturally inclined to perform extraordinary feats. I joined you in them and I wanted to take you still further and you followed me blindly. Your soul and mine joined hands and touched each other's foreheads to convince themselves that the two of them were of the same size. The light from each merged into one.'

The skein of my consciousness made the most extraordinary contortions. Threads went in and came out, each one twisted with another one, and then wriggled to get free and put themselves in order. They now appeared in groups of different colours and, although still very tangled, many of them, if not all of them, seemed to have found their position.

'You loved someone else,' she continued, now beginning not to be a stranger to me. 'I saw her and observed her. I wanted to talk with her, which I did and I got to know her. I found her so unworthy of you that after then I considered myself the victor. It is impossible that I am mistaken.'

On hearing this, my heart, which up to then had stayed calm and mute, asleep like a child in its cradle, started to make so many lively little leaps and to call me in so soft a voice that it caused me real pain. Inside me there was rising what I do not know if I would call a vapour, a wave which at first was lukewarm then burning hot and which came from the depths up to the surface of my being, waking up as it passed everything that was sleeping, a great invasive and overpowering surge which possessed the gift of speech, and as it went up through me it kept saying, 'Get up, everything get up!'

'What's wrong?' the woman continued. 'You're agitated. Your face is getting red... now it's getting pale. Are you going to cry? I am crying, too. Health is returning to your body, as is sensibility to your noble soul. Is it possible that the revelation I have made has affected you? You do not judge my boldness by the common standard, believing that I do not offend decorum, good manners or modesty by saying to a man that I love him. I, for my part, am as pure as the angels and as free as air. The fools who surround me can malign me and malign you, but they will not tarnish my honour, neither will an ideal and heavenly love as it passes from thought to word. If I have concealed this for a long time and pretended to run away from you, it was not because of fear of the idiots but for the benefit of both of us. When I saw you almost dead, when I picked you up with my own arms from the battlefield, when I brought you here and looked after you and took care of you, trying to bring you back to life, I was very afraid that you would die without knowing my secret.'

My stupor came to an end. Mind and heart recovered their pristine existence, but words were slow to come, my, they were slow to come....

'God has heard me,' she added. 'Not only can you hear me, but you are living and you can speak to me and answer me. Tell me that you love me and if you then die, I will always have something of you.'

A heavenly figure, so heavenly that it did not seem of this world, entered me, taking up its quarters and extending itself so completely that there was not a hole in my body that was not filled by it.

'You're not saying even one word in answer to me,' said the voice of my nurse. 'You're not looking at me either. Why are you shutting your eyes? Is this how one answers, sir? You should know that I am not only doubtful, but also jealous. But I can't have displeased you with what I have just done. I won't hide it from you, because I have never lied. My tongue was born for the truth. Perhaps you did not know that your enchanted princess and that rascal of her father were in Salamanca? Who took them there, I do not know. The unfortunate mason was longing for freedom and I gave it to him with the greatest pleasure, getting a safe conduct from the general so that he could leave here and cross the whole of Spain without any hindrance.'

On hearing this, reason, memory, feelings, speech, everything suddenly came back to me violently, in a rush, with a crash, like a cataract falling headlong from the heights of Heaven. I gave a cry, sat up in bed, threw my arms about, and with instinctive brutality hurled the beautiful woman away from me and broke out in exclamations of rage. I looked at the lady and said her name, for now I recognised her.

XXXV

The hospitaller whom I had seen earlier came in when he heard my shouting and both tried to calm me.

'The delirium has started again,' Juan de Dios said.

'I was the cause of this change,' said Miss Fly contritely.

My own weakness overcame me and I fell back on the bed, crushed by the anger that became dully concentrated inside me, finding no voice or strength to express itself outside.

'Poor Señor Araceli,' Juan de Dios said kindly, 'will become mad like me. The Devil has laid his hand on him.'

'Quiet, brother, and don't talk rubbish,' said Miss Fly, covering my arms with the blanket and wiping the sweat from my brow. 'What's all this talk of devils?'

'I know what I am talking about,' the Augustinian continued, looking at me with profound sorrow. 'Poor Don Gabriel is under an evil influence... I have seen it, I have seen it.'

Saying this he detached two thin and sharply tipped fingers from his closed fists and pointed at his eyes with them.[320]

'Go away and look after the other patients,' Miss Fly said cheerfully, 'and don't come and bore us with your nonsense.'

Juan de Dios left and Athenais and I found ourselves alone together once more. Now that I was in complete possession of my thoughts, I said to her,

'Señora, tell me again what you just said. I did not fully understand. I think that neither my senses nor my reason is quite settled. I am delirious as that good man said.'

'I spoke to you for a long time,' Miss Fly said with some alarm.

'Señora, I am very confused about what I saw and heard last night... Really, I saw a beautiful and comforting figure in front of me, I heard some words... but I don't know what they were. In my brain the echoes of distant voices were confused with the mysterious sounds of other ones which I myself may have pronounced... I can't easily distinguish what is real from what is true, for some time I saw objects and faces without recognising them.'

'Without recognising them!'

'I heard words. Some I remember, others not.'

'Try to repeat the substance of all that I told you,' Athenais murmured, pale and serious. 'And if you haven't understood it properly, I'll repeat it to you.'

'In truth, I can't repeat anything. I am terribly confused inside. I thought I saw before me a person whose ideal representation in my dreams will never leave me, a figure I love and respect, because I believe it is the most perfect one God has placed on earth. I thought I heard all sorts of sweet and clear words, mixed up with others I did not understand. I thought at one moment I was listening to the music of Heaven and at the next moment, the crash of a hundred storms that were raging inside a heart. I can't be specific. Finally, I clearly saw you and I recognised you.'

'And did you hear me clearly as well?' she asked, moving her face closer to mine. 'I know one shouldn't have conversations with sick people. I must have disturbed you. But it is true that I was very anxious that you could hear me. If by any unfortunate chance you were to die...'

'From what I heard, señora, the only thing I can remember clearly is that you have given freedom to a person I imprisoned.'

'And does that displease you?' the Warbler asked, terrified.

'It doesn't only displease me, it annoys me very much, very much indeed,' I exclaimed with concern, throwing off the bedclothes to free my arms.

Athenais groaned. After a brief pause, she stared at me proudly and said,

'Señor Araceli, are you so angry because that enchanted bird of the Calle del Cáliz has escaped from you?'

'Yes, that's why, that's why,' I repeated.

'And you're sure you love her?'

'I adore her, I've adored her all my life. For a long time my existence and hers have been so entwined as if they were one. My joy is her joy and her sorrow is my sorrow. Where is she? If she has disappeared again, I swear to you, my dear señora Athenais, that all the ballads of Bernardo, el Cid, Lancelot and Celindos will count for little in my search for her.'

Athenais was pitifully altered. One could say that she was now the sick person and I the nurse. For a long time it seemed to me as if she was waging some sort of horrible battle with herself. She turned her face from me so that I would not see her emotion.

She then gave me a look of the most violent anger which then, without her intending it, changed into one of inexplicable gentleness, until she rose up and with an expression of majestic pride said,

'Señor Araceli, goodbye.'

'Are you going?' I said sadly and taking her hand which she quickly withdrew from mine. 'I will be alone… I deserve your disdain, because I have come back to life and my first words were not to thank this loving friend, this charitable soul who no doubt brought me from the battlefield, who looked after me and helped… Señora, señora! The life which you won from death will look forward with pleasure to the moment when it has to lose itself once more for your sake.'

'Fine words, señor Araceli,' she said solemnly, not approaching me and looking at me pale, sad and serious from afar, like a sibyl in judgment revealing my destiny. 'Fine words, but not enough to conceal the empty vulgarity of your soul. I sift through this empty verbiage and find nothing. You are made of greatness and pettiness.'

'As is everything in creation, everything, señora,' I interrupted.

'No, no,' she said with spirit. 'I know something which is not like that, I know something where all is great. In your life and even in these last few days you have done some admirable things. But you have handed over the very mind which conceived the death of Lord Gray to a vulgar and prosaic housewife like a blank piece of paper for her to write the laundry list on. Your heart, which at times certainly knows how to feel, is of no use to you and you have handed it over to the seamstresses so that they can make a little cushion from it to stick their pins into. Señor Araceli, I am bored here.'

'Señora, señora, for God's sake, don't leave me! I'm still very ill.'

'So my status is no higher than that of a nurse? I am very proud, sir. The hospitaller brother will look after you.'

'You are joking, worthy friend, enchanting Athenais, you are making fun of the true affection, the admiration which you have inspired in me. Sit down at my side, we'll talk about all sorts of things, about the battle, about poor Sir Thomas Parr whom I saw die…'

'I still believe that I am useful for more than just making conversation with idle and bored people,' she replied to me disdainfully. 'Sir, you are treating me with a familiarity that surprises me.'

'Oh, let's recall the unheard-of deeds that we did together. Can you remember Jean-Jean?'

'You really are impertinent. I have helped you enough; I have spent enough hours in your company. While you were delirious, I laughed when I heard the nonsense and foolish absurdities you kept saying but now that you are in your right mind you are just as silly.'

'Well, then, señora, I will become delirious again and talk nonsense as much as you like, provided you keep me company,' I exclaimed merrily. 'I don't want you to leave me while annoyed with me.'

Miss Fly leant against the wall to stop herself falling. I could see that the expression on her face passed from one of senseless fury to deep emotion. Her eyes filled with tears and sensing that her hands could not hide them, she ran quickly from the room. Her initial intention was no doubt to go away, but she remained close by the door where I could see her with difficulty. Nevertheless, I don't know if it was the sighs that I thought I heard or the shadow that projected onto the wall up to the ceiling that were enough to reveal her presence to me. What I have no doubt about is that after being immersed for a long time in sad thoughts, I felt sleepy and slowly descended into the deepest sleep that lasted until the morning. Should I say that when I was on the point of losing the use of all my senses, the strange phenomena that accompanied my painful return to life were repeated? Should I say that above and around my head I thought I saw a winged insect flying, which came and placed its two soft, heavy and burning wings on my brow? This was no more than a repetition of what I had dreamt earlier. The strangest phenomenon of all on that strangest of nights came later, placing a worthy crown on my confused thoughts. And, dear readers, as my confusion had still not been dispelled by this business with the Little Bird, this was that I noticed a black thing, long, not very big, although I could not exactly tell its size, that was hovering over my brow, and this object or ugly beast had two long legs and two pointed wings which opened and closed alternately. It was black all over, rough, stiff and extremely ugly. This horrible crustacean closed itself up and then it looked like a black dagger, and later extended its feet and wings and looked like a scorpion. It slowly came down towards me and when it touched my forehead I felt my whole body go cold. It lashed about, waving its horrible extremities repeatedly, emitting a strident screech, dry and sharp, which put my nerves on edge and then fled.

XXXVI

After a long and deep sleep I awoke in full daylight significantly better. The beautiful brightness of the sun produced a feeling of immense well-being in me and as well as physical relief I felt a definite peaceful repose in my soul. I revelled in my health like a will of the wisp in its beauty.

Two men were at my side, the hospitaller and an army doctor who, after examining me, gave a cheerful prognosis of my illness and ordered me to eat some tasty food if I could find some charitable souls to get me something. He left to go and cut off any number of legs, and the brother, once we were alone, sat down beside me and said sorrowfully,

'Take the advice of a poor penitent, Don Gabriel, and instead of worrying yourself about food for the body, attend to the nourishment of the soul, of which there is a great need.'

'So then, Señor Juan de Dios, am I going to die?' I said to him, suspecting that he wanted to teach me about the system of wild herbs.

'Better death a thousand times,' said the friar lugubriously, 'than to live life like you do. At least, that would be my preference.'

'I don't understand.'

'Señor Araceli, Señor Araceli,' he exclaimed, no longer just anxious but really alarmed, 'think about God, call upon God for His help, rid yourself of all worldly thoughts, abstract yourself. So that we can accomplish this, let us pray, my friend, let us pray fervently for four, five or six hours, without distracting ourselves for a moment and we will be free from the immense, horrible danger that threatens us.'

'But this man is out to kill me,' I said, scared. 'The doctor tells me to eat and here you are offering me a portion of six hours of prayer. Wretched brother, for the love of God, bring me a chicken, a peacock, a lamb, an ox.'

'Lost, irredeemably lost!' he exclaimed in great distress, raising his eyes to Heaven and crossing himself. 'Eating, eating! Gratifying the body with tempting delicacies while the soul is threatened, threatened, Señor Araceli... come back to yourself... Let us pray together, no more than six hours, without an instant's distraction... with the mind fixed on what is above... In this way the Perfidious One will flee, or at least hesitate before putting his infernal hand onto an innocent soul, he will find it bound to Heaven with the holy chains of prayer, and he will perhaps give up his execrable plans.'

'Brother Juan de Dios, get away from me or I don't know what I'll do. You may be raving mad but luckily I am not and I want to have something to eat.'

'For pity's sake, by all the saints, for the salvation of your soul, my dear brother, restrain yourself, curb those frivolous appetites, put a hundred chains onto your lust for chewing, since all sinful affectations enter through the gateway of gastronomy.'

I looked at him with a mixture of anger and amusement, because his austerity, which had started to become grotesque, was becoming tedious yet at the same time was entertaining me. No, I really cannot portray him as he was then, as I saw him at that moment. The brush of Zurbarán[321] would not be able to reproduce on canvas the strange figure of that man who had been reduced to such a sorry state by fasting and the exaltation of his fantasies. No, one would have to turn to the palette of the great Velázquez[322] to find something there that he used for the creation of his immortal fools.

I laughed at him and said,

'Bring me something to eat and then we can pray.'

The hospitaller's only answer was to fall on his knees, take out a prayer book and say to me,

'Repeat what I am going to read.'

'This man is killing me, killing me! Please!' I cried angrily.

Juan de Dios got up and putting his hand on my chest, scared and trembling, he said to me,

'He's coming, he's going to come again!'

'Who?' I asked, tired of this farce.

'Who else can it be, you unfortunate man, who else can it be?' he said dejectedly in a quiet voice. 'Who else can it be other than the infamous enemy of mankind, the black king that rules the realm of shadows as God rules that of light, the one that hates holiness and lays thousands of snares to entrap virtue? Who else can it be other than the unclean beast that possesses the art of transforming himself and beautifying himself, taking on the shapes and clothes that can most easily seduce the unprepared sinner? Who else can it be? What a strange question! I am astonished at how calmly and innocently you speak to me, being, as you are, in the same state as me!'

My peals of laughter echoed round the room.

'I am extremely glad that he is coming,' I said to him. 'How do you know that he's going to come?'

'Because he's already been here, wretched man. Because he has already put his perfidious hands on you as a sign of his possession and dominion over you, because he said he was going to return.'

'I am highly delighted to hear this. And when did I have the honour of his visit? I didn't see anything.'

'How would you have seen him when you were asleep, unfortunate man!' he exclaimed sorrowfully. 'Sleep, sleep! This is where the great danger is. He takes advantage of the occasions when the soul is on the loose and up to mischief, free of the vigilance of prayer. That is why I never sleep, that is why I stay awake.'

'He came while I was asleep?'

'Yes, last night... a dreadful moment! The English lady who looked after you so well had left. I was alone and a bit distracted in my prayers. Without knowing how, I had let my mind fly into voluptuous and rosy regions... worthless sinner, a thousand times worthless! I had put the book on my lap, had shut my eyes and had let myself become drowsy in a delightful lassitude whose vaporous fogs and gentle warmth were entertaining my body and my spirit...'

'And then, when my blessed wretch of a brother was rejoicing in these delights, the earth opened up, and a flame of sulphur shot up...'

'It wasn't the earth that opened, but a door, and he appeared... ah! He appeared in that heavenly form, stolen from those beings in the highest circle of angels, he appeared as he always does when my sinful eyes see him.'

'Brother, brother, I am happy and I might almost believe that you were cured.'

'He appeared, as I have said, and the sight of him turned me into a statue. Another one of a similar appearance was accompanying him, also in the form of a woman, looking older than the first one, the one so hated as much as loved which is the terror of my nights and the horror of my days and the abyss which swallows up my soul.'

'And when they saw me? I adore those demons, Señor Juan de Dios, and I am going to send them a little message right now through you.'

'Through me? Unhappy reprobate! They will come and carry you off with their satanic arts.'

'I want to know what they did, what they said.'

'They said, 'This is where they told us he would be,' and then their eyes, which can see everything in the gloom of horrible night, saw your miserable body and they hurled themselves upon it with howls that seemed like the tenderest of sobs, with wails that seemed like the sweet harmony of maternal love, weeping by the cradle of a dying child.'

'And I was sleeping like a log! Father Juan, you are an imbecile, an idiot! Why didn't you wake me?'

'You were still delirious. The two, ah! Those two most beautiful apparitions, and so finished and perfect that only I with the clear eyes of the soul could see the hand of infernal artifice beneath their dazzling forms, the two women, well, poured out diabolical sparks over your breast and forehead, with such perverted and ingenious alchemy that they seemed like tears of affection. They put their lips of fire onto your hands as if they were kissing them, rearranged your bedclothes, and then...'

'And then?'

'And then they looked for me as if to ask me something, but I, more dead than alive, had hidden myself under that table and I was trembling and dying. Don Gabriel, I was dying wanting to pray but I could not, wanting to turn my eyes from that sight, but still watching it. Finally, they decided to leave... they were already masters of your soul and didn't need anything more.'

'So they went.'

'They went saying they were going to ask for a permit from somebody or other to transfer you to a better place... to hell no doubt. This was how a hospitaller brother who was a great sinner disappeared from the living: one morning they carried him off entirely without leaving a trace of his bodily structure.'

'And then? I am very happy, brother Juan.'

'Then came that lady they call *Doña Flay*, an angelic creature who loves you very much. You began to come out of that atrophy or disorder that the ambassadresses of the black underworld had left you in. The English lady spoke with you for a long time and I, who was listening behind the door, heard her say thousands of affectionate, sweet and enchanting little things to you.'

'And then?'

'And then you became furious and I came in, and the Englishwoman told me to leave, and from what I heard, my Don Gabriel went to sleep. The Englishwoman went in and out, weeping ceaselessly.'

'And nothing more?'

'Yes, there was something more, and without doubt the most terrible and frightening thing, because the tormentor of mankind, the one who, according to one Holy Father, has as his accomplice in his infamous work woman, who is the little furnace for his alchemy and the foundation of his foul creations; the one who torments me and wants me damned came back in again in the same form of a pretty woman in duplicate...'

'And I, was I sleeping again?'

'You were sleeping quietly and calmly. The English lady was at that table wrapping something or other in some paper. They came in... It was a miracle of God that I did not die at that moment... They went up to you and back came the howls that seemed like tears and the chiromantic signs similar to gentle and affectionate caresses.'

'And didn't they say anything? Didn't they say anything to Miss Fly or you?'

'Yes,' he continued after taking a few breaths, as the tiredness in his tightened chest hardly let him speak. 'They said that they now had the permit and they were going to find a litter to transfer you to somewhere they didn't say. But the strangest thing is that on hearing this the English lady, who was no less engrossed, no less taken aback, no less frightened than me, must have known that the glamorous belles were the work of the one who took Jesus to the top of the mountain and the pinnacle of the city, and in awe like me, gave a high-pitched scream and rushed out of the room. I followed her and both of us ran for a long way until she stopped her headlong career and leant her head against a wall, which is where tears were shed, deep sighs were exhaled and vehement words uttered, for which I asked God for forgiveness. An hour later I returned, woke you up and nothing more. All that remains is for us to pray because only prayer and the vigilance of the spirit will drive away the Evil One, just as treacherous sleep, dainty food and worldly talk will summon him.'

Juan de Dios said nothing more, but he was listening to strange sounds from outside and was trembling and pale.

'Here, I'm here, Inesilla... countess!' I exclaimed, recognising the sweet voices I had heard from my bed. 'I'm here alive, well and happy and loving both of you more than my life.'

Ah! Both of them came in and ran to me, desolate. One embraced me on one side,

one on the other. I nearly fainted with joy when the two beloved heads were lying on my breast.

Juan de Dios ran or flew away, I don't know which.

I wanted to speak but my emotions stopped me. They were crying and couldn't say anything either. Finally, Inés raised her eyes to my forehead and looked at it closely with curiosity.

'What are you looking at?' I said to her. 'Am I so disfigured that you can't recognise me?'

'No, it's not that.'

The countess looked as well.

'It's that I've noticed you're missing something,' Inés said, smiling.

I raised my hand to my forehead and there was actually something missing.

'Where have those two long locks of hair that you had there ended up?'

When she said this, her delicate fingers were touching my head.

'Well, I don't know … perhaps in the battle…'

Both of them laughed.

'My dears, I remember having seen in my dreams a nasty cold and black animal above my head and now I understand what it was – a pair of scissors. I have a graze on my temple – can you see it? Those locks were bothering me and the surgeon dealt with them. He's an expert who doesn't forget the smallest detail.'

I had so many questions that I didn't know where to begin.

'So how did the battle end?' I said. 'Where is Lord Wellington?'

'The battle ended like all battles, it finished when they got tired of killing each other,' one of them said, I don't know which.

'But the French were retreating when I fell.'

'They retreated so much,' the countess said, 'that they are still running. Wellington is pressing them closely. Don't worry about all that, they'll manage fine without you. We'll see if they give you a promotion for having taken the eagle.'

'I took an eagle then…'

'A completely golden eagle, with wings open and the beak broken, on a pole and with lightning bolts in its claws. I saw it,' Inés said with satisfaction, expanding on the Imperial insignia with pompous descriptions.

'They found you,' the countess added, 'among many dead and wounded, in an embrace with the corpse of a French standard-bearer, who was biting your arm.'

That was the part of my body that was hurting the most.

'We've been looking for you since the 22nd,' Inés said. 'But until last night it was just running about and more running about without any result. We thought you had died. I went to the great pit where they are burying the poor bodies. There are so many, so many that I could not see all of them… it seemed like a curse of God. If I had had that eagle with me when I saw them, I would have thrown it into the pit as well and then some earth, a lot of earth, on top.'

'Well said, Inesilla, you say the greatest truths in the simplest words. Military glory and the dead in battle should be buried in the same grave… Anyway, my dear ones, I am living to love you very much and to marry one of you, with the prior consent of the other.'

The countess frowned slightly and Inés looked at my hair. The happiness that flooded my soul spilled out into open smiles and joyful expressions, which Inés would have responded to in some way if the seriousness of her mother had allowed it.

'Let's get this rascal out of here,' the countess said, 'and then we'll see. We should give thanks to that English lady who rescued you from the battlefield and who looked after you so well, as we have been told. I know who she is and we have seen her. I met her in El Puerto… We certainly need to speak, sir, you and I.'

'Isn't she here? Athenais, Athenais! She's bound not to come when we need her. It would give me infinite pleasure if you got to know each other, which I think would save me a lot of trouble. Miss Fly is a loyal and generous person. Juan de Dios! That fellow won't come even if he was going to be hanged. He has taken to saying that you are the Devil.'

'That blessed hospitaller?' the countess said. 'The doctor told us that he has already escaped twice from the madhouse… Let's see about getting you fixed up on a stretcher. We'll call another nurse.'

When the countess left, I said to Inés,

'You haven't said anything to me about that person…'

'You'll know everything soon,' she replied, without stopping me from devouring her hands with kisses. 'Come home quickly… try to get up.'

'I can't, my child, I am very weak. That blasted hospitaller was planning to starve me to death today. The Augustinian intent on me not eating anything and Miss Fly driving me crazy with her tittle-tattle…'

'Oh!' said Inés with an enchantingly threatening expression. 'So that Englishwoman has to be with you everywhere? I have a suspicion, a terrible suspicion, which, if it is true… can it be that I am too good, too trusting and innocent and that you are the greatest scoundrel?'

She looked at my forehead again, not just uneasily but with real alarm.

'My darling Inesilla!' I exclaimed. 'If you have suspicions, I will dispel them! Do you doubt me? That cannot be. Nothing has ever happened and it never will. Could I suspect you? Can our faith in the mutual vows we have lived with so long and in our deep adoration for each other be broken?'

'Not up to the present, but now… you're hiding something from me… My mother let slip some words… No, Gabriel, don't deceive me. Tell me, tell me immediately. Miss Fly rescued you from the battlefield. She denied it, but it's true. We have been told so.'

'Me deceive you! That really is a bit rich. Even if I was bad I couldn't have done so even if I had wanted to. But I must tell you the truth, the whole truth, my wife, and I will start right now… Why do you keep looking at my forehead?'

'Because... because,' she said, pale, serious and menacing, 'because Miss Fly cut off that lock of hair. I have guessed it.'

'Why yes, it was her,' I replied with imperturbable serenity.

'Her! And you admit it!' she exclaimed, half-astonished and half-terrified.

Her eyes filled with tears. I did not know what to say to her. However, the truth came out of my heart in an impetuous wave to my lips. Lying, pretending, distorting, dissembling were unworthy of her and me. Sitting up with difficulty, I said to her,

'I will tell you many things that will surprise you, my dear. Both of us should give thanks to that generous woman who rescued me from the dead on the Arapil Grande so that you would not be a widow.'

'Right, let's go,' said the countess, coming in suddenly and interrupting me. 'You will be fine in this litter.'

XXXVII

The house in the Calle del Cáliz, where I have transported my readers twice, and where they will have to follow me to again if they want to hear the end of this faithful account, was the ancestral home of Santorcaz, which he had inherited from his father a year earlier, along with some agricultural land. The large, rambling house was made up of two or three buildings, different in size and structure, which Don Juan de Santorcaz, a villager who had grown rich in the early years of the last century, had bought and knocked together so that they were connected to each other. That dwelling lacked elegance and beauty, but not solidity, nor size, nor comforts, although some rooms were too far from other ones and the corridors were excessive in length, as were in number the staircases one had to use to go from one part to another.

On 22nd July during the battle Santorcaz and his daughter were in the rooms we had seen them in earlier. This last circumstance will make my readers realise that I was not present at what I am about to relate, but if I relate it as a reliable account, if I include it among the matters witnessed by me, it is because I have such faith in the word of those who told me them, as if I had witnessed them with my own eyes and ears, and so this should be taken as truthful and real.

So, the unfortunate Don Luis and his daughter were, as I have said, in the living room; she was lamenting the existence of wars and he was complaining bitterly that his poor state of health was preventing him from being present at the great spectacle of that day, when the famous snakelike door knocker made a sound like thunder and shortly afterwards the single servant who was still serving them and the soldier who was guarding them announced to the solitary owners that a lady wanted to come in. As Miss Fly had been there a few days earlier to give the mason a safe conduct to leave Salamanca and Spain, his spirit cheered up at this, and he ordered them to admit the generous visitor immediately and bring her to them. A few minutes passed and the countess came into the room.

Santorcaz roared like a wounded wild animal when it can't defend itself. For a long time mother and daughter embraced, their tears mingling and oblivious to the rest of creation as if they were the only ones existing in the world. Once they had come to their senses, the mother, watching with terror that furious and gloomy man who was staring at the floor as if he intended, just with his look, to open a hole into which he would disappear, tried to take her daughter with her and said words very like those I had said in similar circumstances.

Those who witnessed my surprise can judge that of Amaranta when Inés broke away from her and in a sea of tears ran with open arms towards the old man in a gesture of affection. The countess watched this incredible move in amazement. When his daughter was close to him Santorcaz turned towards her and put out his arms to stop her approaching.

'Go away from here,' he said. 'I don't want to see you, I don't know you.'

'You're mad!' the girl cried in sorrow. 'If you tell me once more to go, I will go.'

Santorcaz's wild eyes looked from one side of the room to the other, looked at his wife and daughter with equal hatred and, trembling with rage, said again,

'Go away, go away, I've told you to go away. I don't want to see you any more. Leave this house with that woman and don't return.'

'Father,' said Inés, ignoring the old man's frenzy. 'Didn't you say to me that this house was my home? Didn't you give me the keys? Well, I am going to put this lady up in one of the rooms facing the street since it is impossible for her to find any lodging today, and tomorrow the two of us will go and leave you in peace.'

Taking a bunch of keys and rattling them, not entirely without ironic intent, Inés left the room followed by Amaranta, who understood nothing of this tragicomedy.

Once he was on his own, Santorcaz paced round the room, with endless twists and turns like a cog in a waterwheel. His expression showed everything that could be by human physiognomy, from the most terrible rage to the most tender emotion. Then he took up a book, but threw it to the ground after a few minutes. Next he picked up a pen and after scratching on the paper for a short time, he destroyed it and stamped on it. He got up and with an uncertain movement and hesitating steps he went towards the glass door into the next room where there was a dressing table and an empty bed. Kneeling on the ground, he made the bed into a prie-dieu and, leaning his head on it, wept for the whole day.

If Santorcaz had had sharp and very acute hearing, like some species of birds, he would have heard the sound of soft steps in the nearby corridor. If Santorcaz had possessed double sight, which is physically absurd, but does not seem so once one gets to know the mysterious organs of the mind, he would have seen that he was not entirely alone, that a celestial figure was beating its wings in the vicinity of the sad bedroom, that without touching the ground with its light steps, it came and drew near and in a gracious gesture put its head to the door to listen, and then its eyes looked through a crack to see what was happening inside, and as if what it saw and heard pleased it, it illuminated those dark spaces with a smile and left only to return a short while later and do the same. But the poor mason saw nothing of this. That afternoon an English orderly brought him a safe conduct to leave Salamanca, but the mason tore it up. The countess and Inés, except for the times the latter went out, were talking nineteen to the dozen in the rooms on the street. Imagine the task facing the tongues of two women who want to say in one day what they have been silent about for a year. They spoke without stopping, passing from one topic to another, without running out of any, feeling all sorts of emotions, always surprised, always moved, finishing each other's sentences, recounting, praising highly, extolling, commenting, affirming and negating.

This happened on 22nd July. From time to time a distant rumbling and a dull shaking of the earth and the air interrupted them. It was the sound of the cannons of England and France fighting each other where we all know. The two women crossed themselves, raising their eyes to Heaven. The sound of the cannon fire grew louder each time. In the afternoon it was an incessant roar like that of the stormy ocean. Terror got the better of mother and daughter and they fell silent; that is all there is to be said. They were thinking of the number of men swallowed by each roll of the angry sea in the distance.

Night came and the cannon fire ceased. Very late, Tribaldos came to the house. The poor boy was in great distress and, although he put on a show of being brave, he shed some tears.

'Where are you going?' the mother anxiously asked her daughter, seeing that the latter was putting on her coat without saying why.

'To the Arapil,' Inés replied, handing another coat to the countess who put it on without saying anything either.

Inés went to see the old man for a brief moment and then left the house and the city accompanied by her mother and Tribaldos. An immense throng of curious people filled the road. The battle had been horrendous and those who had not seen the banquet wanted to see the leftovers. They walked for a long time, throughout the night, up and down, here and there, without finding the one they were looking for, nor anyone who could give them any information. Close to daybreak they saw Miss Fly who was coming from the battlefield in front of a well-appointed and covered stretcher which was carrying a man found on the Arapil Grande, badly wounded, unconscious and with a horrible bite in his arm.

Inés, the countess and Tribaldos approached Miss Fly to ask her questions, but the latter, impatient to carry on, answered them,

'I don't know a thing. Let me continue. I am carrying Sir Thomas Parr, who is gravely wounded, in this stretcher.'

The women and Tribaldos walked over the battlefield which the light of the dawning day showed to them in all its horror. They saw the stretched and twisted bodies, the features preserving the expressions of fury and terror they had when death surprised them. Thousands of eyes with no brightness or light, like the eyes of marble statues, were looking at the sky without seeing it, hands gripping guns and the hilts of swords, as if they were going to be raised to fire and slash once more. The horses raised their stiff legs and showed their white teeth in lugubrious grimaces. The two disconsolate women saw all this and examined the bodies one by one; they saw the puddles, the ditches, the furrows made by the wheels and the holes that the thousands of feet had opened up in the dance of battle; they saw the crushed wild flowers and the butterflies flying about with their wings stained with blood. They went back to Salamanca, returned that night to the battlefield, no longer just shocked but desperate; they prayed as they went, asking all the living and also the dead.

In the end, after repeated trips and forays inside and outside the city, which took them three days, with brief periods staying and resting in the house in the Calle del Cáliz, they found the one they were looking for in the field dressing station, set up in La Merced. They found him separated from the rest, in an empty room under the care of a poor, demented friar. They made inquiries with the military authority and, in the end, obtained leave to take him away, that is to say, take me away with them.

XXXVIII

They put me up in a bright and pretty room in a comfortable bed which they hurriedly prepared for me. They gave me something to eat for which I was deeply grateful and I began to feel much better. The thing which helped me most in my recovery was an inexplicable happiness that filled my soul. An external symptom of this joy was an expansive joviality that made me laugh for any frivolous reason.

On the evening I came to the house, while the countess was writing letters to every living being in the next room, Inés gave me some supper.

We were alone and I told her all, absolutely all of the almost incredible story of Miss Fly without omitting anything that might prejudice me or augment me in the eyes of my interlocutor. She listened to me with rapt attention, but not without some sadness, and when I finished, I could say that my constant friend had lost the power of speech. I don't know in what vague perplexities her great spirit was floating. Her expression showed a struggle between annoyance and pity, and pride perhaps in a fight with hilarity. But she said nothing and her large eyes looked angrily at me. For my part, the longer her abstracted contemplation lasted, the more I felt inclined to make light of the clouds that were darkening my skies.

'Is it possible that you are still thinking about that?' I said to her.

'I trust that you will show me the blond lock you were paid with for the black one… You're a fine one to think that I will marry you, a libertine, a scoundrel. We will look after you, but once you're well again you can go off with your adored Englishwoman. I don't need you at all.'

She wanted to be serious and she almost succeeded.

'No, I won't go off, no,' I said to her, 'because I love you more than the apple of my eye. I am in love with you because you are a creature from other times, because your soul, señora (I like to address people with *vos*)[323] has joined hands with mine and both will ascend together to the heights where the vulgarity and commonness of mankind will never reach. For you, señora, I will be Bernardo del Carpio, el Cid and Lancelot of the Lake, I will undertake the most extravagant adventures, I will kill half the world and eat the other half.'

'Don't think you can fool me with such nonsense,' she said, laughing in spite of herself.

'Señora!' I exclaimed dramatically. 'You are the lodestone of my existence, the only spouse worthy of the immensity of my soul. I adore the eagles that fly looking the sun in the face, and not hens that can only lay eggs, raise chicks, cluck in farmyards and die for man. Take me, take me with you, señora, to the regions of great emotions and the sublimities of thought. If you leave me, I will cry in the ruins; if you love me, I will be your slave and I will conquer ten kingdoms so that you can put one on each finger.'

'Be quiet, be quiet, silly man, buffoon,' Inés said, trying as best she could to stop laughing.

'Ah, señora and mistress mine!' I continued, intensifying my haughtiness. 'You refuse me. Your heart is unworthy of mine. I thought it was tempered in the fire of passion but it is just a piece of spongy and soft flesh. I asked for it so that I could join it to mine and you throw it to soldiers so that they can stick their bayonets into it. You are unworthy of me, señora. I tell you these sublime things but instead of listening to me, you spend all day sewing. You tremble when I go off to war, you think only of your children instead of thinking of my glory and you occupy yourself in making tasteless stews and odd dishes for me to eat, but I do not eat, señora. In the regions I inhabit, one does not eat. You really are silly. You have insisted on loving me with the sweet and quiet affection typical of seamstresses, shopkeepers, cottagers and corner shop tailors. Ah! Love me ecstatically, frenziedly, deliriously, as Bernardo del Carpio loved Doña Estela and sing of the deeds of the heroes who are the pole star and lighthouse of my life, and become one of those figures from history for me, without caring that my clothes are in tatters, my table is without food and my sons are naked. What am I seeing? Are you laughing? Miserable thing! I'm dying for you and you laugh! I suffer and you rejoice! I'm wasting away and you come up to me fresh, happy and plump!'

Inés cried with laughter, but in such an open and natural manner that all her annoyance was vanishing in those sparks of joy. Our hearts understood each other, like two brothers who quarrel for a moment, only to love each other more.

'I am leaving you because you love another, a vulgar and prosaic one, señora,' I continued, looking at her forehead and making a movement of opening and closing scissors with my thumbs, 'but I want to take a memory of you with me, and so I'll cut off this lock of hair hanging over your forehead.'

On saying this I took her precious head and kissed it a thousand times.

'You're hurting me, you barbarian,' she cried, laughing all the time.

The countess, who was in the next room, came in and when Inés saw her, she went as red as a beetroot and said to her,

'It's Gabriel, who's playing the fool.'

'You mustn't make so much noise while I'm writing. I've still got a lot of letters to do, as I have to write to Wellington, Graham, Castaños, Cabarrús,[324] Azanza, Soult, O'Donnell and King Joseph.'

My beloved mother-in-law had a mania for letter-writing. She wrote to everybody and got a reply from all. Her collection of letters was a very rich historical archive and one day I will dig up many treasures from it.

On the following day my mother-in-law went to call on Miss Fly, with whom, as I have said, she had had dealings in El Puerto and had recognised recently in Salamanca. Athenais paid a return call on the countess on the same day. She came elegantly dressed, dazzling in her beauty and grace. Her escort was Colonel Simpson, as red-faced as ever, vivacious, smartly dressed and elegantly turned out, and honouring as always every object and person with the quadrupled look of his eyes and his spectacles which never tired in their inquiring observations. I had got up and was sitting in a chair without moving during the call, which was not long, but certainly deserved occupying the penultimate place in this true history.

'So you are definitely leaving for England?' the countess said.

'Yes, señora,' Athenais replied, without deigning to give me a glance. 'I am tired of the war and of Spain and I want to be with my father and sisters. If I ever return to Spain, I shall take pleasure in calling on you.'

'But before that perhaps I may have the pleasure of writing to you,' my mother-in-law said, recalling the fact that pens and paper existed in the world. 'I have not yet had time to write to Lord Byron, whom I met in Cádiz.[325] I hope you won't take any bad memories of Spain back with you.'

'Very good ones. I have greatly enjoyed myself in this strange country. I have studied its customs, I have done many drawings of regional costumes and great number of landscapes in pencil and watercolour. I hope that my album will attract attention.'

'You will also have memories of the sad scenes of war,' Amaranta said with some emotion.

'The French respect nothing,' Miss Fly said with the indifference one has when speaking about the weather on calls.

'In their retreat,' Simpson stated, 'they destroyed all the villages on the banks of the Tormes. They will not forgive us for having killed five thousand men, taken seven thousand prisoners with two eagles, six standards and eleven cannon… a magnificent and important battle! I cannot refrain from congratulating Señor de Araceli,' he added, doing me the honour of addressing me, 'for his fine bearing in the action. Brigadier Pack and the honourable General Leith praised you greatly in my presence. I know for a fact that the great Wellington is fully aware of everything favourable about you.'

'In that case,' I said, 'perhaps that will dispel the prejudice that His Excellency has towards me for reasons that I have never been able to understand.'

Athenais went pale but controlled herself immediately. She was not only bold enough to fix her pretty pale blue eyes on me, but to laugh heartily, or so it seemed.

'This gentleman,' she replied with an astonishing jollity given that it was feigned, 'has had the misfortune and good fortune of passing as my lover in the eyes of the gossips in the camp. In Spain, the honour of ladies is at the mercy of anyone malicious.'

'What! Is that possible, señora?' I exclaimed, feigning surprise and what's more, angry surprise. 'Is it possibly because of that extremely lucky meeting of ours? Certainly, I knew nothing about it. And they have dared to slander you! How awful!'

'And they almost suspected that I was married to you,' she added, looking away from me, contrary to what the conventions of conversation required. 'It has amused me greatly, because in truth, although I have much esteem for you as a person…'

'But not so much that I deserve the honour…' I added, completing the sentence. 'That's as clear as water.'

'It all comes from someone seeing us together in the city when, to save you from those vile soldiers, you passed as my servant for few hours,' Athenais said coquettishly and making a funny face. 'And now I should like to know whether out of childish vanity it was you yourself who dared to spread such ridiculous rumours about a noble English lady, who had no intention of falling in love in Spain, not least with a man like you.'

'I, señora! Colonel Simpson is a witness to what I thought about the matter.'

'The rumours,' said the likeable Simpson, 'started among the English officers and began to circulate when Araceli returned from Salamanca and Athenais did not.'

'And you, my dear Sir Abraham Simpson,' said Miss Fly with some annoyance, 'encouraged the circulation of the vulgar stories about me.'

'Permit me to say, my dear Athenais,' Simpson said in Spanish, 'that your conduct has been somewhat strange in this matter. You are proud, I know, you believed you would lower yourself by concerning yourself with the matter… The truth of the matter is that you heard everything and were silent. Your sadness, your silence made one believe…'

'It seems to me that you do not know all the facts,' Athenais said, starting to blush.

'Everyone was talking about the matter, Wellington himself was concerned about it. You were asked as delicately as possible yet you only answered in a vague way. It was said that you were going to request compliance with English laws on marriage, calumny, pure calumny, but that is what they were saying and you did not deny it… I myself drew your attention to such a serious matter, and you remained silent.'

'You don't know all the facts,' Athenais repeated, blushing more deeply, 'and what's more you are very indiscreet.'

'The fact is, in my opinion,' Simpson said, 'you carried delicacy to an unfortunate extreme, my dear Athenais… You felt outraged simply by the idea that it was believed… Well… a woman of your class… I don't want to offend the gentleman, but it's absurd, monstrous. England, señora, would have shaken in its foundations of granite.'

'Yes, in its foundations of granite!' I repeated. 'What would have become of Great Britain!? It's a terrifying thought.'

Miss Fly shot me a terrible look.

'Oh well,' the countess said, 'the rumours circulated, I myself heard them, but there's no use in discussing it any further. Provided Great Britain remains without the slightest stain…'

Miss Fly got up.

'Señora,' I said to her with the greatest deference, 'I would be sorry if you left Spain without me being able to show you the very deep gratitude I feel towards you…'

'For what, sir?' she asked, raising her handkerchief to her charming mouth.

'For your goodness, for your kindness. As long as I live, señora, I will bless the person who rescued me and other unfortunate comrades from the battlefield.'

'You are greatly mistaken!' she exclaimed, laughing. 'I never thought of such a thing. You no doubt wanted me to have done it. Yes, I rescued many, but not you. You have deceived yourself. You saw me in La Merced passing through the rooms and dormitories… I don't want you to give me credit for things I did not do.'

'Well, then, señora, permit me to express my thanks to you for… No, what I want to say is to beg you to bear no ill will towards me for having been the cause, albeit an innocent one, of those ridiculous rumours.'

'Oh, there's no need to mention such a thing. I am very far above such pettiness. Slander! As if it made any difference to me. You, sir! Are you of any importance to me?

You are vain and conceited.'

Miss Fly was making strenuous efforts to maintain in her features that English calm which serves as a model for the majestic impassiveness of sculpture. She looked at the windows, the old paintings, the floor, Inés, at everything except me.

'Well, then, señora, as you have suffered no injury on my account...'

'None, absolutely none. You do yourself too much honour, señor Araceli, and just by asking my pardon for the vile slander, just by associating your person with mine, you are lacking in the restraint, yes, lacking in the consideration that a daughter of Great Britain should inspire wherever people live.'

'Pardon, señora, a thousand pardons. It only remains for me to say that I want to be your most humble servant here and everywhere and at all times of my life. Does this also lack restraint?'

'Yes, it does... but, still, I accept your homage. Thank you, thank you,' she said haughtily. 'Goodbye.'

At the end of the visit, although she was set on laughing a number of times, she only half-succeeded in doing so. Her hands were shaking, destroying the ends of her yellow shawl. She took her leave from the countess fondly, and with great ceremony from Inés and me.

'And might you be so good as to write to us sometimes to tell us how you are?' I said to her.

'Do you care how I am?'

'Very much, very much indeed,' I replied vehemently and in all sincerity.

'Write to you! But that means I will have to remember you. I am very forgetful, señor de Araceli.'

'As long as I live, I shall not forget your generosity, Athenais. It will take a lot to make me forget.'

'Well, not me,' she said, looking at me for the last time.

And in that last look of hers there was so much pride, so much haughtiness and so much vexation that I felt truly pained. Finally, she left the room. The paleness of her face and the fury in her soul gave her a terrible and majestic beauty.

A few moments later that beautiful insect of a thousand colours, which had flitted around me in capricious circles and games for a few days, had disappeared for ever.

Many who had heard me talk about this before claim that Miss Fly never existed, that this part of my story is my own invention for my own enjoyment and to entertain others. But shouldn't one blindly believe the word of an honourable man? Is there any chance that someone who has given proof of such honesty would be capable now of tarnishing his reputation with absurd stories and imaginary inventions which are not founded on truth itself, the daughter of God?

Shortly after the English couple had left us alone, the countess said to Inés,

'My daughter, have you any objection to marrying Gabriel?'

'No, none,' she replied with such self-possession that I was astonished.

With indescribable emotion I kissed her beautiful hand which I held in mine.

'Is your soul calm and content, my daughter?'

'Calm and content,' she replied. 'Poor Miss Fly!'

We looked at each other. A Heaven full of divine light and the inexplicable music of angels floated between our faces… If it was possible to see God, I was doing so now.

'How beautiful it is to be alive!' I exclaimed. 'How well God did to create the two of us, the three of us! Is there any happiness like mine? But what is this, is it living or dying?'

On hearing this, the countess, who had hurried over to embrace us, drew away from us. She stared at the floor sadly. Inés and I thought the same thing at the same time and felt the same sorrow, an intimate and deep pity that disturbed our happiness.

'How is he today?' Amaranta asked.

'Very bad,' Inés replied. 'The two of us will go there. He hasn't seen me for over an hour and a half and he'll be very sullen by now.'

Although I was exhausted and weak I got up and followed her, leaning on her arm.

'I will make a final attempt and I will succeed,' she said close to the mason's den. 'I have watched him closely all day and the poor man's only wish now is to give in.'

XXXIX

Entering the lonely and sad room, we saw Santorcaz sunk in the armchair and attentively reading a book. He looked up at us. Putting her hand on his shoulder, Inés said to him in an affectionately playful tone,

'Father, do you know that I'm getting married?'

'You're getting married?' the old man said in astonishment, dropping the book and looking daggers at us. 'You!'

'Yes,' Inés continued in the same tone. 'I'm getting married to this rogue Gabriel, to an oppressor of the people, to a torturer of humanity, to a crony of despotism.'

Santorcaz tried to speak but emotion made him numb. He tried to laugh and then tried to be serious and even angry, but his face could only display confusion, hesitation and uneasiness.

'And as my husband will have to serve the King and Queen, because that is his job,' Inés continued, 'I shall be obliged, dear Father, to quarrel with you. I have now given myself up to the nobility; I want to go to the court, have a palace, coaches and lots of very fancy servants... That's the way I am.'

'You are joking, Doña Inesita,' Santorcaz said in a bittersweet tone, finally recovering the power of speech. 'So you're just marrying the first one that comes along?'

'I've known him for a long time, as you well know,' she said, laughing. 'I've told you many times. Now, Father, you will stay here with Juan and Ramoncilla and I will go to Madrid with my husband. You will amuse yourself by founding a great lodge and reading books about revolutions and guillotines so that you'll end up driving yourself mad like Don Quijote with his books on chivalry.'

Saying this she embraced the old man and let him kiss her.

'Farewell, farewell,' she repeated. 'As we're not going to see each other again, let's say goodbye to each other properly.'

'You rascal,' he said, hugging her lovingly to his breast and sitting her on his knees. 'Do you think I'm going to let you leave?'

'And do you think I'm going to wait until you let me leave? Father, have you gone crazy? Have you forgotten the person who's been in the house and who has so much power? Don't you know you are a prisoner? Do you think there is no justice or laws or magistrates? Don't even dare to breathe...'

The mason pushed the girl from him, tried to get up, but his aching legs prevented him and hitting the arms of the chair, said,

'Well, that's the last straw... going off and leaving me... Araceli,' he added, speaking to me kindly. 'Now that my daughter has been so weak as to fall in love with you, I give you permission to be her husband, but you and she will stay here with me.'

'You're doing the right thing by pleading,' Inés said, laughing. 'My husband certainly gets on well with masons. He and I, we detest the rabble and adore kings and monks.'

'Well, I'll stay,' Santorcaz said with a slight trace of humour in his voice. 'I will die here. You already know the state of my health, my daughter, it's a miracle I'm alive. During the last few days when you have been cross with me, I have felt that my life was leaving me moment by moment, like a glass emptying. Ah, there's little left, now that I see, now that I'm seeing the black depths.'

'Everything will be all right,' I said, moving my chair closer to that of the sick man. 'We'll take the enemy of kings with us.'

'That's right, that's... Gabriel has spoken with as much skill as Voltaire,' the mason said with a sudden burst of spirit. 'You will take me with you... I don't mind, really.'

'Good, we'll take you,' Inés said, embracing her father. 'We'll take you to Madrid where we have a big house, a very big one, and where we'll have a lot of room because my mother will go off to live in Andalusia with all her servants and never return.'

'Never return!' the sick man said, alarmed. 'Who told you that?'

'She did herself. She will live apart from me while you live.'

'While I live! Now you can see. This shows you how deep is her hatred of me.'

'Quite the opposite, Father,' Inés said gently, 'she's going because you cannot see her and to leave me free to look after you and be with you while you are ill. What I told you just now about leaving you and going off on my own with my husband was in jest.'

Some tears which he would have liked to have held back welled up in the old man's eyes.

'I believe it, but this thing about your mother leaving you to allow me the inestimable benefit of your company seems a sham to me.'

'Don't you believe it?'

'No, why doesn't she dare to come here and say it in front of me?'

'You might want that, dear Father, but why would she come to tell you just that when she's already gone?'

'She's gone! She's gone!' Santorcaz exclaimed with such despair that he remained stunned for a long time.

'Didn't you know? Didn't you hear the voices of some English gentlemen? They are accompanying her to Madrid, from where she'll leave for Andalusia.'

The power of that beautiful and excellent creature over her father was so great that Santorcaz seemed to believe everything she said. He stared at the floor and slowly stroked his beard.

'Search the whole house for her,' Inés continued. 'I'm sure the lady would love to live inside this madhouse.'

'She has gone!' Santorcaz repeated gloomily, speaking to himself.

'And it wasn't easy for me to stay,' she added, playing the fool with enchanting expressions and gestures. 'It was her desire for me to go with her. Somebody there had told her... you can't keep anything secret... that I had become very attached to you. It was only for this reason that she came ready to forgive you, to be reconciled with you... which is entirely natural, as you had loved her a lot and she had loved you... But you are mad... you received her as one receives an enemy... you became furious... you refused to be nice to her. It's taken me a long time to forgive you.'

The tears ran continuously down Santorcaz's face.

'My duty was to flee from this hated house, flee with her, leaving you to the perversities and ill feelings of your heart,' said Inés, who combined the sanctity of angels with something of the astuteness of a diplomat. 'But I remembered that you were prostrate and ill. I told her...'

The mason looked at his daughter, asking as much as it was possible to ask with his eyes.

'I told her, yes,' she continued, 'and as that lady has a good, generous and loving heart and has never, never wished anyone harm and has never lived on hatred, as she can forgive offences and do good to those that hate her... Ah, that's not something you will believe or understand because a heart of iron like yours cannot understand this.'

'Yes, I believe it, I understand it,' said Santorcaz, drying his tears.

'Well, then, she herself agreed that I should not leave you, so that I could console you and give you strength in your final days and as she and you cannot be together in the same place, she decided to leave. We agreed that I would marry the torturer of humanity and that Gabriel and I would take you to live with us.'

'And she went? But can she have gone?' Santorcaz asked with a glimmer of hope.

'She has gone, yes indeed. She came ready to be reconciled with you, to love you as I love you. The poor thing has wept much since finding that after so many years, after so many misfortunes she has suffered because of you, after so much harm that you have done to her, you still refuse to say a Christian word, to wipe away all the faults of your life with one moment of generosity, to rid your conscience and also hers from the weight of an unbearable resentment. She left forgiving you. God will take charge of judging you, when at the moment of judgment, you present to him as the only merits in your existence, that unfeeling and perverse heart, or rather, that nest of serpents, which you have raised and fed every day so that they might grow and live for ever, and bite you here and for eternity in the next life.'

The mason twisted in anguish in his chair. The tears had stopped flowing from his eyes, his face was flushed, his hands tensed, his head thrown back and his breathing was laboured.

'Father!' exclaimed Inés, throwing her arms around his neck. 'Be good, be generous and I will love you even more. Now you know my wish, prepare to fulfil it and my mother will return. I will call her and she will return.'

Santorcaz's muscles tightened and became rigid; he shut his eyes and he looked like a corpse. At the very same moment the door opened and in came the countess, pale and tearful. Walking slowly, she went up to the side of the sick man who was still inert, silent and apparently lifeless. We were all alarmed and went to him and, with the help of Juan and Ramoncilla, we laid him onto his bed and immediately called the doctor who usually looked after him.

Inés and the countess watched him attentively and stared at the gaunt, but still handsome, face of the unfortunate mason. They gazed with fear at that abyss, terrified at what lay in its depths, without fully understanding it.

The doctor, after he had examined him, announced that his end was close, adding that he was amazed that he had lived so long, since the day before he had thought he was almost dead, although he had hidden the fatal prognosis from Inés. Shortly before nightfall, a deep sigh announced to us that he had recovered consciousness again. He opened his eyes, and looking in terror around the whole room, fixed them onto the countess, whose face was illuminated by the dismal light.

'You here again!' he exclaimed gracelessly and with an expression of weariness and anger. 'You here again? You know I hate you. Prison, exile, the scaffold... nothing's too much for you in your persecution of me! Why have you come to disturb my happiness? Go away: why are you gripping my daughter's hand with that yellow hand like the hand of death? Why are you looking at me with those silver eyes that seem like moonbeams?'

'Father, don't speak like that, you're making me afraid,' cried Inés, embracing him, her eyes full of tears.

The countess said nothing and was crying as well.

After that crisis in his mind, Santorcaz fell once more into the deepest torpor and towards dawn he regained consciousness and awoke tranquil and placid. His look was peaceful, his voice clear and calm when he said,

'Inés, my child, dearest angel, are you here?'

'I am here, Father,' she replied, moving affectionately closer to his side. 'Can't you see me?'

Inés trembled when she saw her father's eyes fix on those of the countess.

'Ah,' Santorcaz said, smiling slightly. 'She's there... I can see her... she's coming over here... but why doesn't she speak?'

The countess had taken a few steps towards the bed but remained silent.

'Why doesn't she speak?' the sick man repeated.

'Because she's afraid of you,' Inés said, 'as I am, too, and the poor thing doesn't dare say anything to you. You're not saying anything to her either.'

'Aren't I?' the mason said, surprised. 'I've been speaking to her for two hours... my mouth is dry from so much speaking and she doesn't answer me. Oh!' he added sorrowfully and turned his face away. 'It is too cruel for this unhappy man.'

'Do you love her, Father?' Inés asked, so moved that we hardly heard her words.

'Oh, I do, very much!' the sick man cried, pressing his hand to his heart.

'That's why since you saw her,' the girl continued, 'you have asked her forgiveness for the slight harm you inadvertently caused her. All of us heard you and we praised God for your good behaviour.'

'You all heard me?' he asked in astonishment, looking at all of us. 'You heard me... she heard me... Araceli also heard me? I had said it quietly, very quietly so that only God would hear me and that no one would hear it.'

Amaranta, taking Santorcaz's hand, said,

'It's been a long, long time since I wanted to forgive you. If at any time, after Inés came into my power, you had come to me as a friend... I, too, felt bitter, but misfortune taught me to overcome it...'

Abundant tears cut off her words.

'And I', Santorcaz said gently and with a serene expression, 'I who am about to die, do not know what is going on in my heart. It was born for love. It doesn't know if it has loved or hated all its life.'

After these words all fell silent for a short while. The souls of those three individuals, so united by Nature and so divided by the storms of the world, merged, so to say, in the depths of a religious and solemn meditation on their respective situations. Inés was the first to break the deep silence by saying,

'It is well known, dear Father, that you are a good, honourable and generous man. If you had a reputation for the opposite, it was because you were the victim of slander. But we, my mother and I, and also Araceli, we know you well. That is why we love you so much.'

'Yes,' the mason replied, like a dying man replying to the questions of his confessor.

'If you did some bad things,' Inés continued, 'that is, ones that seemed bad, it was just as a joke... I understand that perfectly... I bet that the persecution wasn't half as bad as you thought... But anyway, it is what it is. What is certain is that you were upset, and with good reason, because you were in love, you wanted to do good, you wanted... But there are proud families... one needs to understand also that a noble family must have a fixed point... God first and then the world where it's not intended that everyone should be equal.'

'But they see themselves as the punishment, or if not punishment, the justice of Providence on earth,' Santorcaz said sharply, looking at Amaranta. 'My lady countess, this very day you have consented to your only daughter and noble heiress marrying a boy from the beaches of La Caleta. A fine pedigree, for sure!'

'It would be better to call him,' the countess replied, 'an honourable, worthy, generous young man of true merit and with prospects.'

'Oh, señora, I, too, was that twenty years ago,' Santorcaz said sadly.

He then closed his eyes, as if to drive painful images away from himself.

'That's true,' Inés said, half-joking, half-seriously, 'but you surrendered to despair, dear Father, you did not have the strength of spirit of this oppressor of the people, you did not fight like him against adversity or win step by step an honourable standing in the world. You let yourself be overcome by misfortune; you ran off to Paris and joined up with those revolutionary rogues who enjoyed killing people at that time. Each of you made the other worse and you all believed that by cutting off other people's heads you gained something, and that those with their heads left on their shoulders counted for more. Then you came to Spain with your heart full of revenge. You wanted us to amuse ourselves here with what they amused themselves with there. People didn't want to give you that pleasure and you entertained yourself with the clowning and nonsense of the masons who, according to them, do a lot and, as I have seen, do nothing...'

'Yes,' the old man said.

'At the same time you tried to harm the person you should have loved the most... I know that if she hadn't despised you as she did despise you, you would have been good, very good, and you would have longed for her...'

'Yes, yes,' he repeated.

'This is clear, God permits such things. Sometimes it seems that two good people come to an agreement to do wicked things, without realising that just by saying a couple of words they would end up embracing each other and loving each other very much.'

'Yes, yes.'

'And I have no doubt,' continued Inés, pouring out a ceaseless torrent of generosity over the soul of the poor, sick man, 'I have no doubt that you seized hold of me because you loved me a lot and wanted me to accompany you.'

Santorcaz did not confirm or deny it.

'Which pleased me a great deal,' she continued. 'You have been a loving father to me. I declare that you are the best of men, that you have loved me, that you are worthy of being respected and loved, as I respect and love you, giving an example to all those here.'

The revolutionary looked at his daughter with an ineffable expression of gratitude. Religion could not have won a soul better.

'I am dying,' Don Luis said with emotion, stretching out his right hand to Amaranta and his left one to his daughter, 'without knowing how God will receive me. I will appear with my load of sins and my load of woes, each one as big as the other so that I don't know which one weighs more. I have breathed vengeance and hatred for so long... I have believed too much in earthly justice; I have had no faith in Providence; I have tried to conquer what I believed was mine through terror and violence; I have had more faith in evil than in the virtue of men; I have seen God as an irritated and tyrannical superior, pledged to protect the inequalities of the world; I have been completely lacking in humility, I have been as proud as Satan and I have mocked the paradise I could never reach; I have done harm while keeping in the depths of my soul some inexplicable interest in the person I hurt; I have chased after the pleasure of revenge as the parched man in the desert chases after imaginary water; I have lived in perpetual anger, tearing apart my heart

with my own fingernails. My spirit did not know any rest until I brought to my side an angel of peace who consoled me with her gentleness, even though I mortified her with my anger. Until then, I did not know of the existence of those two consolatory virtues of the heart, charity and patience. May the two of them fill my soul, may they close my eyes and may they bring me before God.'

As he was saying this, he faded away little by little. He seemed to be sleeping. The two women, kneeling on either side, did not move. I thought he had died, but when I got closer, I saw he was breathing gently. I retired to the next room and Inés followed me shortly after. The two of us agreed to summon the prior of the Augustines, a venerable priest who had been a dear friend of Santorcaz's father's.

In the morning, after the devout spiritual ceremony, Santorcaz asked us to leave him alone with the countess. The two of them talked on their own for a long time but when we heard some noise, we went in and saw Amaranta kneeling at the foot of the bed and him sat up, unsettled, with all the symptoms of a tormenting delirium. With wild eyes he was looking everywhere, but not seeing us, intent only on the imagined objects with which his mind had populated the dark room.

'I'm going,' he said, 'I'm going... goodbye! It's already light... don't tremble... Those steps you hear are those of your father who is coming with an army of armed lackeys to kill me... They won't find me... I will get out through the window in the tower... Good God! They have taken away the ladder, I'll throw myself out, even though I might die... You can well say that my body, found at the foot of these walls, will be your revenge and the shame of this house. Shall I wait? Don't you want me to wait? They are already there, your father is knocking at the door and is calling you... Goodbye, I will throw myself into the open country... There are servants with sticks and muskets down there, too. God is abandoning us because we are criminals. I have thought of a wonderful idea. You are saved... hide there... go to your bedroom. Let me gather up these valuable glasses, these silver candlesticks. I'll take them with me, and I'll try to slip away with my stolen valuables along the cornice of the tower until I reach the roof of the stables. Goodbye... I am going, open the door and shout, '*Stop thief, stop thief!*' God and your father will know of your shameful act if you want to reveal it to them, but not that coarse mob. They saw a man go in, but they don't know who it is and why he came. My darling, be brave, play your part well. Shout, '*Stop thief, stop thief!*' ... Goodbye... I'm going now, I'm stealing away over these slippery and greenish stones... The ones below still haven't seen me. It's vital that they see me... Ah, now those wretches have seen me with my booty of precious objects and they are all shouting, '*Stop thief, stop thief!*' I am so happy! Nobody will know anything, life and my heart; nobody will know anything, anything…'

He fell back, trembling slightly and his soul sank into the ocean without a floor and without a shore. Inés and I approached the lifeless body with religious respect. In our stupor and emotion we thought we heard the sound of black and eternal waters, stirring at the impact of that being who had fallen into them, but what we were hearing was the agitated breathing of the countess, who was crying bitterly, not daring to raise her sinful brow.

XL

Those who want to know how and when I got married, and other details as precious as they are unknown about the almost unchanging peace I have lived in over so many years, will have to read, if they have the patience, what other tongues less tired than mine will tell henceforth. Here I come to the end, to the no small delight of my tired readers and to my great pleasure in having arrived at the greatest occasion of my life, the event of my marriage, the prime cause of the happiness I have enjoyed for sixty years, doing as much good as I can, loved by my family and well thought of by strangers. God has given me what he gives to all when they ask for it through looking for it, and which they look for without ceasing to ask for it. I am a man practical in life and religious in my conscience. Life has been my school and misfortune my teacher. I learnt all and had all.

If you want me to say something more (although others must be responsible for putting me in the public eye again, despite my love of obscurity), you should know that through a series of circumstances, difficult to explain because of their number and complexity, I ended up playing no part in the rest of the war, but the strangest thing was that since I left active service, I began to be promoted with astonishing speed.

Having regained the appreciation and consideration of Lord Wellington, I received many proofs of cordial affection from this distinguished man, and he attended to me and entertained me so much in Madrid that I have always been profoundly grateful for his kindness. One of the happiest days of my life was when we learnt that the Duke of Ciudad Rodrigo had won the Battle of Waterloo.

Soon after the Battle of Salamanca I was promoted to the rank of lieutenant colonel. But my mother-in-law, by the talisman of her uninterrupted correspondence, had me made colonel, then brigadier and, although I still have not recovered from the shock, I found myself one morning made a general.

'This is enough!' I exclaimed in indignation having read my service record. 'If I don't stop this, they are capable of making me a field marshal without any justification for it.'

I asked to go onto the retired list.

My mother-in-law continued writing to improve our well-being in various ways, and with this and incessant work, and the admirable order that my wife established in my house (because my wife was as passionate for order as was my mother-in-law for letters) I acquired what those in antiquity called *aurea mediocritas.*[326] I lived and live comfortably, I was and am almost rich, I had and have a brilliant army of descendants among children, grandchildren and great-grandchildren.

Goodbye, my dear friends. I do not presume to say that you should imitate me, because that would be immodest. But if you are young, if you find yourself ignored by fortune, if you find before your eyes steep mountains, inaccessible heights and you have no ladders or ropes but just strong hands, if you find yourself prevented from realising in the world the generous impulses of thought and the laws of the heart, remember Gabriel Araceli, who was born with nothing and had everything.

END OF THE BATTLE OF SALAMANCA AND THE FIRST SERIES OF THE NATIONAL EPISODES
February-March 1873

Endnotes

Trafalgar

CHAPTER I

1   The Empire of Trebizond was a successor state to part of the Byzantine Empire and was located on the southern shore of the Black Sea. Ruled by emperors of the Komnenos family, it fell to the Ottomans in 1461. The Spanish word for Trebizond is "*Trapisona*" which came to mean a swindle, shady affair or intrigue. It can also mean a confused or rough sea with white caps, an apt allusion for this book.

2   A reference to the picaresque novel *Historia de la vida del Buscón, llamado Don Pablos, exemplo de Vagamundos, y espejo de Tacaños*, by Francisco Gómez de Quevedo y Villegas (1580-1645) published in 1626. The hero is a confidence trickster whose career does not end well.

3   A district at the north-western end of the historic centre of Cádiz.

4   The Battle of Cape St. Vincent took place on 14th February 1797. The British fleet, commanded by Admiral Sir John Jervis, defeated a superior Spanish fleet commanded by Admiral José de Córdoba y Ramos. It was also known as "The Fourteenth" (see Chapter II note 31 and Chapter III, note 42).

5   A beach in Cádiz, near La Viña (see note 3).

6   The enlarged claw of Uca tangeri, a type of fiddler crab, is a great delicacy in Andalusian cuisine.

7   Another district in Cádiz.

8   The Puerta de Tierra or "Land Gate" was built into the old wall surrounding the city in the mid-eighteenth century.

9   The original Spanish phrase is "introductor de embajadores", the name of an official in the Spanish Court who was responsible for overseeing the arrival and departure of foreign ambassadors. The post dates from 1626.

10   A town about 5 miles south-east of Cádiz and an important naval base.

11   The Campo de Gibraltar is a county in the province of Cádiz. After the cession of Gibraltar to the British in 1713 under the Treaty of Utrecht, the main centre became Algeciras.

BENITO PÉREZ GALDÓS

12   A seaport about 12 miles from Cádiz.

13   Medinasidonia or Medina Sidonia is a town about 31 miles inland from Cádiz.

14   A town about 31 miles south of Cádiz and 15 miles from Medina Sidonia.

15   A battle which took place on 19th July 1808 near Bailén, a village in Jaén province, southern Spain. A French army commanded by General Pierre Dupont was decisively beaten by a Spanish army led by General Francisco Castaños. It was the first defeat of Napoleon's Grande Armée and is the subject of *Bailén*, the fourth book in the first series of the *Episodios Nacionales*.

16   Gabriel is referring to two separate incidents. The first is when the people of Madrid rose up against the French occupiers on 2nd May 1808. Many patriots were shot the next day, an event which was the subject of a painting by Goya. This event is covered by Galdós in *El 19 de marzo y el 2 de mayo* (19th March and 2nd May), the third book in the first series of the *Episodios Nacionales*. The second incident occurs after the Battle of Bailén (see note 15), when Joseph I, Napoleon's brother and puppet King of Spain, had abandoned the capital. Napoleon himself then entered Spain to restore his brother to the throne. After heroic resistance, Madrid surrendered to Napoleon on 1st December 1808. These events are covered in the fifth book in the first series of the *Episodios Nacionales*, *Napoleón en Chamartín* (Napoleon at Chamartín).

17   Zaragoza was unsuccessfully besieged by the French from May to August 1808. However, the French under Marshal Lannes began a second siege in December 1808, and after bitter resistance under the command of General José de Palafox, the city surrendered. These events are covered in *Zaragoza*, the sixth book in the first series.

18   The city of Gerona endured a siege from May to December 1809 when General Mariano Álvarez de Castro capitulated to Marshal Augereau, commander of the French forces. The siege is the subject of *Gerona*, the seventh book in the first series.

19   The Battle of the Arapiles (or the Battle of Salamanca as it is more usually known in England) took place on 22nd July 1812 when an Anglo-Portuguese army under the command of the Duke of Wellington, assisted by a Spanish army, decisively defeated a French army commanded by Marshal Marmont. It is the subject of the tenth and final book in the first series, La Batalla de los Arapiles.

20   The original manuscript of Trafalgar referred to Trafalgar, Bailén, San Marcial, Talavera, Zaragoza, Arapiles and Gerona in that order.

CHAPTER II

21   A reference to the painting *Saint Anne teaching the Virgin to read* by Bartolomé Esteban Murillo (1617-1682) in the Prado.

22   Cosme Damián Churruca y Elorza (1761-1805). He was a *Brigadier de la Real Armada* in the Spanish Navy (a rank broadly equivalent to commodore in the Royal Navy). A distinguished scientist as well as having a successful career in the Spanish Navy, he took part in a number of naval actions including the siege of Gibraltar in 1781 and in expeditions to the Straits of Magellan in 1788 and the Antilles in 1792-5. He commanded the 74-gun *San Juan Nepomuceno* in the Combined Fleet (see following note).

23   The Combined Fleet of the French and Spanish fleets under the overall command of Vice Admiral Pierre Charles de Villeneuve.

24   Federico Carlos Gravina y Nápoli (1756-1806). An admiral in the Spanish Navy. He was born in Palermo, Sicily, and joined the Spanish Navy with the help of his uncle who was ambassador in

Madrid. He had a successful naval and diplomatic career in the service of Spain and was appointed commander of the Spanish fleet when hostilities with Great Britain resumed in 1804. At the Battle of Trafalgar his ship was the *Príncipe de Asturias* (118 guns).

25   Cayetano Valdés y Flores Bazán (1767-1834). A *Brigadier de la Real Armada* in the Spanish Navy. He took part in many actions (such as the attack on Algiers in 1775, the Siege of Gibraltar in 1782, and the Battle of Cape St. Vincent in 1797). He also took part in Malaspina's scientific expedition in the Pacific from 1789 to 1794, and in 1792 he circumnavigated Vancouver Island. At the Battle of Trafalgar he commanded the Neptuno (80 guns). He also appears in *Los cien mil hijos de San Luis* (The hundred thousand sons of St. Louis), the sixth book in the second series of the *Episodios Nacionales*.

26   Baltasar Hidalgo de Cisneros (1770-1829). A rear admiral in the Spanish Navy. He took part in the expedition against Algiers in 1775 (see note 33) and the Anglo-Spanish attack on Toulon in 1793. During the Battle of Trafalgar he was a Commodore on board the *Santísima Trinidad*. He subsequently became Minister of the Navy under Fernando VII and Viceroy of the River Plate. He reappears in *Memorias de un cortesano de 1815* (Memories of a courtier of 1815), the second book in the second series of *Episodios Nacionales*.

27   Dionisio Alcalá Galiano (1762-1805). A skilled cartographer, he was part of Alessandro Malaspina's expedition to the Pacific in 1789. With Valdés (see note 5) he circumnavigated Vancouver Island in 1792 and explored the Strait of Juan de Fuca. At the Battle of Trafalgar he was a *Brigadier de la Real Armada* and commanded the *Bahama* (74 guns).

28   Ignacio María de Álava (1750-1817). A vice admiral, he was second in command of the Spanish fleet in Cádiz. At the Battle of Trafalgar his flagship was the Santa Ana (120 guns).

29   See Chapter I, note 2 above.

30   Following the coup of 18 Brumaire in 1797 Napoleon dissolved the Directory and he was appointed First Consul for ten years and then for life in 1802. At the time of Doña Francisca's speech, he had been Emperor since 1804.

31   The Battle of Cape St. Vincent in 1797 (see Chapter 1, note 4).

32   Doña Francisca says, "*el señor generalísimo de mar y tierra*". She is referring to Manuel Godoy (see note 36) who was appointed *Generalísimo de los Ejércitos de Tierra y Mar* in 1801.

33   This is a reference to the attack on Algiers in 1775, a costly venture in which some five thousand Spanish lives were lost.

34   Napoleon I, Emperor of the French since 1804.

35   Charles IV who reigned from 1788 to 1808.

36   Manuel Godoy (1767-1851). Favourite of Charles IV and lover of the Queen, María Luisa. He was appointed Prince of Peace in 1796 following the Treaty of Basel which ended hostilities between France and Spain.

37   The *Tratado de Subsidios*, or the Subsidy Treaty, the name given to a treaty signed on 22nd October 1803 between France and Spain, under which Spain would pay France 72,000 pounds a year instead of supplying ships and troops to France as she had agreed under the earlier Treaty of San Ildefonso in 1796. In return, France would recognize Spain's neutrality in the struggle between France and Great Britain that had resumed following the short-lived Peace of Amiens in 1802. The Subsidy Treaty was one of the more unpopular measures taken by Charles IV and Godoy.

CHAPTER III

38   The last battle in the War of Jenkins' Ear (1739-1748) between Spain and Great Britain. The British Caribbean fleet under Rear Admiral Sir Charles Knowles attempted to intercept a Spanish fleet from New Spain. Although the Spanish lost more men and ships, the result was indecisive.

39   A failed attempt to recover Gibraltar led by the Duke of Crillon (1717-1796), a Frenchman in the service of Spain, who had regained Menorca from the British earlier in 1782.

40   This survey lasted from 1785 to 1786.

41   Antonio de Córdoba y Lasso de la Vega (1740-1811) was a Spanish sailor and scientist. He took part in the attack on Toulon and in the Battle of Cape St. Vincent.

42   The Spanish commander, Admiral José de Córdoba y Ramos (1732-1815), was dismissed from the service and forbidden to appear at court. Sir John Jervis (1735-1823) was created Earl St. Vincent.

43   The *Conde de Regla* (112 guns) was built in 1786 in Havana, Cuba, and broken up in 1811; the *San Joaquín* (70 guns) was built in 1771 in Cartagena and broken up in 1817; the *Real Carlos* (112 guns) was built in 1787 in Havana and sank in the Strait of Gibraltar on 12th/13th July 1801 (see note 46). The *Trinidad* is the *Santísima Trinidad* (140 guns) built in 1769 in Havana and captured at the Battle of Trafalgar.

44   Villeneuve led a combined squadron of French and Spanish ships, the latter commanded by Gravina, to Martinique in the West Indies in April 1805 as part of Napoleon's plans for the invasion of England in the summer of 1805. Villeneuve left for Europe in June 1805, having heard that Nelson was in pursuit.

45   This action took place on 22nd July 1805 when Villeneuve, returning from Martinique, was met by an English squadron under Admiral Sir Robert Calder off Cape Finisterre. The fight (in fog) was indecisive but the Spanish lost two ships, the *San Rafael* (80 guns) and the *Firme* (74 guns) to the English.

46   Gabriel is referring to an incident at night-time in the Second Battle of Algeciras on 13th/14th July 1801 when two Spanish ships of the line, the *Real Carlos* and the *San Hermenegildo*, mistakenly opened fire on each other, collided and blew up with a loss of life of up to 1,700 men.

47   This action took place off the Cape of Santa María in Portugal when four Spanish frigates carrying treasure from South America to Cádiz were met by four English frigates commanded by Commodore Graham Moore. In the ensuing fight one of the Spanish frigates was sunk and the remaining three captured.

CHAPTER IV

48   Nelson. An English translation could be the "Little Lord" or the "Young Gentleman".

49   The *Real Academia Española* was founded in 1713 and is the guardian of the Spanish language. This is achieved by publishing dictionaries and issuing guidance on correct usage.

50   The original Spanish words are *patigurbiar* and *chingurria*. Neither have any meaning so I have tried to create English equivalents consistent with Marcial's wayward treatment of Spanish. *Patigurbiar* could be seen as derived from *pata* (foot, leg or paw) and *gurbión* (a twist used in embroidery or gum from euphorbia plants). *Chingurria* has echoes of *chingarse*, an informal verb meaning to get drunk, which has become a noun in Marcial's vocabulary.

51   Cuthbert Collingwood, 1ˢᵗ Baron Collingwood (1748-1810) took part in three actions during the wars with France: the Glorious First of June in 1794, Cape St. Vincent in 1797, and Trafalgar in 1805 where he was second in command to Nelson. He died at sea off Menorca in 1810.

52   An English translation could be "Old Cramp".

53   Sir Robert Calder (1745-1818) was knighted after the Battle of Cape St. Vincent. In July 1805 he was detached from Cornwallis's fleet blockading Brest to intercept Villeneuve on his return from the West Indies. Following the action off Cape Finisterre (see Chapter III, note 45) Sir Robert Calder was reprimanded at a court martial for not pursuing Villeneuve.

54   An English translation could be "Old Cauldron".

55   Another linguistic creation of Marcial. The Spanish word he uses is *larguea*, which he may have derived from *actuar al largo*, to behave openly.

56   Marcial is referring to the action in the Strait of Gibraltar during the Second Battle of Algeciras in 1801 when two Spanish ships ended up firing at each other, see Chapter III, note 46.

57   The Spanish word for the magazine is *la santabárbara*, a word derived from *Santa Bárbara* (Saint Barbara). She is the patron saint of gunners, and invoked against sudden death, not least from explosions. Marcial plays on this derivation by saying, "...*la santabárbara, y esta señora no se anda con bromas*". The final phrase means "and this lady does not do jokes", but the literal meaning does not make sense in English.

58   Don Alonso calls her the *Soberbio*. HMS *Superb* was a 74 gun third-rate ship of the line launched in 1798. At this time she was commanded by Captain Richard Keats (1757-1834). He was promoted to rear admiral in 1807.

59   The vicuña, a relative of the llama, produces the finest quality wool of all the llama family.

60   1804.

61   José Bustamente y Guerra (1759-1825) was appointed joint leader with Alessandro Malaspina (see Chapter II, note 25 and Chapter VI, note 71) of the expedition to the Pacific from 1789 to 1794. At the time of this incident he was the Commander General of Río de la Plata. From 1810 to 1817 he was Governor General of Guatemala.

62   Another one of Marcial's creations. It is his attempt to pronounce Sir Graham Moore (1764-1843), commodore of the four English frigates. In Spanish, *comodón* can mean someone who is comfort-loving or spoilt.

63   Doña Francisca is alluding to a quotation from Chapter 20 in the First Part of *Don Quixote* when Sancho Panza warns the Don: "*Quien busca el peligro perece en él*" (Whoever looks for danger perishes from it).

64   Doña Francisca uses the phrase "*Rey de las Españas*", literally "King of the Spains". When the Holy Roman Emperor Charles V consolidated the crowns of Castile and Aragon as Charles I, he was named "*Hispaniarum Rex Catholicus*" (Catholic King of the Spains) by Pope Leo X in a bull of 1st April 1516. His son, Philip II, and subsequent monarchs used the title "*Hispaniarum (et Indiarum) Rex*", King of the Spains (and of the Indies).

65   The Second Treaty of San Ildefonso was signed on 18ᵗʰ August 1796 between Spain and the Directory in France and was directed against Great Britain. Among its terms was an obligation on each party to make its fleet available to the other party if requested.

66   Prince Ferdinand, the son of Charles IV, would ascend the Spanish throne in 1808 as Ferdinand VII. Prince Ferdinand was a focus of aristocratic resentment against Godoy.

67   A devotion consisting of special prayers or services on nine successive days.

CHAPTER V

68   A popular dance and singing tradition of Andalusia.

69   Another type of popular Andalusian song.

70   This may be a reference to the play *El sí de las niñas (The Maidens' Consent)* by Leandro Fernández de Moratín. The play is a satire against arranged marriages and was first performed in January 1806.

CHAPTER VI

71   This expedition took place in 1792.

72   Doña Francisca's use of the word "Jewish" here would not be surprising for someone of her class at that time. The monarchs of Spain, Fernando and Isabella, had ordered the expulsion of the Jews from Spain in 1492.

73   Marcial refers to the size of the guns by the weight of the shot that could be fired by the gun, the largest being a "36-pounder". In fact, on the eve of the Battle of Trafalgar, the *Trinidad* had a total of 140 guns, the *Príncipe de Asturias* had 112 guns, and the *Santa Ana* also had 112 guns. The *Rayo* did have 100 guns as stated by Marcial.

74   The Peace of Basel was made in July 1795 between France and Spain. Under its terms, Spain made peace with France and ceded two-thirds of the island of Hispaniola in the Caribbean to France. France restored to Spain territory it had occupied in the Basque Country. Godoy became the "Prince of Peace" as a result of this treaty.

75   The Peace of Amiens, initiated by the Treaty of Amiens of 1802 between Great Britain and France, ended the war between the two countries that had started in 1793. The Peace of Amiens was short-lived, as war between France and Great Britain broke out again in 1803.

76   Villeneuve. See Chapter II, note 23.

CHAPTER VII

77   Don Quixote also leaves for his first adventure by going out through the gate of his yard or *corral* (see Don Quixote, Part I, Chapter 2).

78   Conil de la Frontera is a small seaside town about halfway between Vejer and Cádiz.

79   Gabriel is no doubt referring to Alessandro Malaspina (1754-1810), an Italian nobleman who served for many years in the Spanish Navy. He circumnavigated the world and led important scientific expeditions in the Pacific. He was exiled from Spain in 1802 and died in Italy.

80   Also known as the War of the Pyrenees, the War of Roussillon (1793-1795) was a theatre in the war of the First Coalition against revolutionary France. The war between France and Spain was concluded with the Peace of Basel (see Chapter VI, note 74).

81   A Spanish victory when Spanish forces defeated a French army defending Perpignan on 19th May 1793.

82   General Antonio Ricardos (1727-1794) commanded the Spanish army in the early stages of the War of Roussillon. After his death, the initial successes of Spanish arms were not repeated. A fine portrait of him by Goya is in the Prado Museum in Madrid.

83   Needless to say, this account does not accord with the historical record of the battle.

84   Luis Fermín Carvajal, Conde de la Unión (1752-1794) was a successor to General Ricardos in the War of Roussillon. He was killed in the Battle of the Roure.

85   The Battle of Boulou (1st May 1794) was a French victory whose name appears on the Arc de Triomphe.

86   The Convention was the ruling body in France from 21ˢᵗ September 1792 until 26ᵗʰ October 1795 when it was replaced by the Directory.

87   William Pitt the Younger (1759-1806) was Prime Minister of Great Britain from 1783 to 1801 and from 1804 until his death in 1806.

88   Edmund Burke (1729-1797), born in Ireland, was a noted politician and philosopher. A supporter of the American Revolution, he became a strong opponent of the French Revolution.

89   Frederick North, second Earl of Guilford (1732-1792), usually known as Lord North, was Prime Minister of Great Britain from 1770 to 1782.

90   Charles Cornwallis (1738-1805), 1ˢᵗ Marquess Cornwallis, was a British general and colonial administrator. Despite having surrendered to Washington at the Battle of Yorktown in 1781, he later became Governor General of India and Ireland.

91   King of Great Britain from 1760 to 1820.

92   Two possible candidates are Paul I (1796-1801) and Alexander I (1801-1825).

93   Pedro Pablo Abarca de Bolea, Count of Aranda (1718-1798). He was a figure in the Spanish Enlightenment and a leading diplomat and minister. He became chief minister under Carlos IV in 1792 but was replaced that same year by Godoy, largely because of Aranda's association with reform and his attitude to revolutionary France. An open quarrel in the Council of State with Godoy about continuing the war with France in 1794 led to Aranda's dismissal and internal exile.

94   A mountain massif on the border between Castile (Soria) and Aragón (Zaragoza). Its highest peak, San Miguel, is 7,591 feet above sea level.

95   María Luisa Teresa de Parma (1751-1819), wife of Carlos IV and lover of Godoy.

96   Carlos IV (reigned 1788-1808).

97   El Pardo is a royal palace near Madrid.

98   The seizure of power by Napoleon in 1799 when the Directory was abolished and Napoleon became First Consul.

99   Chiclana de la Frontera is a coastal town about 12 miles from Cádiz.

CHAPTER VIII

100   A street now called Calle Enrique de las Marinas.

101   Collingwood was commanding the blockade of Cádiz in August 1805 while Nelson was on leave in England. Doña Flora is correct in saying that Collingwood only had three ships at the time, but she is being slightly unfair about Villeneuve's performance in that the Combined Fleet did attempt to chase Collingwood as it approached Cádiz.

102   By this time Napoleon had turned his attention from the invasion of England (in which the Combined Fleet was meant to play a crucial role) to military action against Austria. On 19th October 1805 (two days before the Battle of Trafalgar) he defeated the Austrians at the Battle of Ulm.

103   See Chapter II, note 22. The author's description of Churruca closely resembles the portrait of Churruca in the Naval Museum in Madrid.

104   The *Bucentaure* (referred to as the *Bucentauro* by our hero) was an 80-gun ship of the line, constructed in Toulon and launched in 1803.

105   Antonio de Escaño y García de Cáceres (1750-1814) commanded the *Príncipe de Asturias*, which was also the flagship of Gravina. He also appears in *Cádiz*, the eighth book in the first series of the *Episodios Nacionales*.

106   Pierre Dumanoir Le Pelley (1770-1829) flew his flag on the *Formidable*.

107   Charles René Magon de Médine (1763-1805) was on board the *Algésiras*.

108   Julien Marie Cosmao Kerjulien (1761-1825) commanded the *Pluton*. His name is engraved on the Arc de Triomphe.

109   Esprit-Tranquille Maistral (1763-1815) commanded the *Neptune*.

110   In fact, his name was Lavillegris. He commanded the *Mont-Blanc*.

111   Mathieu Anne-Louis de Prigny de Quérieux (1774-1827) was Villeneuve's Chief of Staff aboard the *Bucentaure*.

112   Churruca's speech here closely follows the historical record. See, for example, pages 309-310 in Cesáreo Fernández Duro, *La Armada española desde la unión de los reinos de Castilla y Aragón*, VIII, Madrid, 1902, which can be consulted online: http://www.armada.mde.es/html/historiaarmada/tomo8/tomo_08_14.pdf.

113   See Chapter II, note 22.

114   A reference to the *Academia de Bellas Letras* of Cádiz which existed from 1805 to 1808. One of its founders, Antonio Alcalá Galiano (1789-1865), said of it: "we were considered ridiculous versifiers". See Manuel Ruiz Lagos, *Ilustrados y reformadores en la Baja Andalucía*, Madrid, 1974, pp 49-50.

CHAPTER IX

115   The author uses the *pie* of Burgos which is equivalent to 0.278635 metres.

116   The Escorial or, to give it its full name, the Royal Site of San Lorenzo de El Escorial, is a monastery and palace built for Philip II (1556-1598). It is about 28 miles north-west of Madrid and is a complex of intersecting courtyards, galleries, rooms and passageways.

117   Francisco Javier Uriarte de Borja (1753-1842) held the rank of Commodore (*Brigadier*) and eventually became Admiral of the Fleet (*Capitán General de la Real Armada*). Before Trafalgar he had taken part in a number of actions and voyages, including Algiers in 1775 (see Chapter II, note 33), Toulon in 1793 and the exploration of the Straits of Magellan in 1792 under Antonio de Córdova.

118   The Register (*La Matrícula de Mar)* appeared in 1606 and was formalised in 1737. It was a list of men who were available for service in the Navy and who could receive special privileges as a result.

119   San Jenaro probably refers to San Januario who was a brother of the two patron saints of Cádiz, San Servando and San Germán. All three were martyrs under the reign of Roman Emperor Diocletian (284 305).

120   "*Rayo*" means a flash of lightning.

121   Marcial has a play on words. In Spanish *vela* means a candle or a sail. No doubt the sails on Dumanoir's ship had been reefed too much for Marcial's liking.

122   Marcial's term for the Subsidy Treaty (see Chapter II, note 37).

CHAPTER X

123   The "*Camino de Santiago*" (Way of St James) is the pilgrimage route to the shrine of St. James the Great in the cathedral of Santiago de Compostela in Galicia. The route traditionally starts from many European cities, but the main stretch through northern Spain from the French frontier is about 490 miles long.

CHAPTER XI

124   The *Temeraire* (called the *Temeray* by our hero) was a 98-gun ship launched in 1798 at Chatham. She became famous as the subject of the painting *The Fighting Temeraire tugged to her last berth to be broken up, 1838* by Turner.

125   The *Neptune*, another 98 gun ship, was launched in 1797 at Deptford. She was broken up in 1818.

126   An eyewitness account of the explosion from the British ship *Defence* echoes our hero's description:
"*It was a sight the most awful and grand that can be conceived. In a moment the hull burst into a cloud of smoke and fire. A column of vivid flame shot up to an enormous height in the atmosphere and terminated by expanding into an immense globe, representing, for a few seconds, a prodigious tree in flames, speckled with many dark spots, which the pieces of timber and bodies of men occasioned while they were suspended in the clouds.*"
(*The Battle of Trafalgar* by Martin Robson, Conway Maritime Press, 2005, page 113, quoting from Gardiner, R. (ed.). *The Campaign of Trafalgar 1803-1805*. London, 1996, page 159.)

127   This is a reference to two explicits at the end of the Poem of the Cid (*Poema* or *Cantar de mio Cid*), an epic poem of nearly four thousand lines, thought to have been composed in the twelfth or early thirteenth century. The first is to the name of Per Abbat or Abad, the scribe who signed the only surviving manuscript copy from the fourteenth century. The second is to the phrase "*El romanz es leido, dat nos del vino*" (The romance is now read, give us some wine) which appears in some lines after Per Abbat's signature. No doubt the wine that Marcial wants to give to the greatcoats is powder and shot.

CHAPTER XII

128   Francisco Alcedo y Bustamante (1758-1805).

129   Gabriel's account of Nelson's death broadly summarises the account in *Authentic Narrative of the*

Death of Nelson published in 1807 by Dr. William Beatty, *Victory*'s surgeon. In Beatty's book, Nelson when shot is reported as saying, "They have done for me at last, Hardy."

130   The *Prince*, 98 guns, was commanded by Captain Richard Grindall. She was one of the few ships to suffer no casualties in the battle.

131   This is a play on words by Gabriel. The Spanish word "*seno*" can mean bosom or breast, but it also means a trough between waves.

132   It is unclear which Ordinance Gabriel is referring to. The principal regulations for the Navy were the *Ordinanzas Generales de mi Armada Naval* (General Ordinances for my Navy) issued by Carlos IV in 1793, and the *Real Ordenanza Naval para el Servicio de los Baxeles de S.M.* (Royal Naval Ordinance for the Service of His Majesty's Vessels) published in 1802. Neither contains a specific reference to the requirement for sailors buried at sea to be wrapped up in their hammocks, although this was a common practice in most navies at the time.

CHAPTER XIII
133   In the text, the name is incorrectly spelt "Eurygalus".

134   José de Gardoqui (1755-1816) took part in two expeditions to the Straits of Magellan in 1785 and 1788 and performed hydrographic surveys of the coast of Tierra del Fuego. In 1804 he was given command of the *Santa Ana*, flagship of Álava at Trafalgar. After further promotions and service in Cuba and the Philippines, he died aged 61 in Manila.

135   Juan Ruiz de Apodaca (1754-1835). He later became Viceroy of New Spain from 1816 to 1821.

CHAPTER XIV
136   The *Thémis* was a 40-gun frigate commanded by Captain Nicolas Jugan.

CHAPTER XV
137   The French Fort of Bellegarde was captured in June 1793 by the Spanish after a one-month siege.

138   A commander and number two on the *Elcano*, one of the ships that sailed out of Cádiz after the Battle of Trafalgar to recover dismasted Spanish ships.

139   Epaminondas (c.418-362 B.C.) was a Theban general and statesman who defeated the Spartans at the Battle of Leuctra (371 B.C.). He was an innovator of military tactics, and until his death in the Battle of Mantinea he was a dominant figure in Greece.

140   The opening and closing words of the Roman Catholic mass.

141   Malespina spoke of ninety-five to one hundred *varas* which I have converted into feet.

142   The *Numancia* was the first ironclad in the Spanish Navy. Built in France in 1863, she was commissioned in 1865 and the next year took part in the Chincha Islands War against Peru and Chile. She was the first ironclad to circumnavigate the world in 1866/67. She was decommissioned in 1912 and sold as scrap. In the end she was wrecked on the Portuguese coast in December 1916 while under tow to the breakers in Bilbao. The circumnavigation was covered in *La vuelta al mundo en la Numancia* (Round the world in the *Numancia*) in the fourth series of the *Episodios Nacionales*.

143   The Atlantic Navigator of 1854 describes these as follows:
       "The Juan Vela [*called Juan Bola by Gabriel*] is a large rock lying at the distance of three miles, W. ¼

S., from the castle of Sancti Petri; the depth over it is 2 ½ fathoms.

The Haste Afuera or Outer Haste, lies 3 miles S.W. by W., from Sancti Petri, and 5 ¼ miles N.W. ½ W. from Cape Roche. It is a rocky shoal of 3 fathoms, and near it on the outside are from 14 to 10 fathoms. Large ships should pass at a considerable distance from, and smaller vessels should not come near this shoal, for the sea rolls heavy and breaks over it with a swell.

The Majarrotes is a rocky shoal, about half a league in length, in a S.E. by S. and N.W. by N. direction, in the middle part of which the depth varies from 2 to 4 fathoms. Its N.W. point lies S.S.W., 2 2/3 miles from Sancti Petri, and N.W., 3 ¾ miles, from Cape Roche. Its S.E. point lies S. ½ W., nearly four miles, from Sancti Petri, and N.W. by W., 2 miles, from Cape Roche. On the extremities are 4 ½ fathoms and the sea generally breaks over them."

144   A military fort between Cádiz and San Fernando.

145   These places are all north of the entrance to Cádiz Bay.

146   *Churra* is an ancient breed of sheep from Zamora province.

CHAPTER XVI

147   Gabriel must have been about 31 miles away from Cádiz.

148   The Spanish dollar or pieces of eight.

149   Benito Pérez Galdós notes that these are Nelson's words. They appear in his memorandum written on the *Victory*, off Cádiz, on 9th October 1805 where he set down the "Nelson touch", which he had explained to his officers on 29th September.

150   Alonso Butrón was a midshipman on the *Bahama* and a relative of Alcalá Galiano.

151   The *Bahama* was towed to Gibraltar where she was repaired. She sailed to England and became a prison hulk in the Medway until 1814.

152   "Judge of the footing we are on, when I tell you he [Marqués de Solana, Governor General of Andalusia] offered me his hospitals, and pledged the Spanish honour for the care and cure of our wounded men. Our officers and men who were wrecked in some of the prize ships were most kindly treated: all the country was on the beach to receive them: the priests and women distributing wine, and bread, and fruit amongst them. The soldiers turned out of the barracks to make lodging for them; whilst their allies, the French, were left to shift for themselves, with a guard over them to prevent their doing mischief."

From a letter to J. E. Blackett written on board the *Queen* on 2nd November 1805 which appears in G. L. Newnham Collingwood, FRS, *A selection from the public and private correspondence of Vice-Admiral Lord Collingwood; interspersed with memoirs of his life*. London 1828, pp. 185-6.

153   See Chapter I, note 4.

154   This was incorrect as the *Bahama* succeeded in reaching Gibraltar. See note 151 above.

The Battle of Salamanca

CHAPTER I

155   The "*peseta*", the name of a coin introduced by the French, was equivalent to four "*reales de vellón*" (a *real* of alloy as opposed to the traditional *real* of silver). In 1800 the average annual salary of a male unskilled construction worker in Madrid was 630 *reales de vellón* and that of a skilled worker in the services sector was 3,284. (Source: *Coste de vida y salarios en Madrid, 1680-1800*. Enrique Llopis Angelán and Héctor García Montero, DT-AEHE No. 0901, May 2009.)

156   Miguel José de Azanza (1745-1826) was Minister of Foreign Affairs under Joseph I Bonaparte. After Napoleon's defeat, he left Spain and died in exile in Bordeaux.

157   The Plaza de la Cebada, one of the oldest squares in Madrid, was used for public executions in the nineteenth century.

158   A wry play on words: "*escalera*" means stairs in Spanish.

159   The followers of Juan Martín Díaz (1775-1825), a guerrilla leader of humble origins, who was nicknamed "*El Empecinado*" (The Undaunted). He gives his name to the ninth book of the first series of the *Episodios Nacionales*, "*Juan Martín el Empecinado*".

160   The fairs (*verbenas*) of San Juan and San Pedro are occasions for communal celebrations. The fairs take place in late June when large bonfires are traditionally lit.

161   Joseph's nickname, an allusion to his allegedly heavy drinking, although he was in practice abstemious.

162   The Duke of Wellington.

163   The *Secretaría de Interpretación de Lenguas* (Secretariat for the Interpretation of Languages) was founded by Charles V in 1527 to support the Council of State.

164   The post of *Bibliotecario Mayor* (Chief Librarian) of the National Library of Spain was created in 1721. Moratín occupied the position from 1811 to 1812.

165   *L'École des maris* by Molière, first performed in 1661.

166   Pedro Estala (1757-1815) was an essayist, translator and anthologist. He had been a monk and became rector of Salamanca Seminary. Having been protected by Godoy, he became a follower of Joseph I and in 1809 he published a journal, *El Imparcial o Gaceta Política y Literaria*, which supported the Josephine cause. He died in exile in Auch, France.

167   "*Afrancesado*" ('Frenchified') was the term used to describe a Spaniard who supported Joseph Bonaparte.

168   María Julia Bonaparte (née Clary) (1771-1845), daughter of a rich silk merchant, married Joseph in 1794. Although queen consort of Joseph, she never went to Spain during his reign and remained in Paris.

169   The Society of Philadelphians was a group opposed to Napoleon. Operating in secret and borrowing ideas from masonic rituals and organisation, its members included military figures such as Colonel Oudet (who was killed in suspicious circumstances at the Battle of Wagram in 1809) and General Malet, who was executed following a failed attempt to overthrow Napoleon in 1812 after the retreat from Moscow. Jean-de-Dieu Soult (1769-1851) was commander of the French forces in the Peninsula from 1809 to 1812.

170   José Marchena Ruiz de Cueto (1768-1821). He was a poet and translator who was active in revolutionary circles while in exile in France from 1792 to 1808. In that year he returned to Spain in the service of Joseph and also wrote articles in support of him. He published *Fragmentum Petronii*, purportedly lost verses from Petronius's *Satyricon*, which was so skilfully done that it deceived Latin scholars of the day.

171   Anne Louise Germaine de Staël-Holstein, née Necker (1766-1817), writer, conversationalist and intellectual, played an important role in liberal political and cultural circles in France and Europe. She became a determined opponent of Napoleon.

172   Jean-Paul Marat (1743-1793), Maximilien Robespierre (1758-1794), Louis Legendre (1752-1797) and Jean-Lambert Tallien (1767-1820) were all major figures in the French Revolution.

CHAPTER II
173   Roger-Bernard-Charles Espagnac de Ramefort (1775-1839) was a French-born general in the service of Spain. He took part in many battles in the Peninsular War. He later became Governor of Barcelona and his cruel and reactionary rule there led to his assassination in 1839.

174   Carlos Manuel O'Donnell y Anethan (1772-1830).

175   Julián Sánchez García (1774-1832), nicknamed *el Charro* (the Salamancan), was a noted guerrilla leader of peasant origins. He led a cavalry regiment known as the *Lanceros de Castilla*.

176   Auguste Frédéric Louis Viesse de Marmont (1774-1852). He was transferred to Spain in July 1810 to command the French Army in northern Spain.

177   Bernardo del Carpio appears in a number of mediaeval ballads about resistance against the Moors and Charlemagne. The Carpio was a castle near Salamanca, which was occupied by Bernardo, and the Arapil is a hill near Salamanca, the site of the battle on 22nd July 1812. The Tormes is the river flowing by Salamanca. The original lines are:
"En el Carpio está Bernardo
y el Moro en el Arapil.
Como va el Tormes por medio,
no se pueden combatir."

CHAPTER III
178   Francisco Javier Castaños (1758-1852) was the victor of the Battle of Bailén in 1808.

CHAPTER IV
179   A game originating in the Basque country where two teams strike the ball with the hand, glove or a special basket. Now usually played against a wall, in some traditional variants the teams faced each other over a line or net.

180   See *The nineteenth of March and the second of May* in the Summary of events in the National Episodes between *Trafalgar* and *The Battle of Salamanca*.

181   San Juan de la Cruz (1542-1591) was a reforming member of the Carmelite Order and a mystical poet.

CHAPTER V

182   Fray Luis de León (1527?-1591) was a noted scholar and translator of the Bible. He is now more remembered for his poetry.

183   The Duke of Wellington led a force of about 45,000 British troops, supported by some 33,000 Portuguese regulars.

184   Santa Teresa de Jesús (or Ávila) (1515-1582) became a Carmelite nun at the age of 19 and was a famous mystic, writer and reformer of the Carmelite Order.

CHAPTER VI

185   Dios le Guarde is a small village about 51 miles from Salamanca.

186   Stapleton Cotton (1773-1865), subsequently 1st Viscount Combermere, was an experienced and successful cavalry officer. He had been given overall command of the cavalry under Wellington in 1810. Thomas Graham (1748-1843), later 1st Baron Lynedoch, was Wellington's second in command in early 1812.

187   The Constitution of Cádiz (*La Constitución de Cádiz*) was approved on 19th March 1812 by the Cortes in Cádiz. It was a liberal constitution, abolishing all feudal, aristocratic and ecclesiastical privileges, and established the basis for a liberal and democratic society.

188   Sir Arthur Wellesley became Viscount Wellington of Talavera, and of Wellington in the County of Somerset in August 1809 and Duke of Ciudad Rodrigo, and Grandee of Spain in January 1812.

189   A village about 39 miles from Salamanca.

CHAPTER VII

190   She addressed Gabriel using *vos* as the word for 'you', a mode of address to people much more elevated in the social hierarchy than Gabriel.

191   Joaquín Blake y Joyes (1759-1827) had led the Spanish forces in conjunction with the British led by Beresford in the Battle of Albuera against Soult in May 1811.

192   This incident occurred in *Cádiz*, the eighth book in the first series of the *Episodios Nacionales*.

193   *Salmorejo* is a purée of tomatoes, peppers, garlic and bread similar to *gazpacho*.

194   Major-General Sir Thomas Picton (1758-1815) commanded the 3rd Division in Spain. At the time of this book he would probably have been in England, recovering from wounds he had received at the Battle of Badajoz in April 1812. He was killed at the Battle of Waterloo.

195   General Rowland Hill (1772-1842).

196   A bloody battle indeed where both sides suffered substantial casualties. It was fought in May 1811.

CHAPTER VIII

197   Hercules is the mythical founder of Cádiz.

198   Gabriel's enthusiasm for books of chivalry echoes that of Don Quixote.

199   In Chapter XI of the Second Part of Don Quixote, Don Quixote and Sancho Panza meet a travelling troupe of actors in a strange cart led by the Devil. He tells the Don that they have just performed a play called the *Las Cortes de la Muerte* (The Assembly of Death). It is believed this may be a reference to a play with the same name by Lope de Vega (1562-1635).

200   See the previous note.

201   Puerto de Baños was the name of a battle fought in August 1809 between the French and a Portuguese-Spanish column led by Sir Robert Wilson (1777-1849). It is located near Baños de Montemayor, in the province of Cáceres, Extremadura.

CHAPTER IX

202   André Masséna (1758-1817) commanded the invasion of Portugal in 1810. After defeat at the Battle of Fuentes de Oñoro in May 1811 he was replaced by General Marmont. Masséna was notorious for his corruption, looting and mistresses. One mistress, Mme. Henriette Lebreton, accompanied him throughout the campaign, often wearing the uniform of a cornet of dragoons, decorated with the cross of the Légion d'Honneur.

203   A village 29 miles from Salamanca.

204   Tamames is a village about 34 miles from Salamanca. It was the scene of a battle in 1809.

205   A *partida* was a group of guerrillas who, to varying degrees, began to be organised within the allied military structures.

206   The Battle of Albuera took place on 16th May 1811.

207   Tipoo Sahib, or Tipu Sultan, was the ruler of Mysore, India, and was killed in 1799 at the Battle of Seringapatam fighting British forces led by Wellington.

CHAPTER X

208   The revolt in Madrid on 2nd May 1808 – the *dos de mayo* – brutally put down by the occupying French troops under Murat. The Palace of La Moncloa was one of many locations where summary executions of insurgents took place on 3rd May. These episodes are covered in *El 19 de marzo y el 2 de mayo*, the third book in the first series of the *Episodios Nacionales*.

209   A Spanish victory. The battle is the subject of the fourth book in the first series of the *Episodios Nacionales, Bailén*.

210   The date of Napoleon's entry into Madrid in 1808. The events of this period are covered in *Napoleón en Chamartín*, the fifth book in the first series of the *Episodios Nacionales*.

211   Gabriel's experiences in the siege are related in *Zaragoza*, the sixth book in the first series of the *Episodios Nacionales*.

212   Vicente Cañas Portocarrero, Duque del Parque (1755-1824). Victor of the Battles of Tamames and Carpio in 1809, he was defeated later that year by Kellermann at the Battle of Alba de Tormes.

213   The French siege of Cádiz lasted from February 1810 until August 1812.

214   The Battle of Talavera, 28th July 1809, a victory by Sir Arthur Wellesley that earned him the title of Viscount Wellington.

215   The fight at Arroyomolinos de Montánchez, Cáceres, took place on 28th October 1811.

216   Types of mantillas or shawls.

CHAPTER XI
217   Don Quixote's horse.

218   El Puerto de Santa María is about six miles across the bay from Cádiz. It was one of the bases for the French siege of Cádiz which lasted from 5th February 1810 to 24th August 1812.

219   The ballads ('*Romances*') were an important form of Spanish literature. Initially, they were anonymous folk tales intended for singing, but they were developed into a special literary form by such writers as Lope de Vega and Luis de Góngora.

220   Characters from ballads. Lindaraja was a Moorish beauty living in the Palace of the Alhambra. Tarfe and Bravonel were gallant Moorish heroes. Melisendra was Charlemagne's daughter.

CHAPTER XII
221   *Calva* is a traditional game where players try to hit an elbow-shaped piece of wood in the ground by throwing a cylindrical piece of wood or metal at it.

222   A hamlet not far from Salamanca.

223   A settlement about 50 miles from Salamanca.

224   Joseph I.

225   Villamayor is about 3 miles north-west of the centre of Salamanca.

226   Pigs were traditionally slaughtered on the feast of Saint Martin (11th November).

227   Valverdón is a village on the River Tormes about seven and a half miles north-west of Salamanca.

CHAPTER XIII
228   Fuentesaúco is a town about 21 miles north-east of Salamanca.

229   A rank approximating to sergeant.

230   A proverb about how a liking for something can descend into an addiction.

CHAPTER XIV
231   "*Il n'y a plus de Pyrénées*", words attributed to Louis XIV when his grandson Philip of Anjou was named successor to Carlos II as King of Spain in 1700.

232   "When he went off to war, the crocodile said farewell to his children. Poor old thing, dragging his tail in the dust…". Words from a French nursery rhyme. The tune was used in a one-act operetta by Offenbach, *Tromb-al-ca-zar ou les Criminels dramatiques*, first performed in 1856.

233   A play on Napoleon's words to his soldiers before the Battle of the Pyramids in 1798: "*Soldats… Songez que du haut de ces pyramides quarante siècles vous contemplent*" (Soldiers… remember that from the heights of these pyramids forty centuries are watching you).

234   The *Colegio Trilingüe* was established in the sixteenth century and the building was badly damaged in 1812.

235   See Chapter VII, note 190.

CHAPTER XV

236   *Tú* is the form of 'you' used between good friends, when speaking to children and animals and by social superiors to their inferiors. Jean-Jean continues to use the *vos* form when addressing Gabriel.

237   An extreme revolutionary or republican.

238   Jean-Jean is probably referring to the *Junta Suprema de Gobierno*, which was established in April 1808 by Ferdinand VII to rule Spain during his enforced absence in Bayonne, France. It ceased to operate when Joseph Bonaparte was proclaimed king of Spain in Madrid on 25th July 1808.

239   Paul Charles François Adrien Henri Dieudonné Thiébault (1769-1846) was appointed Governor of Salamanca in 1811.

240   Charles the Bold, the name of the last Valois Duke of Burgundy (1467-1477).

241   *Pied-de-mouton* is the French name for a mushroom, the hedgehog fungus (*Hydnum repandum*).

CHAPTER XVI

242   'Little Rome', a phrase used to describe Salamanca, possibly reflecting the fact that ancient Salamanca also stood on seven hills.

243   This college was founded in 1534 and became part of the University of Salamanca in 1587. It ceased to be a college in 1887.

244   The *Colegio Mayor de Cuenca* was founded in 1500 by a bishop of Málaga who was a native of Cuenca. The building was destroyed by the French.

245   The Benedictines occupied the *Convento de San Vicente*.

246   A *teso* is a low hill with a flat top or a livestock enclosure used in fairs or markets.

247   The Premonstratensians occupied the *Convento de San Norberto de Premonstratenses*, a building dating from about 1570. Part of the cloister still survives.

248   The secular *Colegio de Monte Olivete* (also known as the *Colegio de Santa María y Todos los Santos*) was founded in 1514. The building was destroyed in the Peninsular War.

249   Also known as the Monastery of the Holy Ghost, only the attached church survives today. It has a late Gothic chapel dedicated to *Cristo de los Milagros* (Christ of the Miracles).

CHAPTER XVII

250   The cult of the Supreme Being (*Culte de l'Être suprême*) was instituted in 1794 and promoted by Maximilien Robespierre.

251   The Third Estate (*Le Tiers État*) was the third chamber of the Estates General at the time of the French Revolution. It consisted of everyone in France who was neither a noble nor ordained by the Church and therefore formed by far the largest group in the population. The grievances of the Third Estate were a major cause of the Revolution, and the term 'Third Estate' became associated with revolutionaries both within and outside France.

CHAPTER XVIII

252   Fuenteguinaldo is a village in the province of Salamanca about 70 miles south-west of Salamanca.

253   Toro is a town in the province of Zamora, about 44 miles north of Salamanca.

CHAPTER XIX

254   The Cid is the eponymous hero of the *Cantar* or *Poema de mio Cid*, which celebrates the deeds of a Castilian knight, Rodrigo Díaz de Vivar.

255   Carlos Moor (or Karl Moor) was the hero in Friedrich Schiller's play *Die Räuber* (The Robbers) first performed in 1782.

CHAPTER XX

256   Queen Isabel I of Castile (1451-1504) and King Fernando V of Aragón (1452-1516).

257   Characters from Spanish ballads.

CHAPTER XXII

258   One of the nicknames given to Wellington by his troops was "Old Nosey".

259   Ciruelo means the Escuelas Menores building of the university.

260   Ciruelo is probably referring to the Colegio del Espíritu Santo occupied by the Company of Jesus (the Jesuits).

261   The Convento de San Esteban, a Dominican monastery.

262   The church of Santo Tomás Cantuariense, dedicated to St. Thomas Becket.

263   General Jean-Baptiste Estève de Latour (1768-1837) was commanding the 118th Infantry Regiment of the Line.

264   Jean-Pierre François Bonet (or Bonnet) (1768-1857).

265   Marie-François Auguste de Caffarelli du Falga (1766-1849).

266   Napoleon had begun the invasion of Russia by crossing the River Nieman on 24th June 1812.

267   The correct name of the river is Pregel or Pregolya, which flows through Kaliningrad into the Baltic.

268   Nicolas Charles Oudinot, 1st Duke of Reggio (1767-1848).

269   Properly called Wehlau (now Snamensk), a town on the Pregel in the Russian oblast of Kaliningrad.

270   Michel Ney, Duc d'Elchingen (1769-1815).

271   Jérome-Napoléon Bonaparte (1784-1860), the Emperor's youngest brother.

CHAPTER XXIII

272   A village some four miles from Salamanca.

273   Now a suburb of Salamanca.

274   Locations about 14 miles south-west of Salamanca.

275   As far as I am aware, there has never been a Lord Fly. At the time of this scene the Earl of Chichester was Thomas Pelham, 2nd Earl of Chichester.

CHAPTER XXIV

276   When Napoleon entered Madrid in 1808.

277   A Portuguese word for nostalgia, yearning or longing with melancholic overtones.

278   The Battle of Arroyo Molinos or Arroyomolinos de Montánchez, a clear victory for the allied army, took place on 28th October 1811, some nine months earlier. See Chapter X, note 215.

279   A small town in north-east Portugal about five miles from the Spanish frontier and some 84 miles from Salamanca.

280   Aldealengua is a village about five and a half miles east of Salamanca. It overlooks a ford across the River Tormes.

281   San Morales is a village about nine miles east of Salamanca.

282   Babilafuente is almost 14 miles east of Salamanca.

283   Villorio is just under two miles east of Salamanca.

CHAPTER XXV

284   See Chapter II, note 173.

CHAPTER XXVI

285   A hot, dry wind of the desert.

286   Ceuta, a Spanish territory on the northern shore of Morocco, was notorious for a prison built on Monte Hacho, which was used from the nineteenth century until 1910 and held many political prisoners as well as common criminals.

CHAPTER XXVII

287   The royal palace of El Pardo was a residence of the Spanish kings, just outside Madrid.

288   Doña Jimena Díaz was the wife of the Cid.

289   Cuéllar is a small town in the province of Segovia, about 100 miles north-west of Madrid.

CHAPTER XXVIII

290   Lieutenant-General Sir James Leith (1763-1816) commanded the 5th Infantry Division.

291   When Don Quixote first leaves his house for adventure, Cervantes says in Chapter 2 of the First Part that he "…rode through the ancient and illustrious countryside of Montiel" ("*Y comenzó a caminar por el antiguo y conocido Campo de Montiel*").

292   The River Guareña is a tributary of the Duero.

293   The River Pisuerga flows through Valladolid into the Duero.

294   The River Adaja is about 19 miles south of Valladolid.

295   The River Manzanares flows through Madrid into the River Jarama which is a tributary of the River Tagus.

296   The Abroñigal is a stream flowing into the Manzanares. It is now completely covered by the Madrid ring road.

CHAPTER XXIX

297   Alba de Tormes is about 14 miles south-east of Salamanca. Calvarrasa de Arriba is between the two, about six miles from Salamanca.

298   Calvarrasa de Abajo is a village about six miles east of Salamanca.

299   Sir Denis Pack (c.1772-1823) became the most decorated British officer in the Peninsular War after Wellington.

300   Joseph O'Lawlor (1768-1850) was an Irish-born Spanish general who was attached to Wellington's staff.

301   Brigadier General Sir Benjamin d'Urban (1777-1849) commanded a Portuguese cavalry brigade.

CHAPTER XXX

302   In English in the original text.

CHAPTER XXXI

303   Miguel Ricardo de Álava y Esquivel (1770-1843). Having served as a marine in the Battle of Trafalgar, he was transferred to the Spanish Army. He was a liaison officer of the Spanish Army to the British forces and became a good friend of Wellington.

CHAPTER XXXII

304   Sir Edward Michael Pakenham (1778-1815) was Wellington's brother-in-law. He was killed at the Battle of New Orleans in January 1815.

305   Sir Thomas Bradford (1777-1853).

306   Sir Galbraith Lowry Cole (1772-1842) commanded the Fourth Infantry Division.

307   Sir John Hope (1765-1836) commanded a brigade of the 5th Infantry Division.

308   Claude François Ferey, Baron de Rozengath (1771-1812).

309   Jean Guillaume Barthélemy Thomières (1771-1812).

310   François-Ganivet Desgraviers-Berthelot (1768-1812). He died of wounds on 26th July 1812, four
        days after the battle.

CHAPTER XXXIII
311   William Frederick Spry (1770-1814). He commanded the Third Portuguese Brigade.

312   Sir Henry Clinton (1771-1829) commanded the Sixth Division.

CHAPTER XXXIV
313   Poenco appears in *Cádiz*, the eighth book in the first series of the *Episodios Nacionales*. He runs a
        tavern of dubious reputation and procures girls for Lord Gray, the seducer of Miss Fly's sister.

314   Don Pedro del Congosto also appears in *Cádiz*. An upholder of the tradition of Don Quijote and
        'old' Spain, he is a comical figure who challenges Lord Gray to a duel. Lord Gray accepts, but
        as a joke has Poenco impersonate him. Poenco pretends that he has been mortally wounded by
        Congosto. Lord Gray's followers celebrate Congosto's victory by beating him before carrying him off
        on their shoulders in feigned celebration. Immediately afterwards, Lord Gray and Gabriel fight a real
        duel in which Gabriel kills Lord Gray.

315   Zaide is a Moor who appears in ballads written by Lope de Vega (1562-1635).

316   Abenámar is the Moorish protagonist in the anonymous *Romance of Abenámar*.

317   A Moorish character.

318   Fernán González was a tenth-century count who established the independence of Castile. He was
        then the subject of many ballads.

319   Pedro Ansúrez was a Castilian count of the late tenth and early eleventh centuries.

CHAPTER XXXV
320   This gesture means to watch out and/or that the person making the gesture is clever or knows what
        he's talking about.

CHAPTER XXXVI
321   Francisco de Zurbarán (1598-1664) was a painter noted for his portraits of saints and members of
        the clergy.

322   Diego Velázquez (1599-1660) is seen by many as the greatest Spanish painter. He painted some
        portraits of court fools, jesters and dwarves which are now in the Prado Museum.

CHAPTER XXXVIII
323   *Vos* was used by the common people or people of lowly rank to address the nobility and persons of
        high status. See Chapter VII, note 190.

324   Domingo Cabarrús Galabert (1774-1842) was Minister of Public Finance under Joseph.

325   Lord Byron spent from 30th July to 3rd August 1809 in Cádiz. He took a liking to the city and to its female population in particular. He wrote to his friend Francis Hodgson on 6th August 1809: "*Cadiz, sweet Cadiz! It is the first spot of creation. The beauty of its streets and mansions is only excelled by the loveliness of its inhabitants.*"

CHAPTER XL
326   The Golden Mean.